MUNDO

The LOST OCEAN

Bei Hua

MIRAI

The JADE SEA

Cape
Abuja

The Pinch

The Bash

The Brim

The Bow

The
Crown

The City of
SAN CRISTÓBAL

OCULTA

Also available by Maya Motayne

Nocturna

OCULTA

MAYA MOTAYNE

BALZER + BRAY

An Imprint of HarperCollins*Publishers*

To my parents

THE ICED QUILBEAR

Alfie took a deep breath and knocked on the door.

The sounds of the Pinch echoed around him—babies crying, men swearing, bottles of rum breaking against dank alleyway walls. The afternoon sun was high, bringing a bit of warmth to the cool winter air. He pulled his velvet-lined cloak tighter about his shoulders.

In the far distance he could hear the scattered sounds of chanting—a protest. Ever since the horrors that Sombra's magic had wreaked four months ago, there had been discord in the air, a sense of distrust between Castallan's people and the royal family.

Between the people and himself.

Small, disorganized protests had been sprouting up like weeds, and though his parents told him the unrest would die down in due time, he could see the thinly veiled worry in their eyes.

To make things worse, the people's anger after his release of the dark magic grew heightened with the announcement of the long-planned summit that would bring the Englassen royalty to Castallan next week to negotiate a peace between the two kingdoms.

The bitter resentment permeating the city had been enough for his parents to forbid him from visiting most of the families who had been affected by the dark magic, but he'd begged for the opportunity to do a few himself, as a first step in making things right. A few was better than none, and today's visit would be the very last.

His shadow twisting around his feet, he knew it would be just as painful as the first.

As he waited at the door, he tried to force a casual smile, but feigning nonchalance felt pointless when there was a retinue of red-caped guards flanking him.

Finally, the door swung open, and a woman with dark bags under her eyes stood before him. Like most Castallano women, she wore a long skirt belted high at the waist. The material was rough-spun and full of patches. The sound of children playing rang out behind her.

"Who is knocking on my maldito—" The woman froze, her mouth falling open. She dropped to her knees, pressing her forehead to the ground. "Perdóname, Prince Alfehr."

By now the children had come forward to her side and she quickly tugged each of them to the ground with her, urging them to bow in hushed words.

"No, no," Alfie said, holding out his hand. "Please stand. You need not bow, not tonight."

She stared at his hand before taking it and letting him pull her to her feet.

A soft rain began to fall, and Alfie looked up, raising one hand above his head to hold the drops at bay. Being a water charmer came in handy during the rainy winter months. The guards stood behind him at attention, unfazed. "If you don't mind, could Master Luka and I please come in?"

The woman was still staring at him, mouth agape, as she ushered them in.

Doing what he did best, Luka immediately turned to the children. "Would you three like to play a juego?" he asked, a wide smile on his face.

The children grinned up at him. "What game?" one asked.

"You'll have to catch me to find out!" Luka said, darting about the room. The children followed, laughing, giving Alfie time to talk to their mother.

She showed him to a small wooden table in the kitchen and motioned stiffly toward a chair. Only after Alfie was firmly seated did she sit as well. Her back was so straight Alfie wondered if her spine ached, but he knew there was nothing he could do to ease her nerves about the crown prince sitting in her kitchen.

Alfie cleared his throat. "Your husband was Rodolfo Vargas, yes?"

The woman looked down at the table, her fingers tightly laced. "Sí, he was. Before . . . ," she said, her voice petering off into nothing.

Before Alfie had released Sombra's magic and killed hundreds of Castallano citizens. His throat burned at the memory.

"I'm very sorry for your loss," Alfie offered, his voice wooden to his own ears. Though he meant the words, they sounded terribly meaningless.

"Gracias," she said plainly, looking at him. "But why do you ask about my husband?"

"For the past few months I have been working on a memorial to those who were lost. To complete it, I need something from you. Something of Rodolfo's."

The woman was silent as Alfie described the memorial and why he needed items that belonged to the departed. The memorial would be revealed in a week, so her contribution would be one of the last touches to the project. After he spoke, she sat silently, wringing her hands.

"We don't have much, Your Majesty," she began uneasily. "The things I have left of him . . . they are my treasures."

Alfie clasped his hands in his lap. "Señora, I defer to you completely. If you would rather not, I understand. I have many trinkets from my brother, and I would not be able to part with a single one." Which wasn't entirely truthful, as he had parted with one—a fox figurine that he'd given to Finn. It had looked so right in her palm as she tucked it into her pocket. Alfie shook his head free of those thoughts. "What I ask of you is a sacrifice that you needn't make if you don't wish to."

She looked at him then, and it was as if she was seeing him for the first time. Or maybe she was seeing him not as a prince or as her future king, but as a boy who had lost someone too.

"Wait here, por favor," she added awkwardly. She hurried into the back room of the home. There was no wall there, only a sheet hanging as a partition between rooms. Alfie watched Luka play with the children while he waited.

"Want to see something chévere?" Luka asked, waggling his eyebrows. "Something very, very cool?"

"Luka . . . ," Alfie warned from his seat, but Luka only looked at the cheering children.

"Okay!" Luka said. "You asked for it!" He picked up the two smallest and began to juggle them as easily as if he were juggling eggs. The children squealed with laughter as their oldest sister watched, wide-eyed.

"Luka!" Alfie hissed. "Basta!" Ever since Sombra's magic had granted Luka inhuman strength, he had been juggling everything he could get his hands on. For the last four months Alfie had lived with Luka constantly shouting, "Hey, sourpuss! Look!" only for Alfie to turn and see his cousin juggling his furniture, priceless statues, boulders the size of horses, and now children.

At the sight of Alfie's hard look, Luka rolled his eyes. "*Fiiiiiine.*" Just as their mother parted the curtain and walked back in, Luka caught both siblings, tickling them until they fell to the ground in a fit of giggles.

The mother sank into her chair, clutching something wrapped in a handkerchief. She stared at the bundle for a quiet moment before placing it on the table.

Alfie looked at her for permission, then uncovered it. Inside was an old pocket watch. It was rusted, but Alfie could make out the initials *RV* engraved on the back.

"It was his favorite." She laughed dryly, and then tears were falling down her face. "Even though it never worked."

Alfie held the watch carefully. "Are you sure? I will not be able to return it." The items would disappear when the spellwork was complete. There would be no turning back.

She nodded and the motion seemed to make the tears come faster. "Estoy seguro. I want him to be a part of this."

Alfie watched her, his heart aching in his chest. "I am so sorry, Señora Vargas."

She passed another hand over her eyes. "You talk like you're the one who did it when it was those stuffy dueños' fault that that wild magic was released."

Alfie froze. It was the official statement that the royal family had decided on and delivered to the people. Since dueños studied unknown magic (which, even with the best intentions, could lead to accidents), it was a story that sounded just as true as it was false, and so felt like a sensible way to shift the blame away from Alfie to a distant, faceless group that the people could curse among themselves. The desire to tell the truth ate away at him, but his people already saw him as unworthy compared to Dezmin—he could not add more reason for them to think him a disappointment as heir.

Alfie cleared his throat. "When your child falls and scrapes her knee, do you not feel as if you are responsible?"

The woman glanced at her children, her eyes softening. She nodded.

"A king is the father of his kingdom. When it gets hurt . . . ," he said, his eyes moving to the children as they played with Luka. "He feels as though he is at fault. No matter who is responsible, no matter if it was an accident." Alfie looked away from her, his shadow curling at his feet. "It doesn't matter. The fault is mine."

Before she could speak another word, Alfie stood and bowed. She gasped. Normally, a prince bowed to no commoner, but Alfie would bow to each person he'd harmed. He owed them that much, and so much more.

"I thank you for telling me about your marido," Alfie said. "And for giving me a piece of him. I hope you will be pleased with the memorial. Know that the royal family grieves with you." He looked at her, his eyes stinging as the children showed Luka their handmade toys. Because of him, they would grow up without a father. "Truly."

The woman stared at him, taken aback. "D-de nada," she sputtered.

Alfie turned to the children. The youngest girl dashed to him and pressed a cheek against his knee.

"Luna!" the mother said, but Alfie shot her a smile.

"It's quite all right," he said as the little girl tugged his sleeve. She must have been four years old, too young to see him as anything but a possible playmate.

"Are you staying to eat almuerzo with us?" she asked.

Alfie knelt down, his knee pressing into the dirt floor of the hovel. "My mamá and papá are waiting for us to have lunch with them, otherwise we would love to stay," he said, cupping her soft cheek in his hand. "But let me give you something before I go."

Alfie waved his hand and plucked a ribbon of water from the air. Winter was on its way, and the air had become cool and heavy with moisture. Though it only snowed on the very southern tip of Castallan, it still would get a bit chilly in San Cristóbal. "What's your favorite animal?" he asked her, letting the water slither back and forth between his hands.

The two older siblings gathered around as Luna's forehead scrunched with thought.

"She likes quilbears!" her brother said.

"I know another girl who likes quilbears too," Alfie said, a smile tugging at his lips. He remembered Finn talking about how she'd used quilbear quills to knock out the guardsmen and sneak into the palace vault.

"If I were an animal, I'd be a quilbear," she'd said, sitting up in the palace bed where she'd recovered after they'd defeated Ignacio. Her hefty breakfast sat on a tray in her lap.

"I thought you said you'd be a dragon?" Alfie mused, thinking of her mask the night they'd met at the cambió game.

Finn popped a forkful of mangú into her mouth before speaking. "I'm very complicated," she said with a shrug. "Who says I can't be both?"

His heart aching, Alfie molded the water with fine detail as they watched.

"My brother used to do something like this, but with wood. I lost him not long ago." Alfie wondered if there would ever come a day when he would be able to speak of Dez without it feeling as if all the air had been sucked out of the room, leaving him gasping for breath.

"Like Papá," the elder sister said. While the other two were too young to grasp what had happened, she was old enough to feel her childhood being forever changed by the loss.

"Yes, just like your papá. I hear he was un hombre honorable," Alfie said. The children nodded and he could tell they'd heard these things before, the same way Alfie had heard too many stale phrases after Dez had died. He pushed himself away from those safe, meaningless words and spoke from the heart instead. "I started making my own animals to feel closer to my brother, Dezmin. When I make them, it's like he's still with me."

"But he isn't," the eldest girl said, her voice heartbreakingly flat. "He's gone."

"He is," Alfie agreed, wondering how this child could accept that fact so quickly when he had done such terrible things in denial of his brother's death. "But this is one of the ways I carry him with me. Remember your papá, and find your own ways to keep him with you."

The younger two were still enraptured by the ice figure, but the eldest girl held his gaze for a long moment before nodding solemnly. Alfie stood, mussed the children's hair, and walked to the door, followed by Luka and his guards.

When Alfie was safely out of earshot, the final guardsman presented the woman with a small chest. All families affected by Sombra's magic would be given one. "Please take this as reparations for what you have lost, courtesy of Crown Prince Alfehr."

The guard handed her the compact but weighty chest, which was small enough to balance on her open palms but heavy enough to make her back straighten. Only when the guardsman was gone did she open it and find rows of silver pesos.

THE FACE THIEF UNMASKED

Finn walked through the unfamiliar city, her shoulders squared, her shadow moving like a cat flicked its tongue, her fingers, as always, itching for a dagger.

She'd been calling San Juan home for the last couple of hours, but once she finished her job, she would hop on the nearest ship and find someplace new.

This was the life she'd always wanted, the life she'd had before the prince's wild adventure had pulled her into battles she couldn't have imagined even on her drunkest day, but one thing was very different now.

Finn did not wear a stolen face. She wore her own brown skin, full lips, and riot of dark curls.

The thought made her stomach tighten. She was never this nervous, even when she was thieving. Then again, she was never nervous when she thieved, only excited. But she supposed excitement was just a tastier flavor of anxiety. Her shadow slithered close around her feet, cautious, almost shy.

Wearing her own face at least once a day was a new tradition. Something to work on, something to get used to. Most importantly— a way to dance on Ignacio's grave. Well, if her nightmarish adoptive father even had a grave to dance on.

If she'd done this a few months ago, she would have heard nothing but his voice in her head. Ignacio's persuasive drawl telling her that she had no business wearing her own face when she'd done so many vile things. That she ought to hide behind mask after mask for the rest of her days.

But his voice was long gone, replaced by another one. A kinder one.

Finn pulled her palm-sized journal from her pocket and flipped through the sketches of the many faces she'd donned, the flicker of pages relaxing her. Toward the end of the journal the drawings grew more and more sparse. Lately, she'd felt less inclined to change her face for a job unless she had to, so there was less to draw. It had felt sudden at first, but not long after the incident with Sombra four months ago, she'd realized who was responsible for this change in her.

She was looking right at him.

In the back of the journal, instead of sketches of the faces she'd stolen, were drawings of Alfie. Some were of what she imagined him doing now, reading a book in the library or sitting at his desk in his rooms, his brow furrowed. Some were of moments they'd suffered together—her favorite was the sketch of him asleep at her bedside, his head lying in the cradle of his arms. She tucked it back into her pocket, his words echoing in her head.

I believe you. I believed you then and I believe you now, even if you don't.

It was his voice that made her want to wear the face she'd been born with.

At first it'd been difficult, painful. But soon it began to feel like slipping her hand back into a perfectly sized glove. It felt free. Effortless.

She hadn't realized how much energy it took to be someone else for every moment of the day. Ignacio had made her so ashamed of herself that it had become normal to her. Necessary.

Now wearing new faces was fun, not forced.

She took in a deep breath, walking the square, tossing a vendor a couple of pesos and plucking a cone of freshly fried tostones from his stand. She popped one into her mouth, savoring the salty crunch.

Four months had passed since she and the prince (but mostly her, if she was being honest) had saved the world, and life had been good.

It'd been fantástico, if she said so herself. Ignacio was dead and gone, his voice banished from her head. Her *propio*—a personal magical ability that was unique to each person—was back ever since Ignacio had killed the mobster Kol, and, best of all, with the pesos that she'd stolen from the royal vault as payment after helping the prince save the maldito world, she'd returned with a vengeance to her passion—thieving. Which had brought her here to San Juan, where her latest mark lived.

The cone of fried plantains in her hand, she nearly stumbled into a crowd of children surrounding a man who was making puppets dance to a bachata rhythm. The children laughed as the puppets' hips swayed to the beat.

Finn looked at the puppets, the thought of Ignacio and his

control sending a shiver skittering up her spine. She curled her fingers, summoning a bit of rock up from the ground. Taking it in her hands, she molded it into a flat, sharp-edged disk.

With a flick of her wrist she threw it, letting it fly in a smooth arc straight over the audience and above the puppets' bobbing heads. The disk sliced through the strings with ease, and the wooden dolls fell into piles of bent limbs and frozen faces. Still and free.

"Pinche troublemakers!" the puppeteer cursed as the kids laughed again. "Which one of you did that?"

Finn turned on her heel and stretched her arms over her head, feeling freedom in the movement, no strings holding her in place. No voice in her head waking her up in a cold sweat.

She stuffed the rest of the tostones into her mouth and tossed the cone. The sun was edging closer to the horizon, painting the sky in swaths of pink and orange. There was no more time to waste; she had a job to get to.

"Which one of you did it?!" he shouted again.

While the puppeteer cursed and the children laughed, Finn smiled with her own face. "I did."

THE PUPPET BECOMES THE MASTER

Finn crept through the sweeping hacienda of a very wealthy merchant, her steps light, a new identity slipped over her skin like a fresh coat of paint. So fresh that if someone brushed past her, her face might wipe right off on their shirt.

She walked down a high-ceilinged hall lined with family portraits of a smiling couple with their pipsqueak of a son standing between them. Their clothing was richly embroidered—the woman's silken blouse was a deep violet with floral detailing and was tucked into her elaborate ruffled skirt; the father's dark eyes glinted beneath the wide brim of a sombrero; the little boy's trousers were outfitted in polished gold buttons. Their smiles were wide and assured—the smiles of people who didn't have a care in the world. People who were born rich and would die richer.

Finn smirked up at the painting. They were due for a good thieving.

She'd snuck first into the servants' quarters and unstoppered bottles of sleeping smoke she'd bought, filling the barracks with a sweet-smelling fog that would keep the servants asleep. The merchant, Niurka Herrera, and her husband were gone for the week on business, leaving only the servants, the boy's nanny (already knocked out in her rooms), and the pipsqueak himself to deal with. This would be her easiest one yet. All she had to do was—

"Mamí." A little voice spoke from behind her. "Mamí, is that you?"

Finn grimaced. She'd been very careful throughout her life to ensure that she would never become anyone's mamí.

She turned to see a little boy stepping out of his bedroom and into the dim light of the hall, his curly hair mashed down flat on one side. He rubbed his small, balled fist into his eye in a perfect pantomime of sleepiness. Finn held back a long stream of curses.

"You're home early." He dashed down the hall in his pajamas and wrapped his arms around her legs. "You're home." His words were muffled, his face pressed into her trousers.

Finn froze. None of the other doors down the long hallway had opened; after all, they were empty. Or, in the case of his nanny, the people inside were passed out cold. So long as the boy kept quiet, it would stay that way. Thank the gods she'd put on his mother's face just in case.

She frowned as he squeezed her tighter. She hated kids. They always looked at her like they expected her to kneel down and ruffle their hair. She didn't have time for that mierda. What did he want her to do? Give him a toy? Play a game of tag?

Finn glared at him and internally cursed. She'd been wary of using the sleeping smoke in the kid's room since too high a dose could've killed him. She should've just risked it.

She could just knock him out with a swift hit to the temple. Her hand began to rise.

The boy looked up at her and smiled a gap-toothed grin.

Finn sighed and let her hand drop back to her side. She hated that she had morals. Or some version of morals.

She should've just used the damn vanishing cloak, but the cloak made things too easy. More and more she'd found herself leaving it behind. Invisibility sapped thieving of its excitement. What was the point of stealing if you didn't have to sneak, to plan, to change your face just for fun? What did it matter if you didn't feel that rush of adrenaline at nearly getting caught?

It was just too easy. That was why she'd stopped wearing it. Not because every time she put on the cloak she thought of Alfie, reaching around her to smooth it onto her shoulders, his gaze as soft as his touch. That memory had nothing to do with leaving the cloak behind.

It couldn't. After all, that would be estúpido.

"Mamí, will you tell me a story?" The boy's chin was tilted up, pressing against the spot just above her knee.

"Yes, I'll tell you a maldito story," Finn hissed. "If you quietly go back to your room."

"Maldito is a bad word."

"That's subjective." Finn untangled his arms from around her legs and ushered the boy back into his room, all but shoving him onto his bed and under the sheets.

"Close your eyes," she said impatiently.

The boy yawned and obeyed.

When Finn began to back away from the bed, the boy reached

out and grabbed the leg of her trousers in his small fingers.

"Story first," he said, his eyes sweeping over her as if he'd only just noticed something. "Mamí, why are you wearing pantalones?" Suspicion crawled over his round face.

Finn moved quickly to snuff it out. "Basta, quiet now. Story time, no questions."

"But—"

"Do you want the story or not?" She crossed her arms and leveled her most strict-mother look at him. The suspicion melted off the boy's face, replaced with delight. He looked pointedly at the chair by his bedside. Finn resisted for a moment, not wanting to sit in the rocking chair (why would she need a chair that rocked? What was she, a damned baby?), but for the sake of getting the boy to go to sleep, she perched on the very edge of it, grimacing as it shifted under her weight.

"I'm ready!" he said, watching her with the most genuine excitement Finn had seen in a long while. "Start the story, Mamí!"

"Once upon a time . . . ," Finn began before falling quiet, grappling for words. Her parents had told her stories at bedtime when they were alive, hadn't they? Surely they had, but she couldn't remember them. "There was . . ."

"A prince," the boy sleepily supplied, and Finn sighed through her nose.

"Why does there always have to be a prince?"

The boy stared at her again, confused.

"I mean, sí, once upon a time there was a prince," Finn said hurriedly. "A prince who was too kind for his own good." As the words left her lips, Alfie's warm smile filled her mind.

"What happened to him?"

"He made friends with someone he shouldn't have." Finn shifted, remembering the poison bottle in the prince's room, and leaving it there for Bathtub Boy to drink. "He didn't know any better."

"Who did he make friends with?"

"A thief." Her voice had gone hushed. The boy leaned forward to hear her better.

"What'd they do?" he asked, his words softened and rounded with another tongue-curling yawn.

"They went on an adventure, they stopped someone very, very bad, and then they said goodbye."

"Why?" he asked, and something about that question struck her in the gut. How could a word so small hold so much power?

"Because it's better that way," she said.

He rolled onto his side to face her. "For who?"

"For him. Better for him." Ignacio may have been long gone, but that feeling that she'd bring trouble wherever she went was here to stay, forming a cold pit in her stomach when she thought of the prince and how she'd wanted to stay in San Cristóbal.

"What about for the thief?" he asked, his voice quiet.

"No sé." Finn looked away from his chubby-cheeked face. "I don't know."

And in the way that children took their parents' word as law, the boy didn't question it.

"That's a sad story," he said. His head lolled, his breaths slowing and deepening.

Only when he was finally fast asleep did Finn say, "Sí, it is. Sleep tight, kid."

Finn crept out of the boy's room and back into the hallway. His real mamí wouldn't be home until morning, and Finn needed to rob her blind before then.

She rushed down the hall and around a corner, where a spiral staircase waited. She dashed up the tight stairwell only to run head-first into a stone wall.

"Coño," she mumbled, rubbing her stinging nose with her knuckles.

"Really?" she said to the wall. "En serio?"

Finn pressed her fingertips against the cold, sandy stone. Something was beyond there. Could she shift the stone wall? Force it to open for her? She pushed her awareness into the stones. She could feel the weight of them. These walls were thick—thicker than the rest. Finn grinned.

People only built walls this thick when they were trying to hide something.

But even if she could move the wall apart, that would make too much noise and take too much strength. The whole hacienda would rumble. A thought struck her.

Wasn't this merchant a stone carver?

If so, there had to be a way she could use her carving to open these walls without collapsing the hacienda. Finn pressed her ear into the wall and ran her fingers over its smooth surface again. She could feel nothing but solid rock layered upon solid rock. Nothing.

Wait.

The rock within was in a strange shape. Finn tugged at it with her stone carving and she could feel stone gears begin to move inside, like the inner workings of a clock. Finn gripped the gears and began to turn them. Slowly, the wall began to part. It was as if she were turning the key of a giant windup toy. Finally the wall parted enough for Finn to slide into the room within. Magicked flames sat in the sconces around the circular room, bathing it in soft light. There was a dark wood desk at its center with a ledger and quills. But Finn couldn't care less about that. What drew her eye was the large silver chest that sat at the far end of the room—a coffer where the merchant's money was kept.

Finn took a step toward the chest, her fingers itching to open it. She hardly needed the pesos now when she still had money left over from the royal vault.

She stilled, the prince's voice blooming between her ears.

"You left before I could give you your chest of gold. I never took you as the type to forget a payment."

She'd smirked up at him. "I didn't. I stopped by the vault on my way out. We're square. For now."

And the prince had smiled, his eyes speaking something she both wanted to and was scared to hear. What was he doing now? Pacing in his room? Reading a particularly boring book? A smile tugged gently at her lips.

A blade of sharpened rock sang through the air, pulling her back to the present. With a startled yelp, Finn ducked as the pointed stone skimmed past her nose and buried itself in the wall behind her.

Niurka Herrera stood in the doorway of the room, her face identical to Finn's.

Her heels clicked as she stepped into the room, and though she wore the clothes of a woman who spent her days keeping her hands clean, Finn could see in the way she moved that this woman was a fighter.

"For weeks I've been hearing of wealthy merchants walking into banks and emptying their coffers," she said, her voice slow and sure, as if there was no reason for her to be afraid. "Only to return days later, outraged that their money was gone."

Finn cocked her head in amusement. "How nice for you."

"Didn't take long to realize that it wasn't them emptying out their accounts, but someone who could make themselves look exactly like them." She glanced down at Finn's shadow as if confirming. And then the two were circling one another in the small room, their feet falling against the ground in the same slow, light-footed steps. "You left a path of destruction in your wake. When you robbed Cristina Vidal I knew you were coming my way next. After her, I'm the wealthiest merchant for miles. All I had to do was make it known that I'd be away on business. I knew you'd come running."

"You found me out," Finn said as they moved like predators circling the same prey. "What do you intend to do about it?"

The woman stopped and Finn followed suit. They faced each other, the tension clawing its way forward with each breath they took.

Finn lunged and threw a stone-cloaked punch. The woman pulled a sheath of stone from the ground, fashioning a shield. Finn's fist slammed into it and Niurka leaned into the hit, shoving Finn back with a thrust of her shielded shoulder.

Skidding back on her heels, Finn snarled. Stone-fist was her signature move. It usually worked.

Her shadow zigzagging angrily on the ground, Finn sank into an offensive stance. This woman was not going to take control of the situation, not if Finn could help it.

The air shifted between them then. Finn raised her fists and the woman's arms mimicked hers. She looked strangely confused as her body mirrored Finn's stance.

"Scared now?" Finn said, her fist still smarting from the hit. "It's a little late for that."

Finn dashed forward and so did the woman. They met at the center of the room, and at the exact same time they reached for each other's necks, choking one another. With her free hand, Finn reached for Niurka's wrist, and Niurka did the same to her. They both tugged at one another's hands as they choked each other. Finn squeezed harder, feeling the woman's windpipe buckle beneath her fingers, and in perfect unison, she did the same until Finn could scarcely breathe. Niurka's eyes were wide, not just with the pain of the choking but with something else too—a potent combination of fear and confusion that left Finn's stomach tight.

Her vision going spotty from not being able to breathe, Finn raised her leg and kicked the woman in the stomach. Again, at the exact same time, the woman kicked Finn in the same place.

They each stumbled back, clutching their stomachs.

"How?" the woman gasped. "How are you doing this?"

"Doing what?" Finn forced herself to stand upright as the other woman did the same. "What the hell are you talking about?"

She scratched her nose and so did Niurka. Finn froze. The woman wasn't anticipating every move she made and mimicking her—they were moving *completely in sync with one another.*

Somehow Finn was controlling her movements. She felt the pull of magic within her and knew that this must be some new shade of her *propio*. Her heart shuddered to a halt.

She knew that *propios* developed over time. Some people's *propios* only had a single ability, others' branched out into many. After all, as a child Finn could only change her own face; it had taken years before her *propio* evolved into the ability to change the appearances of others. Now her *propio* had evolved again, and the look in the woman's eyes made the blood drain from Finn's face. It was the same way she'd looked at Ignacio when he bent her to his will until she broke in his hands.

As Finn raised her right hand, Niurka mirrored her, her face a rictus of shock. Every movement that Finn made, the woman did as well. Finn could feel a connection between them, as if Niurka had been transformed into Finn's shadow.

As if she no longer had a will of her own.

Finn shuddered as Ignacio's laugh wormed its way between her ears, victorious and jubilant. It'd been gone for months and now it was back, sighing with pleasure as if he'd just returned home after a long trip.

To think you thought you could get rid of me, Mija. I've been inside you all along.

"Mamí." A voice spoke from the entrance. It was the little boy. His sleepy eyes widened as he looked back and forth between his mother and Finn.

"Alejandro," the woman said, her jaw tense. "Go back to bed. Mamí and her friend are talking." The woman's facial expressions and voice were still her own to control. She shot Finn a pleading look. Something curdled in Finn's stomach. This woman really believed she would kill the boy.

It's not as if you haven't killed a child before, Mija, Ignacio's voice purred. *What's stopping you this time?*

The boy's gaze shifted to the dagger in Finn's hand. His eyes went wide and scared. Scared that she would hurt him. He dashed from the doorway to his mother and wrapped his arms around her legs. Niurka's eyes begged to hold him, but Finn still had her in her grasp, keeping her from her son. Bile crawled up her throat. Finn jerked at the connection between her and the merchant until it snapped, like a string pulled too tight. Niurka gasped in relief, gathering him in her arms.

Her heart pounding in her throat, Finn sprinted out of the room and down the stairs. At the far end of the hall stood a floor-to-ceiling stained glass window, a swirl of reds and blues. Finn leaped, pulling her knees tight to her chest and crossing her arms in front of her face in an X as she broke through the glass.

And as she flew out the window in a spray of colored shards, Ignacio's voice burrowed into her mind once more, alive and well though he was long dead.

Like padre, like hija.

THE MEMORIAL

In the face of tragedy, a king must comfort his people.

Alfie had heard his parents give Dez this advice when they were children—when their grandfather passed and the whole kingdom mourned a beloved ruler, when his mother gave birth to a silent baby who would have been his little sister. Then fate had twisted his world in its grasp and Dez was gone; now Alfie was the one receiving this bleak advice.

"Mijo, you've come a long way," his father said, taking Alfie by the shoulders as they stood before the shimmering palace moat. "We are so proud of you."

His mother beamed. "This memorial was a wonderful idea. And you've been so committed to preparing for the summit, for your future."

Alfie rubbed the back of his neck, grateful for their praise but also discomfited by it. After all, if he hadn't released Sombra, the memorial wouldn't be necessary. And the summit was Dezmin's project, Dezmin's dream. Alfie's stomach tightened at the thought of taking credit for what Dez had spent so long championing.

Alfie forced the voice in his mind to fall quiet. He couldn't wallow today. He needed to focus on unveiling the memorial he'd spent months building. It was a great patchworked wall of stained glass with more colors than he could count, each shade representing a life lost. But, most importantly, he had used items that had belonged to the departed and infused the wall with their essence. When those family members who had offered him the victims' treasures came to visit the memorial, they would see the faces of their lost loved ones reflected in the glass.

It had been a work of complex magic, one he'd poured himself into as penance. The spellwork had forced him to wrestle with the consequences of his actions and, with the help of Paloma, his mentor and teacher of magic since childhood, and his parents, he'd finished it just in time for the unveiling.

He'd done his best to muster up the same vigor for learning the ways of leadership as Dez had. What he'd done was impossible to undo, so he would spend the rest of his life in service to his people. It was almost a relief to take this path. No more fighting, no more endless debating on whether he was good enough to rule. His life was decided for him.

That scared him just as much as it comforted him.

"You're sure you don't want us to come with you?" Queen Amada asked, concerned.

Part of Alfie wanted them to come along. But he was responsible for what had happened. "I'll be fine on my own," he said, forcing his voice to be level and calm. His shadow wriggled at his feet for a moment before he forced it to lie still. "I need to do this myself."

His mother cupped his cheek, her face bright. "Spoken like a true king."

"Rest assured he won't be totally unsupervised!" a voice called, and Alfie turned to see Luka rushing down the palace stairs. "His finest role model will be with him."

The queen laughed as Luka moved to stand beside Alfie. "Behave yourself."

"Siempre," he quipped, but then he gripped Alfie's shoulder and gave him a barely perceptible nod, one that spoke of the seriousness of the situation.

Luka had always had a sunny disposition that matched his butter-yellow magic, but ever since the incidents of four months ago, Alfie could see something behind his eyes that hadn't been there before. Likewise, Luka had been disappearing lately, going off on his own when he and Alfie usually spent their free time together. Alfie wanted to ask what was wrong, but he could tell that Luka did not want to be asked and, in truth, he was afraid to know how his foolishness had hurt his cousin. One day they would have to talk about it, but now was hardly the moment.

With a great rumbling, the stone carvers on the other side of the moat pulled up a path of stone and a carriage rolled down the rock path toward them. The prince swallowed thickly.

"We will be here when you return," King Bolivar said as the carriage came to a stop before them. The footmen held the door open for Alfie, and for a moment, it was as if he were stepping into a lion's gaping mouth instead of a plush carriage.

"Adiós," Alfie said, forcing himself to smile at his parents as he climbed in. Though Luka sat right beside him, Alfie felt utterly alone.

When the carriage finally came to a stop in the Pinch, where the memorial had been built, Alfie's heart seemed to stop with it.

He hadn't even looked out the windows to see the reality of their destination. He felt like a child with his hands clapped over his eyes, as if the monsters could not see him as long as he could not see them. Luka shot him a sympathetic look, but that only made Alfie feel worse.

When he looked away from Luka, he caught an unwanted flash of his reflection in the carriage window. His usually springy black, curly hair sat limp on his head. His brown skin looked sallow. He looked as anxious as he felt. Would the people sense that when he unveiled the memorial?

When the footmen opened the doors, Alfie couldn't bring himself to move.

"Alfie," Luka said, tapping his shoe against Alfie's. "You're ready for this."

Sweat beaded at Alfie's temple. "No, I'm not."

"Exactly. Only a fool would be ready for something like this. A brave person is not ready and does it anyway." Luka gripped him by the shoulder. "You're ready because you're not."

Alfie took a breath. "I don't know how you still believe in me, after everything."

Luka pulled Alfie into a fierce hug. "You might not know how, but I do. So don't worry about it, sourpuss."

"Gracias," Alfie said, his eyes stinging as he finally stepped out of the carriage.

An area in the Pinch that had once been a small, abandoned market square had been cleared for the memorial. When Alfie had first announced the creation of this memorial to the arts council, they'd advocated for it to be built in the Bow, a ring of the city that was much cleaner and more scenic, but Alfie demanded that it be placed in the Pinch, where those most affected by Sombra's destruction lived. Through Ignacio, Sombra had collected most of his shadowless army from the poorer rings before advancing to the palace. It was only right that Alfie build this memorial close to those who were most hurt by what he'd done.

The nobles had complained about having to engage with "riff-raff" from the lower rings when they visited the memorial, but Alfie had pushed back against them, causing even more tension. He wouldn't forsake his poorest citizens just because the nobles were accustomed to keeping their noses high in the air. This was more important than all that.

The guards led him through the gates into the former market square. Where before there had been dilapidated shops and garbage, now there was a quiet pond and stone gardens that encouraged self-reflection and peace. People were spread throughout the place of mourning, and as the guards led him and Luka to the memorial at the far end of the gardens, they murmured and whispered. Alfie didn't have to look to know that they were following them to stand before the memorial. He could feel the weight of their sorrow falling over him like a thick, dark veil.

"Hey," Luka said quietly from beside him. "I'm here. Just keep walking."

Alfie nodded, following the guardsmen numbly up the steps of the dais.

The memorial was a great wall of colored glass curved in a half circle. He wanted his people to feel embraced and shielded when they stood before it, and so he'd designed the wall to encircle them with color and light. On each patch of glass the names of the victims were written.

He had put so much into it that he'd thought he would feel a palpable sense of purpose when he finally shared it with his people. But now, standing before so many saddened faces, he felt completely unprepared. The speech he'd written was plucked from his mind like a petal from a flower.

The guardsmen spread themselves across the dais in a protective formation as Alfie stepped forward to address the somber crowd.

Luka gripped his arm. "You can do this." Then he stepped back, giving Alfie space to speak.

Alfie cleared his throat and murmured a spell to make his voice echo. Fragments of his speech were coming back to him now, snippets that he could barely grasp before they were swept away by the current of his anxiety.

"I stand before you, humbled by your presence." Alfie dropped into a low bow and held it for a long moment, hearing the murmurs of surprise at the sight. He rose and went on. "The loss of our loved ones to a murderous magic is one we will never forget. Today I present to you The Mural of Remembrance. A place to grieve the loss of those who were so unfairly taken from us. With the help of so many of you, this wall has been infused with the essence of your loved ones. When—"

"*Cállate, coward prince!*" a voice shouted from the crowd.

Alfie started, surprised by the hatred that dripped from the voice. The voice had come from the right side of the crowd, but he could not pinpoint it.

The guards tensed, their hands flexing to conjure elements and grip machetes.

"First you let those dueños kill us with their wild magic and now you ask us to open our borders to those Englassen pendejos and offer them peace?!" another voice shouted from the left. "How dare you?"

There was a loud rumbling from the crowd, many angry voices rolling together as one, like a kicked beehive. The air had become charged with such angry energy that it felt as if lightning might strike him dead where he stood.

Luka had rushed to Alfie's side. "I think we need to go—"

Alfie shook his head, unable to speak privately due to the echoing charm he'd cast on himself. But he knew Luka could tell what he was thinking.

This is my responsibility, my fault. I cannot run.

"My good people," Alfie said, his shaking voice betraying his nerves. "I built this memorial to give you the peace you so greatly deserve, just as the summit will grant two kingdoms the peace they've long yearned for."

More shouting erupted, and Alfie knew he'd said the wrong thing. In the blink of an eye the crowd had changed. Instead of somber, solemn faces, there were now only furious ones.

"Englass doesn't want peace, they want control!"

"You think a wall will bring me peace? My family is *dead*!"

The jeers became so overwhelming that Alfie could not hear individual words anymore, but with his *propio* engaged he could see colorful magic moving through the people's bodies with agitation and anger.

Furious citizens began to rush up the dais stairs, their fists raised, their faces twisted in anger.

"Alfie!" Luka cried, pulling him away. "We need to leave!"

"Protect the prince!" a guardswoman shouted. A core group of red-caped guards tightened their circle around Alfie while the others moved forward to block the crowd from reaching him. A whirring sound filled the air. Mouth open, Alfie watched countless ropes tipped with stone grappling hooks surge through the air, controlled by stone carvers in the crowd. The hooks dug into the top of the wall. The throng surged forward as the assailants tugged on the ropes, pulling the wall forward with a horrible screech.

"*No!*" Alfie shouted. He wouldn't let the wall be destroyed, not when so many had given so much for its creation. In the chaos he spotted a mother and her three children fleeing, and he knew without a doubt that it was Señora Vargas, the woman who had given him her husband's watch.

He could not let her sacrifice be in vain. Alfie pulled water from the air and formed disks of ice. He guided the disks through the air, cutting through three ropes.

"Prince Alfehr, get down!"

A guardswoman tackled Alfie and Luka to the ground as the

spot where he had just stood was pelted with large chunks of glass from the wall.

The guards swarmed around them. One tugged Alfie to his feet and forced him to run toward a secure carriage, Luka close behind.

"Stop!" Alfie shouted. "I can help, let me go!"

But then came a great keening and Alfie turned to see the wall of glass teeter forward. His breath caught as he watched it fall, shattering against the stone pedestal it had stood on.

The crowd began to run, scattering like mice under a sudden harsh glare of light. Alfie could see the guardsmen forcing their way into the panicked throngs of people to find those who had attacked, but Alfie knew they wouldn't find them.

The chaos was so intense, it was as if he could no longer hear. The screams had gone muffled and he could only feel and see the bedlam whirling around him. Just before the guardswoman shoved him toward the carriage, Alfie's eyes clung to a lone figure in the crowd—a man who stood still in a labyrinth of chaos. The top half of his face was covered in a black bull-faced mask, nostrils flared and horns jutting from his forehead in sharp points. The mask almost looked like it was moving, a living mass of darkness shifting around the man's face.

Then something heavy and sharp struck Alfie in the back of his head, and all went dark.

THE INFIRMARY

"Dez," Alfie called as he strode into the library.

Sunlight poured through the floor-to-ceiling windows. The jewel-toned leather spines of countless books gleamed on their shelves, begging to be picked up and read.

Dez looked up from the tomes lying open on his desk and smiled brilliantly, beckoning Alfie over. The piles of books were comically high, swaying like flowers in a breeze. The sight of them gave Alfie the inkling that this was not real. It was a dream. But that thought was quiet and far away, a ghost of an echo in the midst of this fantasy. So the prince pushed the thought away and sank further into the illusion.

"What are you studying?" Alfie asked, plopping into the armchair next to his brother.

"I'm doing some research to plan the peace summit with Englass," Dez said, his eyes alight with excitement and purpose. "This will be our kingdom's greatest accomplishment."

Alfie could only nod. Dez and his father had been working on *this for months in anticipation of a summit the next year. It would be Dez's crowning achievement and he hadn't even become king yet. Part of Alfie wanted to be jealous of all his brother was and all he would become, but seeing the look of pride in Dez's eyes, Alfie could only be happy for him. Dez had been born to be king and Alfie had long ago accepted that he'd been born to be something else, something less grand.*

"We are not free until all of us are free," Dezmin went on. "Englassen or otherwise, it doesn't matter. When we convince Englass to end their caste system, we will change the world." Then Dezmin closed his book with a loud snap. He shrugged with an easy laugh. "But I suppose it doesn't really matter now, does it?"

Dez had been working toward this his whole life. Of course it mattered. "What do you mean?"

"It doesn't matter because I'm dead and gone, hermanito," Dezmin said with a grin. "I'm rotting away in that void where you left me." His smile grew too wide then, taking up far too much of his face. No, his smile wasn't widening at all—the flesh around Dez's mouth was rotting away, peeling back until his lips were gone and there were only teeth. Though his heart pounded against his ribs, Alfie was so afraid that he couldn't move, couldn't speak. "And you're going to destroy everything I've worked for."

Alfie woke, his heart pounding and his sweat soaking the pillow under his head. It had been a long time since he'd had a dream like that. Nightmares of Dez falling to pieces had haunted him in that first month after his death, but not so much now. He laid his hand on his chest, willing his heart to slow down.

For a moment he'd thought he was in his room, but he wasn't

in his bed at all. He was in the palace infirmary and the back of his head hurt. Why did it sting so much?

Then the reality of the day struck him—the memorial, the destruction, something hitting him as the guards tried to spirit him away to safety.

He tentatively reached for the back of his head and rubbed it. It was still tender, but he knew that the healers had stopped the worst of the pain. His head aching, he took in the sight around him. The walls of the infirmary were stocked with healing potions. The glass ceiling was a calming mix of blues and greens. But Alfie was anything but calm.

He had never seen the Castallano people like this. They'd stared at him with pure hatred, as if they wanted to see him in pain—he'd hurt them so deeply with his actions, with his foolishness. If he couldn't soothe his own people's pain, how was he supposed to use this summit to undo centuries of oppression and grief? The nightmare he'd just woken up from rang in his sore head. He was going to ruin everything Dezmin had worked for in one fell swoop.

A soft snore drew his attention. Luka sat at his bedside, leaning back in his chair, his mouth wide open as he slept.

"Luka," Alfie said, his voice scratchy. He was parched. How long had he been asleep?

"Five more minutes," Luka whined.

Alfie's head felt too heavy for his body as he slowly sat up and shook Luka's shoulder. "Wake up!"

"I'm awake," Luka said, jolting forward. He stared sleepily before his gaze sharpened. "Alfie, lie back down."

Alfie shook his aching head as he shakily stood. "I have to talk to Mother and Father about the summit."

Luka gripped Alfie's shoulders and pushed him back onto the bed. "No, the only thing you need to do is rest. They are taking care of it and will meet you here when they're done."

Luka pressed Alfie down by the shoulder and, using only an ounce of his newly gained strength, laid Alfie flat in the blink of an eye.

The prince closed his eyes and sighed through his nose. If Luka was holding him down, there was no point in trying to get back up. "What happened after I was knocked out?" Alfie croaked.

Luka leaned back in his chair, frowning. "Honestly, more of what you saw before you got hit in the cabeza—chaos. The memorial shattered and we got you into the carriage while the guards swarmed the crowd." Luka shook his head, his curls bouncing on his forehead. "I've never seen anything like it, Alfie. Things got so out of control so quickly. You've been asleep for hours."

Alfie bent an elbow over his eyes. This was supposed to be the start of him giving back to his people, repairing the damage he'd done. But he'd only made it worse.

"How can we have a summit with the people protesting?" he asked, fear trickling down his spine. This summit would be tense enough as it was, but how would they fare with the Englassen royals if his people were cursing his name and protesting Englass's presence? At the same time, he couldn't blame his people; they had every right to hold Englass's past crimes against them.

Luka pried Alfie's arm off his eyes. "We'll find a way." He shot Alfie a mischievous grin. "After all, we've handled much worse, haven't we?"

Alfie gave a small smile. "I suppose we have." He paused for a long moment, thinking of how they'd trapped Sombra by the skin of their teeth. "Barely."

Luka threw his hands up. "Barely still counts!"

The doors to the infirmary flew open, and Alfie's parents strode to his bedside.

His mother cupped his cheek, her thumb rubbing soft circles against his skin. "You should be asleep." She pressed a kiss to his forehead.

"I'm fine," Alfie lied. His head was pounding, but worse, his heart was broken by the prospect of the memorial in pieces while the people's resentment remained perfectly intact.

"You're not," his father said, his voice soft with concern. "But know this: we're proud of you, Mijo, even if the memorial itself no longer stands."

Alfie's eyes burned as he nodded. "What about the summit? How will we keep the people under control if they're this angry about Englass coming here?"

"You needn't worry about that. The guardsmen will be doubling their patrols around the city," Queen Amada reassured him. "Everything will be fine."

Alfie wanted to believe her, but he could see the fear in his mother's eyes.

"We don't want you focusing on such things, Alfehr," his father said, his brow furrowed. "The people are upset, we know, but this peace summit will give you the opportunity to fix that. To show them the king you will become."

Alfie rubbed the back of his neck. This summit with Englass

was more than just a matter of calling a truce between their nations. Much more was at stake. Castallan's allies had stopped trade with Englass after they'd won back their freedom generations ago. Now only one of the five kingdoms, the winter kingdom of Uppskala, traded with Englass. Because of this, the colonizer kingdom had been in an economic downturn since well before Alfie was born. Last year, Dezmin had realized that Englass might finally be economically desperate enough to make some concessions. So Castallan had extended an olive branch, asking for Englass to join them for a peace summit to put the past behind them and reopen trade between the two kingdoms, which would likely also lead to Castallan's allies agreeing to trade with them too. But only if Englass would make one historic concession—abolish the kingdom's magical caste system.

Englass abided by a strict hierarchy. The nobility believed that only they deserved to use magic; the rest of the kingdom's citizens were made magically impotent through some particularly despicable spellwork. While hundreds of years ago Englass had forced Castallanos to forsake their mother tongue until they could no longer remember how to speak the language of magic, Englass had since perfected spellwork that made it impossible for the body to use the magic it took in. Now they didn't need to make Englassens in the lower castes forget their language of magic as they had done to Alfie's ancestors; they simply made it impossible for them to use it.

The thought shook Alfie to his bones. Not being able to use magic was tantamount to not being allowed to breathe. Englass's declining economic situation had given the two kingdoms the opportunity not only to clear the air but to finally rid the world of magical enslavement for good. Though the summit had been

Dezmin's idea, the people had only been told about it when the summit was finalized after Dez died. So they blamed Alfie for it, grumbling that Dezmin would never let such a thing happen. Living up to Dez was impossible when the people had built him up to be infallible.

Alfie shook his head. This was not about him and his fear of not filling Dez's shoes. This was about freeing thousands in bondage. Guilt knotted in his stomach—how selfish of him to shy away from something so important just because of the protests.

"After this summit, you will be known as the prince who brought Englass into line, who freed the world from magical bondage," his father said. "The people are upset now, but once this summit is over, they will accept and revere you. You will become a symbol of hope and the fight for equality—the prince who ended magical enslavement for good, making the world a safer and freer place for all." The king squeezed Alfie's shoulder. "Your brother would be so proud."

Alfie gripped his father's hand. Seven long months after Dez's death, his father could finally speak about his eldest son without losing himself entirely. It was wonderful, but also painful, because Alfie knew that this meant they were moving on from Dez, leaving him behind. He knew that this was natural, that it was what one had to do to move forward, but it also felt like a betrayal of Dezmin. Alfie forced those thoughts from his mind. Dwelling too much on Dez was what had gotten him and a certain thief into trouble before.

He had to move on.

"I know he would be," Alfie said, his voice thick.

"The memorial will be rebuilt into a plaza," Amada said. "And the beautiful colored glass will be inlaid into its floor. It will still be a place for people to grieve and find solace."

Alfie closed his eyes. He didn't want to hear any more about it. His head still sore, Alfie slowly sat up on his bed, leaning on his elbows and pushing himself upright. He could not keep chasing Dezmin's memory as he had before, but he could keep his brother alive through how he lived his own life. Dez never stayed down; he rose to the occasion no matter how difficult it was.

He swung his feet over the edge of the bed and shakily stood. His shadow wriggled uncertainly as he swayed on his feet before righting itself. Alfie held his head high and gave a resolute nod.

"I'm ready," he said, and in that moment he truly believed it.

His mother embraced him first, then his father joined in, and Alfie leaned into their touch, feeling the sense of safety one could only find in the arms of a loving family.

Luka cocked his head. "So can I join or is this a king-queen-prince-only situation?"

Alfie rolled his eyes before grabbing Luka by the arm and pulling him into the embrace. Enveloped in the love of his family, Alfie couldn't help but feel that even if everything went wrong with the summit, even if his people never stopped hating him, even if he couldn't become the king they deserved, at least he would always have this.

THE FAMILY FEUD

Ever since she could remember, Finn had loved being alone.

She loved the freedom of picking up the few items she called hers and leaving at a moment's notice. No tearful goodbyes, no see you soons, no hasta luegos. No promises to write letters or remember each other fondly. Just her and the world before her, ripe for the taking. Or open like a book, its pages poised for turning. That's what the prince would've said.

She sucked her teeth. Who cared about what the prince would say when she was in this mess?

Ever since she'd discovered the new side of her *propio*, she hadn't gotten a moment to herself.

"So." Ignacio's voice came from beside her. "Where are we going next?"

It had been three days since she'd learned she could control people's bodies with her *propio*, as if they were her own shadow—and since Ignacio had appeared uninvited. She'd walked for miles, hoping to get him out of her head, but no matter what turns she took, he followed.

She'd thought these last four months without him in her life or in her head had been her new beginning, but it was just a dream she'd been rudely awakened from, a short intermission between act one and two of this nightmare.

"Leave me alone," Finn barked over her shoulder.

"Now, let's talk about the wondrous thing that happened with your *propio*—"

"Cállate."

"You made your papá very proud by following in his footsteps."

"*Shut up!*" Finn shouted.

Two fishermen jumped where they walked behind her, looking at one another as if asking which of them had pissed her off.

"No, not you," Finn growled. "I mean him—" She waved a hand at Ignacio before remembering once again that she was the only one who could see him. And that she looked absolutely loca right now. "Just go!" she barked at them. "And stop staring!" She went on as they dashed away from her. "Don't you know it's rude!"

"Never thought I'd see the day when you chided someone else over their manners," Ignacio said with a smirk.

"You're not seeing anything," Finn said. "You're fucking dead."

She stormed through the crowds of the port and made her way to a quieter bit of the dock where only a few small fishermen's dinghies rocked. She didn't need to look behind her to know that Ignacio was following.

Finn leaned on the wood railing and stared out at the water.

Usually a sweeping ocean before her made her feel free, as if it were a single blue road that could carry her wherever she pleased. But now she felt trapped on this dock with a man she could've sworn she'd killed.

"How can this be happening? Why did it just start happening now?" She'd had her *propio* for most of her damn life. Did people still develop different facets of their *propios* when they were nearly nineteen years old?

"For all you know, it didn't appear just now." Ignacio's voice rang out from below her. Finn leaned over the wooden railing to see that he was, somehow, walking on water.

She wanted to spit at him, but that would be a waste of spit.

After glowering down at him in silence for a long moment, Finn finally relented. "What do you mean?"

"You've never faced someone in a fight while wearing their face before, Mija. You've only ever stolen someone's identity to take their place while they were absent. This was the first time it happened because the merchant got home early. Perhaps you would've discovered this part of your *propio* earlier if this situation had occurred before." In the blink of an eye he was gone, reappearing at her side, and she felt his warm breath sliding over the shell of her ear. "Maybe it's been *lying in wait*."

Finn swung a fist at where Ignacio stood beside her, but it simply went through him, as if he were nothing but air.

He was right, though. She'd never faced anyone while wearing their identity, until the merchant. Maybe that was the requirement.

Ignacio leaned against the railing beside her. "It's nice to know that a father can still be surprised by his daughter, even after death.

Then again, none of this is surprising. Not really. I've always known that you had much of me in you."

"How are you still this annoying when you're dead?" she grumbled.

Finn's feet carried her to the farthest reaches of the port, where the fishermen were scarce. She relished the silence as the sun dipped ever closer to the horizon. Sometimes Ignacio would disappear for a while, giving her a break. She could never predict when, but she wasn't going to question it.

Finn frowned as she heard footsteps closing in behind her.

"You couldn't even give me an hour," she sighed with annoyance, looking over her shoulder. But it wasn't Ignacio behind her. It was someone else.

A stranger in a black horned mask.

His fist flew toward her face and Finn stumbled, falling onto her bottom. Before he could jump on her, she pulled a shield of rock up from the ground, creating a makeshift wall between them.

"Who are you?" she shouted. Thrusting her arm before her, she sent the wall of rock flying forward, hoping it would plow through the man, but he simply vaulted over it.

Finn cloaked her fist in a globe of stone and swung for his temple. Quick-footed, he stepped back just in time, but Finn could still destroy that strange mask. It shimmered, even looked a bit fragile. Was it made of glass? Maybe the mask shattering on his face would give her an opening to take him down.

As her fist struck the black horn of the mask, she'd expected a *crack*, but she heard nothing. Her stone-gloved hand moved through it as if it were thickened, dark water. Some of it stained her fingers.

Instead of splattering apart, the paint simply snapped back into shape around the man's face. Even the black drops that clung to Finn's knuckles slipped back to re-form the mask. She'd only glimpsed a sliver of his brown skin before his face was fully covered again.

Finn's jaw dropped. What was this mask made of? But before she could dodge, the man had leaped on her, pinning her to the ground. She felt a pinch at her neck and her body fell slack. When he pulled his hand back she saw a quilbear quill.

Damn it, she thought, her pulse racing. Was this how she would die? After finally killing Ignacio (physically, anyway), would she die now?

"You'll pay for this," Finn said through gritted teeth. "Quilbear venom only lasts for a few minutes, but I will hunt you for the rest of your days."

She glared into his dark eyes through the holes in the mask. His sleeve had rolled up when he landed on her, and etched onto his forearm was a bull tattoo.

Finn's heart sputtered.

That was what his horned mask was—a bull. Both the mask and his tattoo were identical to Kol's tattoo. Just like the bull tattoo the prince had seen when he was under the influence of Sombra's magic and had asked about the people who had killed his brother. This was no regular thief; this was a prince-killer.

Then it struck her. The mask was made of not water or paint but tattoo ink. They were connected. They had to be.

As he raised his hand, his fingers moving toward her neck, Finn willed her body to fight. She'd lived through too much to die now.

And who would tell the prince that this was coming? Who would warn him?

Her mind a haze of panic, she shouted the first question she could think of. "Why did you kill the crown prince?"

His fingers grazing her throat, he went still, seemingly stunned by the question.

But it only stopped him for a moment. His hand touched her neck and Finn was certain he was going to strangle her in the dirt, but he only lifted her head gently off the ground, pulled the strap of her knapsack over her head, and stood.

She was so surprised to still be breathing that she didn't speak— until she saw him going through her things.

"Give me back my bag!" she demanded from the ground. "Keep your filthy hands off my things, pendejo!"

For a moment, he seemed to find nothing of value, but then she saw him pulling something out of the bag, something she couldn't see—

The vanishing cloak. The last thing the prince had given her. Her last connection to him.

Anger swept through her, hot and fierce, but under it was pure desperation for the cloak, for the prince. A desperation she knew was pathetic, but she couldn't hold it back. When he moved to walk away she shouted, "Stop! That's mine!"

He paused, looking down at her, and Finn was annoyed that she couldn't glare at him properly since, from this angle, she couldn't see his eyes through the mask. "The vanishing cloak does not belong to you or to the prince who gave it to you," he said, his voice low and sure. "It belongs to the true king of Castallan. A king who would never let Englass set foot on these shores."

Finn didn't know what to make of that. Was there really this much anger about the peace summit? Enough discontent that people believed the vanishing cloak didn't belong to Alfie's family anymore?

But the man didn't stick around to answer questions. He dropped her bag next to her head and walked away, the cloak tucked under his arm.

"Come back!" she shouted at his retreating figure. She'd be stuck here for another five minutes at least. By then he'd be long gone, along with the cloak. "Coward!"

But the man didn't stop and there was no one to hear her cries.

No one but Ignacio.

"Well, well, well," he tutted. "You do seem to get into trouble whenever I'm away, don't you?"

Finn wished she could disappear into the dirt rather than watch him kneel beside her, but she didn't have the energy to curse the specter of Ignacio.

She flexed her fingers. The venom was finally wearing off, and she knew what she had to do next.

"Not that boy again," Ignacio sighed. "Come now, you can't be serious."

"Stay out of my head," Finn said through gritted teeth. She needed to get back to San Cristóbal to tell Alfie what she'd seen and help him put a stop to these bull-tattooed pendejos once and for all.

"That's not all, though, is it?" Ignacio chided. Finn chewed her lip and Ignacio smiled down at her, like a cat with its paw on a mouse's tail. "You think he'll help you get rid of me."

Finn looked away from him, her face feeling hot. It was Alfie's voice that had pulled her up when Ignacio had made her feel as if the only option was to swim down. He'd given her the courage to fight for who she could be instead of becoming whatever Ignacio wanted.

Alfie's voice had freed her before; maybe he could help her drown out Ignacio once more. In all the cities she'd traveled to, she'd heard people grumbling about the upcoming peace summit with Englass. She knew the prince would be busy with that boring stuff, but he'd have to clear his schedule.

She met Ignacio's eyes, a smirk curving her lips. "He helped me kill you before, didn't he? Who says he can't again?"

Ignacio frowned at her with the disapproving look of a father catching his child eating sweets just before dinner. At the sight of his annoyance, a plume of hope caught in her chest. She had to celebrate the small victories, after all.

She curled her toes, feeling awareness flow back into her body. As soon as she got her land legs back, she'd be trading them for sea legs on the first ship back to San Cristóbal.

THE DENIAL

One week later Finn walked along the deck of a swaying ship as it skirted the eastern shore of Castallan, the sea breeze pushing her curls every which way.

There was only one more night before her ship docked in San Cristóbal and she couldn't sleep. It'd been impossible to get a good night's rest with Ignacio appearing like some unwanted houseguest and the memory of the bull-masked man plaguing her. And so every night, she found herself exploring the deck. If she was going to be bothered by the ghost of a maldito jerk, she'd rather do it with fresh air in her lungs and stars over her head.

The moon hung heavy above the ship, the deck silent, as all the other passengers had long since gone to bed. Well, all except one. There was a man who was a bit too keen on rum, and he tended to drink himself stupid each night until he passed out on the deck. There he was, as always, his back planted against the starboard wall of the ship. His mouth hung open, drool dribbling down his chin. Finn walked past without so much as a glance. The novelty of him had worn off now that she'd witnessed his sloppy behavior for nearly a week.

Her head aching, Finn wished she could just go to bed, but every time she did, she feared she would wake up to Ignacio standing over her.

She wrapped her arms around herself, a chill skittering up her spine.

His presence had begun to subside a little ever since she'd decided to go back to San Cristóbal. Maybe it was a coincidence. Or maybe that meant her decision was the right one. That going back to Alfie was the best call.

She pushed that thought away. She was going to San Cristóbal because they needed to talk about the bull-masked bastard who had stolen the cloak out from under her. Not because she knew the prince tended to bring out the best in her and strip Ignacio's influence off her skin.

Certainly not because she missed him either. This was all business.

The drunk gave several loud, wet snores. Rolling her eyes, Finn turned to look at him.

"I take it you agree with me." She crossed her arms. His response was a piglike snort. "Good to know."

Finn's eyes strayed from the man's face to where his shadow sat stagnant on the ground. He had no *propio*; he was just a regular man who drank too much and thought too little. Her eyes clung to him. She thought of the night she'd controlled the merchant woman. Of how confusing and strange it felt at first, and then not so strange. Then powerful, invigorating, but also terrifying. A fresh part of her *propio* blooming before her like a flower. No, that was far too romantic. More like uncorking a perfectly aged bottle of rum and relishing that first burn as it ran down your throat. All she had to do was engage this new part of her *propio* and she could feel that rush again.

Finn's shadow surged across the deck toward the drunk man's.

"No," Finn said, grinding her heels into the floor to force her shadow to stop. *"No."*

That part of her *propio* was too much like Ignacio. Part of her feared that it would conjure him and, even if it didn't, that it would make him happy, wherever he was—hell, hopefully.

Finn stared at him, her fingers twitching.

One's *propio* developed based on who you were—the events, people, and feelings that shaped you. What did it mean if her *propio* had morphed to be more like Ignacio's? Did it mean they were alike? That he'd shaped her so thoroughly that her magic was changing, infected by his sickness? She shuddered, but the urge to do it again still roared within her.

The problem with discovering the different sides of your *propio* was that once you knew it existed, your body itched to use it. When she'd first engaged her *propio* as a child, the desire to use it was so fierce that she would go to bed with one face and wake with another. To force herself to never use it would be like trying to teach a toddler to stop walking and go back to crawling. It didn't make sense.

She stared at the drunkard again, sweat beading on her forehead despite the night's chill. She didn't want to give in, didn't want to be anything like Ignacio. If she could stifle this part of her *propio*, maybe he would never haunt her again.

But could she truly deny this piece of herself?

Finn paced on the deck, the combination of the man's obnoxious snores and her own loud footsteps forming a cacophonous rhythm.

"Fine, damn it!" Finn finally cursed. Maybe she just needed to get it out of her system. Yes, that made sense, didn't it?

Standing a few feet away from the man, she changed herself until she matched his appearance to a T, from his scraggly beard to his greasy skin to his twig legs. The last time she'd done this with the merchant woman, it had been an accident. Now that she *wanted* it to happen, Finn wasn't exactly sure how.

"Ha!" She threw her arm out and reached for him with wriggling fingers. The man stayed on the ground, smacking his lips loudly in his sleep.

"Come on, pendejo," she grunted, flexing her fingers harder, but after a long moment nothing happened. Finn was struck by how stupid she must look right now. With a gusty sigh, she dropped her arm.

"*Propios* don't come with a maldito manual," she huffed. It wasn't as if she could re-create the situation that had led her to discovering this part of her *propio*. It had just happened. How would she do it now?

Annoyingly, her thoughts strayed to the prince, and the way an intense focus overtook him whenever he called upon magic. It was a stillness that was almost meditative—his body was present, but his mind had gone elsewhere.

Finn took a deep breath and closed her eyes, focusing on the sound of the man's ragged breathing. She didn't know how long she'd been doing it when she felt something pull at her senses like a string that had just come loose. Was this what it felt like when the prince dabbled in his magic coloring or painting or whatever it was that he did—this strange feeling of things unseen, unknown to anyone but him?

Finn reached for the string and pulled, feeling a surge of energy. Goose bumps rose on her skin. When she opened her eyes, the drunkard's body began to move from the ground to match her stance. He rose with his feet firmly planted but his back lifting off the ground until he was upright. He was still passed out cold, but now he stood, his shoulders squared, his back and neck straight. Finn forced herself to smile widely, but the man's face didn't respond.

"So it's just body movements, not facial expressions," she said to the still-sleeping man. "Interesting."

Finn took a step to the right and the man moved in unison. A step to the left yielded the same result.

A smirk on her face, Finn moved to the languid rhythm of a bachata in her head. "One, two, three, four," she counted out the beats, punctuating them with a swish of her hips. The drunkard followed, mirroring her every move. Finn burst into laughter at the sight.

Until the man started blinking awake.

Finn froze as the man yawned, somehow still unaware that he wasn't in control of his body. Should she just hold on to him for now? Or should she disconnect her shadow from his? Would it injure him if she did it too abruptly? Would he fall to the ground?

In the blink of an eye a wave of exhaustion fell over her, along with a splitting migraine and an ache in her bones that could only come from a life of rum and back alley fights. With a shock, she realized that she was feeling what the drunk felt. Mirroring him had brought everything he felt into her mind, as if his feelings were her own. Those awful sensations surged from the man, up the string tethering them together and into her.

After a long moment, the man's eyes slid closed and he fell right back into his drunken stupor. As he fell asleep, the emotions subsided.

Finn sighed in relief.

"Hello, Mija." Ignacio's cool voice sounded from behind her.

Finn jumped where she stood, her connection with the sleeping man snapping like a twig. The man crumpled to the ground in a pile of loose limbs.

"*Coñooooo!*" he growled before settling down on the floor and going right back to sleep, but Finn felt no relief because she knew Ignacio was behind her, grinning his maniacal grin. She shuddered, her focus lost, and her body returned to its original form, shedding the drunk's image.

"Well, well, well," Ignacio drawled, walking around her slowly like a predator circling its limping prey. But that wasn't quite right. That would imply that maybe she could still make a run for it, but how could she run from something that lived in her mind?

Ignacio circled her like a scavenger circled a corpse.

"I see that you're experimenting. Learning your new skill. Very good."

"Shut up," Finn said, pressing the heels of her hands into her eyes. "You're not here."

"Well," Ignacio said, smirking when Finn finally looked at him. "I think we've established that I'm not here physically. But I am here, right in your head." He tapped her forehead. When Finn swiped at his arm, her fingers went through it like smoke. The air rebounded and re-formed into his arm in the blink of an eye. "And why should that be any less real?"

"Why are you coming back as some stupid ghost? Why won't you leave me alone?"

Ignacio walked toward the sleeping man and grimaced, wrinkling his nose as if he could smell the man's stink. "Who can say? What I know is that you decided to become just like me after I died." He frowned at her. "Inconvenient, but I suppose better late than never."

"I am nothing like you," Finn bit out. "Nothing."

"Oh really?" Ignacio pointed at the man. "Then what was that? It looked a lot like me."

"*Cállate!*" Finn shouted.

"I didn't say anything," the drunkard grumbled from where he lay on the floor. "Loca."

"Why not just give in? Look at this sorry excuse of a man." Ignacio gestured at the drunk. "Why not control him, make him walk right into the water and drown himself?"

Finn shook her head. "Why would anyone want to do that?"

"Because you can, Mija. Because that is power. One day you will give in to it. Maybe not tonight, or tomorrow, but someday you will. And that pathetic prince will not be able to stop it for you. He won't be able to stop me from reminding you of just who you are." He smiled wildly. "Not even my death could stop this. How could a sad little boy?"

Finn raised her fists, ready for a fight even if she couldn't touch him, but Ignacio was gone. It was just her and the drunk again. A sigh rasped out of her, dry and weak. She rubbed the back of her hand across her stinging eyes and stared at the lights of Castallan, her mind running from the present toward the prince. Where was he now? Probably in the palace, preparing for the peace summit or reading or something boring. His night couldn't possibly be going half as bad as hers. She bit her lip, nearly cutting it.

Would he be able to help her? Or would this all be for nothing?

She rubbed the back of her neck roughly, as if she could scrub herself clean of Ignacio. At least now she knew how this new part of her *propio* worked. She needed to change herself to match the other person, and then she needed to focus, find that connection between them and tug on it. That was something, wasn't it?

Or was it just taking her one step closer to Ignacio?

Finn dug into her bag until her hand closed over something small. In her palm was the fox figurine that the prince had given her before she'd left San Cristóbal.

Keep it. It suits you.

She smiled at the sight of it, her fingers moving over the fox's snout. She squinted. Was it her imagination or did the fox look angrier? Its teeth were sharper, its mouth curved in a slight snarl, when she remembered it once sitting serenely.

Finn jumped as the drunk man gave a long, winding burp, then sat up and locked his glazed eyes on her. "You're having a rough night, aren't you, muchacha?"

Finn scowled and walked toward the doors to the hull of the ship, where her cot waited. Where she knew she would get little sleep. "Mind your business."

* * *

When the ship finally docked in the clear waters of the Suave the next day, Finn could hardly stop herself from racing down the gangplank and into the port.

The busy dock stank of fish and salt, and the two-faced clock chimed in the near distance. The clock seemed to welcome her home, its panes of red and blue glass melding into purple as it winked at her in the light of the setting sun.

San Cristóbal's port was peppered with foreign ships, and foreign faces as well. In the midst of the crowds of brown-skinned, dark-haired Castallanos she also spotted small groups of blondes and redheads with startlingly pale skin. She'd heard that the summit would feature exhibitions where both Englass and Castallan would display their arts, food, and culture. These must be the common people who would be working on those displays and the crews of ships that had delivered them and other foreign guests to the city. The place was so crowded that Finn could hardly walk without bumping shoulders with someone.

She'd been hearing murmurs, both positive and negative, about the summit in every city she'd dashed through over the last four months, but seeing Englassens here in San Cristóbal was altogether different. There was a strange tension in the air. Some Castallanos looked at the foreigners with unguarded disgust, as if a fight was moments from breaking out. But then she saw the opposite too, such as a vendor handing an Englassen sailor a free sample as they both smiled and laughed.

Finn didn't know on which side she stood. After all, these Englassens weren't the royals who still magically enslaved their own people. These were the lower-class people who weren't allowed to use magic. She shuddered. Finn didn't know how she felt about a possible peace between their kingdoms, but she knew she couldn't blame these people for what their past royals had done here generations ago. But if any of the common Englassens stuck their noses up in the air and shoved that Englassen superiority shit in her face, she'd be more than happy to teach them a lesson.

Now, if the current Englassen royals, the sons and daughters of the people who had enslaved Finn's ancestors, were walking around the Pinch unguarded, that would be a different story. They were still enslaving others and getting rich off their labor. The prince would be the one who had to deal with them. He was probably out of his mind with nerves.

At the thought of him, her eyes took to the horizon, searching. Beyond the port would be the Brim, and somewhere beyond that stood the palace. His palace. Her throat tightened in a way that she could not dismiss as thirst or the beginnings of a cough.

The first time Finn had worked in a circus with Ignacio, she'd watched the performers jitter with energy as they took their bows. She'd never seen anyone look so incandescently happy.

"You see that," an acrobat had said to her. "It's a hell of a feeling, isn't it? Being seen."

"Being seen?" she asked. "But people are seen all the time."

"Not like that," the acrobat said, nodding toward the performers. "Nothing makes you smile brighter than your talents truly being seen."

As Finn began performing herself, she learned the truth in those words. There was something invigorating about the audience's eyes on you, their held breath as you moved through the air—their hope, their trust, their genuine belief that you would land safely on the other side. She got the same feeling when she stole an identity, waltzed into a mark's house, and thieved them for all they were worth. After all, that was a performance in and of itself.

But things had changed. Neither the invigorating roar of a crowd nor the thrill of a well-executed thieving made her feel seen. Not anymore. What made her feel seen were the prince's golden eyes, thoughtful and imploring. The gaze promised that beneath the grime of all that she'd done, she was still flesh and bone. Still human.

Broken, yes, but never beyond repair.

The prince had seen more of her than anyone she knew, and what he'd seen hadn't scared him, hadn't made him turn away. He'd seen her in her entirety and told her that she could be more than Ignacio had made her. And now, with the sudden ability to puppeteer others, she felt Ignacio's spirit within her more than ever, and the strong current of the prince's words had slowed, giving way to Ignacio's laughter and his promise that she would become the little monstro he'd raised her to be. She knew in her heart that the only thing that could possibly snuff out that terrible feeling again was Alfie.

She would tell him about her fight with the man who had stolen the cloak and help him deal with the bull-masked pendejos in any way she could. After he had helped her take down Ignacio, she owed him that much. But after that she'd be on her way. Maybe she only needed to see him one more time, and for him to see her too. To go on one last adventure together and then Ignacio would be gone for good. Then she'd hop on the next ship out of here and get back to her life.

Back to normal.

Her satchel swinging at her hip, Finn pushed through the crowds of the port and the twisty lanes of vibrantly colored pubs and fish markets where tropical fish from the Suave sat ready to be deboned and fried. She couldn't wait to get to the Brim and lose herself in the chaos of the marketplace.

She'd lose herself there and then find herself once more when she found him.

Finn walked through the Pinch with purpose, until she heard angry shouting from farther down the road. Finn followed the sound and the sudden smell of smoke to see a group of people gathered around some burning . . . piñatas?

"*No peace for colonizers! Keep Castallan Englassen-free!*"

Finn squinted up at the smoldering objects. They were clearly in the shape of people. She stared intently at one and then she saw it, big gold eyes painted on the face, a crown resting on curly hair—it was Alfie. The other burning dummies were his parents. Finn was no stranger to hating royals, but her stomach tightened at the sight of Alfie breaking into ash and flames.

She'd left San Cristóbal for four months and everything had gone to hell.

"Oye." Finn gripped one of the chanting protestors by the arm. "Qué fue? Isn't there supposed to be a peace party soon or something? What's with the burning piñatas?"

At the mention of the summit, the man spat at the ground. "We're protesting the royal family. They gave the dueños too much free rein and look what happened—those stuffy bruxos released magic that killed hundreds of us!"

Finn's eyebrows shot up. Clearly the royal family had come up with a story to cover what had really happened. Finn shuddered at the memory of Bathtub Boy almost dying in her arms as Alfie begged her to help him. She could still feel the sudden chill that came with the Sombra's release, as if her body had been frozen from the inside out. Her skin tingled with gooseflesh.

"Now they're holding this disgusting summit with the Englassen royal family to present the fool prince as our future king. He's no king, and we don't want Englassen scum on our land!"

"That maldito Prince Alfehr," a woman said with a scowl. "If Prince Dezmin were still alive, we wouldn't have Englassen animals inside our borders."

"You should shut your mouth," Finn said, her eyes glued to the cheap burning replicas of the very real prince. If it were anyone else's image, she would've laughed. But she couldn't. Not when she knew that seeing this would kill him.

"With him leading us the whole kingdom is—"

"Shut your mouth," Finn seethed.

"—it should've been him who died instead—"

Finn silenced her with a punch to the stomach. The woman bent forward with a gasp, her full weight falling on Finn's fist. Then with an upward jutting of her arms, the burning piñatas were covered in dirt, putting the fires out and leaving nothing but smoking debris.

The protesters, now covered in dirt from Finn's stone carving, turned toward her.

The chanting protestors fell quiet as their eyes locked on the coughing woman who'd fallen to her knees in front of Finn.

"Oye! She punched my wife!" a man cried, dashing to the choking woman's side.

"And she put out the fire!" another shouted.

Finn was a fighter, but she knew when she was outnumbered. With dozens of eyes locked on her, Finn took a tentative step back.

The protestors took a step forward. A tense silence stretched its long fingers until Finn could feel it gripping her about the neck.

"Mierda," she murmured before turning on her heel and running away.

The protesters ran after her, the burning dummies of Alfie jostling on their poles as they gave chase. Finn's arms pumped as she sprinted so fast she was afraid she'd trip over her feet. She raced through the crowds but couldn't shake the protestors off her tail.

Turning a corner, Finn ducked into an alleyway. With her back pressed to the wall, she watched the stampede of protestors run on, leaving her in the dust.

"What the hell did you do, Prince?" she muttered as she caught her breath. She'd never seen the people of San Cristóbal this riled up. And with the peace summit about to begin? She could imagine him now, pacing in his room, his brow furrowed, his fingers itching for a book to help him manage this catastrophe.

Her lips quirked up before she forced them flat. But then, maybe it made more sense to just ask him herself.

Finn poked her head out of the alley to make sure the coast was clear. Once she knew the protestors were long gone, she'd go find the prince.

"Face Thief," a voice called from the dark of the alley.

Finn whirled around, her fists raised, but it was no use as a hand pressed a handkerchief to her nose. She reached for the assailant's neck and gripped hard, relishing the sound of them choking, but it was too late. As her vision began to blur, Finn's grip loosened and she fell into the dark.

THE SOUND

Paloma's lecture on Englassen economics flowed soundlessly around Alfie.

As the sun set over San Cristóbal, its final tendrils of light pouring through the palace windows, he could not get the bull-masked man out of his head.

He'd stood in the chaos of the falling memorial with a chilling calm. And the black bull mask had looked exactly like the tattoo Alfie had seen in his vision in the prison when he'd asked the dark magic why Marco Zelas had helped kill Dez. The very same tattoo that Finn had claimed she saw on Kol's arm. Alfie's skin crawled.

Was the mask related to the bull tattoo? If it was, then how could he learn more about it?

"Prince Alfehr."

Paloma's voice pulled him to the present with a jarring tug.

Alfie blinked. "Sorry, what?"

"I asked if you would like to go over the summit schedule and your duties. Unless you know them so well that you don't need a refresher," she said, raising a brow.

He knew the schedule backward and forward, but he also knew that Paloma wouldn't be satisfied unless they went over it again. "Yes, please, go on."

"The summit will span eight days, tomorrow being the first. The Englassen royals and their advisors will arrive in the afternoon."

Alfie sat straight. "We will greet them and then they will be given time to settle in before the welcome banquet in the evening."

"Correct," Paloma said. "The second day you will begin your morning with trade meetings to discuss what each kingdom can offer the other economically. Keep in mind that—"

"—I am representing my nation and must lead the discussion with knowledge and grace."

"Good," Paloma said with a stern nod. "Your afternoon will be free, but in the evening we will host an art exhibition displaying both Englassen and Castallano art. And on the third day?"

He felt as if he was being asked to recite his ABCs. "We have a meeting on the exchange of magical scholarship in the morning and then the first cultural exhibition in the afternoon." In order to promote friendly relations between Englass and Castallan, the summit would feature exhibitions to celebrate both kingdoms and foster cultural exchange. "And then an early dinner so that our guests have time to rest for the next morning's meeting."

"And the fourth day?" Paloma pressed on.

"We have our first meeting about the abolishment of Englass's caste system." That would be quite the morning.

He had initially thought that they'd jump right into discussion of ending Englass's caste system as soon as the summit began, but his parents did not feel that was the best strategy. His father had told him that though Englass had agreed to consider their demands, they mustn't jump directly into discussions on that topic. First they needed their guests to warm up, and so they would welcome the Englassens to the kingdom and show them what they stood to gain should they come to terms. Then they would get down to the specifics of ending the caste system for good.

"The rest of the day will be free due to the probable intensity of that meeting," Alfie said.

"Good." Paloma nodded. "Carry on."

"On the fifth day we have the second cultural exhibition in the morning. Then afternoon meetings to continue the discussion on the caste system."

"And the sixth day?" Paloma said.

Alfie wanted to bang his head on the desk. "In the morning we will meet to finalize the details of the deconstruction of Englass's caste system and the end of magical enslavement. The rest of the day is free so the meeting may last as long as necessary to reach terms." Alfie didn't wait for her to confirm that he was correct and sped through the rest of the schedule. "The seventh day is a free day for royals to mingle, rest, concluding with a farewell banquet. The Englassen royals return home the morning of the eighth day."

She nodded, satisfied. "Now let us discuss the exchange of scholarship with Englass . . ."

Alfie tried his best to hold on to Paloma's words, but his thoughts pulled him far away.

He'd told Luka about the bull-masked man at the memorial, but he hadn't told his parents. After all, with the protests growing rowdier the closer they got to the summit, they hardly needed another thing to worry about. And what would he tell them? "I'm pretty sure that I saw a man in a bull mask at the memorial that matched a vision I saw of a bull tattoo when I was under the influence of the dark magic I irresponsibly released. We should, perhaps, look into it?"

He shook his head. He hadn't told his parents about the visions Sombra's magic had given him. They'd been shaken enough by the rest of the story. They didn't need more reason to distrust him. He needed to let this go and focus on preparing for the summit, but as he sat through lecture after lecture and watched the servants rush about the palace preparing for the arrival of their Englassen guests, he could think of nothing but the memorial shattering and the masked man standing amid the chaos as if he'd planned it.

A day that should have been about honoring the victims had become a catastrophe. Just thinking of the precious items of the dead that he'd been entrusted with only for them to go to waste, his stomach twisted with guilt and anger. He thought of how reluctantly Señora Vargas had given him her husband's watch, of her children, who would grow up without their papá. It had all been for nothing. All the items he'd been given could not be recovered. Their essences had been absorbed into the memorial and were destroyed with it.

"Prince Alfehr," Paloma snapped.

Alfie jumped in his seat before cradling his head in his hands. "I'm sorry, Paloma," he said, his fingers kneading his temples. "I can't stop thinking about it."

Even after the disastrous memorial, his parents were support-ing him and finally beginning to trust him again, but it still felt as if something dark was looming just out of sight. If things felt right, if he was even slightly hopeful, then something must be wrong.

"Prince Alfehr," Paloma said as gently as he'd ever heard her. "You know that I believe in ruminating on the consequences of one's actions, but don't you think you've suffered enough these last four months? You must let it go."

Alfie hung his head. He knew he had to let go, but it was difficult. Shame was an intoxicating thing. The deeper he sank into it, the more comfortable it felt. When he gave in, there was almost a feeling of relief, of a heavy burden unloaded. There was a calming sense of safety in saying to himself, *Of course I'm a failure. Of course I'm not worthy of the throne. I knew that all along, didn't I?*

"How can I?" he said. "I did too much harm to my people, to those I love," he said, pressing his palms into his eyes. He winced as that last thought conjured up the memory of Luka dying in his arms and then Finn, promising to die with him only a few months ago. He shook his head free of those bleak thoughts. Luka was safe and Finn was gone, never coming back. After all, why would she? His release of the dark magic had empowered her greatest enemy and nearly killed her. It was no wonder that she'd wanted nothing to do with him, that he'd received no letter, no sign of where she was or if she was safe.

Why would she want him to know anyway?

"Prince Alfehr," Paloma said again, her voice resolute. "You made a mistake, this we already know. To let yourself wallow in guilt and self-pity instead of rising to the challenge of this summit would be your second mistake." She crossed her arms, looking away from him and out the window. "Do pull yourself together. As you know, I am not one for pep talks."

Alfie couldn't help but smile at that, and when he saw Paloma's lip quirk, he knew she'd done her best to make him laugh.

He nodded. "You're right. Perdóname."

Paloma stared at him for a long time, and he could tell she knew her "joke" hadn't quite worked. She drummed her fingers on her forearms. "That's enough about the summit schedule for now. I have something more important for you to do, something that may restore some peace to you." Paloma eyed him carefully. "When is the last time you meditated and entered the realm of magic?"

Alfie's spine straightened. The last time he'd done that, Finn had held a dying Luka in her lap, and he'd released Sombra into the world.

Sweat beaded on Alfie's forehead. "You know when," he murmured.

"And you've avoided it since then?"

Alfie nodded.

"Have you avoided the realm of magic completely—have you stopped traveling through it with your *propio*?"

Alfie pressed his lips together. He hated that Paloma knew him so well. Ever since he'd unleashed Sombra's dark power from the realm of magic, the idea of immersing himself in the magic again made him nervous. It reminded him too much of the evil he'd found. He still used his *propio* to see the shades of magic threaded through the world and occasionally to match his magic to another's the way he had at the cambió game where he'd met Finn, but he was far too afraid to use it to return to the realm of magic or travel through its channels.

Magic had once been a sanctuary to sink into, but now it felt like a trap. A home he'd grown up in that now had its windows boarded up and its doors locked for his own good.

"I haven't been able to," he said, his voice threadbare. "I can't."

"Prince Alfehr," Paloma said, her flat voice betraying a hint of concern. "A fine bruxo must have a healthy relationship with the realm of magic and with his own magic as well. Sombra's essence is gone. It is not in the channels of magic where you found it. It is elsewhere, in a place that you cannot possibly reach now."

Alfie clasped his hands behind his back, his grip tight. She was right. It was in Xiomara's void. His feelings about Xiomara—the girl who had disappeared Dez into the darkness but had also helped him save the world from Sombra after he and Finn had broken her out of the Clock Tower—were complicated. In his mind's eye he could still see her falling into the void, letting it close behind her forever, locking him out of the place his brother had been trapped.

I want to make it right, she'd scrawled before she'd died, and the thought of her still put Alfie in such a confusion of anger and remorse that he could hardly stand it. She'd saved them all, but she'd forever stopped him from finding Dez. He still couldn't decide if he was grateful to her or angry with her. He doubted he'd ever settle on one.

Alfie rubbed his stinging eyes. "I can't, Paloma. Not now. I just can't."

"Try," she said. Then she made her way to the door.

Alfie's breath caught. He wanted to make her stay and guide him the way she had when he was a boy. But he knew that this was his journey, and she was not one for hand-holding.

"You'll be fine," she said. "Trust that the magic will welcome you back in. Because it will. But first you must open the door." His teacher walked toward the classroom's exit, and with each step she took, Alfie wanted to beg her to change her mind, to let him avoid the magic for just a little longer. "Prince Alfie," Paloma called just before she stepped out of the room.

"Sí?" he said, hope in his heart. She rarely called him by his nickname; maybe she would let him go this one time.

"You have grown up on tales and histories of kings and queens, some worthy and noble, others driven by greed. Do you recognize a common thread among those who rose to become legends?"

Alfie cocked his head, thinking of the tales he'd heard throughout his childhood. "Confidence?" he said. "Strength?" Two things he sorely lacked.

"No," Paloma said with a shake of her head. "Hesitation."

Alfie stared at her. "What do you mean?"

"The rulers who were consumed by greed and ambition were the confident ones who ran to claim the throne without a second thought, never wondering if they were worthy. They sought glory, not the betterment of their people. At best, they were forgettable rulers; at worst, they were disgraced. Those who became great and loved and remembered were those who hesitated, those who knew the task before them was one not to be taken lightly. Those who were afraid but stepped forward nonetheless."

Alfie felt his throat burning. Her words were so kind that he couldn't look at her.

"The mark of a king does not lie in a haughty, steadfast demeanor brimming with confidence, making decisions at the drop of a hat, completely confident in your own judgment. It lies in the knowledge that to rule a kingdom is to take on an arduous task. It lies in constantly questioning your own motives when making choices that will affect thousands upon thousands of innocents. Know that the voice in your head telling you that you are not worthy, that this task is too great for you to comprehend, may in fact be all the proof you need to know that you *are* worthy. You always have been. Now return to the world of magic and face what you fear so that you can move on and become the king I have always known you could be."

Alfie's eyes stung. He opened his mouth to thank Paloma, to say anything that could possibly reflect his gratitude, but she turned away from him and walked out the door, leaving Alfie swaddled in silence.

Alfie ran a shaking hand through his hair. These last couple of days had been too much. The shadow of what he'd done when he'd released Sombra's magic still hung heavy over him, like a black velvet veil, forever blocking his vision. Then the rage in his people's eyes at the memorial, and now this. She wanted him to return to a place that had ruined him and led him to the most foolish decision of his life. A place that led to more deaths than he could count.

He pressed a hand over his eyes and took a deep breath.

Before everything had happened, he had been working on accessing the realm of magic. It was the mark of a true bruxo—a learned practitioner and scholar of magic. It had been a terrible twist of fate that the first time he'd ever been able to truly enter it, he'd released Sombra's magic into the world. It wouldn't happen again. It couldn't.

Alfie sat cross-legged on the ground and tried to calm his racing heart.

"Breathe," he told himself. "Just breathe."

Alfie closed his eyes and let himself fall into the sound of his own breaths. He didn't know how long it took—it could have been hours—but a calm finally fell over him, sweeping him away from the training room and into the realm of magic. Alfie gasped at the total peace within it. There was no floor, no ceiling, only the beautiful flow of magic. It was breathtaking. Relief poured over him like a healing salve over a raw wound. Paloma was right. The magic had never judged him, never shut him out. After all he'd done when he released Sombra, it still accepted him.

And then came a sound.

A strangled high-pitched keening, like a wounded animal, emanating from every angle. Alfie covered his ears with his hands. There was not supposed to be any sound here. The sound of Sombra's voice was how he'd known he'd found something forbidden. But this was something different altogether. This was not some powerful being pleading for release.

This was a sound of pain and anger and betrayal.

With a shout Alfie broke the connection and opened his eyes to find himself back in the training room. Sweat poured down his face. He pulled his shaking hands away from his ears.

The magic was rejecting him. Pushing him out, shouting in indignation that he dared to enter its realm after what he'd done.

The sound of his people jeering him at the memorial echoed in his head, mixing with the horrible sound of the magic rejecting him from its embrace.

His people didn't want him, and magic didn't want him either.

THE PUBLIC SERVICE
ANNOUNCEMENT

Delegado Julio Rodriguez was having a magnificent evening.

In fact, he was having a magnificent life.

He'd been born rich and, just as a fine vino grew more complex with time, he seemed to grow richer and richer with age. He'd been educated by the kingdom's finest bruxos, and with his family's political past, it was only right that he pursue a position in the royal council of delegados. Without breaking a sweat, he'd become the delegado of San Cristóbal, the capital city, the crown jewel of the kingdom. He'd risen even more quickly after several other delegados were discovered to have been part of the nasty business of assassinating Prince Dezmin. He smiled before admonishing himself and murmuring a silent prayer for the fallen prince.

Still, he couldn't stifle his grin. Even the bleakest of events seemed to work in his favor.

As he walked leisurely through the Bow's stone garden, he breathed a long sigh of contentment.

With retirement on the horizon, his long, cushy career was poised to end on a very lucrative high note—the peace summit. Just the thought of it brought a smile to his face. Though it wasn't the prospect of peace that excited him, not at all. It was the gold, the pesos that would come pouring into the city, that had Julio salivating. Brokering peace with the Englassens would reopen trade and bring a steady stream of pesos pouring into his coffers. Well, the city's coffers. But Julio had no qualms about skimming a bit off the top when no one was watching. After all, he served the people day in and day out. Didn't he deserve a bit of a reward for his civic duty?

Sí, he most certainly did.

He'd fought for the summit. Protests had broken out throughout the kingdom at the prospect of welcoming Englass back onto Castallano soil. But the pesos outweighed it all. After all, Englass had colonized and enslaved his ancestors, not him. That was over a century ago, in the past. Money, however—money was Julio's present and future.

The sweeping stone garden unfurled around him in all its majesty. In it were statues of some of the finest Castallanos in history—the first free king after Englass was overthrown, the first known dueños, and even some delegados. Perhaps one day, he too would be forever immortalized in stone to watch over his kingdom. Pride swelled in his chest.

"Delegado Julio Rodriguez," a voice called from above.

Crouched on the shoulders of one of the stone statues was a masked man. But the black, horned mask was a strange one. It never seemed to stay still. It shimmered, moving fluidly around the man's face as if it were made of smoke or water. The delegado was so distracted by it that he nearly missed the sight of the stranger's white blade slicing through the air.

"Carajo!" he sputtered, his heart pounding in his throat. Julio dodged it, tripping over his own feet. He fell onto his side and his hip broke with a resounding *crack*. He had never been so painfully aware of his age. Before he could rise, another white blade burrowed into his thigh with a wet thunk.

The delegado threw his head back and screamed, rocking back and forth to weather the storm of pain coursing through his leg. He grabbed the blade by its strangely smooth hilt and ripped it from his leg. But it wasn't a blade at all.

It was a sharpened bone.

He dropped it in disgust as hot blood soaked his trousers.

"Who are you?" he asked as he crawled backward, his voice shaking. "What do you want?"

The man leaped off the statue and walked toward the whimpering delegado slowly, carefully, as if he had as much time as Julio had pesos. The stranger ran his hand over his brown forearm and after a terrible *crack*, a bone rose smoothly out of his skin, like a baby tooth cutting through gums.

This man could manipulate his own *bones* and use them as weapons.

He didn't speak a word. He just brandished the bone blade.

"What do you want? Money? I have plenty. However much you're being paid, I can double it!" When the man didn't stop moving toward him, Julio sputtered out, "Triple, quadruple, whatever you need!"

"Your money cannot buy what I need."

"I serve the people," Julio gasped, his hand gripping his bleeding knee. "It's what I've always done. I can serve you too, if you let me."

The man tilted his head, as if considering, and Julio felt hope leap in his chest.

"You serve a different purpose tonight—you'll be a public service announcement."

"Por favor, don't—" he began, but the man only shook his head.

"Get up," the stranger said with a beckoning hand, the moonlight sliding over the bull tattoo on his brown forearm, which matched the mask that covered his eyes and nose. "Or we're going to be late."

Julio struggled to his feet, his eyes stinging, his leg still bleeding. "Where are you taking me?"

"You say you are a servant of the people," the masked man mused. "So I'm taking you to them. To the Pinch."

Julio gave a choking sob as the man led him into the darkness, a knife of bone prodding him forward.

10
THE BREAKDOWN OF THE BAD BEHAVIOR ACCORDS

Alfie approached Luka's door, his hands still shaking.

He needed to talk to someone about the screaming he'd heard in the magic. Or to at least be distracted from it.

He knocked and waited. Nothing. Unable to wait any longer, Alfie threw open the door.

The room was empty. His gaze snagged on the plush pillows piled on Luka's bed. There, leaning against a pillow, was a folded note. Written on the outside of it, in Luka's elegant script, was Alfie's name. He snatched the note off the bed.

If you've come to my rooms hoping to find me,
I'm afraid you'll be at a loss. I am out on a social
endeavor. One that I, very inconsiderately, did not tell
you about.
Oh, how the tables have turned!
Honestly, that phrasing doesn't feel adequate. Let me
begin again.

Oh, how the tables have been FLIPPED and LIT ON FIRE!

Alfie rolled his eyes. Usually Alfie would use his *propio* and one of Luka's things to track him down. But the sound of those horrible screams was so fresh in Alfie's head that he hesitated. He never wanted to hear it again, but he also couldn't stand being alone in the palace without Luka to talk to when he had so much on his mind. And what if Luka was doing something dangerous that Alfie ought to stop him from?

Alfie sighed, his palms slick with sweat. That settled it; he would use his *propio* to travel through the channels of magic and find Luka. After all, maybe he could only hear that terrible sound *in* the realm of magic, not when he traveled straight through it. The realm of magic was a sacred place that Alfie had entered and released Sombra. So it made sense that that place had rejected him, but perhaps the other channels of magic would leave him be.

Or maybe he'd imagined it. Yes, that would be nice.

Alfie nodded, forcing himself to make a decision before he talked himself out of it. If Luka wanted to play a game, then Alfie would make it one for two players. He dashed to Luka's drawers and rifled through the jewelry box until his hand closed around something small and cold. Luka's favorite earring. Alfie rolled his eyes as he weighed the green stud in his hand.

"Really? Must you dress like a pirate out of a romance novela?" Alfie had joked when Luka had put it on for the first time, inspecting himself in the mirror.

"Must you always dress like a librarian who died ten years ago?" Luka had quipped.

The earring was one of Luka's favorites. It ought to be enough to find him.

The last time Alfie had used this method of magical travel, it had been to find Finn.

At the thought of her, the room seemed to fold in on itself before unfurling once more into her room at the inn, where he'd gotten caught in her door. Where they'd met eyes, her looking at him with trust and him gazing at her with gratitude so heavy it could have sent him falling to his knees before her.

Alfie swallowed, his throat suddenly dry.

Four months and he hadn't received a single letter from her. He didn't know why he'd expected one. He'd never verbalized that expectation, but with each passing month something cold had gotten caught in his chest, and Alfie soon recognized it as the absence of letters. The absence of her smirk. Of her voice curving and lilting with a laugh.

The absence of *her*.

Alfie shook away that thought. Luka was out doing something foolish. There was no time to wallow at the idea of nonexistent letters and a girl who likely had moved on, never thinking of the sheltered prince who'd dragged her into a world of trouble.

It would be nice to know where she was and how she was doing. What part of the world was she calling hers now that she had nothing to fear? Did she still carry that weight in her eyes, the look of someone who had been running for so long that they'd forgotten how to walk?

This was ridiculous. He was ridiculous.

He had enough going on without adding Finn. He grabbed his doorknob from his pocket and tossed it at Luka's wall. It spun against the tiled wall before sinking in, awaiting his touch. When he'd first discovered the traveling facet of his *propio*, Alfie needed a way to focus his power, to take the overwhelming concept of traveling through infinite channels of magic and make it as simple as stepping through a door. So the doorknob had become a staple. He needed only the earring and to let his magic change to the corresponding color of Luka's magic.

Alfie let his magic change to Luka's butter yellow, then grabbed the doorknob with his free hand and twisted it. The tunnel of magic opened before him, a starburst of color that he always found comforting. There was no streak of black in it, no darkness like Sombra's magic, just a riot of color welcoming him into its current. He couldn't hear that horrid sound either.

For a moment, Alfie hesitated. Didn't he owe Luka the benefit of the doubt, considering the way Alfie had once disappeared to participate in illegal card games behind his back? But then he remembered the compromise they'd made in the aftermath of Sombra.

"If we do stupid, reckless things, then we do them together, agreed?" Luka had told Alfie months ago, holding out his hand as if they were business associates making a proper agreement. "We shall call it the Bad Behavior Accords."

Alfie had laughed. Luka had given up on stopping Alfie from doing dangerous things in his search for answers about Dez's death and had compromised by joining him.

If Luka was doing something reckless, then Alfie was going to join him. After all, it was in the Accords.

"Ready or not," Alfie said, "here I come." The magic swept Alfie up in its current and carried him to wherever Luka had disappeared to.

As he floated in this space that was both intertwined with his world and also separate, Alfie assured himself that the worst that would happen was he would walk in on Luka with one of his lovers—mentally scarring, but nothing Alfie couldn't handle.

He could feel the currents of magic slowing, getting ready to push him back into the world like a drop of sap welling up from beneath the tree bark to taste the air.

But then came a feeling, something cold and unwanted—the type of spine-shivering sensation Alfie hadn't felt since Sombra had been released.

Alfie's skin prickled into gooseflesh. Somewhere in tunnels of magic came that scream of pain, long and unending. "Hello," Alfie said, his voice shaking. "Who's there?" Maybe it wasn't the magic rejecting him. Maybe it was someone who needed him. "Do you need help?"

But the scream only went on, unyielding and so full of agony that it sank into Alfie's bones. He couldn't stand it. He'd been kidding himself when he thought that it might be someone lost in the magic. He was just hiding from the truth. Magic wanted nothing to do with him.

"I'm sorry," he whispered as the screams rang on. "I'm so sorry."

Finally, Alfie sensed that he was arriving at his destination. The magic tugged him forward until a circle of light opened above him, like a hole in a rainbow ceiling. Usually Alfie stood still and let the magic guide him, but this time he couldn't. He clambered up, his arms stretched over his head, begging the magic to let him out. It pushed Alfie up through the opening, belching him into a smoky room that boomed with noise and stank of stale cerveza. Covered in a cold sweat and his hands still shaking, Alfie blinked the spots out of his eyes. Blinding light arrested him before his vision cleared and he saw where he was.

Alfie stood in the middle of a raised ring with walls of rope. An audience crowded around the elevated arena, shouting and jeering with such vigor that spittle flew past their lips.

"Wait your turn, muchacho!" someone in the roaring crowd shouted.

"Oye, flaco! Who threw a stalk of sugarcane into the ring?" There was a bout of laughter.

That comment pulled him out of the fear of what he'd heard in the magic and dropped him roughly into the present. Alfie sniffed at the joke as the audience chuckled at his lanky frame. So much for trying to build muscle over these last months.

"Alfie!" To his left, Luka was shirtless, holding off the fists of a man twice his size. The man was a knot of muscle, his body so gargantuan that his head looked too small for it. But Luka just yawned as the red-faced man tried to land his punches. Luka leisurely kicked him in the stomach, sending him flying onto the ground, curling around his aching belly.

"Mierda!" Luka dashed over. "What the hell are you doing here?"

"Me?" Alfie said, motioning around him. "What are *you* doing here?"

Luka shrugged good-naturedly, as if Alfie had caught him in the library dozing instead of in a seedy fight club. "What can I say?" Luka's opponent had finally risen from the ground and charged him from behind, and without so much as a glance Luka jutted his elbow back, catching the heavyset man in his thick neck. He crumpled to the ground with a gasp. "I'm good at it."

"Sí," Alfie seethed, shooting Luka a look. "Of course you are." The strength that Sombra's magic had granted Luka had never left him, and it seemed that Luka had been exploring his limits. "You could kill someone, estúpido."

"I could've done that before I became unusually strong too. Lucky for you I have self-control."

Alfie stared at him. "You once ate two entire trays of flan because you were left in the kitchens unsupervised. You have zero self-control."

"Are you really upset with me?" Luka said, tilting his head as if begging Alfie to correct him. "After everything you were doing behind my back before?"

"Oye!" A man had forced himself to the front of the shouting crowd, gripping the ropes of the arena with meaty fists. "You double-team my brother and think I'll just sit and watch?"

"He wasn't double-teamed. The man was outmatched!" Luka crowed, pounding his chest with his fist. "He lost the fight the moment he stepped into the ring with me." He raised his arms and beckoned at the audience, bringing forth waves of loud cheers.

"Luka!" Alfie shouted, his voice quiet in the face of the roaring of the crowd. "Don't antagonize him!" But it was too late.

"You're a cheat!" the man said, and now there were others

behind him looking just as livid. They spat at the ground and cracked their knuckles, their eyes burning. "You broke the rules of the fight by bringing in your skinny friend; now there are no damned rules."

Ten men rushed the ring, ducking under the ropes with an ease that told Alfie they knew their way around a fight club. He and Luka were back-to-back, spinning in slow circles as the men drew nearer, cocooning them in a ring of sweaty, shouting fighters.

"I can't believe you," Alfie said as the men moved closer. He was still shaking from hearing the screaming and now he had to fight?

"You brought me back to life, so why shouldn't I live a little?" Luka winked. A fist flew forward and Luka dodged under the man's arm, charging him like a bull.

A man with his front teeth missing reached forward to grip Alfie by the shirt. Alfie darted back and with a flick of his fingers, a glob of the man's spit flew down the wrong pipe. He broke into a fit of coughs, giving Alfie just the opening he needed.

"*Fuerza!*" But the magic slipped out of his hands. He was so shaken by the screams that he couldn't focus. The man kept running forward. "Damn it, *fuerza!*" The man was sent hurtling away, out of the ring and into the jeering audience.

"*Paralizar!*" Alfie shouted at the bald man surging toward him from the left. He went stiff as a statue and clattered to the ground.

"*Oye! Everyone, stop!*" a man shouted as he stood balancing on the roped boundaries of the ring. "The guards are coming! *Go, go, go!*"

There was a moment of shocked silence before the once-bloodthirsty fighters skittered every which way like mice. Alfie was so relieved to not have been punched bloody that he nearly forgot that there'd be consequences if he and Luka were caught by the guards too.

"Come on!" Luka said, grabbing Alfie by the arm.

"What's going on?" Alfie asked as they ducked under the ropes of the ring.

"I don't know!" Luka shouted over the noise. "Fight clubs are illegal—the guardsmen break them up when they hear about them!"

The place was full of exits, tunnels that ate away at the walls as if they were a stone honeycomb. But each was plugged closed by men trying to wriggle their way out. Then came the sound of armored boots. Red-caped guards were pushing in through one entrance, knocking over those trying to escape. Flashes of crimson poured through all the tunnels.

"Mierda," Alfie cursed. If they were caught out after all they'd done four months ago, then his parents would never let him out of their sight again. They'd only just stopped forcing him to constantly have a retinue of guardsmen around him, even while in the palace. Their trust was too freshly earned now.

"I have an idea," Luka shouted over the chaos. "Let's do firework."

"Qué? Firework only worked when we were younger, lighter, and infinitely dumber."

"Dumber?" Luka questioned while stroking his chin. "Or more innovative?"

"We're not doing it, it won't work."

"It will." Luka grabbed an oil lamp ensconced in the wall. "Because I've got another idea."

Alfie stared at the lamp and understood his cousin's plan immediately. "Ay dioses."

"Hold tight," Luka said. He wrapped an arm around Alfie's shoulders before shattering the lamp on the ground by his feet. He let flame burst into life around his ankles. A great plume of heat surged up around them and in the blink of an eye they were blasting away from the ground like a firework. Alfie scarcely had time to scream as they rushed up to meet the skylight in the roof.

"*Romp*—" he began, hoping to break the glass before they reached it, but too late. He threw his arm over their heads as they burst through the glass and out into the night air.

With a shout, they rolled down the sloped roof before careening off its edge to the hard ground. They lay beside each other on their backs, chests heaving, bones aching.

"Told you it would work," Luka said.

Alfie let out a pained gasp before speaking, his eyes on the dark sky. "You don't get to speak for the rest of the night."

At the sound of boots pounding down the road, they scurried into the alley beside the fight club. But the guards ran on, not even sparing a glance at the seedy spot.

Luka and Alfie looked at each other. Though Alfie knew they should count their blessings for not getting caught and head home, he followed Luka as he dashed through the network of alleyways, following the sound of the guards as they dashed deeper into the Pinch.

"Move! Muevete!" the guards said as they pushed the still civilians out of the way.

Alfie and Luka clung to the outer edges of the wide circle that had formed in the square of the Pinch.

There, on the broad side of a pub, a body was affixed to the wall like a painting, the arms and legs dangling at odd angles while a bloodied white collar attached the man to the wall. Even with the help of the collar, the man's head slumped to one side at a sharp, unnatural angle, as if he'd fallen victim to a noose. With his hood up, Alfie moved through the aghast crowd.

Bile rose up Alfie's throat. It wasn't a white collar—it was made of the man's teeth.

Alfie recoiled, moving back until he bumped into Luka's chest.

The whispers of the crowd threaded through his ears, piercing his thoughts with gruesome details he did not want to know.

"Every bone in his body broken . . ."

"Alfie," Luka said, his voice quiet. He pointed above the corpse and Alfie's gaze followed his finger. What he saw drew his stomach tight. Painted on the wall high above the dead body was the bull tattoo, with a single, chilling message written below it in blood:

NO PEACE FOR COLONIZERS
END THE PEACE SUMMIT
KEEP ENGLASSEN SCUM OUT OF CASTALLAN
OR ELSE

MOTHERHOOD

Finn jolted awake as a wave of ice-cold water crashed over her.

"*Coño!*" she shouted.

She coughed and sputtered beneath the rough—and now thoroughly soaked—sack covering her head. She couldn't see, but her other senses spun to life, gleaning what they could as she choked.

Her spine was pressed to the back of a high-backed chair. Her wrists were tied to the armrests and her ankles to the chair legs. The air was laced with the dank stench of dirt and decay that told her she was underground—in a cellar, probably.

For what must've been the millionth time, Finn thought that if she had a peso for every time she woke up with a sack over her head, she wouldn't need to do the things that led to her waking up with a sack over her head.

In a flash of memory, Finn recalled the last time she'd been trussed up like a turkey in some underground hell—Kol's cellar.

Kol was dead now, her neck snapped like a toothpick at Ignacio's command. Yet Finn felt an overwhelming sense of déjà vu at the memory of the mobster's slow smile when Finn had been delivered to her and forced onto her knees four months ago. At least the chair was a bit of an improvement this time around.

"Where the hell am I?" she shouted, jerking at the ropes that bound her wrists and ankles. The chair was soft and strangely comfortable considering the situation. "Untie me, if you know what's good for you, you cowards!"

There was a flurry of whispering around her, unnerving her further.

"So . . . should we just take it off her?" asked a deep voice.

"No, we should leave it on her head forever," another voice drawled, a girl who sounded as annoyed as Finn felt. "Draw a smiley face on the sack for good measure."

Then came the fleshy sound of a fist smacking skin and a yelp of pain.

Finn rolled her eyes beneath the sack. Had she really just gotten kidnapped by a group of thieflings still wet behind the ears?

There was a whispered argument and then, finally, the sack was pulled off her head. Finn blinked and the dark cellar came to life before her. Her mind spiraled in confusion.

This *was* Kol's cellar, the very cellar where the mobster had broken Finn's wrist and tasked her with stealing the vanishing cloak from the palace vault or else losing her *propio* forever. She'd thought that everything had changed when Ignacio was finally dead, but somehow things were exactly the same.

Only not quite.

The last time she'd found herself in this cellar, Kol's henchmen had stood there, bloodthirsty grins curling their lips, laughing confidently as their leader taunted Finn. Now, though, their faces were oddly somber, almost respectful. None moved forward to hurt her. They looked nervous. Why should they be nervous when she was the one tied up?

"Stop your maldito staring and tell me what you idiots want."

"Go ahead, Pablo," a girl at the front of the horde said, her voice sounding like an audible eye roll. "Let's get this over with."

A tall, burly man stepped forward and stalked toward Finn, his gait purposeful.

"Oh, so this is how you cobardes want to play it? You're gonna set this giant on me while I'm tied down?" Finn uselessly pulled at her restraints, but they wouldn't give, and all the daggers she'd had up her sleeves had been taken. "Really noble of you!" She couldn't keep the warble of panic from her voice as she pressed her back against the chair, her body fighting to move as far from the hulking man as possible.

He came to a stop before her and silently drew out the machete at his hip.

Finn's hands were roped so tightly to the chair that she could barely move her fingers. She couldn't do any stone carving to save her life, literally. So she did what she did best—she lied. "You kill me, and my ghost will haunt you for the rest of your slack-jawed days!"

The man did not speak a word. He raised the machete, its sharp edge gleaming in the dim light. Finn could only screw her eyes shut as the weapon came down in a smooth arc.

She heard the thunk of the blade sinking its teeth into wood, and then the ropes were sliding off her left wrist. She looked up, shocked, as he cut each of her bindings.

"Welcome home," Pablo said, and then they were all dropping into bows, curling forward in a wave of respect. It was only then that she realized she was in the gilded high-backed chair that Kol had been seated in when she'd ordered her henchmen to beat Finn bloody. "You've been knocked out for quite a while. We may have overdone it with the sleeping draught . . . ," he said sheepishly, looking at her as if begging for forgiveness. For mercy. Finn couldn't understand it. "Forgive us, Madre."

"Wait. What?" Finn said. She was no one's mother, yet here they were all staring at her, men and women, some old, but most even younger than her.

The girl who'd told Pablo to set her free stepped forward then. She looked a little younger than Finn. "You're confused." It was the same girl who'd joked about drawing a face on the sack.

"Sí," Finn spat back, her eyes moving over the legion of bowing criminals as she shakily stood from the chair. No one moved to stop her. "You could say that."

"Then let me explain," the girl said. "The rules of thiefdom state that should a thief lord die, there are two paths of succession." She held up a finger. "One, if the thief lord has declared an heir to take their place prior to their death, which Kol did not do," she said bitterly. Then she raised a second finger. "Two, whoever kills the thief lord takes their place. That's you."

"A thief what?" Finn squinted at her. She'd never even heard of that title, let alone known that Kol was one. "And it damn well is *not* me. I didn't kill Kol."

The girl looked at her with the exasperation of a parent watching their child throw their fifth tantrum of the day. "You didn't, but she was killed in your name by a man who is now dead, which makes you next in the line of succession. It's part of the Thief's Code."

"Code?" Finn said. "Isn't the whole point of being a thief that you don't have any laws or codes?"

Pablo, the gargantuan man who'd untied her, sniffed, seeming almost hurt. Without the machete in his hand, he looked like an overgrown child. "We're thieves, not animals."

Finn shook her head, hoping to wake herself up from this strange dream. "Well, then, I just give the thief lord job thing to you, whatever your name is. I don't want it."

"My name is Anabeltilia," the girl sniped. "My friends call me Anabel." She shot Finn a look. "*You* can call me Anabeltilia. And, no, it doesn't work that way. I already told you. There are only two paths of succession. So unless you want me to kill you, you're stuck with the job. You still want to proceed with that method?"

Finn closed her eyes and plopped back into the chair, breathing a long sigh through her nose. "No," she hissed. "I do not."

"Good. We don't have time to kill you tonight. Catching you has taken us too long as is. More trouble than you're worth," she said, giving Finn a hard look.

"How did you find me?" she spat.

The girl rolled her eyes. "Stealing the faces of high-profile merchants and robbing them blind doesn't let you keep a low profile. We had our people track you, and who would've guessed they'd find you getting on a boat back to San Cristóbal. Then all we had to do was wait."

Finn gritted her teeth. The last merchant she'd robbed had said the same thing. She needed to work on being a little more subtle, but in her mind subtle always meant boring.

"Now get up; you need to prepare for a meeting with the other thief lords of Castallan. Tonight."

Finn stared at her. "The who now?"

Anabeltilia kneaded her temples. "This is going to be a very long night. Everyone, get back to work. I have to teach the newborn how to walk."

Finn glared at the girl as the minions—*her* minions, apparently—dispersed. Finn wondered, if she made a run for it, would these thieflings just leave her be and find a new mother duck to imprint on?

"Don't even think about it," Anabeltilia said. "While you were knocked out, we got a bit of your blood."

"And?" Finn asked, nonplussed. "I get a bit of my blood every month, what of it?"

The girl glowered at Finn. "There's desk magic that uses blood to track someone down. I sent yours to the eldest thief lord while you were asleep so that they can catch you if you decide to run. There always needs to be four thief lords. They'll hold you accountable."

Finn fell silent, her thoughts of escape disappearing in a puff of smoke. She still didn't understand what anything meant. What even were thief lords? She crossed her arms.

"Now come with me," the girl said as Finn let out a long, frustrated sigh.

Without a word, Anabeltilia guided Finn deeper into the cellar, where a staircase led even farther down into the dark. The girl held a globe of fire over her palm to light their way.

"Not that I'm not enjoying the silence with an annoying stranger, but could you explain what the hell is going on already?"

"Every kingdom has rule of law—kings and queens or whatever they choose to call themselves. But underneath all that, the street has its own laws, its own rulers. In Castallan, those are the thief lords."

They continued down the stairs into a tight shaft of a hallway, more like a tunnel.

"The kingdom always has four thief lords. One in the northwest, one in the northeast, which is now you, and so on. They run the crime underground of each quadrant."

Finn choked on her own spit. "*I own a quadrant?*"

The girl nodded, not bothering to turn to look at Finn. "Funny, considering you probably can't spell 'quadrant.'"

Finn cocked her head. "Is that how you address your madre?"

The girl didn't take the bait. "You've got a meeting with the rest of the thief lords tonight. I can't prepare you for that. I served Kol closely, but business with the thief lords was always kept secret. I can tell you where to go, but once there you'll have to fend for yourself."

Finally, the girl led her to the end of the hall, where a door stood. She stepped to the side, giving Finn space. "After you."

Finn looked at her with suspicion, but it wasn't as if the girl was going to send her to her death. She would've done that already if she'd really wanted to.

With her chin held high, Finn opened the door and walked in— then almost choked on her own spit again.

The room was small, much smaller than the royal vault, but it was full of chests of gold and silver pesos. She didn't know what she'd done in a past life that let her walk into a trove like this again.

"This was Kol's," Anabeltilia said, sounding less than pleased. "Now it's yours." She rolled her eyes at Finn's shocked look. "You still want to try to escape?"

Finn grinned at the spread before her. Smirking triumphantly at Anabeltilia, she raised her hands in a sweeping motion. With the help of her stone carving, gold and silver pesos flew out of their chests, swirling in the center of the room. In the blink of an eye they'd been stacked into a giant throne. A throne of pesos to burn.

She sauntered up to it and sat, crossing one leg over the other. "Call me Mamá."

"Okay, Mamá." Anabeltilia rolled her eyes. "Get up, you've got somewhere to be tonight."

"En serio? Right now?" Finn sucked her teeth. "Being a single mother is so damn busy."

THE WAR ROOM

Alfie and Luka barreled through the passageway into Alfie's rooms, still shaken.

The sight of the dead delegado was almost enough to make him forget about what he'd heard when he'd traveled through the magic. Almost. But there was no time to think about that now.

The corpse and the message alongside it had frozen Alfie where he stood, but he knew that word would get back to his parents—this news was too gruesome to wait until morning. As soon as they heard, they would be waking him to discuss what had happened and how it would affect the summit. They had to get back to the palace before then. Lucky for Alfie, Luka had set up a tether—magically connected objects that transported bruxos from one place to another—to take them home.

"What?" Luka had said. "A man can't be brilliant *and* guapo?"

The tether had deposited them in the palace's nest of passageways and together they'd dashed straight to Alfie's rooms.

"Quick!" Alfie said. "Change into sleeping clothes before they come for me!"

It was late, after all. They would look strange if they were both dressed as if they'd only just gotten home. Especially Luka, who stood shirtless, still covered in sweat from the fight.

"My nightclothes are in my rooms," Luka said.

"Take a pair of mine, then."

Luka stared at Alfie with absolute disgust.

"Luka, just put them on!" Alfie insisted. "And don't think I'll forget to talk to you about tonight after this." For the last couple of months Luka had been disappearing without telling Alfie where. He'd also sported new bruises several times, telling Alfie that he had taken up sword fighting and martial arts with the palace weapons master. But now Alfie knew that was a lie. Luka had been fighting in seedy pubs, putting himself and everyone on the other side of his fist in danger.

"A literal murder just happened," Luka groused. "Can we talk about this later?"

"You could accidentally kill someone, Luka! What purpose does fighting in the Pinch serve? How could you do something so reckless?"

Luka pulled the pajama shirt over his head, his scowling face popping out of the neck hole. "Are you really asking me that, after everything you got up to four months ago? Illegal gambling? Disappearing for months at a time?"

"That's entirely different. I participated in those illegal games because I wanted to save Dez. What reasons could you possibly have for this?"

"My own!" Luka sniped. "And they're none of your business."

Alfie flinched at the anger in his voice. Tension thickened between them, asking who would strike the next blow.

A knock sounded at the door.

"Come in," Alfie said as he firmly pulled his sleeping shirt straight.

The door swung open to reveal two red-caped guards.

"Prince Alfehr," one said, dropping into a bow. "Master Luka." He bowed again, his expression perplexed.

"The prince had a nightmare," Luka supplied with a shrug.

Alfie had to stop himself from glaring at his cousin.

"The king and queen have requested your presence in the War Room."

Alfie pretended to look surprised as he grabbed a robe to throw over his sleeping clothes. "Of course. Lead the way," Alfie said, and regardless of their fight, Luka was beside him as they walked out of his rooms and followed the guards down the hall.

"Master Luka," a guard began uneasily. "Your presence was not requested—"

"Showing up when I'm not requested is my calling card." Luka squared his shoulders. "If the king and queen take issue with it, they will dismiss me themselves, comprendes?"

Luka hated political meetings; he liked it best when Alfie returned from them and gave him a minute-long summary. Alfie knew that his cousin was coming only because Alfie needed the support. The comfort of it made the fear coiling in his chest loosen slightly.

After their argument, Luka looked tenser than usual, but he bumped his shoulder against Alfie's and gave him a look that seemed to say, *Where you go, I go.*

Alfie nodded, grateful. They would talk about what Luka had been up to later. After a long walk down to the second-lowest level of the palace, they were led through the double doors of the War Room. The sound of arguing hit Alfie like a physical wall. The delegados around the enormous table at the center of the room were shouting and pointing, some red-faced with anger, some ashen with fear. Most simply wore robes over their sleeping clothes, as Alfie did. They must've been called to use their tethers immediately in order to convene in the palace. Alfie could only catch snippets— shouts of "terrorism" and "national security."

At the head of the table stood his parents, fully dressed. When they spotted Alfie at the far side of the room, Alfie's mother raised a silencing hand and squeezed it into a fist.

The delegados fell silent as Alfie and Luka hurried to the king and queen's side.

"Delegados," his mother shouted, her voice carrying across the room. "Now that your future king has arrived, we will convene this meeting about the murder of Julio Rodriguez, Delegado of San Cristóbal."

A hushed murmur swept through the room at that, whispers of "Dioses bless him and his family" and "Descansa en paz."

"King Bolivar and I have requested your presence to discuss the fate of the peace summit, whether we should or should not proceed tomorrow. There is still time to get word to our guests that they ought to return home. The Englassen royal family hasn't arrived yet. Only the ships of their servants and dignitaries wait in the port."

The king nodded, his face grave. "We will hear your arguments, but, as always, the final decision will fall on my and Queen Amada's shoulders." The king stared at the delegados with a hard look of challenge. Silence drowned the room.

"Your Majesties," Paloma said from the far side of the table, where a group of dueños had been brought in for guidance. "May I speak first? I have news about the delegado's death."

An annoyed muttering came from the delegados. While the dueños' main focus was studying unknown forms of magic in order to uphold the balance of magic, the focus of the delegados was more economic, to say the least. They were two groups that seldom got along but nonetheless begrudgingly respected one another.

The queen nodded at her. "By all means."

"After careful examination of the body, we have concluded that the assailant used *propio* magic to kill the delegado." Paloma's lips curved into a grimace. "It appears that the murderer's *propio* lets him manipulate bones."

Alfie's stomach tightened. That was how the man's teeth had been removed. *Propio* magic was supposed to be a reflection of who you were, of your very soul. What kind of person's *propio* was the manipulation of bones?

"It is the recommendation of the dueños that we take this seriously. A person with this kind of power is unspeakably dangerous. We believe the summit must be postponed until the murderer and any of his cohorts are caught."

"The dueños are right. We must end the summit before it begins!" a man shouted from the far end of the table as Paloma stepped away.

The man went on. "With an anti-Englass murderer on the loose and the already shaky state of Englassen-Castallano affairs, should we proceed with the summit so that the relationship between our kingdoms deteriorates even more? While our intentions are good, this could risk our international standing."

A murmur of agreement swept through the room before a red-faced man interrupted.

"And how do you think we'll look if we cancel the summit like a bunch of cobardes? A politician was found dead in the Pinch between a bar and a brothel." The man threw his hands up. "Is this that strange? He probably just got mixed up with the wrong people. We all know Julio was no angel."

Another round of murmurs followed as the man leaned over the table, splaying his hands wide. The sand began re-forming into the shape of San Cristóbal from a bird's-eye view. Alfie recognized the domed rooftop of the palace at its center. With a deft twist of his fingers, the delegado made guardsmen out of sand, placing them strategically throughout the city.

"We already have guardsmen out searching. I say we continue the peace summit with the city heavily guarded. Simple. Should he strike again, we cover up the murder before our guests can even hear of it."

The room grew louder until another woman shouted over the noise. "And risk having terrorists murder more delegados?"

"Well, perhaps if Julio hadn't been out and about in the Pinch doing who knows what, maybe he would still be alive," the delegado sniffed.

Jeers of agreement and tutting about impropriety sounded around the room. Alfie frowned; there was something disgusting about the way the man referred to the Pinch. As if death was deserved there. The Pinch and places like it were full of good people; he could only think of the family he'd visited, how she'd kindly given him her fallen husband's watch. The delegados represented the people of Castallan, but they didn't seem to know them or care much about them. This was something he would have to rectify when he became king.

"Fine—if you're not worried for the lives of your delegado brethren, then what of our guests? What will happen if an Englassen citizen is killed? Ridículo!"

Gustavo Veras, a red-faced man with a mustache, stood up. Alfie's stomach knotted uneasily. Gustavo never had anything good to say. "The summit must go on! Your Majesties, the people are angry after the horrors they experienced with Sombra's release. And rightfully so!" The room fell silent for a long moment and Alfie felt his face grow hot as every delegado turned to look at him. Though the public did not know that he was responsible for what had happened or that Sombra's essence specifically had been released, the delegados and the dueños knew and were sworn to secrecy. For the good of the cities they governed, it was only right that they know about the existence of this kind of threat. "With that hovering over our kingdom, we cannot just cancel the summit. Bringing Englass into line is the prince's chance to earn the trust of the people!"

Another round of grumbling filled the War Room. Some sounds of agreement and others of protest. It was hard to tell what opinion was winning out. Alfie shot Luka a look, but Luka only shrugged as if silently saying, *I've got no clue.*

"I, for one, believe we ought to listen to the people," a voice rang out from the far end of the table. It was a slender man with sharp features and carefully groomed facial hair. "Can we blame them for not wanting our former colonizers welcomed on our shores?" he said, raising his chin with a look of thinly veiled disgust. "This summit should never have been arranged in the first place. There will be other ways for the prince to earn the trust of his people, ways that don't include cozying up to our enemies."

"Hush, Delegado Culebra," Gustavo said with a sharp laugh. "We have no time for your pettiness. Keep your family politics out of this meeting."

The thin man flushed, his jaw tightening as Gustavo laughed on.

Of course Diego Culebra was still disagreeing about the summit. He'd been fiercely against it since before Dez had passed. The Culebra family were next in line for the throne and were constantly whispering behind their hands about how much better they would be as the ruling family. Instead they made their wealth as successful merchants of the gems they mined from their family's caves and quarries. It was almost a guarantee that Diego Culebra would oppose the royal family's position on any given issue. Even if King Bolivar were to pass a law to put pesos directly in the Culebra coffers, they would still disagree out of stubborn, petty principle. Alfie could tell by his mother's face that she was trying very hard to not roll her eyes at the man.

"And what of the enslaved Englassen people who have had their magic robbed from them?" Claritza Espaillat, delegado of Santiago, said. "You want them to continue to suffer for generations to come? Have you no empathy? If we can rid the world of Englass's caste system, then we should regardless of the risks."

Before the delegados could react to her impassioned words, Delegado Culebra crossed his arms. "I waste no sympathy on Englassens, thank you very much."

Several delegados shouted in agreement, and Alfie winced. Before this, all the delegados who did not want the summit had had to begrudgingly accept that it was happening, but now that there was a possibility of cancellation, the anti-Englass rhetoric was revealing itself once more. Many delegados and citizens felt that Englass should never be forgiven for what they'd done, which Alfie understood. Anger was always easy to understand; it was fast and all-consuming that way. But this summit presented them with the chance to free an entire nation of magically enslaved people. Wasn't that more important than holding a grudge?

As the arguments continued around him, Alfie thought of the man in the bull mask at the memorial and of seeing the bull symbol again at the murder scene. Should he tell his parents that he'd seen the symbol before, when the dark magic had shown it to him? He knew it would only hurt them to know that he'd turned to the dark magic for answers on Dez's death. But now it seemed imperative that they know. What if he held back this secret and things went disastrously?

Alfie watched his parents. They stood at the head of the table, watching the delegados debate back and forth, but every now and then they held each other's gaze, and Alfie knew that they'd already come to a decision. They were only waiting for the right moment to say it.

Alfie's mother opened her mouth to speak, and Alfie knew he couldn't wait any longer.

"Wait!" Alfie said, his face burning as the delegados and his parents turned to him, falling silent. "I have information to share before a decision is made."

Queen Amada raised an eyebrow, and King Bolivar said, "By all means, speak your mind."

"I have seen the symbol painted above Delegado Rodriguez's body before."

A great murmuring swept through the room.

"Where, Mijo?" the queen asked, touching his arm.

Alfie could feel his ears burning. "Under the influence of Sombra's magic, I had a vision that—"

The room exploded with sound then—sighs of disbelief and even some laughter. Alfie's mother pulled her hand away from him, her eyes wide. His father looked furious, his face all flared nostrils and clenched jaw. He turned away from Alfie and gripped the rim of the table.

"*Silencio!*" King Bolivar shouted and the room fell still once more. "Our decision has been made."

The queen stepped forward. "The peace summit will continue as planned. The murderer is only one man, after all. We will work our guardsmen to the bone to find the culprit before he strikes again. We will increase security to keep our guests and ourselves safe. The ending of Englass's caste system and the establishment of Prince Alfehr as future king are too important to jeopardize. Only now are the Englassens finally in a desperate enough position to agree to end their vile practices. Who knows how long it will last? We must strike while the opportunity presents itself."

The room boomed with sound again, some shouts of praise, others of anger.

"This meeting is adjourned," the king said, a thundering finality in his voice.

The delegados fell quiet as they pulled their tethers from their pockets and bags and spoke the secret words of magic that would spirit them back home.

Then there was only Alfie, Luka, the king and queen, the dueños who had been summoned to attend the meeting, and the palace guards.

His jaw tight, the king said, "Leave us."

The dueños and the guards filed out, but Luka stayed beside Alfie.

"Luka," Queen Amada said. "This conversation is not for you."

Luka squared his shoulders in a valiant effort to look more intimidating, but he quickly wilted under the queen's gaze. "I'd like to stay anyway," he managed.

"Luka," the king began, but Alfie interjected before his cousin could get into trouble on his account.

"It's all right," Alfie said to him. "Go."

After a long look, Luka hesitantly walked out of the room. Alfie watched him go, desperately wishing he could follow.

"A vision, Alfehr?" his mother said as soon as the doors closed. "Are you out of your mind?"

His father looked too angry even to speak.

"It's the truth, Mamá," he said. "I saw it when I asked Sombra to show me why Marco Zelas was involved with Dez's death. I—"

"*Enough!*" she shouted before taking a long, calming breath. "Mijo, what makes you think you can trust what you saw under the influence of something of pure evil, something that nearly destroyed our kingdom because of your carelessness?"

Alfie looked away from the heat of her glare. For the last four months he'd never stopped apologizing for what he'd done, but he knew it didn't matter. He wouldn't ever be able to atone for the mistake he'd made.

"Do you have any idea how weak, how unhinged you looked in front of the delegados?" his father asked, his voice tense. "After your brother's death we worked hard to position you as the rightful leader of our kingdom, and you decide that now is the time to mention a vision? Not only a vision, but one given to you while under Sombra's influence?"

"I'm sorry," Alfie said. It was all he could think to say. "I wanted you to know the truth before you made a decision. I asked the dark magic to show me why Marco Zelas got involved. It showed me a tattoo of the exact bull symbol painted on the wall above the delegado's corpse. If Zelas was part of it, then it isn't just one man. It must mean that this group had something to do with Dez's death. Isn't that worth knowing?" he pleaded.

"The only truth I see here is a prince who is proving himself to be a disappointment to his kingdom."

"We could protect you before by saying what you did four months ago was done out of grief for Dez, but we cannot make excuses anymore," the queen said.

"You will prepare for the peace summit and you will prove

yourself a reliable leader. If you don't," his mother said, her voice grave, "we won't be able to protect you from the consequences. Is that understood?"

Alfie swallowed thickly. "Yes," he finally said. "I understand."

Alfie left the War Room, his shadow circling close at his feet like a shamed dog tucks its tail between its legs.

The peace summit was happening even if he didn't think it was safe. He would have to pretend to agree with his parents, but as he walked the palace halls with slumped shoulders, he remembered that in a matter of years this kingdom's future would rest in his hands. And what kind of king would he be if he did nothing when he knew in his heart that danger was afoot?

As he made his way through the halls of the palace, Alfie squared his shoulders.

It was his duty to protect his people, even if his parents did not approve, even if it made the delegados see him as unstable. So there was nothing left to do but the exact same thing that had gotten him into trouble four months ago—walk into the night looking for things that did not want to be found.

But first he found Luka waiting for him in the hallway.

"You know I have your back," Luka said, falling into step with him.

"I know," Alfie said before looking at his best friend. "Thank you."

Luka nodded. "And I think I know exactly where we need to start. Have I mentioned that I got a tattoo?"

"*Qué?*"

Luka grabbed Alfie's arm and pulled him down the hall. Even

at this hour, it was full of servants readying the palace for the summit. There was even a small retinue of Englassen servants who had
arrived early to prepare the rooms for the Englassen royal family.
They'd brought trunks upon trunks of clothing and other items to
ensure the royal family's comfort during their stay. They stuck out
like sore thumbs, pale skin and fair hair in a sea of brown skin and
dark eyes. Though they looked markedly different from the Castallano servants, they were united by the look of absolute stress on
their faces.

As Luka pulled Alfie around a sharp corner, the two collided
with an Englassen servant. The boy fell onto his backside, staring up
at Alfie in shock. Without a moment's hesitation he pushed himself
onto his knees and pressed his forehead onto the floor. In practiced
Castallano he said, "Forgive me, Prince Alfehr. I was careless."

Alfie instantly felt bad for feeling uncomfortable with having
Englassen people in the palace. Thus far all the servants had been
perfectly kind.

"It's quite all right. In fact, it's my fault, and for that I am sorry.
Please rise."

The boy rose slowly, his green eyes darting away from Alfie's
face and to the floor. He had a murky dark brown magic that
reminded Alfie of the color that formed when he would mix all his
paints as a child. It hurt Alfie to know that he could still see the
magic welling within the servant, but that the boy could not use it.
All Englassen servants were magically bound. Like everyone else,
they took in the shimmering, free magic just as one drew breath.
As they did so, they gave the free magic color—but unlike everyone
else, including their own nobility, they could not release it. He'd

seen the Englassen servants around the palace, each full of colorful magic, of potential, but unable to access it. It made the summit feel all the more important.

"What is your name?" Alfie asked him.

"James, Your Majesty," the boy said. He looked to be a little younger than Alfie himself. Probably Luka's age.

"James, please forgive me. My cousin and I were rushing. I hope you will excuse us."

"Of course, Your Highness," he said, bowing once more.

Luka dragged Alfie around the bowing Englassen and dashed down the hall to an empty classroom.

"Sorry, James!" Luka called as they dashed away. "It's Castallano tradition for the prince to haphazardly run into at least two people per day, not to worry!"

As they rushed into the classroom Alfie heard James exhale sharply through his nose, as if he was trying to hold back a chuckle.

"Did you see that?" Luka chimed in beside him. "I just made an Englassen laugh. We can cancel the summit, all is well."

"Luka, what did you drag me in here to tell me?"

"I got a tattoo," he said before pulling the sleep shirt off his head.

"Yes, you said that," Alfie said. "But why are you getting naked?"

Luka stared at himself, moving in a circle like a dog chasing its own tail. "Because the tattoo is enchanted to move around my body, and I can't seem to find it," he said, pulling off his pantalones.

Alfie looked away with a grimace. "Why would you get a tattoo that moved around your body? And what does your tattoo have to do with stopping the bull-masked people?"

"To answer your first question," Luka said while inspecting his leg, "I got a moving tattoo so I could ask my lovers to find it." He winked. "It moves in a set pattern that goes from leg to hip, up the back, around the shoulder, down the chest . . ."

Alfie rubbed his temples as Luka charted the path over his skin. "You're the worst."

"And the man I got the tattoo from is well-connected in the tattoo world. I'll find him and see if he knows where the bull tattoo came from."

It wasn't the easiest route, but it was something. "If we can find the artist who did the tattoo, we might be able to find out who the members of the group are."

"Ha! Here it is," Luka said, hopping over to Alfie on one foot, presenting his bent knee. "See?"

"Dioses, put some clothes on," Alfie said, but he caught a glimpse of the tattoo before he looked pointedly away. "You got a tattoo of a gravehopper?"

Gravehoppers were seen as bad omens. The jumping bugs were often found making their homes near fresh graves because they were attracted to the scent of the incense Castallanos left for their loved ones who had passed. Some even believed that if you heard a gravehopper, it meant that death was hot on your heels.

Luka's smile faltered, as if he'd only just remembered what the tattoo was. "It's nothing," he said, quickly putting his clothes back on.

"It's not nothing," Alfie said, wringing his hands. Luka had gone through a deep sadness after Sombra had been dispatched, an immense guilt about getting to live when so many died after Alfie chose to save him. Luka had told him he was fine now, but if he'd gotten a tattoo of a gravehopper, Alfie doubted it. He had a feeling this was part of the reason why Luka was being so reckless in fight clubs. "Luka, are you—"

"I'm fine," Luka said, now fully dressed and avoiding Alfie's eyes. "I'll try to set something up with the tattoo guy and we'll go from here, all right?"

"Luka, we have to—"

"I don't want to talk about it," Luka shouted. Alfie jumped where he stood and Luka looked at him guiltily. "I'm sorry, I just don't want to right now."

"Very well." Alfie nodded, trying to hide his worry as Luka finished dressing. "But if you ever want to . . ."

"I know." Luka gripped him by the shoulder. "It's been a long day; let's get some rest."

"All right," Alfie agreed, forcing a small smile, but he knew that Luka could see the worry in his eyes as they walked out of the classroom and back into the hall.

THE THIEF LORDS OF CASTALLAN

Finn stood before a burbling fountain, her head spinning with new information.

The fountain was a gaudy thing in a quiet corner of the Bow—the richest ring of the city aside from the palace grounds themselves. It was as over-the-top as the surrounding haciendas—a woman in a flowing gown with her arms outstretched as she spun on her toes, frozen mid-dance.

Finn thought of her nights sitting on the figurehead of the ship, her feet swinging as they bobbed toward another horizon. Even with Kol's enticing treasure trove waiting for her, Finn couldn't help but wonder why she'd ever left the damn boat. Why hadn't she just stayed on it and gone to some other city? Maybe even some other continent. Why had she decided to come back to San Cristóbal in the first place?

She knew the answer—it was tall, dimpled, and looked at her like she could be more.

"Estúpida," Finn muttered to herself.

Pinching the bridge of her nose, she approached the fountain just as Anabeltilia had told her. She pressed a coin into the statue's hand, and the coin was somehow absorbed into the stone palm, disappearing from sight. The statue turned its head and looked at her, its eyes as dead as a doll's. Yet it moved smoothly, as if it were made of flesh, joint, and bone, not rock. Though she'd been warned about this, Finn still jumped, goose bumps sprouting on her skin.

"I have to pay a statue to attend a meeting I don't even want to go to?" Finn had asked Anabeltilia.

The girl only nodded as if this were all normal. "I didn't make the rules."

As the statue regarded her with its soulless eyes Finn fidgeted, afraid it would strike her down. But the statue only nodded, and the white floor of the fountain beneath its feet began to shift into a spiral staircase that sank into the dark. Water from the fountain trickled down the stairs, and the statue slowly returned to its previous pose. Finn grimaced. According to Anabeltilia, there were three other thief lords in Castallan. Each controlled the illegal underbelly of a quadrant of the continent. Kol had controlled the northeast, including the capital.

If Finn had known Kol was *that* powerful, she might have been less brash when they'd first met.

Well, maybe.

The thief lords seldom gathered in person, but tonight's meeting was apparently mandatory. A few days ago, Finn had owned nothing but her wits and what she could fit in her bag. Now she owned a quarter of the continent's thieves, spread throughout endless cities like crumbs on a table.

Of course, she owned this illegally, but the responsibility weighed on her as if she'd been born with a crown on her head. She thought of the prince, of how his throat worked when he talked about his fear of ruling. She'd assumed he was being dramatic, but now she could see the truth in the anxiety that had thrummed through him.

Finn was barely responsible enough to look after herself, let alone an entire quadrant of the continent, but if they really had her blood and could track her by it, then did she have a choice?

"Who says you have to look after anyone, Mija?" Ignacio's voice crooned in her head.

Finn nearly tumbled down the stairs at his sudden intrusion. "Stop it."

"You were more than capable of killing even before this new side of your *propio* appeared. And now? You are absolutely *lethal*. Kill whoever stands in your way and leave. You know you want to."

Finn paused on the stairs and counted down from ten until his voice finally faded and the only proof of his presence was the cold sweat coating her skin. She needed to be sharp. She was about to face some of the finest thieves that Castallan had to offer. The last thing she needed was Ignacio's voice upending her confidence.

Finn trudged down the tight spiral staircase until it opened into a long hall with walls of dark rock. From the far end of the hall she heard the soft voice of a woman and the raucous laughter of a man. Following the scent of cigarillo smoke, she walked down the corridor until she stood before a set of open double doors that led into a parlor of sorts.

The room was spare, with a large square table at its center where three people sat. Finn cocked her head as she saw that the table was piled high with desserts. Flans drizzled with dulce de leche, tiered cakes with pineapple jam between each layer, spiced breads, and bowls of habichuelas con dulce. She could smell the spiced cocoa in the mugs at the table and she spotted a corked bottle of coquito. It was as if she'd stepped into a child's fantasy of the perfect dinner.

The thief lords fell silent as she moved to stand in the doorway. At the head of the table was a woman with a riot of curly white hair. She must've been at least seventy years old and wore a white eye patch detailed with lace and pearls. Finn had a feeling she had one to match every outfit. She looked at Finn with a gentle smile, like an abuela welcoming home a grandchild. Finn frowned; she would've felt more comfortable if the woman had glared at her or tried to pin her to the wall with a dagger. And speaking of daggers, behind the woman was an expansive wall with dozens of machetes jutting off it, blade first. Finn squinted at it. She liked a good blade just as much as the next bad thief, but it was an off-putting choice of decoration.

To her left was a man old enough to be Finn's young father. His hair was dark but streaked with gray, and his jaw was covered in a thick coat of stubble. He watched her, amused, as he took a long drag of his cigar, then exhaled a stream of purple smoke. The last person at the table was a boy who couldn't be older than twelve. He drummed his fingers on the wood, clearly impatient. Who brought a little kid to a meeting of thieves?

"So you're Kol's replacement, eh?" the man said. He pointed to the empty chair across from the old woman. "Take your seat; we don't have all night."

"We have as long as I say we need to make things right, Rodrigo," the older woman said before taking a delicate sip of her spiced cocoa, steam rising from the mug in curls.

Rodrigo stiffened. "Of course, Emeraude. As you say."

Well, it was clear who the jefa was here.

Finn took her place at the table while the old woman scanned her appraisingly, almost as if she were expecting something. If she was waiting for Finn to grovel for her approval, she'd be waiting a long time. Finn threw her boots up onto the table. Emeraude raised a white eyebrow as a bit of mud sprinkled onto the flan.

"This your grandson?" Finn jerked her thumb at the young boy to her right.

The boy looked at her as if she'd asked if he was a cucaracha. The man burst out laughing.

"Ah, unfortunately, I don't have any grandbabies," Emeraude said, her tone light. "Having grandchildren would mean carrying a man's child, and you'd sooner see me carry myself off the edge of a cliff."

Finn thought that was a fair response.

"The boy is Elian," Rodrigo said. He spoke a clearer, slower dialect than those in the capital city. In San Cristóbal people spoke so fast that the ends of words were lost in the mad dash. It was an accent she'd come to love. This man must be from southern Castallan. "He's thief lord of the southwest territory. I wouldn't cross him."

Finn rolled her eyes at the man before looking at Elian. The boy stared at her, as if to say, *Try me.*

She glared back, crossing her arms as if to say, *Do your worst, muchachito.*

A moment too late, she saw his shadow twist at his feet.

Shit.

He looked pleased that she'd noticed. His green eyes flickered down and then back up to hers as emotion rose in Finn's chest like a tidal wave. First, a strange motherly affection that made her want to reach out and hold the boy, protect him. The feeling swelled so quickly that her arm began to rise, reaching out to stroke his cheek.

The boy smirked then, like a fisherman surveying a cod flopping on his hook, and the feeling took a sharp dive. Goose bumps spread over her skin and her throat clenched. She feared this boy—feared him as if she'd watched him take a knife to everyone she loved while promising to save her for last. She pulled back her hand, a scream building in her throat. Just as she opened her mouth to shriek, the boy let her go.

He looked away from her, a small smile quirking his lips. Finn's fingers dug into her crossed arms as she gasped for breath.

He could manipulate emotions with his *propio*. Finn tried uselessly to get her heart to slow its pace as the boy went back to drumming his fingers on the table, as if she were nothing to worry about. She wanted to blast him out of his seat with a stone-cloaked fist.

"Te lo dije," Rodrigo said with a wink as Finn caught her breath. "I'm Rodrigo. I run the southeast. And Emeraude"—he gestured at the older woman—"runs the northwest. Pobrecita really doesn't know anything, does she?"

All three of them laughed.

"All right, all right," Finn grumbled. "Enough. We're here for a reason, aren't we? Get on with it or I'm out the door."

Emeraude's finger traced the delicate rim of her teacup. "She has a point. We're here to discuss the summit and the bull-masked group."

Finn's pulse jumped. The thief lords knew about them?

"I've been calling them Los Toros," the woman went on. "For obvious reasons."

"They've taken down our Englassen connections in our three quadrants." Rodrigo turned to Finn. "Have you seen the same here?"

Finn blinked at him. "Qué?"

"She doesn't even know what we're talking about," he sighed to Emeraude. "How long have you been a thief lord?"

Finn thought for a moment. "What time is it?"

His jaw went slack. "You haven't even been a thief lord for a full day?"

"Nope."

"Then we'll have to explain Los Toros," Emeraude said, eyeing an exasperated Rodrigo.

Finn nodded. Playing dumb seemed like the right move. She didn't need these people to know that she knew about Los Toros already.

"I'll explain it since Elian isn't much of a talker," Rodrigo said. "Los Toros, as Emeraude has nicknamed them, is a new gang that sprang up out of nowhere a few months ago. All we know is that they seem to be an anti-Englass nationalist group."

Emeraude nodded. "They likely emerged in response to the announcement of the peace summit."

"For the last month, they've been killing our connections to the Englassen black market, making it clear that they stand against anyone who is working with Englass in any way," Rodrigo complained. "Very annoying."

"Wait," Finn said, her brow furrowed. After seeing the protests against the royal family for inviting Englass over, Finn was surprised to see the thief lords defend that decision. "Don't you hate Englass too?"

"Oh, absolutely," Emeraude said.

At the same time Rodrigo leaned back in his chair and said, "Colonizing pendejos don't deserve to make peace with us."

Elian nodded, crossing his arms. As he shifted she noticed that Elian and Rodrigo were wearing matching necklaces. Small stoppered vials hung on their necks. She rolled her eyes; men had the worst fashion sense. Or maybe it was a thief lord thing and the old lady had one too. She pushed away those thoughts. She wasn't here to analyze thief lord fashion.

"If you hate Englass too, then why are you so upset about a group of people who are against making peace with them?" she asked.

"Because we hate Englass but we love dinero." Rodrigo smirked.

"For years we have worked in black market trading with Englassen thieves. But on both sides we stand to make even more money once our kingdoms open their borders to one another. What Englass did to our ancestors is personal," Emeraude said, her jaw tense. "But this is just business."

"We have a stake in this summit, and Los Toros is endangering it." Rodrigo grimaced, his face pinched as if he tasted something sour.

"That, and we don't like new gangs in our territory," Emeraude said, steel in her voice.

"I can't believe after today's murder, we find ourselves on the same side as the royal family—protect the summit at all costs." Rodrigo shook his head. "The old thief lords are rolling in their graves."

"Today's murder?" Finn choked on her spit. She'd only been here for a day and someone had been killed? Maybe Ignacio was right. Maybe she did bring chaos wherever she went. "And the royals already know about it and Los Toros?"

She'd thought she'd be bringing some fresh information to Alfie when she told him about the bull-masked thief. Now it felt like she was coming empty-handed. Would he even want to see her?

"You really are out of the loop, aren't you?" Rodrigo said with a laugh. "Today, Los Toros murdered a delegado who was in favor of the peace summit. They are threatening to continue the murders if the summit goes on."

"We have a few spies in the palace. Servants who will tell us what they hear in exchange for a couple pesos." Emeraude folded her hands on the table. "They apparently had a meeting about it earlier tonight. Thankfully, they're going to go on with the summit, but they'll be increasing security, trying to hunt them down themselves."

"We've got our people searching for them in our quadrants too," Rodrigo said, crossing his arms. "I can't believe we're actually helping the royals with something. Dioses."

"We expect you to mobilize la Familia to do the same," Emeraude said, her sharp-eyed gaze on Finn. "Now, with the summit beginning, we can only assume that Los Toros will focus their efforts on the capital. Your people know these streets better than anyone else. They could be the key to finding Los Toros and ending this before it costs us too many pesos to say."

Finn was too surprised to speak. Over the past few days her life had changed so quickly. She'd been free from Ignacio, then suddenly caged by him again. She'd seen the bull tattoo that Alfie had described, but before she could tell him about it, she'd been made a thief lord and pulled into a mission whose goal just so happened to be putting a stop to Los Toros. Everything seemed both random and oddly connected.

"All right," Finn finally said. "I'll get la Familia on it." As much as she hated cooperating without a fight, it was in her best interest to do so if she wanted to help the prince.

"Good," Emeraude said. "We'll be meeting periodically throughout the summit to check in and discuss how to ensure it goes smoothly." She looked pointedly at Rodrigo and Elian. "I'll see you both in two days' time."

"Of course," Rodrigo said as he stood and dropped into a bow. "Nice to meet you, new Kol." He winked.

"It's Finn," she said.

When Finn got out of her chair, itching to get to the prince and tell him everything, Emeraude pinned her down with a look. "You, stay."

With a barely stifled snort of laughter, Rodrigo took his leave, Elian following close behind.

"I'm not a dog," Finn growled.

"Ay, mi amor, even a dog would've known better than to put its feet on my table. I'd like to acquaint myself a bit more with you. Alone."

Cursing under her breath, Finn sat back down.

"Well?" she asked, annoyed. "What do you want?"

Emeraude poured a glass of coquito and pushed it across the table. "I can tell you're not the type to look for allies, but I think we could help each other, even understand each other."

Finn rolled her eyes and stared at the dessert-laden table. "I think we're a bit different. I don't hide who I am, while you've got this sweet little abuela act going on."

"Excuse me?"

"The whole flan-and-cookies act? Why are you doing this, pretending to be some sweet old lady when you've already got the other two thief lords afraid to disobey you? What's the point in acting all sweet?"

Finn despised the idea that women had to be motherly, smiley creatures to be saved or protected or fallen in love with. People born to set the table instead of claiming a seat.

"Oh, Face Thief. I know all about you. First, you say that you don't hide, when your *propio* in and of itself is a way to hide." Finn started at the sound of her moniker. How did this vieja know anything about her?

Emeraude laughed, dimples emerging in her wrinkled cheeks. "And what makes you think it's an act?" When Finn said nothing, Emeraude smiled, producing a spoon to stir her cocoa. "Muchacha, you are very sure in your opinions, aren't you?"

"Sí, when I'm right. And I'm always right." Finn leaned forward, her fists on the table. "Now, how do you know that I'm the Face Thief?" The other two had clearly had no idea who she was.

"I'll get to that in a moment," Emeraude said, waving a dismissive hand.

Finn's nostrils flared. Why did old people have to be so difficult? Emeraude could die any second; she should tell her now while she still had life in her.

"But this 'abuela thing' is no act. I've always been this way, well before I became a thief lord. It's quite a story—"

"If it were an act, it would be an interesting story," Finn said, stifling a yawn. "But if it isn't, and you're just this annoying generally, then I don't need to hear it."

Emeraude's gaze sharpened. "I think you do, Face Thief. I was born long before you were—"

"Obviously."

"It was a different world back then. I was raised to cook, clean, and run a household. But I was lucky because I actually enjoyed those tasks, especially the cooking." She motioned at the cakes on the table. Then her gaze turned sharp. "And don't think I missed that joke. Respect your elders or I'll break my chancleta on your culo and you'll never live to see this age, oíste?"

Finn rolled her eyes again.

"When I was born, it was even harder for a woman to be anything but married," she said with a shrug, as if it were an insurmountable fact. "So I got married, like a good girl does. When Manolo first started pursuing me, my family pushed me to be with him because they knew he had the money and connections to give me a good life. But they didn't know what his actual job was. Would you care to take a guess?"

Finn rolled her neck from side to side. "A really, really boring storyteller?"

Emeraude didn't rise to the bait. "He was the thief lord who ran the northwest territory before me."

Finn stared at her. As she'd recently come to learn, the only way to become a thief lord was to inherit the position after one died—or to kill them yourself. Finn had a feeling it was going to be the latter. Men weren't keen on giving up their power to anyone, let alone a woman, let alone their wife.

"I learned a lot from him. He was an incomparable thief lord, but . . . ," she said, her voice petering out as she gestured to her eye patch. "He was not a great husband."

Finn's brows rose. "He took your eye?"

Emeraude nodded, taking a slow sip of her coquito. "He caught me having an affair a few years in. Told me that if I was going to use my eyes to look at men who weren't him, then I didn't need eyes. He took one and told me to consider my second eye a gift."

Finn's spine straightened, and Ignacio's glinting grin filled her mind, a half-moon hanging in a dark sky. And how that smile would crumple and twist when Finn dared to make a friend. When she dared to look at anyone but him.

Emeraude shook her head. "I wanted to leave, tried many times, but Manolo had connections everywhere. No one wanted to anger a thief lord by helping me, and everyone wanted to earn his favor by catching me and returning me to him like a lost cat. Years passed and the beatings went on—a blur of bruises and broken bones, until something in me finally cracked," she said, her jaw tightening. "I knew that Manolo's connections would stop me from being free, so the only logical solution was to make those connections my own." She shrugged, as if it were nothing. "He took my eye, I took his life. Seemed like an even trade."

Finn nodded, her voice gruff. "Sounds more than fair to me."

Emeraude looked at her then, awareness in her single eye. Suddenly feeling vulnerable and horribly exposed, Finn sat farther back in her seat.

"I've had my people look into you, muchacha. I'm sure you understand the kind of man my husband was very well."

Finn could only nod. "I did. Not anymore. You've told me your life story; now, how do you know who I am and why did you ask me to stay? If you're looking to trade horror stories, I'm not the one."

"I asked you to stay because I have a proposition for you." Emeraude pushed a plate of cookies her way.

Finn frowned. The last time she'd made a deal with a thief lord, she'd ended up inside a dead pig, but, then again, she could use whatever information the woman knew about Kol, the bull tattoo, and the murder that had just been done in its name. "Get on with it."

"I'm the longest-living thief lord in all of Castallan."

Finn rolled her eyes. "Congratulations on outliving most trees."

"Listen to me," she snapped. "I know you don't want this position. I can get you out of it."

Finn stared at her. "I thought the only way to get out of this was to die."

"Most of the time, yes," Emeraude said as she absentmindedly swept crumbs off the table. "But in certain circumstances . . ." She leaned back in her chair, crossing her legs beneath her gown. "I know you don't want to be thief lord, and you certainly didn't escape that man to end up living a life you didn't choose."

Finn put her elbows on the table, steepled her hands, and rested her chin on her fingers. "Keep talking, Abuela."

"I can offer you a way out, in exchange for answers. I know much of what went on leading up to Kol's death. That's how I knew about you—a face-stealing thief who Kol sent on some impossible quest while she plotted to poison the crown prince."

There was no way Emeraude knew everything that had happened—only she and the prince knew that. But the vieja had put a lot of the pieces together.

"Our kind don't play with politics, with the killing of royals. We have our own laws to abide by," Emeraude said. "Then I remembered that Kol had a bull tattoo, just like the Los Toros symbol. It can't be a coincidence. Interfering with the royals is against the sacred thief lord bylaws. If we can prove that Kol was a part of it, then her actions would be grounds for ending her reign as thief lord."

Finn squinted at her. "But she's already dead. How does that help me?"

"If Kol was involved in trying to assassinate a royal, it would be against the thief lord bylaws, which would mean that her line of succession is no longer eligible to be thief lords. You would be free to go. My people haven't been able to figure much out about them, how Kol was connected to them, or who convinced her to try to kill a prince. We have no real proof of anything but hearsay. But a girl who can change her face like that? A girl who is now in control of Kol's people?" Emeraude snapped her fingers. "She could come in handy, dig up the truth, entiendes?"

Finn crossed her arms, considering. "I get you answers and I get out of being thief lord?"

Emeraude nodded. "Free as a bird."

If Finn were a dog she'd be wagging her tail. This was a perfect deal. She wanted to know what Kol was up to as well, and the prince would too, since that would help them learn more about the bull-masked people. She would've sought out this information about Kol and the tattoo one way or another, but now she would get rewarded for it with her freedom. She'd never have to see a single member of la Familia again. She could do as she liked and live as she pleased.

Her life would be hers again.

Finn squinted at Emeraude. "What do you get out of this? You can't just want answers for no reason."

Emeraude smiled. "You're a smart one, muchacha. If I can prove that Kol was up to something that went against the Thief's Code, then the senior thief lord gets to pick her replacement. You would no longer be the heir to her throne since she herself had broken the rules. I can install a puppet thief lord to take over her quadrant after you leave. Then I'll be running half of Castallan and Elian and Rodrigo wouldn't be able to do a thing about it."

Finn stared at the woman for a moment. She was a lot smarter than she'd anticipated.

"So that's why you're asking me for help without the other two here. You don't want them to know about this plan for you to pick this quadrant's new thief lord."

"Exactly," Emeraude said. "If they knew I was pursuing this, they would find a way to bury the information about whatever Kol was up to. The last thing they want is me getting a puppet to run the most profitable quadrant of the kingdom. I've had my eye on this quadrant for decades; I won't let those two get in the way. Right now they know nothing of Kol's tattoo and her connection to Los Toros. I'd like to keep it that way."

Finn considered the vieja's words. Now that her intentions were clear, Finn was less nervous about working with her.

"If you want out of this job, you'll need me. So either you can help me or you can die. The choice is yours," Emeraude said, her eye glinting with the knowledge that Finn only had one valid choice. "Do we have a deal?"

"Coño," Finn sighed. She was already tired of making deals

with mobsters, and she'd only done it once before.

But she wasn't meant to run a normal family, let alone a family of mobsters. Anything that would let her be free again was worth agreeing to. "Deal."

"Good. You'll report to me. The others needn't know that we're doing this, oíste?"

"Fine with me." Finn pushed her chair and moved to stand. It wasn't as if she had any allegiance to the creepy kid and the guy who laughed too much.

"Esperate, at least try some flan before you go." Finn was about to argue when Emeraude added, "Or take some home for later? You're looking thin. You should eat more. Can't solve a murder mystery on an empty stomach."

Finn stared at her. How could someone be a sweet abuela and a killer all at once? "How would you know that I'm looking thin if you just met me?"

"I just know," she said with a wave of her hand. "Some flan to take home?"

Finn watched the dulce de leche dribble off the side of the flan and finally gave in. If she was hiring her for a job, it's not like Emeraude would poison her, and she could always do with some flan. "Fine."

Emeraude rang a bell and a servant came in with a glass container. Emeraude cut a thick wedge—making sure to give Finn the piece that had been speckled with the mud from Finn's shoes—and carefully placed it in the container. She added some cookies in as well. "And you can call me abuela if you want, muchacha. I don't mind."

"You minding was the whole point of doing it."

The woman grinned and Finn was annoyed by how quickly she

was beginning to like her.

"You know," Emeraude said as she spooned another dollop of dulce de leche into the container, "last week was Manolo's birthday."

Finn could hardly imagine the woman baking a cake in his honor. "What'd you do?"

"Laugh," Emeraude said. Then she threw her head back and did just that. "Now, I have one lead for you to start with. . . ."

"Who?" Finn asked, resisting the urge to lean forward.

"The man who brewed the poison Kol used to try to kill the prince. Hidalgo Venoso."

When Finn emerged from the fountain, her mind was abuzz with too many thoughts to keep straight.

For one, she'd been robbed by a bull-masked pendejo, the vanishing cloak long gone. Second, she'd shown up in the city on the same day that a murder had been committed by someone in Los Toros, and now with Emeraude's deal, she had all the motivation she needed to find out exactly what Kol had been up to with the masked gang. The prince would be happy to help, she knew—after all, this would help him finally figure out what had happened to his brother. Even though he was in the middle of preparing for the summit, he'd be glad to see her. She hoped.

"Just because he makes you feel all warm and gooey inside doesn't mean he'll be happy to see you," Ignacio laughed.

She whirled around and there he was, leaning against the fountain as if he owned it.

"Shut up," she said, turning her back on him. "You're not real."

"I think we've established that," Ignacio said. "But are you sure you want to get involved with that little boy again? He's a weakling, but he's still an honorable prince. What could he want to do with you now that you don't have me to fight?"

"What I do is none of your business," she bit out, walking away from the statue without looking back.

"You entered his life by accident," he said with a laugh. "He never wanted you there. He kept you around out of desperation because he couldn't face me alone. He'll pretend he's glad to see you, but you'll see the truth on his face—that he wants nothing to do with you."

"Stop it," Finn said, hating how small and afraid her voice had become. She sounded like a child, like the child he owned.

"Wherever you go, you bring trouble. You will bring him nothing but pain."

Finn pressed her hands to her face, her nails digging into the flesh of her cheeks. Her mind unearthed that foul memory of what she'd done with Ignacio at her side—the boy choking as Ignacio told her to squeeze his neck tighter and tighter. When Finn finally dropped her hands, she wore a new face. A new identity. A clean slate. She felt safer.

"See," Ignacio said, his voice hushed. "Doesn't that feel better?"

When Finn turned to face him, he was gone. Wrapping her arms around herself, she let an exhausted sigh sag out of her. At least she was alone, for now.

Her feet heavy, she began her long walk to the palace and the prince within it.

THE REUNION

Cold rain sluiced down Finn's face and back as she scaled the side of the palace, Alfie's balcony looming overhead.

Using her stone carving, she pulled stones from the palace outward to fashion footholds and handholds for herself. It would've been easy if not for the maldito rain.

It was long past midnight and she wondered if she would be waking him. Finn froze mid-reach at that thought before shaking her head. Who cared if he had to be woken up?

"Stupid," she grumbled to herself as she continued to climb.

But she couldn't stop thinking about what Ignacio had said—would he be happy to see her?

Finn lost her footing. With a yelp she slid down the side of the palace for a few feet before catching her wits and gripping on to the palace wall once more. "Shit."

Sinking her fingers into the stones for leverage, Finn shook the water out of her eyes. "You're here to get out of being thief lord and maybe get Ignacio out of your head. That's all."

Finn finally reached the prince's balcony. She pulled herself over the side and landed on her backside with a wet *plop*. Her legs and arms aching, Finn stood up from the ground and waited for a long moment before approaching the balcony door. Though it was late, beyond the sheer blue curtains on the other side of the glass balcony doors, Finn could see the soft glow of light.

He was awake.

She swallowed. Why was she so nervous? He was just a boy, one she'd saved more times than she could count. He should be nervous to see her, not the other way around.

But then he was also a boy who'd looked at her with soft gold eyes and promised to die with her, promised that now, in this moment, she was more than she ever believed she could be.

As the rain dripped off her, Finn wished she hadn't climbed the side of this palace or stepped on the ship or left that city in the southern port of Castallan, because this anticipation rising within her meant too many things. It meant that when she eventually left the prince, and she would, it would hurt. Without even greeting him, she was already in pain from the loss, suffering from the goodbye. It was stifling. He was stifling. If standing outside his doors was this unbearable, what would happen when she stepped inside?

Did she even matter to him anymore? They'd only known each other for a few days. Four months apart trumped that, didn't it? This was stupid. She was stupid for coming here.

Before Finn could turn back to the balcony and climb down, a flash of movement beyond the curtains caught her gaze. Finn leaned forward, peering through the sliver of space between the curtains, and there stood the prince.

Naked.

The towel draped over his desk chair told her that he'd just come out of the bath. She couldn't stop her eyes from skimming up past his toes and ankles and knees and up and up and . . .

Some part of Finn knew that the appropriate thing to do would be to look away. But no part of Finn had ever been appropriate.

She didn't realize how close she'd gotten to the glass door until her nose bumped against it and her breathing had left a circle of steam. She rubbed her nose and scoffed at herself. It wasn't as if she'd never seen a man naked before. This was nothing.

She kept watching.

The prince slipped into his sleeping trousers and perched on the edge of his bed. He massaged his head in his hands, looking stressed. He had the strange talent of making anxiety look endearing. She was annoyed at herself for smiling.

She raised a hand, her fingers grazing the balcony's doorknob before the double doors swung open and inward at her touch. Finn jumped, dumbfounded.

Alfie turned, his gaze holding her where she stood. The look on his face was one Finn could not begin to describe. Hope and heart-break rising, cresting, and shattering in quick cycles, as if he was elated that she was here but knew it couldn't be for long. She wore a new face, but she could tell he knew it was her. He knew her beyond the flesh and bone to something else.

She gestured at the balcony doors. "It just swung open," she said awkwardly. It was the only thing she could think to say, and his grin at the sound of her voice was so soft and vulnerable that she had to believe it was the right choice of words.

"I know." He sounded breathless, as if he were the one who'd scaled the side of the palace.

"It just swings open for anyone?" Finn asked. "What kind of idiot would do that?"

His smile brightened and Finn felt annoyingly shy, as if she wanted to cover her face with her hands and shout insults at him until he went away.

"I magicked the door to open for some people. Mamá and Papá, Luka, Dezmin." He stood, and the light clung to his skin, pooling in the hollows of his collarbones and sweeping over the smooth muscles of his chest and stomach. "You."

He said that last word as if she was a wish made real. Real and soaked to the bone, standing at his balcony doors.

He walked as if the world had tilted on its axis with the sole purpose of delivering him to her. Just as her feet had moved with a mind of their own when they'd said goodbye months ago, she dashed those last steps into his open embrace, her arms twining around his bare waist.

"You're here," Alfie said, as if he couldn't quite believe it himself. "You're really here."

"I am," she said, unsure of what else to say.

Suddenly conscious of the press of her wet clothes to his bare skin, Finn pulled away.

His eyes fell on her face with new wonder. "There you are."

"What?" Finn asked. Then she caught a glimpse of herself in the mirror behind him. Ignacio had made her feel such intense shame after her meeting with the thief lords that she'd donned a new face, running away from her own and all she'd done. But as they embraced, the new face she'd fashioned melted away like butter.

Her clothes were soaked, and they'd left their mark after their hug. His chest glistened with rainwater. The band of his sleeping trousers had gotten wet too. She knew she'd been staring for too long when Alfie's face reddened and he hurried back to his bed and grabbed his sleeping shirt, pulling it over his head in one swift motion. Finn looked away. Somehow watching him put clothes on seemed too intimate.

"You must be freezing," he said when he was dressed. "Let me help you." He outstretched a hand and looked at her, waiting for her to say yes. He always waited to see if it was what she wanted. She'd missed that. She nodded, and the prince made a plucking motion with his hand, as if he'd caught a handkerchief in midair.

At the delicate pull of his fingers, every drop of rainwater slipped off her body to hover over his open palm. A shudder ran up her spine. It was an odd feeling, as if thousands of fingertips had passed over her skin all at once, the touch featherlight but leaving trails of goose bumps. He hadn't touched her, not directly, but she wondered if that was how it would feel. Slow and delicate. Careful and deliberate. She fingered the sleeve of her shirt, the hairs rising on the back of her neck.

Alfie directed the water into a nearby vase.

He opened his mouth to speak, but Finn beat him to it. "I lost the cloak," she blurted out.

Alfie stared at her. "Qué?"

"I said I lost the stupid cloak," she said, crossing her arms. "Are you deaf?"

Alfie stared at her for a long moment and Finn watched his

face carefully. She wanted to see anger twist his features, or at least annoyance. She wanted to see his shadow whip around. She was used to that. It was what she knew best. Maybe that was why Ignacio was back in her mind. Maybe she would always look for pain because it was her native language.

But the prince did no such thing. His shadow stretched gently toward her. "Tell me what happened," he said, and even when he spoke in a command, it sounded optional, gentle. He looked at her as if he'd already forgiven her, when she didn't even ask him to.

She hated it.

"It's a long story," she said, her voice going quiet.

Alfie stepped away from her and perched on the edge of his bed, giving her space. "I have time." He nodded at her encouragingly and, after a deep breath, Finn explained everything. Her encounter with the bull-masked thief and how she thought the mask and the tattoo were connected. How the mask had been made of some strange, liquid substance that wouldn't break. How she'd been kidnapped by la Familia and made a thief lord. How she could only get out of being a thief lord if she could solve the mystery of what Kol was up to and how it connected to Los Toros and tonight's murder.

When she finally finished, Alfie stared at her, wide-eyed. She could see the wheels spinning in his mind. "So they're called Los Toros, then?"

"That's what Emeraude calls them; no one knows what they call themselves. They're an underground Castallano organization that's against peace with Englass. That's all the vieja knows so far. The rest is on me."

"No," Alfie said, resolute. "The rest is on us." Then he caught himself. "If you'll let me help, of course."

Finn tilted her head, pretending to consider. "You could be useful, I suppose."

"Then we'll work on this together," he said, his smile looking touchably soft. "We'll figure out what's going on with Los Toros so that you can be free and I can stop them from hurting anyone else. Maybe get you the cloak back too if we can manage it." He crossed his arms. "I don't understand why they felt the need to take it—or how they knew you had it."

Finn shook her head, not wanting to tell him what the thief had said, but she knew she had to. "He said that the cloak belonged to the rightful king of Castallan, and now that your family invited Englass here, you no longer are the rightful royal family."

Alfie flinched as if he'd been struck. "Oh."

"Don't let it get to you," Finn said, feeling useless as the prince's face crumpled.

He swallowed thickly, holding out his hand, his eyes finding hers. "We'll figure it out," he finally said. "Together."

"Deal," Finn said, grasping his hand. The warmth of their palms pressed together made her feel the need to change the subject. "What's been going on, Prince?" she asked, pulling her hand away. "I ran into a mob of people burning piñatas of you."

Alfie rubbed the back of his neck, the smile slipping off his face. "They're burning effigies of me, not piñatas."

Finn didn't know what an effigy was, but it made more sense than a piñata. "I wondered why they would burn something that was full of candy. . . ."

"The people are upset about what happened with Sombra."

He explained the tale that the royal family had spun—that the dueños had been studying some experimental magic that had gone rogue. That seemed like a smart lie to Finn. It pushed the blame onto a group of people instead of one person, and no matter how much people disliked dueños, they still respected them.

"Then why are they blaming your family?"

Alfie shook his head. "Because the responsibility for a kingdom will always lie with those who rule it. And the people are upset about Englassen royalty coming for the peace summit at my family's invitation too—all their anger has found its target in us. It's been awful," he admitted. "An angry crowd confronted me as I was unveiling a memorial to those taken by Sombra," he said, looking shaken enough that Finn wanted to throw a barrage of daggers at whoever had made him feel that way. "They destroyed it, nearly attacked Luka and me too. And I know I saw a man in the very same black bull mask there. Or I thought I saw him; I'd hoped I was just seeing things in the chaos. But now I know it was true. I knew something was coming before tonight's murder even happened. Los Toros had something to do with my brother's death, and they're back." The prince's eyes were clouded, but Finn could see the pain beneath.

"Mierda." Finn plopped onto the bed beside him. "If they were brave enough to show up to the memorial ceremony where you were surrounded by guards, they must not be afraid at all."

Alfie bit his lip. "They're planning something. Something that makes them feel confident."

Los Toros aside, things were messy enough. What had been the point in lying about Alfie releasing Sombra's magic if it was all going to blow up in his face regardless? "And this peace summit thing is still happening in the middle of all this?" Finn asked.

"After a meeting with the delegados, my parents decided that the summit would proceed regardless of the risk. It starts tomorrow," Alfie sighed into his hands. "The people have connected that we are having the summit in part to present me as the future ruler of Castallan to the world. But I'm not the ruler they want." Alfie gave a pained laugh. Finn didn't like the way it sounded, the way she could hear his heartbreak folded into it. "They wanted Dez. Now they're stuck with me. All this has combined with their anger at having Englass on Castallano soil and what happened when Sombra was released—a single storm against my family and me. And that's all without Los Toros murdering a delegado who supported the summit."

"Coño," Finn said.

Alfie nodded. "We've got no time to waste. Luka is working on finding out the origin of the tattoo. He's got some connection with a tattoo artist. He's hoping his connection can tell him which tattoo artist is doing Los Toros' tattoos."

"Then maybe we can track them down from there," Finn said with a nod.

"Exactly," Alfie said. "That's all I've got thus far."

"Well," Finn began uneasily. "That's not all you've got."

The prince raised a brow.

"Emeraude gave us our first lead," Finn said. "But you won't like it." Maybe she shouldn't have even told him about this one. It might've been better to pursue it on her own.

"I don't like most things." Alfie shrugged. "Tell me."

Finally, Finn said, "She gave me the name of the person Kol hired to make the poison that almost killed Bathtub Boy. He might know what Kol was up to."

Alfie fell silent, and she knew his mind had gone to that awful night when Luka had nearly died in his arms.

The vase that he'd filled with water from Finn's soaked clothes shook and spilled over. Finn pretended not to notice.

Alfie bit the inside of his cheek. "I suppose we have to explore every possible lead."

"We do," she said, and she hoped he heard what she'd truly wished to say. *I'm sorry this is happening to you. I wish it weren't.* She drummed her fingers on her thighs. "I didn't mean to lose the cloak."

Alfie looked at her for a long moment, as if he'd forgotten all about that. Though, in the midst of everything else going on, the loss of the cloak seemed small. "I gave it to you. It was yours to do with as you pleased." His lips curved down into a frown. "Though I wish it was still yours instead of being stolen by some crimi 'al."

Finn cocked her head. "*I'm* some criminal."

"You're different." He tensed, and Finn knew it'd slipped off his tongue before he could stop himself.

They both looked away from each other, just as a curious child jerks her hand away from a lit candle, fingers singed by the heat.

"I'm just surprised you're not upset," Finn admitted.

Alfie rubbed the back of his neck. "I'm not happy to hear it's gone, but the cloak was always supposed to go to the rightful king of Castallan next. I never felt like that was me. In my mind, it wasn't mine to keep." He shook his head. "But with everything else we have on our plates, it can't be our priority. After all, the only time I'd need the cloak would be for my betrothal ceremony." He gave another dry laugh. "That's not happening anytime soon."

Finn stiffened. She'd always known that the prince would get married—after all, a king needed to produce heirs—but the reality of it struck her now like a slap in the face.

"What's the cloak have to do with that nonsense?" she spat, her voice coming out rougher than she intended.

"The cloak represents the weight of generations before me, and its invisibility represents how we carry our ancestors forward though we cannot see them," Alfie said. She could tell the thought of it overwhelmed him. "The weight of history. When we enter a new union, a marriage, we bring all who came before with us. So part of our betrothal ceremony is wrapping the groom and the bride in the cloak. It represents taking our ancestors with us as we step into the future. That, and the cloak was key in helping us reclaim our freedom, so it was adopted into our betrothal ceremonies as a reminder of what we fought for. Father and Mother wrapped each other in it when they had their ceremony. Dezmin was supposed to wear it next." Alfie's voice grew quiet then. "Instead it's me. Someday, anyway. It's not important now."

The thought of him getting married had made something inside her coil uncomfortably tight, and she wondered if he could tell. If he looked at her with his *propio* now, would he see something that would tell him how she felt? The thought drove her to her feet.

"Now that we've told each other what we need to know," Finn said brusquely, "I'll be on my way." She stood and made her way back to the balcony doors.

She couldn't help but relish the panic that bloomed on his face.

"You're leaving already?" he asked, following her outside.

"Prince, you have a peace summit starting tomorrow. I suddenly have about fifty children to handle, and Kol's mystery to solve. I'll come back to you as soon as I've given la Familia instructions on tracking Los Toros and set up the meeting with the poison master."

The hopeful look on Alfie's face curdled. It wouldn't be easy for him to look the man who'd nearly killed Bathtub Boy in the face.

"You don't have to come to that meeting, if you don't want to," she said, her eyes moving away from his face. Her voice had come out uncomfortably kind, and she didn't want to see his reaction to it.

"No, I'll come," he said resolutely. "I've faced worse with you."

Finn nodded, feeling a hint of pride at the bravery in his voice. "That you have."

With that, Finn dashed out the doors, hopped over the railing, and began to climb down.

"Finn," Alfie called, and when she looked up at him, his face was haloed by the glow of the moon. "Hold on," he said. In his hand was a piece of parchment. He looked at it, his brow furrowing with focus, and murmured words of magic. Then he held it out to her. "Take this."

She took it hesitantly. "I'm not much of a writer."

"It's for us to communicate," he said. "I've magicked it to mirror another piece of parchment in my room. Whatever you write on there, I'll see, and vice versa. This way, we can keep each other updated on what we discover and when we should meet."

"Got it." Finn nodded. She remembered how he'd done this to stay in contact with Bathtub Boy while he and Finn had gone to the

Clock Tower. It was strange how it felt as if that had been ages ago yet also mere seconds ago.

"Be careful," he said, leaning over the railing as if the closer he got the more weight his words would have.

"I won't." Finn smirked up at him. He was close enough that they could've brushed noses. "You risk everything when you risk nothing."

Before he could speak another word, she scaled back down the palace wall. Even without looking, she knew the prince's eyes followed her all the way down.

RALLYING THE TROOPS

After Finn got back to Kol's pub—her pub now, she supposed—she threw herself onto what was once Kol's bed and fell into a deep sleep.

Only to be awakened the next morning by something prodding her.

"I will stab you," she grumbled into the pillow. "Many, many times."

"You need to get up," came Anabeltilia's monotone.

"I'm the mother here, aren't I?" Finn groused as she sat up. "I don't *need* to do anything."

"The whole of la Familia has gathered in the pub for you to give new orders." The girl crossed her arms. "So get off your culo."

"Who the hell scheduled that?" Finn asked, rubbing her eyes.

"Me," Anabeltilia spat. "Because if you don't tell them what to do next, they'll jump ship. Plenty already have since we haven't had a thief lord in charge for months."

"So they can leave but I can't?" Finn complained. "Makes perfect sense." How come she was the only one being held at knifepoint to this maldito job?

"They wouldn't dare leave a leader like Kol, someone they feared and respected. That's what held them here for years. That's what keeps any thief loyal to their lord. Without that, they'll disappear on you like that." She snapped her fingers.

Finn's mind jolted awake at that. La Familia was her best resource for helping the prince find Los Toros so that she could be rid of this job. She needed them.

"Fine." Finn rolled out of bed with a groan. "Did you get me the meeting with Hidalgo Venoso?" The poison master was the only lead they had to go on. She was anxious to get to it.

"Yes, you're meeting with the poison master this afternoon." She rolled her eyes before giving Finn the details.

"Good." As soon as she'd come back from the meeting with the thief lords last night, she'd asked Anabeltilia to set it up. Emeraude had told her that since he was one of Kol's associates, he'd be more comfortable talking with Kol's replacement than to a rival thief lord. Otherwise the vieja would've done it herself.

Finn wrote a quick note to Alfie about where to meet in a few hours. She hoped he'd be able to get away from that stuffy summit in time. She glanced at the clock. He'd be meeting with the Englassens now. He'd better make it quick.

"Now leave so I can get ready," Finn said with a dismissive wave of her hand.

After a quick wash and a change of clothes, Finn stood on the rum-slick bar of the pub with the entirety of la Familia standing before her. The cellar was where Kol had stripped her of her dignity and her *propio*—she wasn't going to be holding meetings there anytime soon, so the pub would have to do.

Now, in the light of the tavern as opposed to the dark of the cellar, Finn took a long look at the motley crew before her. She could've sworn that there'd been more of them when Kol had captured her. And weren't there older, seasoned-looking thieves back then? The majority left were around her age if not younger, naive and painfully unsure of themselves.

"Is this everyone?" Finn muttered to Anabeltilia, who stood behind the bar, waiting for Finn's command.

"Many of the older recruits took off when Kol died, and more still when they first saw you yesterday. This is all we've got left in the city."

"So you're telling me that what I've got left is the absolute bottom of the barrel."

Her face impassive, Anabeltilia said, "If you turn the barrel over and scrape its actual bottom then, sí, you've got this."

Mierda, Finn thought. If she wanted to get out of this thief lord mess, she needed to get Emeraude the information she needed about what Kol was up to when she decided to kill Alfie. She'd hoped to have the best of Kol's minions at her command, but instead she was left with amateurs. They chattered to one another as she stood on the bar, surveying them with her hands clasped behind her back, waiting for them to fall silent. But the fools just kept talking.

"You're their leader now," Anabeltilia pressed, gesturing at the crowd. "So lead them."

Finn gave a loud *"Ah-hem!"*

Still, they kept talking. Finn could feel Anabeltilia's smile unfurling behind her; she didn't need to turn around to confirm it.

"*Oye!*" Finn shouted. "Listen up, pendejos! By now you all know who I am, so there's no point in a flashy introduction. So tell me, what were you idiots responsible for when Kol was here?" Only silence met her ears. "Don't be shy! Not a one of you was this shy when Kol had you all beat the shit out of me four months ago, were you?"

Bodies stiffened and shifted awkwardly.

"Well?" Finn crossed her arms.

One by one, voices in the crowd began to pipe up from all directions.

"Reconnaissance work on other thieves in the kingdom!"

"Debt collecting!"

"I'm a chef! I cooked anything that la Madre requested."

"Silencing our enemies," one gruff voice added.

"Just say murder, idiota," another one said.

Finn raised her hands. "Basta!" They fell silent again. "Everything you just said doesn't matter anymore. You're not doing that. Forget you ever did it." Finn cocked her head, thinking better of it. She pointed at the man who'd said he was a chef. "Except you. I'll be giving you a list of my favorite foods later." The man's smile was incandescent. "The rest of you have new jobs—the same job, actually. You're all on the hunt for people who have this tattoo." Finn held up a sketch of the Los Toros tattoo that she'd drawn on a long swath of paper Anabeltilia had given her. "Along with wearing matching black horned bull masks." Last night Emeraude had told her that witnesses claimed the killer of the delegado had also worn a matching mask. The same mask she'd seen on the man who'd stolen the cloak. Alfie had seen a dark bull mask at the memorial too. For now she would have to assume that that was Los Toros' uniform. "That's your one job."

"So we find them," a man said slowly. "Then we kill 'em?"

Finn pinched the bridge of her nose. "No, that's not what I said. You will watch them and collect information for me. I want every Los Toros sighting—every crime, every murder, everything—reported to Anabeltilia and she'll mark it on this map." Finn unfurled a map of San Cristóbal that Anabeltilia had secured for her. From what she'd heard of the gruesome murder done in its name, she had a feeling that Los Toros would make mincemeat of la Familia. There was no use wasting her resources. Finn only wanted them to find Los Toros so that she and the prince could handle things themselves.

"So . . . ," a woman said. "We're not killing anyone?"

"Yes," Finn said between clenched teeth.

"Yes, we're killing people?" a man said hopefully.

"No, no," Finn said, gritting her teeth. "You're not killing anyone."

There was a wave of confused murmuring.

Finn stared at the whispering fools. This was why she'd always liked to work alone. She couldn't wait to be out of this job. It was nice to have help, but involving other people meant more risk of mistakes being made. Mistakes being made in her name as the new Madre. She made enough mistakes on her own; she didn't have time to deal with theirs too. The thieves were all chattering among themselves now until the pub filled with sound. Finn rubbed her temples, feeling a headache blooming between her ears.

"Quién soy yo?" Finn's voice thundered over the noise. When

they only stared at her, she repeated it louder, her chin raised. "*Who am I?*"

"La Madre," they chorused. Finn grimaced, but ran with it anyway. It was her card to play now.

"Do you question la Madre?"

"*No!*"

"That's what I thought. Now go. Report back to Anabeltilia." Finn shot the girl a look. "And she will report back to me." Finn would have her mark Los Toros' whereabouts on a map of the city. Maybe she could pinpoint their stronghold that way.

With that, the thieves and Finn's new personal chef left the pub with purpose.

"I'll get the map started," Anabeltilia said mirthlessly. The girl was too damned obedient. Finn couldn't help but be suspicious of her and her motives. Yet another reason she preferred to work alone—no one can stab you in the back if there's no one behind you.

"Why haven't you tried to kill me yet?" she asked, seeing no reason to beat around the bush. "Don't you want this stupid job? You wanted to be la Madre after Kol, yet you do whatever I say without a fight."

Anabeltilia stared at her for a long moment. "Kol took me in off the street and told me that one day, when I was older and ready, I might take her place. Before your friend killed her—"

"He was not my friend."

Anabeltilia didn't even pause. "I asked if I was ready then and she said not yet. I'm not ready, so I can't kill you." She shrugged nonchalantly. "Me as the leader right now is not what she wanted for la Familia. I'll respect her wishes, even if I can't respect you."

Finn's brows rose. She was surprised to hear about such loyalty toward Kol. It was odd to think that such a monster of a woman had inspired such devotion. "Fair enough. Then get me meetings with any other people Kol worked with often too. I want their names and what their relationships to her were. Got that?"

Anabeltilia nodded.

"Good," Finn said. Today was the first day of the peace summit, so she doubted the prince would have time to meet. In the meantime, she would do all she could from here, set up whatever meetings she could to get them closer to figuring out the truth about Kol and Los Toros. She wondered how Alfie was feeling, though she already knew the answer. Nervous. Meeting with the poison master this afternoon probably wouldn't help that feeling, but they needed to follow any lead they could.

"You know," Anabeltilia said, genuine surprise in her tone, "you handled yourself pretty well. You're not bad at this."

Finn squinted at her. "I'm taking that as an insult."

"Fine by me," Anabeltilia retorted.

THE ARRIVAL

That morning, Alfie snapped upright in his bed, his chest heaving, the sounds of the horrible screams in the magic echoing between his ears. Another night, another nightmare.

When he was little and would have bad dreams, his mother said she would come to check on him only to see his shadow twisting about on the bed. Alfie would bet that his shadow had tossed and turned with him all night. Maybe this was all stress—the odd dreams, the screams in the magic. He wiped the sweat from his brow. He didn't have time to wonder about it now. He needed to focus on today, on the arrival of the Englassen royals.

What did the peace summit and Englass's presence have in store for him and his people? Would Los Toros strike again? Would protestors continue to burn his image no matter how the summit went? There were too many questions to consider.

On top of all that was the warmth that had bloomed in his chest when Finn walked through his balcony doors. That moment had been a layer of sweet cream atop a bitter cup of café. It was strange how it felt as if both ages and only seconds had passed since they'd last seen each other, and now they were entangled in yet another adventure, with the cloak once again mixed into the chaos. Something so sacred to his family was in the hands of people who hated them. His stomach twisted at the thought. What did they intend to do with the cloak? Even more concerning, how did they know Finn had it? Though she'd come with bad news to deliver, her presence was enough for a spark of happiness to catch alight in the sea of anxiety.

But he could barely cheer himself with Finn's return thanks to the memory of the terrible, haunting screams he'd heard in the channels of magic and his nightmare. Could it be that magic truly was turning against him? That thought snuffed out the giddy joy he'd felt at seeing her.

Alfie forced himself out of bed. He would rather face the reality of the peace summit than think on that last question. He had so much to tell Luka and no idea of when he'd be able to if they were surrounded by his parents and Englassen nobility all day. Luka had no clue that Finn was back and about everything she'd said. He would have to pull him aside at some point.

Alfie had just finished dressing when a knock sounded at his door. Perfect timing. Alfie rushed to open his doors, but instead of Luka he found his mother, a careful smile on her face. A smile that told him they were not going to discuss what he'd said in the War Room about seeing the bull symbol while under Sombra's influence.

"Good morning, mi bebé." The queen stroked his cheek with a soft hand. She only called him her baby when she was trying to smother some tension. "Did you sleep well?"

"Yes," he lied, and he could tell that she knew he was lying, but she didn't press him on it as she usually would. The rift between them seemed to widen by another inch.

"It's time to receive our guests," she said. "Are you ready?"

Alfie held back a sigh. "Is it possible to be?"

His mother smiled, and Alfie felt the knot in his stomach loosen slightly.

"I suppose not." She took his hand gently. "But we can certainly pretend."

Dressed in their finest, Alfie, Luka, and his parents took a carriage eastward, only a few miles from the palace. His parents had commissioned a new port, separate from the one in the Pinch, for their foreign guests to dock. There was no smell of the fish market at this port, only a freshly polished wood deck that rocked gently in the clear blue water. Bruxos who were well-versed in spellwork that encouraged plant growth had magicked a grove just beyond the dock for the royal families to meet in.

A great circle of flowers had been planted at the valley's center. It was divided in two, one half showing the Englassen flag in lush white and blue petals, and the other Castallan's flag exemplified by red and gold blooms—a representation of their kingdoms peacefully sharing this world.

Alfie knew that this meeting was about peace, and goodwill, and dusting the ash off burnt bridges and building them anew, but the sight of the Englassen flag blooming on Castallano land drew his stomach tight. If he couldn't stand the sight of their flag, what would he do when he had to face the Englassen royals in person?

"It's like we're sharing a big cake," Luka said, trying to lighten the mood as they waited, stiff-backed, for their guests to arrive. Alfie could only stare at the Englassen slice and think of how their blade had cleaved into Castallano land, shoveling an extra portion onto their plate while the rest of the world had simply looked away.

"Yes," Alfie said, resisting the urge to stomp on the Englassen flag. "Just like a cake."

Luka knocked his shoulder against Alfie's, murmuring, "Be as angry as you like." He poked Alfie on the temple. "In there. What we really feel about these bastards we keep on the inside."

Alfie gave Luka a playful shove. "Easier said than done."

"Better done than starting a war." And for once Luka's joke caused a tense silence instead of laughter. Then something drew Luka's eyes over Alfie's shoulder toward the ocean. "So much for building a new port."

Alfie turned and saw a black spot dotting the horizon. He squinted for a long moment as it grew closer, larger. Then he finally saw it—white and blue—Englass's colors.

The Englassen royals had arrived in a great silk air balloon and a fleet of less grand balloons followed behind them, likely carrying the lesser nobles and dignitaries who had come to witness the peace summit. As the royals' balloon hovered above land, white braided ropes fell from the balloon's basket. Acrobats in intricate costumes swung from the ropes with graceful twists and spins. The acrobats landed, and with spoken magic and waves of their arms, the silk ropes began to twist into the ground, pulling the balloon down gently.

Upon a closer look Alfie could see that this balloon's basket was not made of wicker but of plants woven together, a flying garden. Flowers native to Englass bloomed on the greenery holding the basket together—roses, bluebells, and snowdrops. Birds were perched here and there, building nests. It was a marvel of magic and nature, a flying ecosystem that represented their kingdom.

One by one, the other balloons touched ground with soft thunks, and Alfie was struck by the weight of history stacked upon this moment. Englassens were setting foot on Castallano soil with the intention of seeking peace rather than slavery and colonization. True, they may be open to peace only because they now needed Castallan's help economically, but still, it was something. It had to be something. His shadow curled anxiously around his feet.

Alfie watched as the Englassen royals stepped out of their luxurious hot air balloon. They strode toward the flag garden, their retinue of servants and dignitaries in tow. Some of the Englassen servants who had been sent to Castallan early had come to the port as well. They walked to the balloons to receive the royals and help unload the luggage.

Alfie had spent the last four months studying Englassen culture and the way they used magic. In truth, he'd studied it even before then when he had been trying to bring Dez back, but this time he'd studied their magic to try to better understand them. In Castallan, the relationship between magic and man was deferential—man bowed to the power of magic and accepted its gifts. In Englass it was different. When they spoke to magic, they spoke in commands. They did not ask; they demanded. He wondered how the two countries would be able to understand each other when they were so wildly different.

Alfie watched them approach; their clothing in tones of pale yellows, whites, and beiges looked muted compared to the jewel tones and vibrant hues that he and his family wore. Alfie wondered what they thought of his clothes—did they find them clownishly bright?

When he looked at them, he could think of nothing but the differences they would have to overcome to make this summit a success—all while he and Finn were hunting down Los Toros.

"Breathe, sourpuss," Luka murmured. "You're forgetting to breathe."

The prince nodded and inhaled as the Englassen royal family— King Alistair, Queen Elinore, and twins Prince Marsden and Princess Vesper—approached the garden with a sure stride. They took their place beside their floral flag.

The Englassen royals faced them, looking aloof and calm. Their chins were a little high for Alfie's taste, but then Alfie caught the green eyes of Princess Vesper as she ran her fingers over her red hair, and he saw a familiar anxiety in her face, a nervousness that matched his own. She gave him a nearly imperceptible nod, as if she knew exactly what he was thinking. As if she too were rooting for this to work out. Alfie's shoulders relaxed.

Then came King Alistair's voice in slow, carefully spoken Castallano. "Thank you for hosting us for this historic summit. We are humbled by the opportunity to reopen communication between our great kingdoms." He raised a fist and tapped his heart in the traditional Englassen greeting of respect.

Alfie looked at his parents. They were silent for a beat too long before the queen nodded in deference. "The pleasure is ours. In Castallan we do not blame anyone for the sins of their fathers. Peace is for all, is it not?" Her voice was a hair strained, and Alfie leaned

closer to her so that the backs of their hands touched. She pressed
her knuckles to his, a quiet thank-you.

"It is," Queen Elinore replied with a stiff nod. While the
Englassen king and their children were redheads, the queen's hair
was blonde, looking startlingly fair beside her family. Another
silence writhed between them.

At least everyone was feeling awkward and not just him, Alfie
thought.

Luka coughed quietly into his fist.

Alfie watched Vesper gently prod Prince Marsden with her
elbow before shooting her brother an encouraging nod.

The prince took a step forward and bowed, his red hair fanning
out over his forehead. "May we present a gift?" he asked, his voice
tense. Alfie couldn't help but notice that the prince was a behemoth,
taller than Alfie himself with a jaw like an anvil. Alfie could feel
himself squaring his shoulders, trying to take up more space despite
his slender frame. "We are most eager to thank our gracious hosts,"
Marsden said.

Alfie didn't have to look at his parents to know this was his cue.
Prince Marsden was heir to the Englassen throne. He was presenting
this gift to the entire Castallano royal family, but this summit was
about the two of them spearheading a future of prosperity and peace
between their kingdoms. It was Alfie who must accept the gift.

Alfie bent into a deep bow. "It would be our honor to receive it."

Alfie had the feeling that Marsden was sizing him up, evaluat-
ing him, but nothing in the Englassen prince's face betrayed whether
Alfie measured up or fell short.

Prince Marsden snapped his fingers and a servant came forth

carrying two bundles of white fur in his arms. It was James, the Englassen servant with the muddy brown magic Alfie had run into after the meeting with the delegados. At first, he thought James was carrying the fur muffs that Englassens wore during their snowy winter months, until one of the bundles of fur lifted its head and gave a whimper.

"We present you with Englass's finest beast," King Alistair said as James deposited the white puppies at the royal family's feet with a bow. "The Englassen hunting hound."

Luka shot Alfie a look of pure joy. Though they'd begged as children, Queen Amada had never allowed any pets in the palace. But now she certainly couldn't refuse. When the puppy sniffed at Alfie's boot before rising on its hind legs to press its paws against his calf, Alfie couldn't stop himself from scooping it into his arms and letting it nibble his fingers.

"They are . . . lovely," Queen Amada said as Luka picked up the other dog. "Are you certain they will be comfortable here? Perhaps a cooler temperature would be preferred?"

"Englassens are adaptable," Queen Elinore assured her. "Our hounds are no different."

"And not to worry," Princess Vesper said. "These are a breed that stay small—the size of a foal, not a full-grown horse. Perfect for house pets."

"How wonderful," Queen Amada said, and Alfie had to bury his face in the puppy's neck to hide his laughter at the thinly veiled dismay in her voice.

"My servant James will train the pups for you for the duration of our stay." Marsden looked at the servant boy. "Isn't that right,

James?"

"Yes, Your Highness. Of course," James said, bowing deeply. He shook a bit as he rose and Alfie wondered why the boy looked so nervous. He'd seemed calm enough after Alfie had bumped into him in the hall. Perhaps he was unnerved standing before so many royals at once. Alfie looked between James and the Englassen prince. Or maybe it was for another reason.

"We thank you for your generous gifts," King Bolivar said. "Please, let us escort you back to the palace, where you may rest before the banquet."

"We are much obliged," Prince Marsden said with a bow.

Alfie smiled at the puppy. Maybe this summit wouldn't be as terrible as he thought.

At that, Alfie felt something warming in his cloak pocket.

The parchment that he had connected to Finn! It was magicked to warm up whenever it was used. As the royal families boarded their carriages Alfie opened the note.

Meeting with the poison master at noon.

Alfie scratched his puppy behind the ears. This one lovely moment had made him forget about what was at stake should Los Toros be left unchecked. The Englassen royal family would be resting for a few hours before tonight's banquet. He had time to meet Finn and the poison master in that small window of time between summit obligations.

As his parents spoke of the successful arrival of the Englassens,

Alfie leaned close to Luka and murmured, "Meet me in my rooms when we get home. We have to talk."

Luka nodded, whispering back, "Later. I've got the tattoo lead to follow up on before the banquet tonight."

"I've got a lead too." He couldn't hold back his smile as he said, "Finn's back."

Luka's eyes widened as Alfie scrawled on the parchment.

Tell me where to meet you and I'll be there.

"You should draw a little heart next to your note," Luka said. "Just a little corazón or two. Perhaps a nude drawing of yourself with a knife between your teeth. She'd like that."

Alfie's face grew hot. "Shut up." He pointedly looked away from Luka for the rest of the ride, but he didn't need to look to know Luka was smirking.

THE GRAVEHOPPER

After escorting the Englassen royals to the palace to rest, Luka had a few hours to kill.

Just enough time for him to go after his lead before tonight's banquet. He'd wanted to talk to Alfie about Finn—well, if he was being honest, he'd wanted to *tease* Alfie about Finn, but neither of them had time. Luka had his lead to follow and Alfie and Finn had theirs. He'd have to save his quips for later.

He sauntered into the chic social club in the Bow, his eyes searching for a familiar face. Or, to be honest, a familiar set of broad shoulders. The face had been fairly forgettable.

Luka scanned the people perched on plush sofas and chaise longues as servants carried around finger foods. Skinny shoulders, hunched shoulders, soft shoulders—there! At a booth tucked into the back of the lounge, Hernando nursed a glass of rum and a plate of finger foods, his arms an explosion of colorful tattoos. He was a nobleman's son who'd gotten into tattoo artistry to spite his parents. Hernando put up the front of being rough enough for a life in the

Pinch, but he always ended up here, back where he'd started—in the safe haven of the Bow. His immature, rebellious spirit had been far too good for Luka to resist.

Luka slid into the booth across from him. He curled his lips into his most charming smile, and that was a very high bar if he said so himself. "Well hello, Hernando. Long time no see."

Hernando choked on his rum mid-sip and glared at Luka. "You told me you would send for me within the week," he huffed, motioning to a passing servant to refill his glass. "I gave you that tattoo months ago."

"And you said you'd be amazing in bed," Luka hissed back. "It seems we both lied."

The servant poured the rum into Hernando's glass. The boy didn't say a word, didn't even look away from his glass until it was replenished. Then he tossed it right in Luka's face.

Luka sputtered, blowing rum out his nostrils as Hernando stared at him, looking satisfied.

Luka licked his lips. "Well, at least you spilled good rum on me."

"What do you want?"

"Information." Luka pulled Finn's drawing of the tattoo from his pocket. "Do you recognize this tattoo?"

Hernando looked at it for a long moment. "I recognize it as the mark above the dead delegado's body." He looked at Luka, his eyes narrowing. "What are you up to? You're an idiot, but not this much of an idiot."

"You only had me for one night. How do you know how much of an idiot I am?"

"Trust me, it only takes one." Then he went silent, his fingers tracing the lines of the sketch.

"A friend of mine swears he has seen it as a tattoo."

Hernando tilted his head, as if the tattoo could speak and he had finally heard its voice. He started in his seat, snatched the sketch off the bar, and pushed it against Luka's chest.

Luka eyed him. "You recognize it, then?"

"Yes, and you ought to stop asking questions," Hernando said before dropping a few pesos on the table. He grabbed his jacket and headed for the door, Luka close behind.

"Esperate," Luka called, following him into the quiet streets of the Bow. "I have money, I'll pay you!" He pulled a pouch of pesos from his pocket.

"Use it to buy some sense," Hernando spat, and kept walking.

Luka chased after him and gripped him by the shoulder. There were no crowds for Hernando to disappear into here as there were in the Pinch. There was nothing but small groups of nobles taking walks with their parasols. Some saw Luka and whispered behind their hands.

"Please, Nando," Luka said. "Just tell me. It's important."

Hernando sighed through his nose and snatched the purse of pesos from Luka's hand. "Fine. I don't recognize the specific tattoo, but I do recognize the style. It was crafted by the Tattooed King," Hernando hissed, looking around as if he were afraid someone would hear him.

Luka squinted at him. "The who?"

"The Tattooed King," he said, reverence and fear in his voice. "Ernesto Puente. Have you never heard of him?"

"Please," Luka said. "I know the real king. Of course I have no

clue what you're talking about." He looked at Hernando nonchalantly, but he was already worried by the boy's reaction. Hernando
may have been a little soft from being raised in the Bow, but he still
spent his nights tattooing in the Pinch. He didn't scare easy.

"He's a legend. His tattoos are . . ." Hernando shuddered.
"They're alive."

Luka shrugged. "So? The tattoo you gave me moves too."

Hernando shook his head. "That's different. The tattoo I gave
you moves in a fixed pattern. His tattoos . . . they're living things."
He swallowed in a way that made Luka's stomach tighten. "Every
gang worth their salt goes to him for their mark. His clientele is the
very lowest of the low. You don't want to mess with him."

Luka forced himself to smile debonairly. "He should be worried
about me."

"I'm not joking."

"Neither am I," Luka said, finally dropping his act and shooting Hernando a serious look. "I wouldn't ask if it wasn't important.
Where can I find him?" When Hernando didn't respond, Luka took
his hands in his own. Not all of that one night had been bad—maybe
it would help. "Por favor," he said, insistent.

Hernando looked at him for a long moment. "There's no stopping you, is there?"

"You already know the answer to that."

"It'll take me a few days to get the information." He pulled his
hands free of Luka's.

"Gracias," Luka said. "Truly, this is really important." When it
came to seeing ex-lovers, less was always more, so Luka said a quick
goodbye and turned to leave.

"You didn't have to go so quickly, you know?" Hernando said, stopping Luka mid-step. "That night. You could've stayed."

Luka's smile froze on his face. "We don't need to talk about that." Luka had such a talent for focusing on the good that he sometimes forgot the bad altogether. So when someone mentioned a bad thing, it felt like a fresh punch.

He'd fallen asleep in Hernando's arms only to wake in a cold sweat, thinking that he was bleeding from his eyes and ears again, just like the night he'd been poisoned.

"You woke up so upset, then you asked for the tattoo and then you just left. I—"

"It's fine," Luka snapped, his voice more terse than he'd intended. "It's fine, really."

"You kept repeating—"

"Thank you again," Luka interrupted. He didn't want to hear Hernando say it because he remembered it all too well.

Everyone dies but me, everyone but me. Why not me?

He strode away, pulling his hood up. The tattoo he'd asked for was of a gravehopper—a hopping insect that was often found in graveyards.

Their lot in life was the same as Luka's—they were always surrounded by death, but never died themselves.

THE POISON MASTER

"You're late," Finn said as Alfie came to a halt where she leaned on the side of a pub.

"I know," he said, catching his breath. First he'd had to change into more common clothing before sneaking out (he hadn't arranged a tether for today), and with that horrible screaming he'd heard in the currents of magic yesterday and in his nightmare this morning, Alfie couldn't bring himself to use his *propio* to travel again. Then, while on the way, he'd gotten distracted by seeing Englassen servants strolling throughout the lower rings of the city, and suddenly he was running very late. He'd nearly forgotten how long it took to get places via carriage and on foot. How did Luka have time to get into so much trouble when he always had to travel the normal way? "The welcome reception for the Englassen royals ran long," Alfie lied. He didn't want her to know what he'd heard, the suffering that rang through the realm of magic—a place that had once been peaceful. He didn't want her to look at him and reach the same conclusion he had—that the realm of magic was rejecting him, punishing him for what he'd done when he'd freed Sombra.

Finn rolled her eyes, uninterested. "Let me change your face a bit before we go in."

Alfie watched her as she took his face in her hands and molded it so he wouldn't have to keep wearing a hood to hide his identity.

Anyone else would have immediately asked him a long list of questions about what the Englassens were like, but Finn was refreshingly unconcerned. It reminded him of when he'd caught her trying to steal the vanishing cloak from the palace. He'd explained to her then how important the cloak was to their history and their culture.

"And you still want to take it? You're not at all concerned with what it means to people?" he'd asked.

"No," she'd said without pause, and even though Alfie's jaw had been sore from her elbowing him in the face, he'd felt comforted by how little stock she put in the royal traditions he'd been lectured about all his life.

He knew how important the cloak was, yet he'd still given it to her. Part of him wanted to say that he'd only done so because he'd promised it to her in exchange for her help defeating Sombra, but he knew that wasn't it. Not entirely. Maybe it was his own small act of defiance against the idea of a political marriage—a future decided for him.

Or maybe it was because a small, quiet part of him hoped it would be her shoulders that he would wrap the cloak around.

"What are you smiling about?" Finn asked, bringing Alfie back to the present. She pulled her hands away from his face, and only then did he realize that he'd been leaning into her touch.

"Nothing," he said a little too quickly. "This is where we're meeting him?"

"Sí."

Alfie looked at the pub's awning before exhaling sharply through his nose. "It's a bit on the nose, don't you think?"

Finn squinted at the pub's sign and shrugged. "This is where he and Kol used to meet. She had a sense of humor, it seems. A twisted one, but one all the same."

They stood beneath the awning of a pub called Veneno—Poison. Of course this was where Kol and the poison master used to meet. Alfie took in a deep breath, his shadow whipping around his feet. He didn't want to meet with this man, but he might have information on Los Toros and what Kol had been up to. He hadn't even told Luka that he was going to meet with this man. After all, Luka was already skittish about what had happened the night he'd drunk the poison and Sombra had been released. Alfie didn't want the rift between them to widen. But still, coming to meet this man reminded him of why he was so angry at Luka for running off to fight clubs. Alfie had almost lost him once, had felt the pain of thinking his best friend was dead. Why was Luka tempting fate by jumping into every dangerous thing he could find?

Finn watched him closely. She'd made her reservations about letting him attend this meeting clear—she knew him too well to believe it would be easy for him to stay calm when they met with the man who had nearly killed Luka. The man who had led him down a path to release Sombra.

His mind was split between anxiety about what was to come

and blistering anger. He needed to stay calm so that they could learn what they could from this man, but a baser part of himself screamed that he should grip the man by the neck before he could speak his first word.

"Before we go in, I have one question for you," Finn said.

Alfie stared down at her. Was she going to tell him to go home? Could she sense how unnerved this meeting made him feel? "By all means," Alfie said, his voice tight.

Finn was silent for a long moment before she spoke again. "The Englassens," she began. "You're being careful around them, right?"

Alfie blinked. He hadn't expected her to be concerned with his manners. "Yes, of course. We're all being very polite."

"That's not what I mean," Finn said. "Just be careful. When people own you once, it's hard for them to look at you as anything else. Trust me." She looked away. "I would know."

Alfie knew she was thinking of Ignacio, and it pained him that even in death that horrible man still haunted her, and there was nothing he could do about it. No matter how much he wanted to help, he knew he shouldn't bring Ignacio up. The way she healed from that man's wounds was her business alone. He let it be.

But her distrust in the Englassens spoke to more than her time with Ignacio. It also spoke to the weight of the bad blood between the kingdoms. The fact that even Finn, someone who cared little for politics and royals, distrusted the Englassens spoke volumes about how deeply his people reviled them. Whether they lived in the bowels of the Pinch or the gardens of the Bow, Castallanos would never forget what Englass had done to their ancestors. But things were different now; peace was within reach.

"We'll be careful," he said, "They're here because they need our help; it's they who are in a position of weakness. You don't have to worry for me."

"I wasn't," she sniped.

"You weren't," Alfie agreed, smiling.

"I hear their skin burns if they're in the sun for more than a minute." Finn glanced at him, changing the subject. "That true?"

Alfie had to stop himself from snorting. "Yes, their skin is delicate. Princess Vesper looked quite red by the time we got back to the palace. It's commonplace in Englass to carry a parasol at all times to protect the skin."

"Pfft. Too delicate to face the maldito sun. Pendejos." With that, she led him to the pub's door while Alfie smiled at her back. "We're here for information. Try to keep your wits about you. I told you we'd do this your stupid way—"

"Is questioning the man instead of beating him bloody stupid?"

"Sí. Don't ask stupid questions." Finn scowled. "We'll meet with him and do it your way. You watch him with your magic color thing—"

"My *propio*," Alfie interjected with an eye roll. He would watch the man's magic to see if he was telling the truth or not. Magic moved through the body almost like a heartbeat. When one lied, the magic sped up, moving erratically. Though he was too afraid to use his *propio* to travel through the channels of magic, he was still comfortable using it to see the colors of magic, as that aspect of his abilities didn't conjure those terrible screams.

"Then, if asking him questions gets us nowhere"—Finn flexed her fingers and a dagger flew out of her sleeve and into her waiting hand—"we do it my way."

"Very well," Alfie said, his jaw tight. He was angry with himself both for wanting to let Finn beat the man and for wanting to try to keep this meeting as civil as possible. Both felt wrong, like a failing on his part. And how would he react if the poison master had devastating information for them concerning Los Toros and Dezmin's death?

"Whatever you're thinking," Finn said, poking his furrowed brow, "stop."

"Sorry." Alfie shook his head. "We're here for the truth, nothing more, nothing less." If he made it sound simple, perhaps it would become simple.

As always, Finn seemed to see through him in a moment. "Everybody wants to know the truth, but very few are ready to hear it. Nothing about this is going to be easy."

"You're right," Alfie said, both bothered and comforted by what she'd said. There was something calming in embracing the difficulty of what was to come instead of hiding from it.

"I know," she said before opening the door. "Let's get this over with, then."

Finn and Alfie stepped into the shoddy pub. It was loud with sailors playing rounds of exploding dominoes, and couples flirting over pints of cerveza. Just as they'd discussed, he and Finn approached the bar and sat on two stools. Alfie wrung his hands in his lap. But that betrayed nervousness and the last thing he wanted to do was look nervous in front of this man. He pressed his palms on the bar before grimacing and pulling them back. Now his hands were sticky.

"When is he arriving?" Alfie asked as he charmed water from the air to clean his hands.

"Any minute now," Finn said quietly, looking as nonchalant as Alfie was nervous.

Alfie scanned the bar. There were couples tangled up in a twist of limbs, drunks who shouted loudly with their friends as they began another rousing round of a drinking game, and, of course, there were the silent drinkers who looked as if they were drinking to forget. Finn had changed his face enough that no eyes lingered on him. He was just another boy in a bar, waiting to be served.

Finn sucked her teeth. "Stop looking around like that."

"Like what?"

"Like a prince pretending to be part of the city's most notorious gang," Finn said. "He'll sit on the stool next to me when he arrives." She gestured to the empty chair to her right. "So try to act natural for once in your life."

Alfie forced himself to keep his eyes to himself, drumming his fingers on his thighs to give his nerves a more subtle outlet.

An absolutely sauced man stumbled up to the bar and threw himself onto the stool next to Finn. "Oye, barkeep!" he slurred. "I'll take a—"

Without a moment's hesitation Finn shot out her leg, kicking him out of the seat. With a cry, he fell to the ground.

"Seat's taken," Finn said.

The man stared up at her, so uselessly drunk that he could only be confused and not angry. "By who?"

"Señor," Alfie began, wanting to defuse the situation, "I—"

But Finn didn't let him finish. In the blink of an eye she stabbed the cushion of the stool with a dagger. "By my best friend. She loves meeting new people. She's got a really sharp wit, so she makes friends easy." Finn gripped the dagger and twisted it deeper into the stool.

With a fearful gurgle the man crawled away, his eyes never leaving Finn.

"You told me to act natural and that's what you do?" Alfie said.

"Welcome to the Pinch," Finn snorted. "That was exactly what Kol would do if she were here. Trust me. This isn't some cute little lounge where nobles gossip behind their gloved hands and eat finger foods. The only way to act natural in the Pinch is with a dagger in your hand."

Before Alfie could respond, a squat man with a shiny bald spot approached the bar and looked pointedly at the stool.

"What's your poison?" the man asked her, nodding toward the bottles behind the bar, just as Finn had told Alfie he would. So this was him. The man who had started everything.

Alfie's hands curled into fists on his lap.

Finn looked at him, her chin raised high with the authority of someone who ruled over the deadliest gang in this city. "Yours."

The man nodded and Finn pulled her dagger free of the stool, letting him sit. Alfie engaged his *propio* and watched the man. His magic was mucus green, a color as appalling as the man himself.

"You are the new Madre, then?" he said, his voice slick, as if he had too much saliva in his mouth.

Finn stiffened. Alfie didn't have to ask her to know she did not like to be referred to as Madre, but she had a part to play.

"Sí, and this is my second-in-command." She gestured to Alfie.

The prince forced himself to nod solemnly, trying to play the part of a stoic accomplice.

"How can I be of service to la Familia?" Hidalgo asked, his eyes still focused forward on the rows of bottles.

"You can answer my questions," Finn said.

The man straightened in his chair. "Kol never came to me with questions, only orders for my products."

Finn casually spun the dagger, letting it glide back and forth across her fingers. "I don't know if you've noticed, but I'm not Kol. Things are different now, entiendes?"

A flop sweat was gathering at Hidalgo's upper lip. He nodded shakily. The flow of his magic began to speed up with anxiety. Alfie was happy to see him looking nervous—he deserved discomfort, deserved to feel every ounce of pain he'd caused. Alfie winced as his nails cut into the flesh of his palms. When he opened his fists, red half-moon cuts were welling with blood.

"Around four months ago, Kol had you make a poison for her. A poison to be mixed into liquid. It caused bleeding from the eyes, ears, and mouth."

"Oh yes," Hidalgo said, his shoulders relaxing. His gaze took on a faraway look, as if he were recalling a work of art that he'd given away to be hung above someone else's fireplace. Anger roared inside Alfie. What kind of monster would look so enraptured at the thought of killing someone else? Alfie could see now that making poisons was not simply a job for this man, it was a passion. He felt sick to his stomach.

"*Dolor Eterna*," Hidalgo said wistfully. "She asked for something that would cause real pain, long-lasting. Usually Kol was quite

practical. She asked for poisons of efficiency, one sip and dead,"
he went on, his voice quickening with excitement. "But that night
she wanted something that would take hours. First a fever, then
the bleeding, then slipping fitfully in and out of conscious, terrible
hallucinations for as long as a day. And then," he sighed, as if he
were bringing a great concerto to a flourishing close, "death."

Alfie didn't know when it had happened, but his hands were
gripping the bar again, so tightly that his fingers shook. He'd only
seen Luka suffer through the first moments of the poison, and there
had been so much more pain to come. Meanwhile, this man was so
comforted by the memory of his cruel poison that the flow of his
magic had slowed and calmed. Alfie wanted to take the man by the
shoulders and shake him, make him understand what he'd done.

Alfie started at a sudden, gentle touch on his wrist. Her eyes
still on the poison master, Finn had reached back and gripped Alfie
by the wrist. She knew without looking at him what he felt, how
close he was to teetering off the edge and into a sea of his own fury.
Alfie relaxed slightly, his jaw unclenching. He tried to focus on the
warmth of her fingers instead of the anger that threatened to burn
him from the inside out.

"Did you know who the poison was made for?" Finn asked.
This was a question Alfie wanted answered, though he wasn't sure
how he would react if the answer was yes.

The poison master shook his head. "No, I never know who will
be gifted with my product. I receive orders, and I craft them. That
is all."

Alfie breathed a quiet sigh through his nose. He couldn't tell
if he was glad to hear that or disappointed that he didn't have

more reason to punish the man.

"Did Kol give you any information on who she was working with when it came to her plan to use the poison?"

Alfie raised his eyebrows. Finn's question was a bit blunt, but, then again, he supposed there was no point in beating around the bush. They'd come for specific information. They might as well ask him directly.

The man froze. "Kol works alone, does she not?"

Hidalgo's magic was quickening again. The question was clearly distressing him.

Finn leaned closer to him. The blade of her dagger glinted in the light. She caught his gaze with a hard look, holding him hostage. "I don't know, does she?"

The man's eyes skittered away from hers, like a mouse dashing back into its hole. He stood shakily from his seat. "I bottle death, I do not answer questions. Should you need my products—"

Alfie reached over Finn and gripped the man tightly by the arm. "You will sit down and answer our questions. Do you have any idea how much pain you've caused? You say you bottle death as if you're some artist, but you're a coward. Sending others to their graves without the common courtesy of looking them in the eye."

"Let go of me, boy," Hidalgo spat. "Or you'll find yourself suffering the same fate."

As the threat left his lips, Finn got to her feet. The bar's patrons had all turned to watch the fight unfold. "Watch your mouth—" Finn began, but Alfie couldn't stop himself. He stood from his seat, grabbed the man by the back of his neck, and pressed his face to the filthy, sticky bar.

"Hijo de puta!" Hidalgo sputtered. "Let me go."

Finn's eyes went wide. "Alf—"

"You will answer our questions, whether you like it or not," Alfie said through gritted teeth as he pinned Hidalgo's arm painfully behind his back, pressing him harder against the bar.

The man cried out, his eyes wide with fear and brimming with tears. Of course this weak, crying man spent his life making poisons—he was too much of a coward to meet an opponent face-to-face.

"Do you know anything about a gang that wears bull masks?" Alfie asked, his eyes focusing on the man's magic.

"No," Hidalgo yelped. "I know nothing."

Alfie watched the man's slimy magic. It squirmed quickly because of the stress and pain of the moment, but Alfie knew the difference between how magic moved when one was nervous and how it moved when one was lying. This man was telling the truth. Alfie looked at Finn and knew she could tell from his expression that the man was being honest.

"Do you have any information on Kol's allies, who she was working with, or the bull tattoo that was on her arm?"

"I only know that it matches the symbol found with that delegado's body, nothing more! I swear it!"

Alfie watched the man's magic carefully. He was telling the truth again. He had nothing that would help them. But Alfie refused to leave empty-handed.

"Your poison almost took my best friend from me," Alfie said, his voice thick with emotion. "I watched him bleed and whimper as he nearly died in my arms. Do you care at all?" When Hidalgo only lay there, slack-jawed, Alfie put more weight on his twisted arm until he cried out again. *"Answer me! And do not lie. You will regret it if you do, oíste?"*

Finn gripped Alfie by the shoulder then, and when he turned to look at her he was afraid he'd find shame and disapproval on her face. But her solemn expression told him to feel what he felt, to do what he must to get the answers he needed to let go. Her eyes told him that she would be behind him no matter what he chose.

Tears slid over the bridge of Hidalgo's nose and onto the bar. "I don't," he admitted. "I don't care."

Alfie's jaw was clenched so tightly he feared his teeth would break. If he twisted the man's arm just a little more, he could dislocate it, cause him an ounce of the pain he'd caused Luka. A mere fraction of the suffering that he deserved. He could snatch Finn's dagger from her hand and cut his throat, end it all right now.

He wanted to do it. His mind shouted at him to do it, to dole out the punishment Hidalgo had earned, but he couldn't. His fingers twitched as the man whimpered and cried pathetically. He met Finn's eyes and let the man go.

"You have one week to leave this city and never return. And no matter where you run, if I ever hear that you are working in this vile trade of yours again, I will hunt you down and finish what I started. Do you understand me?"

Hidalgo nodded before wiping the snot from his nose and running from the bar, nearly tripping over his feet on his way out.

The pub was painfully silent as Alfie sat back down on his stool, Finn's hand still on his shoulder.

"What are you pendejos looking at?" Finn barked. She sliced her dagger expertly through the air. "Keep your eyes to yourselves or I'll come and take them, oíste?"

With that, everyone turned back to their tables and the bar exploded with sound once more.

Alfie scrubbed a hand across his stinging eyes. He'd truly wanted to end the man's life, to watch the light fade from his eyes and feel his filthy future crumble to nothing in his hands. He had nearly surrendered to something dark inside himself. Something feral and unrecognizable to him. The prince was struck by a memory of when he and Finn had only just met and he'd had to kill a man infected by the dark magic.

"One bad thing doesn't undo all the good, Prince," she'd told him solemnly. "It takes more than this to lose yourself, trust me. I've seen it."

He'd looked at her with a fear so deep he could feel it in his bones and asked, "Will you stop me if I get too close?"

He turned to Finn now, his eyes wide and afraid. "You didn't try to stop me," he said, shame welling inside him. "I was so close to going too far."

"I knew you wouldn't," she said.

"How?" he said, pressing the heels of his hands into his eyes.

"Because I know you," she said, as if it were the simplest thing in the world.

He held her gaze for a long moment and Alfie worried about how he was looking at her. He had been rubbed raw by the inter-action with Hidalgo and knew he couldn't hide anything from her now. He didn't know what she would discover if this went on.

"Come on," she said, finally ending the silence. "Let's get out of here."

Alfie nodded wordlessly, feeling more tired than he had in a long while. Together the two of them walked out of the pub and into the afternoon sun. And after all this, he still needed to rush home to prepare for tonight's banquet.

A tired sigh sagged out of him. When he'd finally collected himself, he turned to her. "Gracias, Finn."

"You say that too much."

"Or perhaps you've just heard it far too little," he offered. "I'm working to remedy that."

Finn looked away from him, but he could've sworn he saw a small smile before she flattened it back into a smirk.

"Well," Finn said brusquely, changing the subject as easily as she changed her face. "We got nothing from Hidalgo. I'm going to interview Kol's associates, see what I can dig up. Maybe we can find a new lead that way."

"That's smart." Alfie nodded. "Using your position as thief lord to our advantage. Luka is looking into the tattoo artist lead today. I'll let you know if his contact has any information. And I can try to attend some of the meetings with you, if you like," he offered, "but the summit will keep me busy for much of the day."

"It's all right, Prince," Finn said as she twirled a dagger in her hands. "I have my own ways of making sure someone is telling the truth. I'll manage without you."

A soft smile curved his lips. He wondered how he'd lasted this long without her.

An emotion sat so heavy on his tongue that he feared he wouldn't be able to take another step until he unburdened himself. "I've really missed you, Finn."

The moment the words left his lips, Alfie wished he could grip them by their tails and shove them right back down. He clasped his hands behind his back as Finn stared forward, seeming to think seriously about what he'd said. She was making the same face Luka made when he studied mathematics. She waited so long to speak that Alfie wondered if he'd offended her or if she was just trying to torture him.

The thief shot him a sideways glance, her eyes alight. "I know."

THE GIFT

After Alfie and Finn parted ways in the Pinch, he came to a realization that shook him to his bones—unless he used his *propio* magic to get home, he would be late for the banquet.

Standing in an alley between pubs, Alfie squeezed the stained glass doorknob in his hand. Stepping into the currents of magic used to bring him such comfort. Now it only brought him crippling fear and sweaty palms.

Alfie swallowed thickly as he pressed the doorknob into the side of the pub, letting it sink into the wood. He couldn't be late to this banquet. It was out of the question. He would have to face the magic's wrath no matter how much it scared him.

Sweat beading on his forehead, Alfie let his blue magic engulf the doorknob and stammered, "*V-voy.*"

The wall opened into the colorway of magic, and before he could lose his nerve, Alfie forced himself to step in. For a blissful moment, there was only the calming silence of the colorful streams as they carried him home. Alfie sighed at the peaceful quiet. Maybe the screams were temporary; maybe the magic felt that it had punished him enough.

Maybe everything was okay again.

But Alfie was wrong. He felt it before he heard it. His skin prickled with gooseflesh and the hairs on the back of his neck stood on end a few breaths before the screams found him once more, shrieks of acute pain and suffering that made Alfie's eyes tear. The currents of magic despised him so much that they shouted as if in pain when he traveled through them. Each time it was a new wound in his flesh, a fresh gush of blood.

"I just want to go home," he murmured, clapping his hands over his ears. "I'm sorry. I'm sorry."

When he stumbled into his bedroom, he was covered in a cold sweat, the doorknob gripped tight in his hand. He wanted to lie on his bed and forget about how flippantly the poison master had spoken of the substance that had nearly killed Luka, forget about the damage he'd done to the currents of magic that had once embraced him, but there was no time. Still smelling of the pub, Alfie rushed to the palace baths, scrubbed himself clean, and hurriedly got dressed.

He wearily walked the palace halls, his shadow dragging behind him. As soon as he got to the banquet hall, he would be made to stand and smile and greet every guest. The thought made his eyes drift closed as he turned the corner. He couldn't believe it was still only the first day of the summit. He felt exhausted enough to have gone through a whole month of political events.

"You look tired, Prince Alfehr."

Alfie froze mid-step. He hadn't heard that voice in over a decade, but he would never forget it. He *couldn't* forget it, even if he tried.

Alfie turned. Behind him stood the royal diviner. The woman who'd told him he had no future to speak of. Her wrinkles were deeper now, her long black curls streaked with more silver than before, but her eyes were exactly the same—so light they might have been translucent.

After divining Dezmin and then Alfie, she'd left the palace to travel and continue honing her ability to see the unseen—whatever that meant. And Alfie had been glad to see her go. She'd come back briefly for Dez's funeral, but Alfie had been in such a haze of grief he had barely noticed. Now she stood before him once again, and Alfie wished he could disappear.

"Diviner Lucila," he said. "What are you doing here?" The question flew out of his mouth before he realized how rude it sounded. When he moved to apologize, she waved a long-fingered hand.

"In light of all that has happened, your mother and father asked me to return in case they needed guidance. I've only just arrived."

Alfie nodded dumbly, unable to speak, her voice echoing painfully in his head.

I cannot divine him. There is a piece missing, an important one. Without it I cannot see the prince's future.

A new fury rose in him like a tidal wave. Why hadn't his parents told him she was back? Did they think he wouldn't be able to handle it? Now he'd been blindsided yet again.

Well, he thought. *Am I handling it properly?*

Alfie plucked that thought from his mind and tossed it away.

"Diviner Lucila," Alfie said before dropping into a stiff bow. "I'm expected at dinner, if you'll excuse m—"

"One moment," she said, her thin arm outstretched. Her fingers moved as if she were grasping at invisible things in the air. "Something's changed. Something's different. You're due for another divining."

Alfie stared at her. Was this her idea of a joke? Did she mean to bring him back to her divining chambers to mock him, to tell him there still was no future for her to see?

"Excuse me?" he said, anxiety and anger churning in his stomach.

"Sooner rather than later would be best, don't you think?"

Alfie gaped at her. As if he would ever subject himself to that again.

"I'll just need something from you before then." The diviner closed the space between them, and before Alfie could move, she'd plucked a hair from his head. He started at the sudden sting. "I'll see you soon, Your Majesty." She turned on her heel and walked away, moving as if she followed a higher path only she could see.

"Wait, what?" Alfie asked, rubbing his scalp.

But, as always, the diviner only answered the questions she wanted to answer. She disappeared around the corner, never turning to acknowledge his question.

Alfie took a deep breath, his mind abuzz with too many questions and fears to count. Handling Los Toros, this summit, and the screams he heard in the magic were enough without the prospect of another divining. He knew he would not be visiting her anytime soon.

Alfie's mother and father were at the doors to the banquet hall waiting to greet guests when Alfie came to stand stiffly beside them.

"Is there a reason why neither of you told me the diviner was here?" Alfie asked through a tight smile as Englassen and Castallano dignitaries paused before them to bow and be greeted.

As they passed, his mother gripped his arm. "Considering every-thing that has gone wrong, we wanted her here to advise," she said quickly as another Englassen guest approached.

"It would have been nice to know," Alfie said through gritted teeth when the guest was out of earshot. They were aware of how he felt about her and yet they'd said nothing.

"Alfie, not now. There are more important matters to attend to." He could hear the exasperation in his father's voice. After his outburst in the War Room they'd run out of patience with him.

Alfie bristled. He was being dismissed like a toddler. "Fine," he said tensely as they went on with the greeting.

Nursing his wounded pride, he took his seat at the banquet table. After the guests were all seated, King Bolivar cleared his throat and began his opening speech. Alfie had heard him practice it several times, but his father was such a fine speaker that it sounded fresh. He had a way of pulling all eyes to him even if he was only comment-ing on the weather.

Dez had that gift too, Alfie thought with a sting.

"Let us break bread and forge new paths of peace and prosperity, not only for us, but for our sons and daughters, who will inherit this world long after we are gone," King Bolivar said, ending his opening speech as he stood at the head of the expansive table.

The banquet hall erupted in applause as the king took his seat and motioned for all to begin eating. Alfie was seated across from Prince Marsden. The seating chart had purposefully mixed the guests to force interaction between different kingdoms, but Alfie knew that he and Marsden had been placed near each other because they represented the future his father spoke of.

Alfie shot the Englassen prince a cautious smile and Marsden awkwardly returned it.

With a delicately held fork, Marsden took a bite of his chorizo and his eyes widened. He coughed into his fist, his cheeks reddening.

Alfie fought to keep his face neutral as the prince gasped. It was no secret that Englassen food tended to be on the blander side compared to Castallano cuisine.

Luka leaned closer to Alfie, whispering. "They stole all our spices and sold them off but never thought to use any in their own maldito food."

Alfie nearly burst into laughter, his shoulders shaking though no noise came out. Englass had colonized Castallan for generations, forcing them to farm and then taking their crops and spices to sell abroad, but it seemed that those spices had never found their way into any Englassen kitchens. Luka dabbed delicately at his lips with a cloth to hide his grin, but Marsden's tearing eyes were on them, and Alfie could swear he spotted a hint of embarrassment on his face. Alfie knew it wasn't kind to laugh at another, but he needed it after his encounter with the diviner.

Vesper patted Marsden on the shoulder, but the way her lips were mashed into a flat line told Alfie that she was suppressing a laugh as well.

"Excuse me," Marsden wheezed when the coughing fit finally faded. The Englassen prince snapped his fingers and James, the servant Alfie had bumped into before, came to remove the offending chorizo from his plate. Luka rolled his eyes so dramatically that Alfie had to elbow him to get him to stop.

James's hands shook as he removed the sausage, his eyes looking pointedly away from Marsden. Even for an Englassen, he looked a bit pale, almost sick. Marsden watched James like a hawk as he moved.

Maybe James wasn't sick; maybe he was just afraid.

Alfie wanted to say something, but he didn't know what. It wasn't his place to comment on how another royal treated his servants, especially when they were in the middle of tenuous negotiations, but still, something felt wrong. Luka shot him a look and Alfie knew he'd noticed it too.

"Prince Alfehr," Vesper said as her brother recovered. "I hear you have a lovely library here. Is it open to guests?"

Alfie grinned at the question, glad to be distracted. He didn't need to look at Luka to know that he was rolling his eyes again. "Our library is indeed quite expansive, and of course it's open to you anytime, Princess Vesper. Honestly, it's my favorite place in the palace," Alfie admitted, and she nodded in a way that told him she too had lost many nights to the pages of a book. "I'd be happy to accompany you there whenever you'd like."

"I will have to take you up on that," she said, her face looking more animated than Alfie had seen thus far. Certainly warmer than Marsden's. Something about the Englassen princess felt different than her brother. Alfie couldn't quite put his finger on it, but he already found himself feeling more comfortable around her.

Desk magic nerds of a feather flock together, Finn's voice echoed between his ears. Alfie felt a smile spread on his face.

What was she doing tonight now that the poison master had led nowhere? he wondered. What face was she wearing?

Was she thinking of him as often as he thought of her?

"Alfie," Luka whispered to him when Vesper and Marsden were busy talking to each other. "My contact is going to get us a meeting with the tattoo artist who made the bull tattoo."

Alfie's eyes widened. He hadn't had high hopes for Luka's source, but he was glad to hear that he would have something of note to report back to Finn. "He knew who the artist was?"

Luka nodded. "Apparently he's quite famoso and also . . . a bit dangerous."

"What?"

Luka waved his hand. "We'll deal with that when we get to it."

Alfie wanted to hear more, but the two delegados to his left asked his opinion on Castallan's sugarcane trade and Alfie politely answered, doing his best to show that he understood his kingdom's agricultural economics. The delegados were still lukewarm toward him after his outburst at the meeting in the War Room, but also because most of them still wished that it were Dez who would take the throne, not Alfie. This summit felt like a battle on two fronts— he had to impress Englass, but he also had to prove himself to his own people. The fight left him mentally drained, and he barely touched his dinner.

As the banquet went on, Alfie noticed an elderly Englassen dignitary across the table looking at him. Alfie wondered if he had food on his face.

"I'm sorry for staring, Your Highness," she said. "Your skin is such a lovely color, like coffee mixed with cream or perhaps a cinnamon stick."

Alfie stiffened awkwardly before giving a simple "Thank you."

The Englassens had long exoticized Castallanos' skin color and features. They didn't seem to realize how uncomfortable it was to be compared to food, seen as some sweet oddity, a dessert to pick off a tray and savor. He'd already seen several Englassens stare at his hair but, thankfully, none of them had said anything about his curls. Yet.

"Ah yes." Luka smiled pointedly at the woman. "And you have wonderful skin of mayonnaise. The best of all sandwich spreads. Lovely!"

Alfie nearly choked on his water as the woman's brow furrowed, seemingly confused by being compared to a food herself, though comfortable comparing Alfie to one.

"Thank you," Alfie murmured to him. Things were rough between him and Luka now because of Luka's sudden interest in fight clubs, but he knew his cousin would always have his back.

Luka shot him a knowing smile before getting back to his dinner.

The banquet was nearly at its end when Prince Marsden stood and waited for the table to fall silent so that he could speak.

"We are grateful to Castallan's illustrious royal family for their hospitality. On behalf of my people," Marsden said, his voice carrying across the long table, "I would like to thank them once again for the opportunity to mend the rift between our nations." He paused, and the room filled with applause.

Alfie couldn't help but notice that some of the delegados looked less than pleased as the Englassen prince spoke. Especially Delegado Culebra and his cronies, who sat at the far end of the table, frowns on their faces.

"I have one more gift to bestow upon Prince Alfehr," Marsden announced. Alfie's face grew hot as all eyes turned to him. "From one future king to another. May today mark the beginning of a fruitful friendship." Marsden snapped his fingers, and Alfie winced. If that was how Marsden treated his own people, Alfie wondered how he would behave during negotiations.

Before Alfie could dwell on it, a pair of servants stepped forward through the doors of the banquet hall carrying a hefty chest. "You are too kind," Alfie said, trying his best to hide his discomfort. He hated receiving gifts in general, let alone in a room full of people watching him.

The Englassen servants strained as they carried the hefty chest and Alfie's chest ached at the sight. They could not use magic to carry the gift. Instead, they were made to struggle in a room full of privileged royals who could have helped them with just a simple word of magic. Slowly they walked along the long side of the table, lugging the chest. Alfie could hear them breathing heavily as he waited.

One of the two servants stumbled and Alfie watched his side of the chest fall from his hands. It would strike his foot if no one stopped it.

"*Parar!*" Alfie said, his hand outstretched.

The chest froze in midair, just inches above the servant's toe. The look on his face was first shock, followed by gratitude.

"I'm happy to take it from here, gracias," Alfie said to the two servants. They froze, staring at him in pure panic. It struck Alfie that this kind of kindness had never been extended to them before. His stomach soured at the thought of a life with not only no magic, but also no dignity.

"Prince Alfehr," Marsden said with a surprised laugh. "It is their honor to carry it for you."

"I can manage," Alfie insisted. He could see his parents tensing, unsure of what to say.

"Please," Marsden said. "This work is their purpose and they are happy to do it. Bring the chest," he said to them. The servants scrambled to grab the chest, but with a word of magic Alfie let it float to him. It was the Englassen way to deny their people the magic they deserved by birthright. They seemed to truly believe that their people were happy to serve, and that they were born for no other purpose. Alfie couldn't understand it. He couldn't stand to watch them struggle. That was why they were here, after all, to negotiate the end of Englass's caste system. If Marsden was so insistent that Alfie not help the servants, how was he going to react to freeing the servants from magical bondage?

"Just because something is," Alfie said as the chest arrived to levitate before him, "doesn't mean it should be that way." He'd said it so quietly that only Marsden and those very close could hear him.

The room fell silent as Marsden opened and closed his mouth a few times. When Vesper touched his arm, Marsden finally spoke. "Of course, as you wish." The air had grown hot and still. Delegados and Englassen dignitaries alike fidgeted in their seats. The banquet had been pleasant, but good food and vino had not distracted them from the difficult task that lay ahead.

"I bet it's a nice pair of socks," Luka murmured beside him, but not even his cousin's jokes could break the tension.

With a word of magic Marsden opened the chest and revealed neatly stacked sheaths of preserved parchment. Alfie only looked at them, unsure of what the gift could mean, until he recognized the script on the papers.

"These are written in classical Castallano script," he said, his voice hushed, as if the parchment would fall apart if he spoke too loudly.

"Within this chest you will find the remains of Castallano texts from centuries ago. From our time of occupation," Marsden said with an awkward cough. "We thought it best to return them to their home."

Alfie's spine straightened. These were the words of his ancestors, stolen from his people and left to gather dust in a box. The Englassen royals had come to a meeting for peace, but with this gift they'd done nothing but remind Alfie's family of the past violence that hung over Castallan like a shadow. He was surprised that they'd even gone through the trouble of preserving the artifacts.

Alfie didn't realize that his fingers were curled tight around the chest until his knuckles began to ache. So many of their treasures had been stolen and destroyed by Englass during colonization. The vanishing cloak had been one of the few that were left, and thanks to Alfie that was gone too. Guilt and anger knotted his stomach.

"We thank you for this," his mother said, rising from her seat at the far end of the table and coming to his side. Alfie could barely hear her over the blood roaring in his ears. "We look forward to adding it to our collection of Castallano history."

Alfie's fingers twitched; words of magic sprouted in his mind. Not magic to defend, but to attack. Magic that Finn would use, if she ever used desk magic.

"Yes," King Bolivar said tersely as he came to stand at Alfie's other side, putting a hand on his son's shoulder. Alfie could feel the warning in his father's grip. *Stay calm*, his touch said.

Alfie said nothing, his eyes on Marsden. He could feel his nostrils flaring. His shadow whipped about his feet. Only when his father squeezed his shoulder did Alfie compose himself.

"Yes, thank you," Alfie heard himself say, though he could hardly believe that he hadn't shouted an insult instead.

"You are most welcome," Marsden said with a bow, and Alfie followed suit, his mind screaming as the banquet finally came to a quiet, tense close.

"Alfie," his mother said when they met in the king's study after the banquet. "If we are going to end this summit with the historic agreement that we all hope for, you must try to control your emotions. The summit has only just begun and you're already flustered."

Alfie kneaded his temples as his parents watched him. "How are you two so calm? They presented something they stole from us as a *gift*. It's . . ."

"Insensitive," King Bolivar offered from where he sat behind his dark wood desk. "Despicable. Mijo, we could go on for days. You must remember, to the oppressor, their mere presence, their willingness to speak with us, seems like a gift. Just as they believe that forcing their people into enslavement is a gift."

"It was just difficult," Alfie admitted as he pressed the heels of his hands into his eyes. "Watching those servants struggle, watching them not be able to perform magic, and then the gift." He shook his head. "Forgive me, it was too much."

"Mijo," his mother said before gently rubbing his shoulder. "It's all right to feel angry on the behalf of those servant boys. It's all right to recognize how thoughtless their gift was, but if you let your emotions get the best of you, then you will fail the people you hope to protect. Those two servants will live the rest of their lives without knowing the joy of magic and so will thousands more in Englass. For them, you must keep a cool head."

When she pulled him into a hug, Alfie tucked his face into her shoulder. He still had so much to learn. He needed to keep his eye on the horizon, on the larger goals at hand.

"I understand. I'll be better," he said as he pulled away.

"Go get some rest," King Bolivar said before standing and ruffling Alfie's hair. "Tomorrow will likely ask even more of us than did today."

Alfie nodded and made his way to the door. Before he stepped out he turned back to his parents. "Mamá, Papá."

"Yes, mi vida," she said.

"Thank you."

With that, Alfie headed to his rooms. Luka had promised to talk to him tonight about the information he'd gotten from the tattoo artist, but knowing Luka, he wouldn't come until after he'd had a midnight snack.

Alfie didn't want to be alone with his own thoughts any longer, but now that the Englassen royal family was in the palace, roaming the halls seemed like a death trap of sorts. With a frustrated sigh, Alfie tucked his hands into his pockets. His fingers met the dry, crisp edge of the parchment he used to reach Finn.

Maybe she would want to hear what Luka had to say in person. That was a valid reason to ask her to come over. Perfectly valid.

Alfie flopped onto his back and pressed a hand over his face. This back-and-forth was childish. Finn should be present to hear what Luka had to report. Simple as that. There was nothing else to it.

Before he lost his nerve, Alfie strode to his desk, unfurled the parchment, and wrote a message.

THE SHAPE OF PROTECTION

That night, Finn watched Anabeltilia set up the large map of San Cristóbal in her office above Kol's pub. *Her* pub. She would never get used to that.

After a long afternoon of interrogating the poison master with Alfie, and an even longer evening dealing with the individual and very stupid queries of the members of la Familia, Anabeltilia sat with Finn and made a list of Kol's associates so that they could decide which ones would be worth meeting with for questioning about what Kol had been up to.

Finn hated every single moment of it.

Who knew that being a thief lord involved so much grunt work? Was this why Kol was always in such a bad mood?

"Madre," a voice sounded from the door. It was her chef struggling with a tray of food. Kol had been the mother of all pendejas, but bless her for having a cook on staff. "I've brought your second lunch."

Finn clapped her hands. "Well, come in already. I won't wait all day. This is cutting it very close to first dinner."

Anabeltilia rolled her eyes as the man put a heavy tray on the desk. A plate of ropa vieja with a side of tostones along with a steaming bowl of sancocho. Finn tucked in, crumbs raining onto her lap.

"I'm labeling any possible sightings of Los Toros that have been reported by la Familia in blue, like you asked," Anabeltilia went on, sounding bored as usual. "The location of the murder," she said, pressing a crimson tack into a point in the Pinch, "is in red."

"Fine," Finn said, her mouth full. Having a chef was nice, but she still prayed to whatever dioses were listening that she and the prince would solve this mystery fast so that she could get out of this babysitting job. It was odd to be making plans that would hold her in this city for who knew how long.

"Will you be seeing Emeraude again soon?" Anabeltilia asked, trying and failing to make her voice sound casual.

Finn wiped her mouth with the back of her hand. "Why do you want to know?"

She looked at Finn over her shoulder. "Because she's amazing. Killed her husband and took his place, becoming the longest-reigning thief lord in history."

"But she hates Kol and it sounds like Kol hated her," Finn said. "Why would you like her?"

"I served Kol and respected her," Anabeltilia said. "Doesn't mean we shared every opinion. Emeraude is a *legend*."

She spoke as if she was talking about a god. Finn laughed and popped a tostone into her mouth. "Do you want me to bring her a fan letter for you? Or maybe you want to bake her something?"

Anabeltilia's eyes widened. "Do you think she would like that?"

Before Finn could fall into another fit of laughter, the map threatened to fall off the wall and Anabeltilia lurched forward to catch it. As she did, her shirt rode up and Finn spotted scars lining her back. They were healed, but the sight of them made her wince.

"Who gave you those?" Finn asked.

"Gave me what?" Anabeltilia asked, sounding exasperated.

"The scars on your back."

The girl froze before carefully affixing the map to the wall again. "None of your business."

A cold pit formed in Finn's stomach. "Was it Kol?"

The girl's silence was answer enough. For a moment, Finn was surprised by how loyal Anabeltilia was to Kol, how protective she was of her memory if she beat her like that. But then didn't she herself spend her childhood returning to Ignacio, wanting to make him proud, wanting so desperately to be whatever he wanted her to be?

"I miss it too," Ignacio said, suddenly beside her. "It's all right to miss your papá. It's only natural."

Finn kept her eyes forward, refusing to acknowledge him.

"You know, you don't have to speak well of her," Finn said. "She's dead."

Anabeltilia whirled around, fury in her eyes. "Kol gave me everything. A place to stay, a job, a life. So watch your tongue."

"See, this—this is a very good daughter," Ignacio said as he circled the girl. "You should take note."

"It's possible for one person to give you everything and take everything from you at the same time," Finn said. "The smartest, worst abusers do both."

Ignacio rolled his eyes. "You speak as if you've won, but I'm still here, Mija."

She held Anabeltilia's gaze for a long moment. As tears gathered at the corners of the girl's eyes, Finn did her the courtesy of looking away with a shrug.

"You don't want to listen to me, that's fine."

Anabeltilia said nothing, only turned to the map, her back tense.

Happy for an excuse to get out of the silent room, Finn jumped when she felt the parchment warming in her pocket. She hadn't expected to hear from him again so soon.

She unfolded it and read Alfie's elegant script.

Luka has new information. Can you meet tonight?

Finn put a check mark next to the sentence and got to her feet. She looked at Anabeltilia, her brow furrowing. With Ignacio still smiling at her, Finn couldn't help but wonder how many specters were chasing this girl too?

"When you finish with the map, take the night off," Finn said as she made her way to the door.

"I don't need the night off," Anabeltilia seethed. "I'm fine."

Finn wanted to say, "No, you're not. I'm not either," but she knew it was no use. "Suit yourself," she said, walking out the door. Regardless of her new title, she wasn't this girl's mother. With everything she had on her plate, she didn't have the time to help Anabeltilia too. Still, Finn couldn't get the scars out of her head as she walked away.

* * *

When the prince's balcony doors swung open, he and Bathtub Boy were waiting for her.

Finn strode right past them and plopped onto the edge of Alfie's bed.

"Long time no see," Luka said to her, a grin on his face. "I hear you're thief royalty now. Congrats! I'm sorry to have missed your coronation."

"No hard feelings," Finn said with a grin. "It's good to see you fully dressed." She smirked, remembering the first time she saw him in the royal baths, the day he'd earned his nickname.

"The night is still young; who knows?"

"Both of you are ridículo," Alfie said, exasperation lacing his words, but Finn could see that he was barely succeeding at suppressing a smile himself. His shadow zoomed around his feet.

Finn stared pointedly at it and raised an eyebrow. "Nice to know that you're excited to see me."

Luka snorted and Alfie looked away, his hand rubbing the nape of his neck.

Satisfied, Finn crossed her arms. "So what did you learn from your tattoo connection?"

"The man who did those tattoos is infamous. He's called the Tattooed King."

"More royalty," Finn said, unimpressed.

Alfie shot her a warning look. "He's supposed to be quite dangerous, and getting a meeting with him cost a fortune."

"He charges for meetings?" Finn asked, tapping her chin. "Maybe *I* should charge for meetings. . . ."

"Finn," Alfie said. "Focus."

"My contact is seeing if he can arrange a meeting. Whenever it happens, I don't want Alfie going alone. I say we get the good old trio together and go as a team," Luka said, gesturing at all of them as if they were about to form a bachata band.

Finn didn't like the idea of the prince going alone either. "We're not a trio, but yeah, I agree. We should go together."

"Definitely a trio," Luka corrected her. "My contact told me that this guy doesn't tolerate tardiness. So whenever this meeting is, no one can be late, entiendes?"

Finn waved a dismissive hand. "Yes, Mother."

"I hear that's your name now," Luka said.

Alfie sighed through his nose. "The two of you are unbearable apart and insufferable together."

"Thank you," Finn and Luka said in unison.

"Now that that's settled," Luka said before faking a yawn. "I'm tired and I think the two of you have other things to discuss." He winked at Alfie.

Finn squinted at him. "Really? That's all you have to say?"

At the same time Alfie pointedly said, "Are you leaving because you have *plans*?" Clearly the prince had his suspicions about where Luka was going.

Luka strode to the door. "Finn, an absolute pleasure as always." He shot Alfie a look. "And no, Alfie, I don't have any *plans*, don't worry your pretty little head about that. I won't be far." Luka rolled his eyes, but Finn could see the deeper frustration beneath. "Have fun!"

Finn snorted as he closed the door behind him.

Alfie wrung his hands and Finn felt the sudden urge to stare at either the floor or the ceiling, nothing in between.

"You wanted to tell me something?" she asked.

Alfie shook his head, forcing an awkward laugh. "No, not really," he admitted. "Luka just likes to be . . ."

"Annoying?" Finn offered. Alfie finally met her eyes then, and she hated the warmth that pooled in her stomach when he did.

"Exactamente."

A heavy silence stretched through the room and Finn could sense that they both had something to say, but neither wanted to go first. She'd come back to Castallan for him, to rid herself of Ignacio once more. She'd thought just seeing him would be enough to banish Ignacio from her mind, but it wasn't. Ignacio's ghost still haunted her and she wondered if she had to talk to Alfie about it to make it all go away.

Finn sucked her teeth. She hated talking.

"I—" Finn said.

At the same time Alfie said, "Well—"

"You go first," they said at the same time. Their shadows bobbed on the ground awkwardly, surging closer to one another and then retreating.

Another silence crested between them until Finn finally admitted, "I don't want to."

"Me either," Alfie said, leaning on the wall behind him. Then his face lit up. The prince was too expressive for his own good. Finn could practically see the idea bubbling up in his mind. "Can I try something?" he asked her.

Finn nodded. It wasn't as if she had anything to lose.

Alfie opened his desk drawer and pulled out a thick piece of chalk. Crouching on the open floor in front of his bed, he began drawing something on the tiles.

He swatted at her feet, a smile curving his lips. "Some space, please."

Finn obliged with a smirk, raising her feet and letting him work. "You've gotten bossier since we last met." She let one foot drop so that her ankle was draped over his shoulder.

Alfie froze for a long moment before wrapping his hand around her ankle. Finn blinked. Bossier *and* braver.

"Just holding on for balance," he said. His voice had gone quiet and Finn had to lean forward to hear him. "Is that all right?"

"It's fine," she said, waiting until he looked away before she swallowed.

When he was done, he gently took her leg off his shoulder and stood. Finn had been so distracted that she hadn't looked down at what he was drawing. It was a shape that was a triangle with a white circle in the center. He'd drawn countless lines connecting from the circle to the sides. Words of magic and symbols she didn't recognize were written along its sides and in the middle.

"It's a bruxo's triangle," Alfie said.

"What does it mean?" she asked as he put the chalk away and wiped the white dust from his hands.

"It's a very common shape in written spellwork."

"Ah," Finn said, rolling her eyes. "Desk magic."

"It's often used in protection spells, but it can also be used to trap people inside and harm them," he said. Finn raised her eyebrows. "But let's think of it as the former, not the latter. Dez would say it's the shape of protection, of trust." His face went painfully tight and Finn wondered if the prince would ever be able to mention his brother without looking so lost. "The most important pieces of it are each of the three corners and the circle in the center. Those have to be done properly for it to work. Usually special spellwork and certain ingredients need to be placed at those four points."

Finn could see that the unknown symbols were clustered around those four areas.

"When I was little and I wanted to talk about something that made me uncomfortable, my brother would draw this shape on the floor and we would step into it and tell each other our secrets. The bruxo's triangle was a symbol that we and our secrets were safe." Alfie looked away from her then, rubbing the back of his neck. "It sounds infantile, I know, but I thought it might help. . . ."

"It does sound a bit dumb." Finn nodded, watching his face drop. Then she stepped into the center of the triangle, holding his gaze. "Let's do it anyway."

With a feather-soft smile, Alfie stepped in too and sat cross-legged on the floor. Finn followed suit.

"Do I still have to go first?" Alfie asked after the silence had stretched too long for comfort.

"Mm-hmm."

"What happened to ladies first?" Alfie joked uneasily.

Finn cocked her head nonchalantly, hoping the gesture hid her discomfort. "I don't know if you've heard, but I'm not a lady, I'm a lord."

"Fine, I'll start," Alfie sighed. He wrung his hands in his lap for a long moment before finally speaking. "After everything we did to stop Sombra, I've been afraid to use my *propio*."

Finn stared at him. His *propio* made him afraid too? How was it that they were so different, yet their lives seemed to move parallel to each other?

"All parts of your *propio*?"

He shook his head and Finn spotted dark circles under his eyes. "No, not all of it. I used my *propio* to make sure the poison master was telling the truth yesterday, remember? I've been afraid to go back into the channels of magic because the last time I did . . . ," he said, his voice tapering off.

"You released Sombra," Finn said for him.

Alfie nodded, clearing his throat before he continued. "The realm of magic, the physical place I had to go to release Sombra, is connected to the magic channels I use to travel with my *propio*. I was afraid that the realm of magic and all the channels connected to it would reject me for what I'd done, that I didn't deserve to use it in that way anymore. And I was right."

Finn's eyes widened as the prince told her of the screams he heard whenever he traveled through the magic.

"So I'm afraid of using my *propio* to travel through the magic the way I used to. The rest of my *propio*, I'm fine with." He rubbed the back of his neck. "Or at least I am for now. Who knows, maybe at some point I'll start hearing the screams when I touch any part of it."

Finn didn't know what to say. She was hardly an expert on magic but, then again, she had become something of an expert on the prince.

"Prince," she said. "I don't know much about the realm of magic, but I know you're stressed. About the summit, about Los Toros." She looked at him pointedly. "Probably about your general existence too. You don't look like you've been sleeping. Maybe all this has to do with that."

Alfie tilted his head. "You're not wrong. I haven't been sleeping much." He looked away from her then before mumbling, "Bad dreams . . ." But he moved on from that before Finn could even ask about it. "Access to the realm of magic is the mark of a skilled bruxo. It's a reflection of being in tune with magic as a whole. Only the most skilled bruxos and dueños can do it. I can't shake the feeling that the sound I'm hearing is the realm of magic punishing me for what I did, telling me I'm no longer welcome there."

Finn blew a stray curl out of her face. "If that's what the realm is doing, then it's stupid."

Alfie burst into laughter. He wiped the tears from the corners of his eyes before he could finally speak again. "I'm sorry," he said. "I just have never heard anyone call it stupid like that."

Finn grinned. It was nice to see him laugh. "Either way, I think things will get better if you just relax for once in your maldito life. Doesn't magic behave differently based on our emotions, or some sappy mierda like that?"

Alfie considered for a moment before nodding. "It does," he said. "The user colors the magic, not the other way around. Maybe I am manifesting the sound myself. . . ."

In that moment, the prince's tense shoulders finally relaxed. "Thank you," he breathed, and Finn found herself struck by how wonderful those two words could sound from the right person. "I feel so much better."

"You're welcome," she muttered, pointedly looking away from him. She traced the lines of the triangle, leaving her fingertip coated in white dust. "Well, I suppose my work is done." She stood, but the prince grabbed her wrist gently.

"No, it's your turn," he said. "I told you my secret, now you tell me yours. Fair is fair."

"I'm not usually one for fair," she said, thinking of how he'd said that to her months ago at the dock when she'd showed him her true face. How many times had she thought about the day they'd gone their separate ways? She'd repeated their goodbye in her head so many times that it felt as if she'd lived a handful of lifetimes with that moment as the common thread.

Alfie tugged her arm gently with a look so open and vulnerable that it made her want to pry herself open to match him. She hated it. "Make an exception. Please."

Finn let him pull her down, as if she were a balloon he held by the string, one that he would let float away whenever it pleased. He let go of her when she was back on the ground and her wrist felt annoyingly cold.

"You're not the only one scared of their *propio*," she admitted.

When she didn't speak again, the prince nodded. "What happened?"

"I found a new ability, a new part of my *propio*," she said. When Alfie quirked an eyebrow, Finn sighed and began to transform until he was looking at a mirror image of himself.

"Huh." Alfie stared. "Luka is right; my neck *is* oddly long, isn't it?"

Finn rolled her eyes. There was nothing wrong with his neck, but she wasn't going to tell him that. She focused and felt the connection between them. He gave a soft gasp. He could feel it too.

Finn was afraid to show him what she could do, how she could control him. Would he look at her in fear the way she did Ignacio? Would he shout for the guards? Finn bit the inside of her cheek.

"Here we go," she said before standing. Alfie's eyes widened as he stood in perfect unison. She raised her left arm and Alfie followed. Then her right.

Disgust pooled in her stomach. She severed the connection between them and transformed back into herself. "I can control people, just like . . ."

Alfie nodded in understanding. "Like Ignacio." When she said nothing, Alfie's hands found her shoulders. "Finn, you're still nothing like him."

"Don't lie to me," she said, her face feeling hot. "You saw what I can do, felt it. I controlled you, like you were a puppet."

"You did," Alfie admitted. "But you didn't hurt me. And you have to mirror me while you control me. That's different than Ignacio."

To Finn, it would never be different enough. She looked away from him, wanting to talk about anything else. Her eyes traced the chalk lines of the triangle. "You drew the triangle, but you didn't actually engage any magic, did you?"

He shook his head. "When Dez did this it was just a symbol. A representation of trust." He paused for a long moment. "Trust and love."

Finn's eyes met his and it occurred to her that magic could be spoken and drawn in chalk or invoked when controlling an element, but there was also another kind of magic. The type of magic born when trust bloomed between two people, trust that could survive the worst of your faults and secrets, your greatest fears.

Finn shook her head free of that thought. "How exactly can a triangle be used to hurt people?"

Alfie looked surprised—it wasn't like her to ask questions about desk magic. But she would listen to just about anything to change the subject, to stop thinking about what it meant for the prince to draw a shape of love and protection around her, and how safe she felt within it.

"There are lots of ways, really," he began, and she could see the gears turning in his mind, years of magic lessons unfurling. "But there is a legend about ancient Castallan. It is said that there were two warring kings, the northern king and the southern king. Each wanted the continent for themselves."

"Typical men," Finn said, rolling her eyes.

"They had spent years battling each other's armies only to end in stalemate after stalemate, so they finally decided to fight one on one—no armies at their sides, nothing but their machetes and their wits."

Finn leaned forward. "Now we're getting somewhere."

"Everyone knew the two kings were equally matched, so onlookers expected that they would simply fight for days and days until they both collapsed dead, but that's not what happened."

"Good," Finn said. "That would be boring."

"The northern king chose the location of the battle, a cliff high in the mountains. The southern king took the position closest to the cliff's edge and the northern king took the side closer to safety. Before the southern king even raised his machete, the northern king spoke a word of magic and the ground fell from beneath the southern king. He fell to his death."

"So the northern king won because he fought dirty. I can respect that."

Alfie tilted his head. "The lesson of the fable was brains over brawn, but I suppose that's one way of looking at it."

"So where does the triangle come in?"

"The story goes that the northern king had drawn a triangle on the side of the cliff where the southern king stood. He spoke a word of magic and that side of the cliff crumbled away," Alfie explained. "Essentially, bruxo triangles can be used to destroy whatever is within them. I've drawn mine clearly in white chalk, but one can easily hide the written magic and wait for its prey to step right into a trap. But they just as easily can be used as a form of safety, to protect all within. It's a sacred and powerful symbol that, like magic, is influenced by the intentions of the user. So it has been used for good just as often as it's been used for evil."

"That's funny," Finn said with a chuckle. Alfie shot her a questioning look. "How the same things that are meant to protect you can hurt you too."

His eyes told her that he knew she was thinking of Ignacio. He shook his head. "It's not funny."

"I guess you had to be there," Finn joked, but her laugh sounded broken.

"I was there with you." Alfie tilted his head before gently taking her hand in his. "And I still am."

His words conjured a flood of memory, of him fighting at her side in the face of the monster that Ignacio had become and the monster she feared that she herself was. And the prince was right; he was still here. Part of her knew he always would be.

In that moment, she knew she was free from Ignacio. She knew it the way a baby knew to cry when it was born, the way a flower knew to grow up toward the sun instead of down into the dark. She was free. Alfie had freed her.

Finn didn't know who started leaning forward first, but it was as if the triangle had drawn tighter around them, guiding them forward to each other. The prince ducked his head down and his nose brushed hers before he met her eyes, silently asking a question.

Finn answered, rising on her tiptoes, her hand wrapping around the back of his neck, her thumb rubbing the same spot that he always rubbed himself when he was nervous.

"Did you really think that would work?" Ignacio said from just outside the triangle.

Finn jumped back, stumbling out of the triangle. Why was he still here? Why did he still haunt her even after she had spoken to Alfie about it?

Alfie's eyes flew wide. "I'm sorry, did I—"

"You didn't do anything," she said, her heart pounding in her chest, her eyes burning. "I just have to—I have to go. I'll see you for the tattoo thing when Luka sets it up."

"Finn," Alfie began, but she didn't wait. Finn dashed out the balcony doors and began climbing, not looking up to catch his eye.

"Maybe you should've let him kiss you," Ignacio said with a laugh. "Isn't that how all the stories end? A kiss from a prince fixes everything."

"Stop it," she said, but she knew it would be no use.

If the prince's kindness couldn't banish Ignacio, nothing would. She would be haunted by him until she died and, at this rate, probably after too.

THE SEARCH FOR TROUBLE

Luka moved through the empty palace gardens as if he were looking for something he'd lost on the way home.

As if he'd been at his bedroom doors only to find a hole in his pocket from which something precious had slipped. He moved as if retracing his own steps, following bread crumbs. But Luka hadn't lost anything. Still, he went searching. But what he sought couldn't be held in his hand or tucked into his pocket.

What he was looking for was trouble, a distraction—anything to quiet his thoughts.

Lately, he'd proven himself adept at finding it in fight clubs. He could catch its scent like a truffle pig snuffling for spoils in the dirt.

Luka stuffed his hands into his pockets. He'd thought he'd want to stay with Alfie and Finn longer, if only to watch Alfie fall over himself for her, and Finn pretend not to care, but as soon as all three of them were in the room, he'd wanted to get out, like a fly buzzing against a closed window.

When he saw them together, all he could think of was walking into the Blue Room four months ago and falling ill, his head on Finn's lap and his veins full of poison as Alfie sobbed.

Something had changed in all of them that night.

Luka knew he should feel lucky to be alive. He did. But he still couldn't shake the feeling that he shouldn't be. He'd avoided death one too many times. He had hardly deserved it the first time, let alone this time too.

A chill passed over him as he remembered what he'd spent over a decade hiding behind quips and charming grins—the little tombstones next to the large ones, the estate once filled with his family's laughter suddenly silent.

That was enough luck for one person.

Luck and a curse now that he stood here without them. How had he made it through again when so many died after Sombra's release? And not only did he live, but Luka thrived. Thanks to what had happened, he'd become unnaturally strong, capable of juggling boulders without breaking a sweat. He was full of vitality and life while so many bodies fell away to ash. He couldn't understand it. He didn't know if he ever would. But every time he saw Alfie, every time the prince brought up Sombra, it was all he could think about.

I'm here and they are not.

That ache inside, that empty space that death should have crawled into and claimed as its own, had built some sort of craving in him. A craving for trouble, a craving to tempt death if it was always going to elude him anyway. A craving that sent him running into fight clubs and gambling halls and made him excited to meet the supposedly dangerous Tattooed King to learn more about Los Toros.

Something within him was burning, as if he'd swallowed a lump of coal, and he could do nothing but exhale steam like some sort of dragon from a children's tale.

His mind a tangle of grief and gratitude, Luka stood before the garden's pond, catching his reflection in its moving mirror.

"Stop! Heel! Sit!" a voice called in the night. Luka turned and saw two puppies charging toward the pond with James, the servant Marsden had tasked with training the dogs, following close behind.

The puppies, leashes and all, paid Luka no mind before jumping right into the pond, splashing Luka with cool water.

James came to a halt at the pond's edge, gripping his knees. "I'm . . . so . . . sorry," he said between gasps, motioning at the puppies. "They love the water." Then, upon realizing that it was Luka, James's green eyes went wide, and he dropped into a low bow. "Please forgive me, Master Luka! I did not mean to disturb you."

"Oh, it's nothing," Luka said. "Please don't worry." He tried to make reassuring eye contact, but the boy kept looking away and Luka couldn't help but think he looked like a dog who had been beaten, one who feared that every outstretched hand would strike. He'd looked so afraid when Marsden had made him take away his chorizo, and Luka himself was almost afraid to ask why.

The puppies pulled themselves out of the pond, zooming about in circles and shaking the water off their coats.

"This was supposed to be their last walk of the night before bed," James said, his shoulders relaxing slightly. "And of course they get themselves soaked."

The puppies pressed their wet paws to Luka's pant leg as he petted their floppy ears. "You could just use a drying sp—" Luka began before stopping. Of course James couldn't use any spellwork to dry the dogs; he was an Englassen servant and was forbidden from using magic. "Sorry," Luka said sheepishly.

"You have nothing to apologize for, Master Luka," James said.

"Just Luka is fine," he said. "Really. Let me dry the dogs." Before James could stop him, Luka put a hand on each puppy's head. "*Secar.*" In the blink of an eye the two dogs were fluffy once more.

James gripped their leashes, pulling them back before they could jump into the pond again. "Thank you. And truly, I'm sorry for interrupting you."

"You have nothing to be sorry for either," Luka said. "I appreciated the company." Maybe there were things besides alcohol and fight clubs that could distract him from his dreary thoughts.

When James didn't respond, Luka looked up from the puppies and saw the boy rocking forward on his heels, his eyes rolling back into his head.

"James!" Luka said before leaping up to catch him in his arms.

James was a bit shorter, so when he fell against Luka, his forehead met the crook of Luka's neck. Where their skin met, Luka felt a searing, unnatural heat. The boy had a terrible fever. Thanks to his strength, Luka held him easily with one arm and gently shook the boy. "James?"

"So sorry," James slurred feverishly; leaning back against Luka's crooked arm, he blinked, noticing how easily Luka held him in place. "Wow, you're quite strong."

"Thank you." Luka smiled. He usually loved a good compliment, but he couldn't fully enjoy it. James's face was so close to his that he could feel the strength of his fever. Luka was a flame caster, so he ran hotter than most, and even to him, James felt far too warm. "You might need medical attention because you're quite hot." Luka paused, tilting his head. "That sounds like a pickup line but it wasn't. But I will no doubt be using it as such at some point."

James jumped free of Luka's hold, his face flushed, his eyes more alert. "That was inappropriate of me." He swayed on his feet, look- ing truly ill. "Please don't tell Prince Marsden that this happened. Or anyone. Please."

Something in the way James said that made Luka's heart ache. Did Marsden punish his servants if they took ill? Luka wouldn't be surprised. Marsden didn't seem like a nice person to his equals, let alone to his servants.

"I won't, it's all right. Let me take you to the infirmary," Luka insisted. "You're burning up."

Panic pinched James's face taut. "No, it's not necessary. I'm just a bit under the weather. I must go." James tugged the leashes gently until the puppies stopped sniffing Luka's shoes. "Please forget that this happened." He bowed again, the puppies jumping at his face as he did. "And thank you for drying them, Master Luka."

"Just Luka," he corrected.

"That I cannot do," James said with a small smile. "I think I've been improper enough for one night." In that moment, Luka caught a glimpse of a James who hadn't been ground into ash, who joked and held the slightest glint of mischief in his eyes. This was a James that Luka wanted to see more of.

Before Luka could say another word, James led the dogs away. Luka watched the strange boy disappear into the night and won- dered what secrets he was keeping behind his skittish, kind eyes.

Alone again, Luka's thoughts began to edge toward the tombstones, toward a past he could not outrun. He looked over his shoulder at Alfie's balcony. He'd told Alfie he wouldn't go anywhere tonight, but what Alfie didn't know wouldn't hurt him. He would go have some good rum and company in the Bow and maybe a fight in the Pinch while Alfie and Finn had each other.

THE STOLEN HEART

Just before midnight on the first day of the peace summit, Arturo Camacho stood before the fireplace in his hacienda.

The walls of the study were a mix of warm oranges and yellows, as if he'd captured the sunset within them. When the hacienda had first been built on the riches of his family's merchant business, he'd held his infant son in his arms and said, "It will always be the golden hour in this family, in your life."

Now his son was nearly twelve years old and life indeed had been golden. And it seemed that soon things would be even more so.

After all, he'd invested more gold in the peace summit than a sunset could capture. He was a merchant, and the more peace there was between countries, the more trade and the more gold flowed into his coffers for his son and the very surprise baby on the way.

He crossed his arms, his jaw tight as he watched the flames crackle. So long, of course, as this foolish group of vagabonds with the bull symbol would stop their meddling. There had been talk about canceling the peace summit to stop the violence, but Arturo had made his thoughts clear to his representative delegado. No peace summit meant no more funding for the delegado's lofty plans. The delegado had changed his tune quickly and rallied his colleagues to fight to keep the peace summit. Now that the summit had begun, there was no stopping it. Arturo let his shoulders relax. He was in the clear. The protestors had lost.

"Papí?"

Arturo jumped before whirling around to see his son, Antonio, standing behind him, his face soft with sleep.

"Mijo, what are you doing up? It's tarde."

Antonio gave a long yawn. "I got thirsty."

Arturo smiled. "Go get some agua and get back to bed, oíste?"

"Okay, Papí," the little boy said, turning on his heel and padding toward the kitchens.

A smile softening his sharp features, Arturo turned back to the fireplace, but his jaw went slack at the sight before him.

It looked as if worms were wriggling out of the wall of the fireplace. No, not worms, fingers. In the blink of an eye, a man stepped through the fireplace as if through air. He wore dark clothes and a horned bull mask.

Arturo's heart sputtered in his chest. "How did you . . . ?"

The man in the bull mask simply stood before him, gesturing at the ground where his shadow paced back and forth on the floor, like a cat's tail whipping about at the sight of prey. *Propio* magic.

"You come with me quietly, and the boy lives. You make a fuss . . ." He paused as if daring Arturo to even consider that option. "The boy dies, and you come with me in pieces, oíste?"

Arturo's mouth went dry. He could hear his heartbeat pounding in his ears. But above that roaring rush of blood was the sound of his son pouring himself a glass of water.

His mind too frantic to form words of magic, Arturo called upon the stone walls of his home, pelting fist-sized stones haphazardly at the stranger. But the masked man only stepped forward and the bricks moved *through* him, slamming into the fireplace behind him. In three quick strides he'd gripped Arturo, one hand about his neck, the other on his chest. His palms were hot, as if a fire burned beneath his skin.

"You know," he said in a whisper, "it's not only brick and wood and stone that I can move through. I can move through flesh and bone too." With only the slightest pressure against Arturo's chest, the man's fingers began to sink into his skin. Arturo gasped in pain. "Think how easy it would be to sink my hand into that boy's chest and pull his heart free."

"Papí?" came Antonio's voice again, but the masked man held him fast. He couldn't turn to see his son. That broke him more than the pain of this man's fingernails beneath his skin ever could. "Papí, who is that?"

"Say goodbye to your son. Most don't get the chance," the stranger said, and for a moment he sounded apologetic, but his voice was cold when he went on. "Then we go out the way I came."

Arturo could only nod and mash his lips tightly together to keep from screaming as the man pulled his bloody fingers out from his skin. With a tight grip on Arturo's shoulder, the man turned him around to face his son. Arturo looked at the face of his son one last time. He took in the dimples that the boy had gotten from his mother, the curls he'd gotten from him, the nose that had traveled generations to land between those soft brown eyes.

"Papí?" Antonio said, his voice growing hushed with fear, his glass of water shaking in his hand.

"It's okay, Mijo. Papí's talking with a friend. Go to bed."

As the man tugged him backward toward the hearth, Arturo felt a chill crawl over his skin—the man's *propio* magic. And suddenly he was sinking into the cool wall of the fireplace too.

"Te amo," he said when only his head could be seen. "Sleep well, Mijo."

Then Arturo Camacho was gone, and Antonio could only stare at the wall that had swallowed his father and the masked stranger.

The glass of water fell from his shaking hand and shattered on the ground.

THE LEGACY

"I'm sorry," the queen said, her voice shaking. "You mean to tell me that his heart was pulled from his chest?"

Alfie himself couldn't believe what Paloma had just told them. They had been woken so early on the second morning of the summit that the moon was still visible. He was still reeling from his almost-kiss with Finn and how she'd run from him as if she'd been burned. Dressed in their sleeping clothes, the royal family had gathered to hear a report of another murder by Los Toros. Alfie stared at the dueña, hoping that this was somehow metaphorical, but Paloma only nodded.

"According to Arturo's son, the masked man pulled him through the wall. We can only assume that he used the same *propio* to pull his heart from his chest."

Alfie shuddered. Los Toros were a gang of bruxos with monstrous *propios*, that was for certain. How many were there and how many more Castallanos would die at their hands?

The king pressed a hand over his eyes, worry pulling his skin taut. "The delegados have been alerted. We'll need to have another meeting."

"Has the situation been properly dealt with?" the queen asked.

Paloma nodded. "The body was removed. We used memory spellwork on anyone found in the area, including a few Englassen servants. We could not catch everyone, but it is highly unlikely that this will get back to the Englassen royals."

His mother let out a breath. "Good."

Alfie shook his head, his shadow surging nervously around his feet. "But how long can we cover this up before the Englassen royals hear about it? Before they learn that we brought them here in the middle of a rash of anti-Englass murders?"

His father stared at him. "What are you suggesting?"

"Perhaps we need to cut the summit short, send the Englassens away before things get worse," Alfie said. "We could resume the summit when things are safe."

"Out of the question," his mother said. "Alfie, do you know how much time it took to broker this summit? It has taken generations for Englass to reach a point where they are willing to consider dismantling their caste system. We cannot simply tell the Englassens to go home and come back another time. They might never return."

"And if we continue, it could very well end in disaster," Alfie nearly shouted. "How can you not see that?"

"I agree with the prince," Paloma said before his parents could argue against him. "This was already a tenuous situation without these added variables."

The king shook his head. "The summit only lasts seven days longer. We will find a way to make this work."

"But Papá—"

"We will finish this summit, both for those still in bondage and to complete your brother's legacy. I will not hear another word about it!" the king thundered.

Alfie started. So this was why his parents were clinging so tightly to the summit. Not only because they wanted to end enslavement in Englass, but also for Dez. Dez had been the one to ask their father if they could leverage Englass's falling economic standing to get them to end their caste system. It would be his victory if he were still here. Alfie didn't know how to feel about this. His parents were far from perfect, he knew that, but to keep the summit going when lives were at stake just to honor Dezmin's memory felt selfish. But then, Alfie knew all too well that grief made you selfish.

"Alfie," his father began, his voice quiet with shame as the queen took his arm in hers. "I'm sorry. I—"

"It's all right," Alfie said. "I understand." He himself had done foolish things for Dez, things that had put their entire kingdom in danger. He could forgive his father for this, even if he didn't agree.

"We will strengthen security to keep our guests safe and unaware of these horrible events," the queen said. "And we will catch the culprits before they can harm anyone else. The summit has already begun. If we were going to postpone it, it would have had to happen before. Now we have no choice but to see it through. Paloma—"

"I will fetch the captain of the royal guard," Paloma said, anticipating the request before the queen could speak it.

"Thank you," the king said as the dueña strode out of the room.

"We will put a reward out for the capture of the bull-masked criminals. A hefty reward," his mother said, her voice resolute.

"They won't be able to strike without someone trying to capture them. The guardsmen will spread the word throughout the rings. With such a bounty, even the city's criminal underworld will be on the hunt for them."

The king and Alfie nodded. Finn would certainly be hearing about this soon. If they couldn't track down Los Toros themselves, then maybe the people could. With a price on their heads, Los Toros might back off. It was their best chance of keeping the summit safe. When Alfie bid his parents farewell, he dashed down the hallways to find Luka and tell him what had happened. But when he let himself into Luka's rooms, they were empty.

Alfie exhaled sharply in frustration. At this hour, he knew where Luka was—getting into trouble somewhere in the Pinch.

Frustration crawled over his skin. Why had Luka chosen now of all times to cause more trouble? Alfie knew he had complicated feelings about what had happened with the release of Sombra, but that hardly gave him the excuse to act so thoughtlessly. No matter how many times Alfie pressed him to talk about it, he wouldn't. Luka wouldn't even let him try to help.

But what angered Alfie the most was that Luka kept disappearing on him when he needed him. And for what? Some silly fight that he was guaranteed to win thanks to his strength? Was he doing it for the ego boost?

Alfie trudged back to his rooms and scrawled a note to Finn about tonight's murder before crawling into his bed. He hoped Luka's connection would help get them a meeting with the Tattooed King soon. Los Toros weren't stopping their attacks, so they needed to follow every lead as quickly as possible.

As he finally fell back asleep, hoping to catch a few more hours'
rest before the sun rose, he thought of the desperation on his father's
face when he demanded that they continue the summit for Dez.
Alfie felt strangely grateful that at least he wasn't the only one in his
family who was willing to make rash decisions in Dez's name.

THE MEETING OF GHOSTS

The sun was only just beginning to rise on the second morning of the summit as Finn stared at the statue that would lead her down to Emeraude's underground quarters.

She had barely slept after Ignacio's appearance in Alfie's rooms. For a moment, everything had felt right. She'd felt safe, cured of Ignacio for good. Then he'd appeared, as if waiting to let her feel an ounce of freedom before snatching it away from her.

Finn had wanted nothing more than to stay in bed, but Emeraude had told her to come update her after she'd interrogated the poison master yesterday. Finn had very little to report, but she still had to show up.

With a frustrated sigh she pressed a peso into the statue's outstretched hand and watched it eerily come to life. Finn trudged down the tight spiral staircase and followed the scent of spun sugar straight to where Emeraude sat waiting at her pastry-laden table.

"You're late," Emeraude tutted.

"And you're old," Finn retorted. "Are we done trading truths for the day?"

Emeraude shot her a quelling look and motioned for her to sit. "So," she said as she poured Finn a cup of café. "You spoke to the poison master?"

"I did," Finn admitted, drumming her fingers on the table. Her shadow zigzagged agitatedly at her feet.

"And you learned nothing?" Emeraude guessed.

Finn threw up her hands, too exhausted to hold anything back. "He didn't know anything we could use. He's just a cowardly man who got his power from making poisons."

"You're certain he wasn't lying?" Emeraude asked. "He's a criminal. It would hardly be surprising if he were mentiroso."

Finn shook her head. "I brought an"—Finn grasped at straws for the right word—"associate whose *propio* makes him sensitive to lying. The poison master was telling the truth."

Emeraude sighed, looking more than a little disappointed. "I'm sorry to hear that. I'd hoped the poison master would have some value, but like most men in the world, he did not. What is your next plan of action?"

Finn leaned back in her chair and told her about interrogating Kol's associates. She'd already asked Anabeltilia to set it up.

Emeraude nodded. "This sounds like as good a place as any to start. I expect you to report back to me as soon as those meetings are over. Understood? If I am going to get you out of this position I expect results."

Finn downed the café and wiped her mouth with the back of her hand, her mind far away. She couldn't get Ignacio out of her head.

"Don't you have any rum?"

Emeraude stared at her. "It's the morning."

"I know that," she bit out. Before Emeraude could respond, everything that had bubbled inside Finn last night came to a head. She grabbed the cup and tossed it at the wall, feeling a brief moment of satisfaction at hearing it shatter.

Emeraude looked at her, calm in the face of the sudden destruction. "Are you all right, Face Thief?" she asked. "You look like you've seen a ghost."

"*Have* you seen a ghost?" Ignacio asked, suddenly beside her. "Or have you seen your reality?"

Finn gritted her teeth, refusing to look the apparition in the face. "Can I ask you a question?" she asked.

Emeraude looked at her with concern, which only made Finn want to disappear into a dark, deep hole. "Of course."

"Your husband . . . ," Finn began as she wrung her hands in her lap. "Do you ever still hear him? Or see him?"

"You're speaking of my dead husband?"

"Sí."

"The one I killed?"

"Yes," Finn said. "Him. Do you still see him?"

Emeraude looked at her for a long moment before piling a small plate high with cinnamon cookies and pushing it toward Finn. "Every day."

Finn felt the blood drain from her face. "Cada día? You can't be serious."

Emeraude only nodded, looking strangely at peace. "A day hasn't passed where I haven't heard his voice in my head calling me worthless or felt him shake his head at the freedoms I gained when I took his life."

Finn's throat had gone bone dry. She hadn't expected that answer, hadn't expected the possibility that Ignacio would be living inside her head for the rest of her days—months, sure, maybe years, but not forever.

"The bond between a father and a daughter never dies, Mija," Ignacio tutted. "A little stab in the back can only do so much."

Finn shook her head, as if Ignacio were a bit of water caught in her ear. "Then how do you live?" she demanded, her voice more desperate than she'd intended. "How do you go on with him following you around?"

Her breathing ragged, Finn didn't move when the mobster reached across the table and took her hand.

"Ay, muchacha, let me tell you a hard truth. We are all haunted houses, full of the ghosts of our pasts. The ghosts of men who have wronged us and told us that we were born nothing, are nothing, and will die nothing."

Finn tore her hand away. It was all getting too close, too personal, and the more Emeraude spoke, the more she was rubbed raw and bloody.

"Just as the ones who love us leave an indelible mark on our spirits, so do those who hurt us. We turn to the voices of the former when we need guidance and support, but the voices of the latter tend to rise and swell when we doubt ourselves, when we hate ourselves. When we are taking steps to better ourselves and do what's right, that's when those voices speak up and make us stray from our best path."

"What do I do to stop it?" Finn asked, her voice thick.

"You keep going. Keep putting space between you and them and eventually the voice will quiet down."

"But it never goes away?" Finn asked, scrubbing at her eyes with the back of her hand.

"No." Emeraude shook her head. "Not completely. But you will reach a point where you only hear it when you are making the right choices in life. Now when I hear Manolo, I smile."

"Why?" Finn asked.

"Because when I hear him trying to cut me down, I know that I am rising higher than he ever thought I could. When he tells you to stop," Emeraude said with a blazing look, "you keep going."

Finn nodded, her eyes still stinging, but when she looked around her, Ignacio was gone.

At least for now.

As Finn walked out of Emeraude's chambers, the parchment in her pocket began to warm. Finn didn't want to read it, didn't want to have to answer if the prince asked why she'd run away last night like a child.

Muttering a curse, Finn unfolded the parchment.

Another murder in the Pinch last night. Is there anything I can do to help you with interviewing Kol's people? I want to do everything I can to stop this.

Finn's eyes widened. That had not been what she was expecting. She quickly scribbled back that she could handle interviewing Kol's people on her own. After all, the prince had a summit to run; she couldn't rely on him to show up for a slew of interviews. Yes, that's why Finn told him he didn't need to come to the interviews. It'd be rude to ask that of him when he was so busy with the summit.

Not because the memory of standing in the bruxo's triangle with him made her nervous. Never that.

Finn hurried back to the Pinch, where she was certain Anabeltilia was putting another red tack on their map.

25

THE HUNTER AND THE PREY

"We hope to prove that Englass will make an excellent partner in trade. There are many unique exports that can only be found in our kingdom," Marsden droned from where he stood before the great oval table. Half the seats were taken up by the Englassen royals, their advisors, and other dignitaries. The other half belonged to the Castallanos. "As you all must know," Marsden continued haughtily, "Englass has some of the finest timber in the world . . ."

Alfie wondered if this was how Luka felt just before he fell asleep during history lectures. He scowled. Luka had been annoyingly flippant this morning when Alfie asked him where he'd gone last night. Alfie had caught him sneaking back in just before breakfast, bruised and stinking of alcohol. Now, though they sat beside each other at this boring meeting, it felt as if there was a vast chasm between them.

The second day of the summit had just begun. This morning was the very first of the meetings between the two kingdoms. Alfie, as well as the Castallano economists, had already done their

presentation on what Castallan had to offer should trade reopen—
everything from sugarcane to mangoes to an endless list of spices
and herbs native to their land.

As they privately took breakfast before the meeting (while Luka
nursed his hangover in his rooms), his parents had warned him that
this meeting would be far from eventful.

"Mijo, this meeting is about setting the table, not eating the
meal."

"What do you mean?" Alfie tucked into his breakfast of yucca,
fried eggs, and avocado.

"Today we will discuss how we can help one another should
we successfully reach an agreement to reopen trade," his mother
explained, spooning a bit of avena into her mouth. "The Englassen
royals know that we are going to ask them to dismantle their caste
system, but before we officially do so, we must show them why it's
worth the trouble on their part."

"Of course," Alfie said, his voice rough. "We have to convince
them that it's a good idea to stop enslaving their own people."

His mother shot him a look.

"I know, I know." Alfie sighed, remembering what they'd told
him after the banquet. "Less emotion, more negotiation, but isn't
this unnecessarily beating around the bush? Wouldn't it be better to
leap in headfirst?"

King Bolivar shook his head. "Think of us as the hunter and
Englass as the skittish prey. Is it more effective to run after it, arms
outstretched, or lay your trap and wait?"

Alfie couldn't argue with that, so now he sat in this unsurpris-
ingly boring meeting, understanding that though it felt unnecessary,

it was, in its way, just as important as the meetings about the actual dismantling of the caste system.

Luka's head lolled onto his shoulder. He was asleep, mouth wide open.

"Luka," Alfie hissed, righting him in his chair.

Luka startled awake with a yelp.

Marsden paused mid-sentence. "Do you have a question, Master Luka?"

Luka quickly threw on his signature charming grin. "Absolutely not. I'm just so excited about timber. By all means, Prince Marsden, carry on."

Alfie looked down at his lap to hide his face until Marsden continued his presentation.

"Tired from your late night?" Alfie muttered.

"Are we still talking about that?" Luka sniped back.

Alfie crossed his arms, looking pointedly away from his cousin.

After last night's murder, Alfie had tried to think of ne t steps on his own. But he'd come up with nothing aside from waitiıg on Luka's contact for a meeting with the Tattooed King and seeing if Finn's interviews with Kol's associates led to anything. She'd written on their parchment that she was hosting the meetings today and would get back to him if she learned anything of note.

Alfie's stomach tightened at the thought of her. Last night, something had bloomed between them while they stood in that triangle, and everything inside him told him to pull her close, to kiss her. It had seemed as if she'd wanted to, and then suddenly she'd lurched away like a child who'd gotten too close to a hot stove.

Had he misread the situation? Should he apologize?

Alfie straightened, chiding himself. Now was not the time to focus on an almost-kiss, or any kiss for that matter. Though it had been a while since he'd last had one. . . . Alfie shook his head. He and Finn had a mystery to solve and a murderous syndicate to find. Clearly, he'd misunderstood her, and while he preferred to talk things through, bringing it up would only embarrass her. She would just change the subject. He'd pretend it hadn't happened for her sake.

Alfie started as Marsden and the Englassen advisors finished their presentation and the room sounded with polite applause.

King Bolivar stood with a jovial smile. "This morning has been most fruitful. We have learned much about how we might help each other as future allies." Then his face grew a shade more serious. "We look forward to speaking soon about what compromises must be made in order to make these economic proposals a reality."

The mood in the room shifted slightly.

"Of course," King Alistair said, his voice as stoic as ever. "We know that such a prosperous future comes at a cost. We do not shy away from discussing this."

Alfie's eyebrows rose. It was a strange way to discuss compromise. The Englassen king had made it clear that he believed Englass would be losing more than it could gain through this. Alistair seemed to think that freeing the enslaved Englassens was an annoyance, a cost to him. How could he not think of them as people with lives he'd stolen when he'd deemed them unworthy of magic? How could anyone listen to him speak about the suffering of his own people with such flippancy? It made Alfie all the more certain that this summit had to go well. Lives were at stake.

While Alfie was silently fuming, King Bolivar didn't miss a

beat. "Very well; tomorrow morning we shall begin discussing the exchange of scholarship between Castallano and Englassen bruxos. Until then."

Alfie didn't know how his father managed to keep his cool. That gene had certainly skipped a generation.

With the meeting over, Englassens and Castallanos alike began filing out of the room.

"I'm going to take a nap until tonight's art exhibition," Luka said with a yawn. They all had free time now until the evening. "You'll wake me if something of importance comes up?"

"How can I wake you if you're never in the palace?" Alfie asked, his tone short.

Luka's jaw tightened. "Just find me if you need me. I'll be around tonight."

Alfie bristled. How kind of Luka to grace him with his presence for the night. "Fine."

With that, Luka sauntered out of the room and Alfie followed. Without Luka to distract him, he wanted nothing more than to disappear to a quiet place where no one of consequence would find him. Where there would be no one he had to impress with his political prowess, no one he had to smile at even if they made him uncomfortable. Just him and silence.

The answer came to mind without hesitation—the library.

Once he got there, he could write to Finn and ask if she'd discovered anything—and also see if she was okay. The way she'd left his rooms last night didn't sit right with him.

"Prince Alfehr," Marsden called from behind him as a flood of royals and dignitaries exited the meeting room.

Alfie resisted the urge to curse under his breath. Finn was rubbing off on him a bit too much. He turned to greet the Englassen prince. "Yes, Prince Marsden."

Marsden came to an awkward halt before Alfie, his arms stiffly at his sides. Marsden constantly gave the impression that he was trying to be jovial but didn't quite know how. Perhaps Alfie had judged him too harshly at first. Perhaps his stiffness was anxiety, not haughtiness.

Marsden cleared his throat. "I only wanted to say that your presentation on the ways in which importing Castallano sugarcane into Englass would benefit both countries was quite well said."

Alfie's brows rose in surprise. "Thank you, Prince Marsden. The discussion you led on Englass's timber trade was riveting." It was not. They both had presented extremely boring information and Alfie had a feeling that they both knew it, but this was part of the game, part of the point of a peace summit. They needed to thaw the ice between their nations after generations of bad blood, and though the conversation was awkward, Alfie was comforted to see Marsden trying.

"And I hope you and your family enjoy yesterday's gift," Marsden said, clasping his hands behind his back.

The thought of the stolen documents brought Alfie's opinion of the Englassen prince right back down to barely tolerable.

His mother's words sounded in his head. *If you let your emotions get the best of you, then you will fail the people you hope to protect.*

But Finn's fiery voice chased his mother's out with a *Forget about propriety, Prince. Punch him in the face.*

Alfie pushed that last suggestion away.

"Of course," Alfie said through gritted teeth. "We appreciate your generosity."

Marsden nodded, looking pleased, and Alfie wished he could say something to wipe the smug look off his face. But he wasn't Finn; he was a prince. He knew better, even though it was painfully annoying to know better. The two bowed to each other and Alfie tried his best not to rush away before anyone else could try to talk to him.

As Alfie finally strode into the library, the tension in his shoulders subsided at the sight of the books, and of so many worlds left unexplored. Until his eyes found Princess Vesper seated at his favorite reading desk, a stack of books beside her.

He held back a sigh. It seemed he couldn't escape the Englassen royals. The last thing he wanted was to have to keep up political appearances for another minute. He couldn't even rely on Luka anymore as someone to talk to when he was frustrated, and now he couldn't rely on the library as a safe space either. Alfie began to back out of the library, but, of course, the moment he moved, she saw him.

"Prince Alfehr," she said, standing and dropping into a curtsy. "I trust you had an informative trade meeting."

Alfie had to stop himself from wincing. There was that political small talk again. He strode to her desk and bowed deeply. "Yes, it was very eye-opening." He'd nearly fallen asleep, so in actuality it was eye-closing, but he knew better than to say that.

Vesper looked about the library, which was empty aside from its attendants, before saying, "It's quite all right; I know it was boring. That is why I did not attend. I have no desire to hear my brother wax poetic about Englassen timber."

Alfie stared, surprised.

"That's one of the perks of being the spare and not the heir," she admitted, tracing her finger along the page of the book in front of her.

Alfie looked away from her and at the shelves of books around them. He could still hear Dez's laugh whenever he stepped in here. "I was the spare once, until I wasn't," he said quietly.

Vesper's face grew tight. He could tell that she knew she'd said the wrong thing.

"I apologize. I didn't mean to speak so flippantly," she said. "My condolences on the loss of your late brother."

"Thank you," Alfie said, moving to sit at the empty armchair, but he didn't want to stay on that topic any longer. The last thing he needed to do was cry in front of her. "I can't say that I don't miss being the spare sometimes." She and her brother were trying to connect with him, in their own stilted way. The least he could do was reciprocate. "It would have been nice to be here instead of talking about the potential grain trade between our kingdoms."

Vesper exhaled sharply through her nose, a hint at the laugh she was holding in, and Alfie couldn't help but give a bark of laughter himself. He hadn't expected the quiet princess to have a sense of humor. "Have you found anything interesting to read in our library?"

Vesper nodded, flipping the book over so that Alfie could see the title.

"Our nations have been enemies for so long that our resources on Castallano history are very few. I've been lost in your histories all morning."

Alfie smiled. It was nice to see such an effort on her part to understand him and his people.

"The feeling is mutual. Perhaps we could trade books sometime. I would be grateful to read up on Englassen history."

Vesper pounded her fist to her chest. "It would be my honor."

A surprisingly comfortable silence passed over them until Vesper broke it. "Prince Alfehr, there is something I wish to talk to you about. If you have a moment," she said quietly.

Alfie straightened, wondering if the topic would be something formal and political like what he'd spoken about in the meeting. "Of course."

Vesper looked at him for a long moment before she spoke again. "I just wanted to say . . ." She clasped her hands in front of her. "I'm excited by the prospect of finally ending the caste system," she blurted.

Alfie stared at her, willing his mouth to stay closed. He hadn't expected to hear any of the Englassen royals say that aloud. After all, they benefited off the magical enslavement of their lower class. Yet she'd just said it.

"You are?" Alfie asked. Then he caught himself. "I'm sorry. It is rude of me to assume your stance on this issue. Please forgive me, Princess Vesper."

"No," she said. "Please don't apologize. It's more than fair of you to assume otherwise."

Alfie was still so confused by her confession that he could barely string a sentence together. "May I ask why?"

Vesper's face grew solemn then as she folded her hands in her lap. "Well—"

The doors to the library opened and Prince Marsden strode in, and by the way Vesper's eyes widened at the sight of him, Alfie knew she did not want him to hear what they were talking about.

"There you are, Vesper." Marsden bowed to Alfie. "Prince Alfehr, so nice to see you again so soon."

Alfie returned the bow. "And you."

"Father and Mother are looking for us. Did you get the books I asked for?" he said with the tone of a man speaking to a disappointing servant. Alfie bristled at the way he addressed her.

"Of course," Vesper said, pointing to the stack of books next to her. "Right here."

"Very well," Marsden said. "Let's be off, then. Mother and Father are waiting."

Alfie was surprised Marsden didn't snap his fingers at her.

Marsden collected the books and held his arm out to Vesper. Her eyes flickered to Alfie for a moment before she took his arm.

"It was nice to see you, Prince Alfehr," she said with a curtsy.

"The feeling is mutual," Alfie said with a bow as Marsden led her away.

As the Englassen royals left, Marsden's eyes darted between Alfie and Vesper, a dash of suspicion on his face. But when he noticed Alfie's eyes on him, Marsden's expression changed to one of nonchalance.

He gave Alfie a nod and then walked out the door.

THE LAST IDIOT OF THE DAY

While the prince sat through his meeting, Finn was in the middle of a series of her own.

She gave a tongue-curling yawn as the moon rose on the second night of the summit. She couldn't remember the last time she had been *this* bored, yet the man just kept on talking. She found that men usually couldn't tell when no one wanted to listen to them anymore. Or did they just ignore the fact that no one wanted to listen to them? Honestly, she didn't know.

"Stop," Finn said, raising a hand while she leaned her elbow on Kol's desk. "You don't have the information I'm looking for." She cocked her head toward the door. "Go."

While the prince and Bathtub Boy were going to some art exhibition tonight, whatever the hell that was, Finn was stuck in her office trying to get any useful information she could out of Kol's contacts. But she'd been interviewing all day and had gotten nowhere. Now she was stuck listening to Kol's weapons supplier talk about her weapons of choice—"Scissors. Really big scissors. She liked weapons where, after you stab someone and the blade's all up in there, you can open the scissors and stab them even more, from the *inside*"—which was both disgusting and interesting, but not what Finn was looking for. She wanted to figure out Kol's relation to Los Toros, not what her favorite toys were.

The weapons dealer gave a nervous laugh. "But there is so much more for me to tell you about weaponry! There's artistry! They are more than just tools with sharp bits—"

"You know, I'd have to disagree," Finn said as she slammed a dagger into the desk and stood, leaning over the table. "I'm simple. I think the sharp bit is what makes the weapon. Sharp bits give so many things the potential to be lethal." Before the man could speak, Finn pointed at the desk's left corner. "For example, this desk has a pointed corner. Seems like nothing, right? Nada. But what if I slammed your head into that point over and over and over again?"

Finn watched the man's Adam's apple bob. Sweat beaded his thin upper lip.

"Or let's say—hypothetically, of course." Finn smiled. "If I were to throw you out a window. Like the one right there." Finn pointed to the far end of the room. "You would fall and land terribly and then your bones would break. They'd become sharp bits inside you. Some would get so sharp and bent that they'd shoot right out of your skin, stabbing you from the inside out."

The man's chest was heaving now, his body quaking in the chair.

Finn rolled her eyes. "Get out before I make testing your own weapons on you my new distraction."

Without a word, the thin man scampered out of the room, his bag clanging with endless types of blades that he'd so kindly described to Finn. In great detail.

"Anabeltilia," Finn called as she banged her head against Kol's desk. "Send in the next idiot!"

"The next idiot is the last idiot," Anabeltilia said, leaning against the door frame. "The one you've been most excited about."

Finn sat up at the desk. In looking through Kol's papers, she'd found that Kol had been funneling money to someone for years. All in secret, no names, just a silent money trail from Kol to this unknown person. Finn had tasked la Familia with tracking them down and they had.

Finn was sure that this would be the start of finally unraveling the maddening mystery of Kol. It had to be.

"Send them in," Finn said.

The man was short and wore a wide-brimmed hat that covered his eyes.

This, Finn thought. *This is what an important person looks like. This is the person who is going to give me the information I need.*

"You are the new Madre?" he asked, his voice quiet.

"Sí," Finn said. "And you're here to explain your relationship with Kol to me."

The man shifted in his seat. "Our relationship was private."

Finn could hardly stand the wait. This was it. It had to be.

She lunged across the desk and gripped the man by his cloak. "I am the new Madre. You will tell me the truth or you will suffer, entiendes?"

The man's thick mustache twitched. "I was sworn to secrecy."

"What are spilled secrets to a dead woman?" Finn pressed a

dagger to his throat. "I could cut your throat and you could go ask her yourself."

The man's lips quivered before he finally nodded. "Fine, I'll tell you." Then he pointed at the ground just to the left of Finn's desk. "The answer is there, just beneath the floorboards."

Finn squinted at the man suspiciously before stepping over to where he pointed. She tapped the ground with the toe of her boot. It made a hollow sound—the sound of hidden treasure.

Finn got on her knees and used her dagger to pry the floorboard up. With one great pull, it finally broke free, falling away like a loose baby tooth.

What would she find? Letters between Kol and Los Toros? Secret plans? Maps to their hideaways? Her heart pounding, Finn stared into the dark space beneath the floor, her eyes adjusting until she finally saw what the mobster had hidden. Finn reached in and grabbed one.

"*Teacups?*" In her hand was a mint-green teacup with a silver handle. It was decorated with elephants. Oddly, most of them had an elephant design. "Kol had a stash of teacups?"

The man nodded, his eyes darting back and forth around the room as if he feared Kol's ghost would appear to punish him. "She had a love for delicate things, but collecting such objects would be bad for her reputation. She commissioned me in secret, paying me handsomely for my work."

Finn stared at the man, slack-jawed. "So that's it, then?" she asked, flabbergasted. "You made teacups for Kol. That was your secret relationship."

"Oh well, not just teacups, of course," he said. "There were saucers too. The occasional plate. Obviously, she had a thing for elephants. To each their own! She often asked them to be made in pairs so that she could gift the teacups to her associates. Sometimes she'd have me inscribe little messages or images on them for colleagues, or occasionally lovers. I must say it got a little spicy at times—"

Before the man could finish his sentence, Finn grabbed him by the collar and slammed him against the nearest wall.

"You were the last idiot. The very last one, and this—this is what you tell me?!" She pulled him forward before slamming him into the wall again.

"I—I beg your pardon," the man sputtered, his glasses askew. "I was one of Kol's most important persons. The only one above me was Luis Manuel with the weird *propio*."

Finn's fingers loosened on the man's cloak. "Who?"

The man looked away. "I shouldn't say—"

"I will break a bone for every teacup I find in this shithole," Finn growled.

"Luis Manuel Dejesus!" the man yelped. "He has the ability to know someone's *propio* just by looking at them. Kol called upon him often. That's all I know, I swear!"

Finn blinked. It wasn't exactly related to Los Toros, but it was something. Plus, the murders carried out by Los Toros had been done using strange *propios*. Maybe the man could help identify the killers? Or at least point her in the right direction.

She let go of the man's cloak. "You get to live, but only if you run very, very fast."

The man dashed out the door, barreling into Anabeltilia as he went.

"For the record," Anabeltilia said, rubbing her shoulder, "I had no idea about the teacups. Or the *propio*-seeing guy."

"Find him and set up a meeting as soon as possible," Finn commanded. She'd need to tell the prince about this new lead. When she looked up, she saw Anabeltilia still standing there. "I'm done with idiots for the day, so you can go too."

After Anabeltilia shrugged and walked out the door, Finn pulled the parchment from her pocket. She pressed her quill to the paper but couldn't bring herself to write out of embarrassment. She hoped Alfie wouldn't bring up what happened with the triangle last night, but maybe the best way to move on from that was for her to start a new conversation.

Finn stared at the parchment before cursing at herself. "Just get it over with."

> *No new lead. Might have something in a couple days.*
> *Anything on your end?*

The *propio* seer was a good idea but hardly a lead worth writing to him about until Anabeltilia could find him and set up a meeting.

She tossed the parchment on the table and looked away from it, drumming her fingernails on her thighs. Within minutes the prince's elegant script appeared on the parchment.

> *Unfortunately I have nothing of importance to report.*

Hopefully Luka's contact will secure the meeting with
the Tattooed King soon.

Finn tapped her quill on her desk, unsure of what to say. Since she'd first arrived in San Cristóbal they'd seen each other every night, but there was no real reason to do so tonight. Did he still want her to come?

She grimaced at the memory of what had happened last time she was in his rooms. How she'd heard Ignacio and fled like a child. She shouldn't go see him. There was no reason to. Finn chewed on a dirty fingernail before scribbling on the parchment once more.

Should we meet tonight?

Waiting for the response was a strange kind of madness. Finn paced the room, her eyes shifting back to the parchment with every other step until a message appeared.

If you like.

Finn stared at that. What would it mean if she said she wanted to? Did he want her to want to? Did it matter to him at all? Why was she the one who had to decide? Why did it feel like they both had things to say that they simply weren't saying?

With an exasperated sigh, Finn scribbled another message.

Fine, see you some other time.

After a few very long minutes, Alfie responded.

Very well.

"Very well," Finn said, mimicking his stupid, bookish voice as she flopped back into her desk chair. "Very well and very stupid."

THE ART EXHIBITION

Alfie strode down the famous Castallano beach, Punto Higuey, where the art exhibition was being staged.

The second night of the summit was finally coming to a close, and while he wasn't looking forward to more smiling and making small talk, he was thankful for a chance to distract himself from everything with his kingdom's stunning art.

The white sand was covered with tents of brilliant colors filled with works of art from each kingdom. Palm trees and mango trees adorned with glowing candles were planted throughout the area. The sand had been magicked so that it would be easier to walk on.

Englassens and Castallanos alike moved through the beach, observing pieces of art from paintings to sculpture to tapestries. Servants weaved through the groups of guests with rum, vino, and Castallano finger foods.

No matter how exquisite the pieces were, it was hard to focus on the beauty before him instead of his endless anxieties. Despite the reward for information on Los Toros, would there be yet another horrific murder done in their name tonight? His family was on edge, waiting in case there was another bloody scene to be hidden from their guests.

And then there were his nerves about the strange exchange he and Finn had had through the parchment. Why had it felt as if neither of them was saying what they actually wanted to say? Had she decided not to visit tonight because he'd made her uncomfortable when he'd tried to kiss her? He'd left the decision up to her, but maybe that had been the wrong way to handle this. Maybe she'd wanted him to say that he *wanted* her to come over.

Alfie sighed deeply through his nose. He wouldn't know how to fix it until he saw her face-to-face again. He was surely better at communicating in person, right? Or so he hoped.

Tired of aimlessly and anxiously moving past the art pieces without really looking at them, Alfie coasted to a stop in front of an enormous painting.

He took in the colorful figures on the canvas. It was a painting of the pantheon of the gods. Castallan had an endless array of gods to worship, from minor ones like the god of sewing and the goddess of rum and spirits, to the gods of legend like Luz, the goddess of light. Each one was recognizable by the garb they wore and the wild colors of their skin. Some deities were brown like Alfie; others were blue, green, magenta. But only one was obsidian, tinged faintly with blue. The color of a dark night.

Sombra.

While the other gods were drawn in the heavens above Mundo,

Sombra was drawn falling from the sky, cast away by his kin. His face twisted in fury, he raised a fist at the heavens, as if cursing them for disregarding him.

Alfie's heart began to race at the sight of the humans below, unaware of the darkness that would befall them at Sombra's hand. Had the gods known what would happen when they tossed Sombra aside? Had they known that generations upon generations later, Alfie would release him and cause unimaginable harm to his people? Goose bumps rose on his flesh at the memory of Luka whimpering in his arms, and Sombra's hypnotic voice offering to help, to stop his cousin's suffering.

For a price. One that his people had paid dearly.

"What are we looking at here?" Luka said, popping up beside Alfie, a glass of vino in his hand. Luka tilted his head and scanned the portrait.

They hadn't spoken since they'd sniped at the meeting this morning. Luka had a habit of pretending all was well instead of talking about what was wrong, and Alfie couldn't help but go along with it. With Sombra's image before him, he didn't want to fight with Luka; he just wanted to be with his friend.

Luka stared at the painting, his eyes narrowing at the sight of Sombra. "Nope," he announced, taking Alfie by the shoulders, guiding him away from the portrait and down a lane of new art pieces as they smiled and waved at guests. "And we're circling, and we're mingling, and we're not looking at that painting and getting sad."

"I know, I know," Alfie said, grateful for Luka's push. "But do you ever think about it?" he asked him, his voice quiet as his shadow drew close around his feet. "About him?"

Luka hadn't seen everything that he and Finn had, but he'd been there for that final battle in the palace. He'd seen the stone hands come to life, the terrifying dragon. He'd seen Finn being possessed by Sombra's will. But even though Luka had always pointedly avoided the conversation, ever since Alfie had seen his gravehopper tattoo, he knew that something had undoubtedly changed in Luka since Sombra.

Luka looked at him for a long moment, his smile slipping.

"More vino, Prince Alfehr and Master Luka?" a servant asked.

His easy grin back in place, Luka winked at the servant. "You're right on time." He downed the rest of his wine and exchanged his empty glass for a full one, then hurried away.

Alfie followed close behind as Luka swiped two tostones topped with sautéed shrimp from a servant's tray and popped them into his mouth. Whenever Luka didn't want to talk about something, he tended to eat and drink more than he should.

Luka closed his eyes and hummed with satisfaction. "See that right there, that's art."

"Luka," Alfie said, gripping him by the arm. "You won't talk to me. Does it have to do with why you're disappearing all the time, fighting in the Pinch—"

"Because I don't want to talk to you about it," Luka said quietly, his smile pasted on as guests lingered around nearby paintings. "When everything happened with Dezmin, you disappeared on a ship for months because you didn't want to talk about it. Would it kill you to extend the same courtesy to me?"

Alfie opened his mouth to speak but couldn't find the words.

Luka was right. He himself had needed space after Dezmin had been taken. If Luka also needed time to think things through, then the least Alfie could do was give him that time.

"I'm sorry," Alfie said. He didn't want to let it go, but it didn't feel like he had a choice. He hadn't exactly been reasonable when he was going through losing Dezmin. "You're right."

With a huff, Luka turned toward the painting they'd drifted to a stop in front of. "I know." He shot Alfie a look, then rolled his eyes. "Calmate. You looking all concerned takes the fun out of being right."

Alfie gave a snort of laughter. Luka would talk to him when he was ready, and all would be well again. He had to believe that. As the two came to pause before a painting, so did Marsden and Vesper, with James the servant trailing close behind.

They bowed to one another and said their greetings, then an awkward silence passed among them before Luka began.

"How are you enjoying the art exhibition?" Luka asked jovially, looking at the two royals but making sure to meet eyes with James as well.

James looked as if he wanted to wish himself invisible. Alfie had a feeling that being around Marsden made most people wish they were invisible. Taking a second look at James, Alfie noticed that he looked a bit pale, almost sick. He hoped he was all right.

"It's beautiful," Princess Vesper said. "We know so little about each other artistically. It's a wonderful chance to learn."

Marsden nodded stiffly beside her. "Agreed, it is quite educational."

Another silence.

"Who are the people in this piece?" Vesper asked.

The painting before them was of the families that rose to prominence after Englass had been expelled from the country. Alfie winced. This was the wrong painting to discuss with the Englassens.

Alfie could see Luka stifling a grimace before saying, "These are the forefathers and foremothers of our country. They were instrumental in, erm . . . reclaiming Castallan."

The strokes of the painting were bold and bright—the faces of their ancestors shined with pride, but were also drawn and tired, drained from a rebellion that claimed so many lives. Alfie could only think of the vanishing cloak again and of how instrumental it had been to their freedom. Now it was long lost to Los Toros—a group that thought his family didn't deserve to have it. Alfie felt a wave of shame as he met the gazes of his painted forefathers. Would he ever get the cloak back? Would they think him unworthy of it like Los Toros?

"It is . . . ," Marsden began slowly, "very vivid." He looked at Alfie and Luka, and Alfie could tell he was trying to decide whether he should apologize or say something to soothe the tension. Seeming to think better of it, he closed his mouth instead.

Alfie was annoyed by his silence, but part of him knew he would be just as annoyed if Marsden had tried to say something repentant. What would mere words accomplish in the face of all that had happened between their people? It seemed there was no right answer.

Vesper gripped her brother's arm. "There's still so much art to see. We'll let you two enjoy this one." She shot Alfie a look that told him she knew what he was thinking and that the only answer was to give each other space. He was grateful for it.

"Come along, James," Marsden barked, and Alfie watched the boy walk away, his feet padding on the sand. He could've sworn that Luka's eyes were following him.

"Well," Luka said. "That was fun."

"Only five more days," Alfie murmured, feeling the stress knotting in his back and shoulders. His eyes clung to the painting. He knew his parents had chosen it with purpose, to make it clear that Castallan was proud of its past. But the longer Alfie looked at the artwork, the more he feared that their kingdoms would never become civil.

Alfie stared at the looks on the faces of Castallan's forefathers and foremothers. His stomach tightened uncomfortably as he wondered what they would think of his peace summit.

"I know what you're thinking," Luka murmured. "Don't go there. You'll never be able to know what they would've thought about where we are now. We have to do what's right for the kingdom today instead of worrying about the past."

Alfie stared at Luka. "When did you get so wise?"

Luka shrugged. "I always have been. I just didn't want to intimidate you."

Alfie laughed.

"I know you don't care for him," Luka muttered. "Especially after his gift. But I think we ought to try to spend some time alone with Prince Marsden and Princess Vesper. Something more casual."

Alfie's brows rose. "You really think that's a good idea?"

"Trying to get to know each other is hard enough, let alone doing so with everyone's parents watching and generations of bad blood hanging over us," Luka said. "If we want this to work, it might be better if we can get to know each other outside all this."

Alfie nodded. Maybe freeing themselves from the eyes of their parents and politics would help. That is, if he could get through a full conversation with Marsden.

At the thought of the prince, Alfie remembered that he still hadn't told Luka about his conversation with Vesper in the library.

"Luka," he said, leaning closer to him to make sure no one else would hear. "Vesper told me that she's excited for the dissolution of the caste system."

"*Qué?*" Luka reeled back, nearly knocking over a servant with a tray of wine. "I didn't know any noble Englassens actually felt that way."

"Neither did I," Alfie said. He wished Marsden hadn't interrupted them. It had seemed like there was more she wanted to say.

Luka shook his head in disbelief. "What exactly did she say?"

As the exhibition wound down, Alfie explained the conversation to Luka. "It felt like she wanted to say more, but then Marsden showed up." Alfie remembered the look Marsden had given him. "I don't think he liked seeing her and me alone together."

Luka snorted as they paused before a painting of the Englassen countryside. "Honestly, I think he just dislikes most things."

"Ladies and gentlemen," Alfie's mother called from where she stood at the center of the exhibition. Bolivar stood beside her, his hand in hers. "We would like to close tonight's exhibition with a fireworks show that will honor the beauty of both our kingdoms. We hope you enjoy!" She gestured to the skies above with a flourish as the guests applauded.

The fireworks burst into life, lighting the sky in a myriad of colors. It reminded Alfie of the realm of magic and all the hues he'd seen there, and the screams he'd heard. Alfie pushed those thoughts away. He could relax for one night. Well, at least he could try.

The fireworks burst into the shapes of famous Englassen animals, such as bears and hounds. Alfie spotted a Castallano quil-bear bounding across the clouds. Castallano orange blossoms and Englassen snowdrops bloomed among the stars, their petals glimmering. The show was a sight to behold. Distracting enough that for a moment Alfie let himself release his worries and look at it with awe, the way he and Dezmin would lie on their backs in the garden and stargaze with absolute wonder on their faces. His heart both warmed and broke at the memory.

Alfie waited for the final planned image to appear in the sky—the Castallano and the Englassen flags, side by side in solidarity. But that never appeared. When the last fireworks burst in the air, they took the form of a bull's face, its nostrils flared.

Los Toros.

Alfie's eyes found his father, who was already speaking to a guardsman. Were Los Toros here, waiting to strike? If so, surely the attack would've started now?

Or maybe they were simply sending a message—that they were not done yet.

Not skipping a beat, Luka began clapping loudly after the snarling bull firework faded. He smiled broadly at the nearest Englassen guests. "Lovely, wasn't it?"

Alfie could spot his mother shooting him and Luka a look of relief as she clapped along, but he knew what was on her mind.

The bounty may have postponed another murder, but it clearly hadn't completely scared off Los Toros. If they were bold enough to infiltrate a royal exhibition to tamper with the fireworks, how long until they did something worse? What would the third day of the summit have in store for them tomorrow?

CLOSE COMBAT

"Don't be such a scaredy gato," Dezmin teased as he pulled himself onto the tree branch, his bare feet scuttling up the trunk.

"I'm not scared." Alfie watched him from the ground, digging his heels into the earth. "I just don't like being so high up."

Dezmin smiled at him from an even higher branch. He had the agility of a monkey when he was in a tree. "Get used to it, hermanito. You're going to be as tall as this tree one day."

Alfie felt his face go hot. Mami and Papi had been saying how fast he was growing. How he might soon be taller than Dez. His brother had never taken offense to the comparison. He'd just grinned and said that if Alfie got taller than him, then he could stand on Alfie's shoulders to climb even bigger trees.

When Alfie looked up next, Dez was so high, Alfie could hardly see him. The tree had stretched up into a mountain.

"Dez!" he shouted, his voice high with adolescence. "Come down! Ten cuidado!"

Dez laughed from his perch in the tree. "Be careful and be

boring mean the same thing, Alfie."

But then Dezmin rocked forward on the branch and he was careening down to Alfie, his arms windmilling.

He slammed into the ground, and a terrible bone-shattering crack sounded in the air.

Covered in blood, Dez shrieked in agony, gripping at the exposed bone poking through his skin. The scream was unending, carrying through the air until all the light was snuffed out and there was only darkness and the sound of his brother in excruciating pain.

A series of loud knocks woke Alfie, and he snapped upright in his bed, soaked in sweat.

He stared at his door, trying to catch his breath. "One minute," he croaked as he climbed out of bed on the third morning of the summit.

When was the last time he'd dreamed about Dez falling out of that tree in the palace gardens? They'd been so small back then. When Dez had broken his leg that day, it was one of the few times Alfie had seen his brother look afraid. It wasn't a memory he liked to revisit.

He opened the door only to have a lively-looking Luka rush through.

"Guess what?" he said as Alfie closed the door, still too dazed to speak. "Guess what, guess what!"

Alfie glanced at the clock. "Luka, it's so early." He was usually the early bird dragging Luka out of bed.

"No murder!" Luka nearly shouted.

"What?" Alfie asked, blinking.

"No murders by Los Toros last night!" Luka said with a wild grin. "The bounty on their heads must be scaring them!"

Alfie was almost relieved enough to forget about the nightmare. He'd been certain that the fireworks stunt last night was foreshadowing something worse. He'd expected to wake up to another murder this morning. But maybe tampering with fireworks was all they could muster with the bounty on their heads. Maybe the group was retreating, at least for the moment. Maybe they *would* be able to get through this summit in peace after all. Alfie fell back, perching on the edge of his bed.

"Thank the dioses," he mumbled. "But you must know that just because they didn't do anything murderous last night doesn't mean they're gone, Luka. It's not over. They tampered with the fireworks for a reason."

"They tampered with the fireworks because they could hardly do anything else while they hid. They probably already had that set up before the bounty was announced."

Alfie cocked his head. He hadn't thought of that. Maybe the fireworks weren't a retaliation for the bounty. Maybe that had already been in motion and now they were lying low?

"No matter what stressful thing you're thinking about, it's better than waking up to another murder. That's something worthy of celebration!"

"It's something," Alfie admitted. "But it isn't everything." At least he wouldn't have to face his parents for yet another tense meeting about corpses that had to be spirited away before the Englassens caught wind of them.

"I thought it'd be worth an early morning wake-up call," Luka laughed before staring at Alfie, his smile slipping. "Why are you so sweaty?"

Alfie didn't know if he wanted to ruin this small moment of hope by mentioning his nightmare, but he also knew that Luka could smell a lie from a mile away.

"I had a bad dream," Alfie admitted, wiping his forehead with the back of his hand. His shadow drooped at his feet, tired from the restless night. "About Dez."

Luka sat next to him and gently bumped his shoulder against Alfie's. "The same one as before?"

Back when Dez had first been lost, Alfie had had nightmare after nightmare of watching Dez fall into the black void, unable to save him, but those days had thankfully passed. "No, not exactly," Alfie said. "I dreamed of the day he broke his leg."

Luka furrowed his brow. "Back when he tried to climb the tallest tree in the palace gardens?"

Alfie nodded. "He just kept screaming and screaming in pain and everything went dark." Alfie shuddered at the memory. "I've been thinking of him so much lately."

Luka nodded. "It's only natural. This summit was his dream. Of course he would be on your mind more than usual."

"But . . . ," Alfie began. Part of him wondered if the dreams meant something. If he was doing something wrong? Maybe he wasn't doing what Dez would've wanted and that was bringing up these thoughts.

"I know you," Luka insisted, pulling Alfie away from his spiraling thoughts. "Do not overthink a bad dream. It means nothing."

Alfie sighed deeply through his nose, loosening the dream's hold on him. The longer he was awake, the hazier it got. "You're right," he said. "Thank you."

"De nada," Luka said with his signature grin. "Have you heard from Finn lately? Haven't seen her since I left you two alone the night before yesterday."

Alfie shook his head, feeling his face grow warm as Luka smirked. He hadn't had a real conversation with her, in person or otherwise, since that night when they'd stood in the triangle and she'd risen on her toes, her thumb rubbing the back of his neck. He pushed that thought away. He'd overstepped and now she was skittish. He didn't know if he should write her and tell her to come over or if he should leave her be. It had only been a day, but each time he looked at the unchanging parchment, it felt like ages.

"Not really," Alfie said, forcing a casual shrug. Luka didn't know about the triangle situation and he wanted to keep it that way. "I sent her a message about the fireworks last night. Neither of us have any new leads to share, and she's busy with la Familia."

Luka's smile widened. "Well, my contact is supposed to meet me with the information about the Tattooed King at this afternoon's cultural exhibition, so you'll have an excuse to see her tonight."

"Luka—"

"You're welcome. Now that I have delivered the news of the day, I'll take my leave." Before Alfie could admonish him, Luka was moving on. "We have another very boring meeting to get ready for and then a likely *incredibly* boring cultural exhibition in the afternoon. So, for the love of the gods, bathe and get that sweat off you or you'll scare our guests with your rancid smell." With a laugh,

Luka bounced off the bed and dashed to the doors as Alfie tossed a pillow at Luka's back.

Luka had been wrong. The meeting was actually quite interesting.

The third day of the summit began with a discussion of a potential exchange of magical scholarship between Englass and Castallan. Scholars and dueños—Paloma included—spoke about the knowledge each kingdom had to offer the other and about all they could learn about the mysteries of magic if the two kingdoms were to join forces.

Englass used magic so differently from Castallan. While Castallanos saw themselves as conduits for magic and its gifts, Englassens saw magic as a source of power to channel and control. Alfie couldn't help but marvel at the differences. It was not an interpretation of magic that he agreed with, but it was interesting nonetheless. At least to him. Meanwhile, the meeting left Luka on the verge of falling asleep for a full two hours. Only Alfie's persistent nudges kept him awake.

The Englassen scholars even mentioned that they had made impressive preliminary discoveries in their research of *propio* magic that they would be ready to share soon. Alfie was eager to hear more. He couldn't help but think of how four short months ago he'd been scouring Englass's books for a way to move Xiomara's *propio* from her body to his so he could find Dezmin. Now he simply wanted to learn for the sake of learning. It was progress.

It's forgetting about Dezmin, leaving him behind, a quiet part of his mind whispered, but Alfie let those thoughts fizzle into nothing. He had to move on.

This meeting was so placid that Alfie found himself forgetting that discussions like these were mere preparation for the meeting where they would finally ask Englass to dissolve their caste system for good. Alfie was certain *that* meeting would be far more tense. The stakes wouldn't be cultural exchange or scholarship; they would be improving the lives of thousands of enslaved Englassens. He couldn't let these less strained sessions lull him into a false sense of security. He needed to stay sharp for when the real work was to be done.

After a short post-meeting rest, the royal families boarded carriages to the Brim for the next cultural exhibition. Luka, Alfie, and his parents shared one carriage, and Alfie was happy to see there was a little less tension in the air than there had been. Of course, after yesterday's unscheduled fireworks display, they were all a bit on edge, but there was the silver lining of Los Toros falling silent for the moment.

The theme of the second cultural exhibition was war—which seemed a bit on the nose. Of course, that wasn't what it was officially called. Today's exhibition would show how each kingdom learned and applied each form of magic. Yes, there would be presentations of beautiful illusions that left viewers gaping in wonderment, but much of it would show how each nation used magic in combat.

Alfie warily asked, "If this is a peace summit, why would we have an exhibition that highlights violence?"

Luka nodded. "I hate to admit when sourpuss has a point, but he has a point."

"It would be foolish to ignore the past violence between our kingdoms," Queen Amada said. "To rule a kingdom is to understand the art of war. We honor the bloody past that led us to a peaceful present. And Englassen culture honors the ability to fight and defend oneself. This is a nod to that and an opportunity for them to showcase their own cultural feats."

Alfie nodded at that. He'd forgotten that Englassen culture took pride in sword fighting. From what he'd read, before a wedding it was customary for the families to bond through dueling and the practice of martial arts. It was all very different from what he knew.

"Also, Mijo, you are right to say that this is a peace summit, but we must give each kingdom the chance to show their strength." The king jokingly flexed a bicep. "That's how I caught your mother's attention."

"Ugh," Luka said, covering his face in embarrassment.

"Papá," Alfie said, his voice shaky with laughter. "Please."

"The old act old and the young make fun. But when we try to act young they make fun of us too," the king laughed.

"Who says we're old?" the queen huffed.

"The dictionary," Luka murmured, yelping as the queen swatted him on the arm.

"What your father means to say," the queen went on, her eyes narrowed, "is that though we are celebrating peace, it is important that we give each kingdom the opportunity to show off, to boast their militaristic strength. Though it seems counterintuitive, it helps deflate tension. War is too big an elefante in the room to ignore. Especially at a peace summit."

When they arrived, the Brim had been transformed. Instead of twisting lanes of shops and stalls, the space had been cleared to make way for grand platforms where representatives from the two nations demonstrated their finest weaponry and offensive magic.

One platform, its floor painted in the colors of the Englassen flag, featured fighters performing duels with the thin sabers that Englass was known for. Likewise, the Castallano platform showcased the mastery of the Castallano machete as well as duels fought with spoken magic and martial arts.

All around him mock battles ended in handshakes and back slaps and cheers from the audience. Everyone—except of course for Delegado Culebra and his surly-looking crew of anti-peace summit followers—looked content to learn from one another. Alfie relaxed. Maybe today would go smoothly.

And then he heard the shouting.

"*No peace for colonizers!*"

Alfie's heart sputtered. The blockades that kept the common people away from the nobles touring the cultural exhibition were suddenly overrun by protestors, many of them wearing what appeared to be a cheap imitation of Los Toros' bull masks.

"*No peace for colonizers!*"

Alfie's parents stared at one another as the guards moved to make the protestors disperse, but before they could stop them, a rotting tomato sailed through the air toward Prince Marsden.

Alfie thrust out his hand. "*Parar!*" The tomato stopped midair, just before it hit the Englassen prince. A drop of red liquid dripped onto his white cravat. Marsden stepped away from the hovering fruit, picking at the stain on his shirt as he glared at the jeering protestors.

"Guards," King Bolivar said, his voice low and controlled. "Please escort the protestors out of the exhibition. They may continue their protest off the premises." But Alfie knew that his father had said that just for show, and that the guardsmen would be taking anyone wearing Los Toros paraphernalia to the palace to be questioned later. These protocols had been decided after the first murder.

The guardsmen made quick work of the protestors, aggressively guiding them out of the exhibition area, but Alfie could not take his eyes off them. The hatred rolled off them in waves and doused him in a sticky layer of shame. By the looks of them, Alfie was sure that they must simply be copycats—not actual members of Los Toros, but common folk who took up their cause. Still, part of Alfie wondered, had any of them managed to meet members of Los Toros? Or did any of them know anything about where they were hiding? He wanted this exhibition to end so that he could go straight to the dungeons where he knew the masked protestors would be taken. His father shot him a look that said he was thinking the same thing.

Bolivar turned to the Englassens. "We apologize for that incident. Know that you are most welcome in our kingdom."

The Englassen queen raised an eyebrow. "And yet you permit your subjects to say otherwise."

A string of silence coiled tight in the air. "We allow our people the right of self-expression. What they choose to express is their own decision."

Marsden gave a surprised bark of a laugh. "So they won't be punished for their insolence?" He picked at the spot of red on his shirt. "I assumed the guards were taking them to be flogged at the very least."

Alfie stared at the Englassen prince. The protestors would only be questioned to see whether they had any information on Los Toros—if they hadn't been wearing the bull masks, they would have been left to protest in peace. They wouldn't be punished or hurt for exercising their right to protest. There would only be consequences if they were truly connected to Los Toros and the murders, but that seemed unlikely. His voice rougher and lower than he'd intended, Alfie said, "That is not our way."

It was so like an Englassen to want swift punishment for protest. After all, Marsden's people had been comfortable punishing Alfie's ancestors for generations. What would flogging a few people mean to Marsden?

He and Marsden held each other's gaze for a long moment and Alfie could feel the tension sprouting between them, like thorned flowers bursting from the ground in the heat of spring.

"The exhibition looks lovely," Vesper said awkwardly, shattering the silence, her eyes moving between Alfie and Marsden. Alfie cleared his throat and looked away from the prince.

"Shall we move on?" King Bolivar asked, motioning toward the platforms before them. The other royals followed as he led them forward, but Vesper lingered near Alfie, which in turn seemed to make Marsden linger as well.

"If only James had come along," Marsden said, frowning at his shirt. He spoke a quick word of magic to clean it. "He would have stepped in front of me and borne the brunt of the fruit."

Alfie wondered if Marsden ever thought before he spoke.

"Where is he?" Luka asked, quickly adding, "He's almost always with you; it's strange that he's not here."

"He was under the weather." Marsden shrugged. "He's a delicate thing." He tilted his head, thinking. "Why were some of those shouting people wearing bull masks?"

Alfie's throat went dry. "I have no clue," he said a little too quickly.

"Does it matter what they choose to wear?" Luka said, clearly trying to draw Marsden's attention away from the protest. "Are you looking for fashion advice?" The joke was enough to make Marsden laugh quietly. Alfie shot Luka a grateful look. "Come, Prince Marsden, there's a stall with fine Englassen sabers this way. I would love to hear your thoughts on which is best," Luka said with a forced grin.

Marsden's spine straightened with interest. "Of course," he said. "Lead the way."

Alfie mouthed *Thank you* to Luka as he led Marsden away. Luke knew Alfie better than anyone, and while Alfie was generally a calm person, Marsden seemed to bring something out of him that was decidedly *not* calm. Plus, Alfie knew that Luka wanted him and Vesper to have a moment alone so he could finally find out why she was happy to see the Englassen caste system end.

"Would you mind if I walk with you?" Vesper asked quietly. She shifted in embarrassment, her hair obscuring part of her face. Alfie felt a sudden stab of guilt. She clearly sensed the tension between him and her brother and was constantly trying to defuse it.

"Of course." He offered her his arm with a smile.

Together, with a small retinue of guards hovering around them, they passed a platform where an Englassen and a Castallano fought a friendly duel. Their blades clashed as they moved—the Englassen fighter with more structured, stiff movements while the Castallano was more fluid, dancelike.

"I hoped to get a moment alone with you so that we could

continue our talk from yesterday, in the library."

"Of course." Alfie nodded, trying to hide the curiosity from his face, but then Vesper's eyes flickered toward the guards, hesitation keeping her lips closed. He turned to the trio of guards flanking them. "Would you give the princess and I some space, please."

The guards nodded and stepped a little farther away. Close enough to protect should the occasion call for it, but far enough that they could speak privately.

"Please," Alfie said. "Go on."

"When I was little, I had a servant girl who was about my age. She would clean my rooms and brush my hair before bed," Vesper said, her voice quiet as the duel continued, the clangs of swords obscuring their words. "I was so young that I didn't fully see the difference between a servant and myself. Not completely, anyway. I thought we were friends."

Alfie nodded. He'd had a similar situation as a boy, when he and the servant children would play together. Sometime after he had been divined, they had turned away from him, as if overnight Alfie had become untouchable.

When he'd cried about it, Dezmin had held him, saying, "Being a prince comes with immense power and privilege."

"You sound like Papí," Alfie grumbled into the crook of his neck.

"I know," Dezmin laughed. "But he's right. And with that privilege, you and I both have the power to hurt or help those children and their families. They keep away from you now because they don't know which you will grow up to choose—help or hurt." He pulled back from the embrace, looking Alfie in the eyes before saying, "You mustn't blame them for that."

"But I don't want to hurt anyone," Alfie argued. "I wouldn't!"

"And you won't," Dezmin said, wiping Alfie's tears. "But because of that power, they fear us. They have every right to. You cannot befriend them the way you want to, but when you grow up and I become king we will make the world a better place for them. That is the kind of friendship a royal can have with his people," Dez said, shrugging one shoulder before grinning down at Alfie. "And you don't need any other friends. Not when you've got me."

And Alfie had indeed had Dezmin, but for far too short a time.

"I tried to teach her magic," Vesper whispered to him, her eyes moving away from him and toward the floor.

Alfie stared at her. Not only was it forbidden to teach the lower classes magic in Englass, but it was impossible for them to even perform magic. The lower classes were made magically impotent through Englassen spellwork.

"But how could you teach her?" Alfie murmured back. "It would be impossible for her to learn."

"I was a child; I didn't know any better. I hadn't fully grasped the caste system. I knew she was common," she admitted. "But I thought that because she was my friend she should be allowed to learn magic. Of course, no matter how much I taught her, she couldn't perform any spellwork. I was so frustrated that I took her to my mother and threw a fit about it." She gave a broken laugh, but it petered out as quickly as it came. Her face paled. "I will never forget my mother's face when I told her I was trying to teach the girl magic. She slapped me so hard that I lost my footing." Her voice had gone quieter still. She gingerly touched her cheek, as if it still ached years later. "The little girl was taken away. I never saw her again."

Alfie's stomach dropped at the thought of the poor child struggling to learn something unfairly forbidden to her. Why should she suffer for wanting something that was so natural? "But it wasn't her fault," Alfie said, horrified. "You are a princess; whether she wanted to learn or not, she could hardly refuse you when you decided to try to teach her."

"I know," Vesper said shortly, her tone terse. She pressed her fingers to her temples. "Forgive me; it's still difficult to talk about. I told my parents that it was my fault—the girl hadn't asked to learn magic, I'd demanded that she let me teach her. But they wouldn't listen. She'd committed treason, and she paid the price."

Alfie looked away, his stomach souring. He knew what happened in Englass if someone in the lower class was discovered even attempting to perform magic—they were executed. They weren't done the kindness of being killed painlessly with magic, as magic was not to be wasted on them. Instead, they were hanged.

Alfie's skin went cold. A child killed for trying to learn magic. In Alfie's eyes it was the same as being killed for breathing, for simply being alive. It was too cruel to comprehend.

"Why would you tell me this?" he asked, anger and disgust boiling inside him. This hardly made him look at her parents with respect.

Vesper met his gaze, her eyes resolute and her voice was so low and quiet Alfie had to lean forward to hear her. "Because I cannot change things, Prince Alfehr. I cannot go back in time and stop myself from teaching her, and I cannot make my brother change the future. But you can." The look of hope in her eyes was so unguarded that Alfie felt as if he should look away. "What your kingdom asks is what I want for my people. I hope you step forward and do what needs to be done for that little girl and the ones who came after her."

Alfie felt as if he was seeing the princess for the first time. She'd seemed shy and agreeable, nothing more, nothing less. But now he could see that she was a girl who believed in what was right but had been beaten into submission by the restrictions of her homeland.

Someone who, under different circumstances, might have been his friend.

"I understand," Alfie said, a sense of hope stirring inside him. He still didn't know if he could trust her, but he knew that ending the caste system was the right thing to do, not just for the kingdoms participating in this summit but for the whole world. "I will do everything I can."

"Thank you," she said quietly. "I know it won't be easy. My family can be intimidating, especially Marsden."

Intimidating was not the word Alfie would use. He'd say haughty. He held his tongue, but Vesper seemed to read it on his face.

"My brother can be difficult to get to know in general, let alone under circumstances like these. I wish we could have met as normal people, not under all this pressure," she said, gesturing vaguely around them.

Luka had said the same thing—that perhaps they needed to spend some time with Marsden and Vesper without their parents present, without all the pomp and circumstance of the summit to weigh them down. If he wanted to change the lives of thousands of Englassens, maybe he needed to try harder to meet Marsden halfway.

"I know what you mean," Alfie agreed. "What if we all spend some time together in the library or perhaps one of the more secluded palace towers?" He and Luka had spent many nights there as children lying on their backs and stargazing. It was one of the few places that felt separate from the rest of the palace. His parents and Paloma seldom went up there.

Vesper shook her head gently. "I don't think that will work. Just being in the palace sets Marsden on edge. It can put me on edge too, if I'm being honest." Her eyes widened, as if she'd misspoken. "Not that I don't enjoy being here. I do—"

Alfie watched the princess sputter. She reminded him of himself before Luka and Dezmin had dragged him out of his shell. Nervous and unsure of herself, questioning every word. Of course, Alfie still did those things, but he liked to think he had better control over his anxiety now. He raised a calming hand. "It's quite all right, Princess Vesper. I know what you mean."

"Even being here, outside the palace walls, feels a bit better." Her eyes darted to the other side of the platform, where his parents chatted with the Englassen king and queen. "But still, the pressure follows."

Alfie didn't want to make this suggestion. Los Toros were still out there, even if they'd chosen not to strike last night. But the hopeless look on Vesper's face tugged at him. He and Marsden needed to get along for the future of both of their kingdoms, and if that included him and Luka sneaking Vesper and Marsden out of the palace for an evening, then maybe it'd be worth it, dangers aside.

"This might sound outlandish," Alfie began, clearing his throat. "You, of course, can say no, but would you and Prince Marsden be interested in spending some time in San Cristóbal without our parents or chaperones?" Her eyes brightened so quickly that Alfie had to tack on, "Just a quick outing, for us all to loosen up and get to know each other." He could ask Finn to disguise their appearances so there was no way any of them would be recognized.

She smiled, and it looked so genuine that Alfie had to think that though this idea was Luka-level ridiculous, it might be the right call. "My brother and I would love that. We'll be ready tonight."

Alfie blinked at her. "Tonight?"

"Sooner rather than later would be best." Her face tensed, the smile slipping away. "Especially considering tomorrow's agenda."

Alfie's shoulders tightened. She was right. If he and Marsden were going to try to understand each other better, it was probably best to do it before tomorrow's tense meeting on abolishing Englass's caste system.

What about Los Toros? his mind asked as Vesper watched him, waiting for his answer. Thus far all the Englassens had seen of Los Toros were a bunch of copycats, disgruntled citizens who were easily led away by guards. Maybe now was the time to do this. Would waiting for another night make it any more dangerous?

He looked at Vesper's hopeful face. She seemed like she truly wanted to end the caste system and thought that doing this would help. She knew her brother better than anyone else. Perhaps he should trust her and take the plunge. If there was any way to save thousands from a life of magical bondage, shouldn't he pursue it?

"Very well," Alfie finally said. Vesper's face lit up. "This will have to be a secret among us four, of course."

"Of course," she agreed.

"I'll talk to Luka and see what we can do."

The princess squeezed his arm. "Thank you, Prince Alfehr."

"It's my pleasure," Alfie lied, his stomach twisting with anxiety.

With that, the two royals watched the match unfold before them. At the end, the Englassen fighter and the Castallano fighter bowed to one another and shook hands, earning a cheer from the crowd. Alfie could only hope this summit would end the same way.

THE INTERROGATION

By the time the exhibition was over, the masked protestors were in the palace dungeons, ready to be questioned. Alfie's stomach knotted with nerves. The summit had only gone on for three days and yet there had already been so much chaos.

After excusing himself and wishing Vesper and Marsden a pleasant afternoon, Alfie dashed down the halls to attend the interrogation. When he reached the twisting stairwell to the dungeons, it was lined with guardsmen. They bowed as Alfie walked briskly past them. He rushed down the stairs, only slowing his stride when he reached the bottom.

"Come mierda, hijo de puta," a man grumbled from a cell before spitting in his direction.

Alfie raised a hand, and the glob of spit stopped before it hit his shoulder. At first, anger swept through him, hot and fast. But a wave of guilt doused the fire, turning it to hissing steam. Maybe this man had lost a loved one to Sombra and was looking for someone to blame, just as the people at the memorial had.

Instead of flinging the saliva back in the man's face, Alfie let it drop to the ground and then walked on, leaving the man to stare after him, silent.

At the end of the hall, Maria, the head of the royal guard, stood in a cell where a cowering man was chained to the ground. The king and queen stood outside, watching from behind a wall of guardsmen, unseen by the captured protestors. When Alfie moved to stand beside them, his mother took him by the arm, her grip firm.

"Who do you work for?" Maria demanded. "Who is running this group?"

The man shook his head. "W-W-We don't know!"

Maria summoned a plume of fire in her palm. "You can either tell me the truth or I can burn your tongue. Which would you prefer?" She leaned forward and held the flame just beneath his chin.

Alfie had known Maria since he was a boy, but he'd never heard her speak like this. It must be for show. His kingdom didn't hurt its people simply for protesting. Perhaps the guardsmen were stressed from the constant fear of Los Toros attacking—he could see it in the tense set of their shoulders as they roamed today's cultural exhibition. That was why Maria was getting carried away with this show of force—that must be it.

"I'm telling the truth!" the man cried as he pressed himself against the wall, jutting his chin up, away from the flame. "We only wanted to take up a symbol to make a point! To stand up for our kingdom." He was gaining steam now, glaring up at Maria regardless of the fear in his eyes. "We are against this summit and the maldito Englassens! Our royal family can't even protect us from the wild magics their own dueños release and now they bring in our kingdom's greatest enemies? Disgusting!"

Alfie flinched. The man sounded just like the member of Los Toros who had stolen the cloak from Finn—because of this summit he didn't believe that Alfie or his family were worthy of this throne. He saw them as betrayers of their ancestors' legacy. Did Los Toros actually represent what his people truly thought of him? Alfie's heart ached at the thought. But before he could dwell on that any longer, Maria raised her hand to strike the man.

"You will show the royal family the proper respect," she said, her voice snapping like a whip.

Alfie stepped forward, pulling himself free of his mother's grasp. "Stop!" he said. He'd been wrong. He had truly believed they were different from Englass, but clearly, they weren't so different after all. The fear Los Toros had stoked was leading them down a path they'd never intended to take—one that had civilians in cells and Maria willing to strike one down. Who were they becoming in the name of protecting themselves and the summit from this threat?

"Stop," he said again. He wouldn't let it happen, not as long as he was the future king of Castallan. Exhaustion seeped into his bones. He was tired of this summit, tired of being a disappointment, tired of hearing his people curse his name for bringing Englass here, but he knew that this wasn't right. Alfie stepped out from behind the curtain of guards and walked into the cell. He nodded at Maria. She reluctantly moved away from the man, her fists clenched.

"Alfehr—"

"I'm fine, Mamá. It's all right." As Alfie stepped into the torch-light, the prisoner's mouth fell open. "You say that you are against us, that you hate us, but now you're silent."

The man's mouth opened and closed soundlessly, like a caught fish gasping for water.

Alfie grabbed the man's chained arms and pulled up each sleeve. No tattoo. Alfie couldn't decide if he was relieved or disappointed.

"I believe this man is telling the truth," Alfie said to Maria. "As I said before, I am familiar with this organization." Alfie could feel his parents tensing behind him as they remembered his outburst about seeing the symbol of Los Toros while under the influence of Sombra's magic. But there was no avoiding the topic now. His stomach knotting tight under the heat of his parents' gaze, Alfie continued. "The members do not simply don masks. They also have a tattoo. Feel free to search this man more thoroughly, but I'm sure the tattoo is usually on the forearm." After all, that was where Marco Zelas's had been, and Finn had told him that Kol's tattoo was in the same place. "I doubt anyone caught at the exhibition is actually part of Los Toros." He looked down at the quivering man. "They're just angry and afraid." What hurt the most was that Alfie could hardly blame them.

King Bolivar nodded, his nostrils flaring with anger. "Search the prisoners for bull tattoos. Report back to me with your findings." He leveled the prisoner with a searing glare. "Then release everyone not related to Los Toros. May you all take this as a warning. Do not pretend to be a gang of murderers unless you are ready for the consequences. Next time we may not be so lenient." Silence curdled in the dungeons as Bolivar turned on his heel. "Come along, Alfehr," he said before striding down the dank halls, but Alfie did not follow. Instead, he looked down at the prisoner.

"I know you hate me and my family," he said, his voice soft. To rule a kingdom of people who loved him was terrifying enough, but to sit on the throne of a kingdom that despised him? That shook him to his bones. He wanted to fix it, to repair the shattered trust between them, but he wasn't naive enough to think he could do it now, with one conversation.

He could not sit down with every citizen of Castallan and explain how things had gone so wrong four months ago. Instead, he told the man a simple truth. "Know that you are free to hate me now and you will be free to hate me when I am king too." Alfie stepped out of the cell before thinking better of it and turning back to the man. "But know also that I don't hate you."

Alfie turned and followed his parents, leaving the man behind.

When he returned to his rooms, Luka was waiting for him.

"What happened?" he asked, jumping to his feet.

Alfie shook his head. "None of them were members of Los Toros. Just angry people looking for a cause to take up. Mamá and Papá are declaring the rest of the week a holiday and cutting taxes to keep the people happy and dissuade them from jumping into any more protests like today's."

Luka fell silent for a moment. "You sound disappointed."

Alfie stared at him. "You're not?"

"Alfie, it might be another hint that the real Los Toros are too afraid to show themselves anymore. That the bounty has scared them off," Luka said. "Try to be a little optimistic, sourpuss."

Alfie sighed. "I mean, that's possible," he admitted. "I just have a bad feeling—"

"You *always* have a bad feeling," Luka said. "Try having a good one instead."

Alfie couldn't argue with that. Maybe he was thinking too much. Los Toros hadn't committed a murder the night before. Now it was evening once again and still nothing had happened. Maybe they had finally gotten the situation under control. He had to hope so.

"You're right." Alfie kneaded his temples, his shadow curling about his feet.

"Can you repeat that?" Luka asked with a grin.

"Cállate," Alfie laughed, finally feeling the tension ease out of his shoulders. Luka was right. He needed to take this for what it was—a good sign. Facing some protestors was much better than having to hide another one of Los Toros' murders. This was a win—a small one, but a win all the same.

"Now we can relax for the night," Luka said with a contented sigh, flopping onto his back onto Alfie's bed.

Alfie had waited all his life for Luka to want to stay in for a night, so it pained him to correct him. "Actually, you and I have plans with Marsden and Vesper."

Luka snapped forward on the bed. "¿Qué?!"

Alfie explained as Luka nodded along. "In the end, I think she's right. If Marsden and I are ever going to get along with each other, we need to get away from all the pomp and circumstance."

"Good to know I was right. Though, of course, I already knew that," Luka said triumphantly. "So what shall we do? Maybe grab some food and rum and take them to one of the northern towers for conversation and stargazing? No one ever bothers us there."

"No—"

"You're right, you're right," Luka said with a wave of his hand. "Sounds too much like a date. Plus you'd probably throw Marsden over the side of the tower—"

"Luka," Alfie interrupted. "Listen. We are putting on disguises and taking Marsden and Vesper out to see San Cristóbal."

Luka's eyes widened. "For once, you came up with the more dangerous option. Why now?"

Alfie rolled his eyes. "It's not my decision—Vesper feels that Marsden won't properly loosen up unless we're out of the palace, completely away from our parents. And I want to ask Vesper more about how she feels about disbanding the caste system. I have a feeling she might be able to give me some insight into how to ensure the summit goes smoothly." Since Vesper was the only Englassen who seemed excited to end the caste system, he wanted to know what she had to say, but, still, it was a risk. If he took the Englassen royals out of the palace without guards, anything could happen. Even without the threat of Los Toros, it wasn't the smartest thing to do. "Maybe we should just cancel it."

"Alfie," Luka said, his gaze sharp. "I know what you're thinking, but we can't predict what Los Toros are going to do, or if they're going to strike again. We've got to take their absence last night as a good sign and hope for the best. This outing might be what we need to get you and Marsden to a better place politically and to find out exactly what's on Vesper's mind. And we need to do it before tomorrow's meeting about the caste system. It has to be tonight."

Alfie sighed deeply. Luka was right, but Alfie still had his reservations. "And if Los Toros do attack?"

"I don't know if you remember this wondrous fact," Luka said, standing and making his way to Alfie's writing desk.

"Don't—" Alfie said, knowing where this was going.

"But I am unnaturally strong." With one hand, Luka casually tossed Alfie's desk so high into the air that it hit the ceiling, shattering into chunks of wood. Luka winced as a desk leg hit him on the head. Alfie ducked out of the way. "Okay, that was not how I wanted that to go."

Alfie pinched the bridge of his nose in exasperation and murmured, "*Reparar*." The desk quickly came back together.

"What I mean to emphasize," Luka said, "is that I have great physical strength and you are one of the finest bruxos in this kingdom. You helped defeat Sombra! We can protect Vesper and Marsden if something happens, and it's more than likely that nothing will happen anyway."

"You're right," Alfie relented. In all likelihood it would be fine. And maybe he and Marsden would come out of this as friends? He shook his head free of that thought. Too ambitious. Maybe they'd come out of it . . . civil.

"I'll tell Vesper at dinner. We'll meet them at the library tonight," Alfie finally said. "I assume you have tethers set up to take you into the city?"

"Is the sky blue?" Luka said. "Is love eternal? Am I guapo?"

"Basta," Alfie laughed.

"And in even more news," Luka said. "Once I got away from Marsden at the exhibition by distracting him with shiny, pretty swords—"

"Thank you for that," Alfie added gratefully. It had been nice of

Luka to pull the prince away.

"You are not welcome," Luka quipped. "Once I got away from him, I met up with my contact. We have a meeting with the Tattooed King tomorrow night."

"Really?" Alfie said. They'd only been waiting for an appointment for a couple of days, but he'd been starting to think it would never happen.

"I aim to please," Luka said, raising his hands as if trying to ward off the applause.

Alfie spotted a purple mottled mark on his knuckles. "What happened? Are you all right?" he asked.

Luka pulled his hands back. "It's fine. Nothing to worry about."

Luka wasn't talented in healing magic. "Let me help—" Alfie could see now that his knuckles were bruised. Clearly from a fight.

A tense silence stretched between them.

Luka's face had gone tight and Alfie knew he looked the same. Luka wasn't going to listen to him, so what was the point? Still, he wished he could understand why Luka was choosing to put himself in harm's way, but every time he asked it ended in them arguing.

Alfie pulled the parchment out of his pocket. "I've got to tell Finn about the meeting."

Tomorrow's Tattooed King meeting was more than enough reason to ask her to come by tonight regardless of their awkward moment in the bruxo's triangle. His face warmed with embarrassment at the memory. Part of him would rather just talk about it, but he knew Finn. That would be the last thing she'd want to do. Frustration raked its nails over him. He couldn't talk to Luka about his fight club forays, and he couldn't ask what had happened between him and Finn so she would forgive him. He felt like a stoppered bottle of a fizzy drink, the questions building up inside him with nowhere to go.

Alfie pushed those thoughts away. Figuring out Kol's connection to Los Toros and stopping the gang came first. He needed to stop getting distracted and tell Finn what had happened so that they could move forward with this meeting.

Plus, he could use her help in disguising Vesper and Marsden before they snuck out tonight. There was a fair amount of Englassen commoners out and about in San Cristóbal—the royal family's servants, as well as the ship crews that had brought the rest of the Englassen dignitaries and representatives, were free to explore San Cristóbal during their time here. So Vesper and Marsden wouldn't look completely out of place, though their telltale red hair was a bit eye-catching. It would be better if Finn could alter that, in addition to Luka's and Alfie's faces.

He quickly wrote to tell her about the Tattooed King meeting tomorrow and that he needed her help for a favor tonight. He'd explain it once she got here. Alfie watched the parchment, waiting for a response but afraid of what he'd find.

He thought of how her breath had ghosted over his lips that night, the foreshadowing of a kiss—the flash of lightning before the rumble of thunder. But the sound had never landed. Just a flash of light with no final crescendo.

He watched the parchment, his pulse thrumming beneath his skin.

THE BOUNTY

While the prince and Bathtub Boy enjoyed yet another cultural exhibition, Finn was stuck in a meeting with the thief lords.

"Two more of my associates with connections to Englass's markets have disappeared," Rodrigo said, his jaw tight. "Elian has lost a few too. Los Toros, as Emeraude calls them, are thorough."

The boy nodded and raised three fingers.

Emeraude shook her head, frustration creasing her brows. "The fact that they can spread their forces among all four quadrants means their numbers are nothing to joke about. Finn, what news of your quadrant?"

Finn jolted in her seat. "What?"

Emeraude shot her a look. "San Cristóbal, where Los Toros have murdered two delegados, is in your quadrant. Have you nothing to report about how la Familia is handling this?"

In truth, Finn didn't have much to say. Her people were proving to be about as useful as she'd thought they'd be. And Los Toros were proving to be just as difficult to track.

"Right . . . ," Finn said, watching Elian's and Rodrigo's heads swivel toward her. "Los Toros infiltrated a royal event last night," she blurted. The prince had told her as much through their parchment. "They tampered with the enchanted fireworks the royals had set up for the Englassens. One of the fireworks formed an angry bull's face."

Rodrigo clapped his hands, laughing. "Ah, it all makes sense now," he said to Emeraude. "That's why they put a bounty on their heads."

Finn just blinked, and Emeraude sighed. "You don't know about the bounty."

Finn crossed her arms. "I'm a busy woman."

"Last night the royals announced a bounty on Los Toros," Rodrigo said. "Anyone who comes forward with good information on the group will be rewarded handsomely. The monarchs must be truly desperate if they're relying on us to clean up their mess."

"Everyone is on high alert," Emeraude said. "Including the guards. They all want to be the ones to track down Los Toros and gain the royals' praise. They're grabbing whoever they can find with any visible tattoos, hoping to catch them."

Finn had never felt better about deciding not to get that tattoo a few years ago. She wondered how the prince and his family were doing. A bounty wouldn't solve the immediate problem of figuring out how they got into the palace grounds undetected. "Well, that's all I've got on Los Toros."

"How did you learn about Los Toros and the fireworks?" Rodrigo asked, his eyes narrowed.

Finn shrugged. "I have connections everywhere." She didn't

need any of them to know about her relationship to the prince.

What even *was* her relationship to the prince?

She thought of standing in the chalk lines of that triangle, her hand on the back of his neck, his nose brushing hers.

"No need to flush," Rodrigo laughed. "I won't press you any further."

"I hate to say it," Emeraude sighed, drumming her fingers on the table as Rodrigo took a cookie slathered in dulce de leche, "but perhaps we should help the royals."

Rodrigo choked on his cookie. "Excuse me?"

Finn stared at Emeraude, surprised. The vieja had no love for the royal family; she'd made that abundantly clear.

"We need the summit to go well for our own interests," Emeraude said. "This is business."

"What are you suggesting?" Finn asked.

"Would you like me to guard the palace myself?" Rodrigo said, sarcasm dripping from his voice.

Emeraude shot him a quelling look. "If Los Toros are smart, they'll try to attack the Englassens directly. No more dropping bodies in the Pinch. They'll do something drastic. We should have our people around whenever the royals bring the Englassens out to see the city. I'm surprised that nothing happened at their cultural exhibition in the Brim today. Dumb luck. They surely will attack any day now. If we pool our resources, we might be able to catch them before they ruin the summit."

Finn couldn't help but nod. The prince could use some help. "If getting through this summit without the whole thing erupting is what you all—we want," Finn corrected herself. "Then it sounds like the right thing to do."

Rodrigo shook his head. "We don't meddle so directly in royal affairs. If they decide to take the Englassens out for another field trip then they'll have to handle the consequences."

Elian inclined his head in agreement, and Emeraude sighed.

"The least you both could do is take the day to think about it," Emeraude said. "The next exhibition is tomorrow."

"To a thief, reputation is everything. I won't tarnish mine by helping the royals." Rodrigo stood from the table, looming tall over Emeraude. "Is that all for today?"

Emeraude raised her chin. "Yes, that is all. Be here again in two days' time for another update."

"As you wish." Rodrigo grabbed a cookie, then strode to the staircase, Elian in tow, neither staying a moment longer than necessary.

"I swear he disagrees with my suggestions just to anger me," Emeraude muttered, rubbing her temples. "And the boy always follows him."

Finn didn't know what to say to that. Helping protect the summit made sense since the thief lords had a stake in it, but Rodrigo also had a point. It would be damaging to the thief lords' reputation to side with the royals and be their unofficial guards.

"Forget about them," Emeraude said. "Now that they're gone, tell me where you are with Kol's connection to Los Toros." Emeraude poured her a glass of rum. "And you were brilliant, by the way."

Finn stared at her. "Of course I was," she said. "But which time are you talking about?"

Emeraude laughed. "Pretending you were oblivious to the

bounty placed on Los Toros by the royals. Brilliant. They would never guess that you and I are working together."

Finn stopped herself from scowling. She really needed to get better at this stupid job, even if she did plan to be free of it as soon as possible. "Of course. All according to plan."

"Now tell me what you've learned, muchacha."

Finn told her about how interviewing Kol's associates had mostly gotten her nowhere, aside from the possibility of meeting with the *propio* seer—the man who could identify someone's *propio* just by looking at them. Thus far Anabeltilia hadn't been able to track him down, so the chances of talking to him were low.

"Kol told me about that man," Emeraude said. "His skill could certainly be useful in finding the murderers. If I remember correctly he travels often. My people are spread thin trying to track Los Toros in my quadrant, but I can task them with looking for him as well if it's proving too difficult for your second-in-command."

Finn nodded in thanks. She didn't like relying on the help of others, but she would do it for the prince. "And we have a new lead," Finn said before explaining how Luka was using his contact to secure a meeting with the Tattooed King.

"I see," Emeraude said, straightening in her seat. "If I'd known that the mask was made of ink, I might have assumed that it was Ernesto's work. Only he could make tattoos like that."

"Wait, you know the Tattooed King?" Finn asked. "Should we say we know you?"

"It would hardly help your case," Emeraude said, and Finn had a feeling she was holding something back.

"Bad blood?"

"I told you that I tried to run from my husband many times," she said, her eyes darkening, "but he had connections everywhere, and everyone wanted to curry favor with him. What better way to do that than to return his wife to him?"

"The Tattooed King caught you and took you back to your husband?"

"He did, kicking and screaming. Before he was the Tattooed King, he was just a thief with something to prove in the criminal underworld. He used me to launch his reputation and get funding for his tattoo parlor, but I paid him back for that." The air turned cold and Finn had a feeling that she'd really left her mark on the man. "Let's just say, I wouldn't tell him you know me."

Finn swallowed. "Got it."

While she wanted to interrogate the pendejo who had sent Emeraude back to her husband, part of her had also hoped that Luka never got the meeting set up. She, Alfie, and Luka were supposed to go see the Tattooed King together. But after what had happened between her and Alfie in the triangle and the way she'd run off when Ignacio appeared, the thought of seeing him in person made her stomach tighten. Scribbling on the parchment was all right, but she wasn't ready to face him. Not yet. At the same time, she wished she had a reason to scale his tower and walk through those balcony doors again. To stand where they stood and maybe try again. Maybe. Finn pushed those thoughts away, her face burning.

"That's all I've got, vieja," Finn said, standing from her seat. "If we get it set up, I'll tell you what we learn."

"I look forward to hearing how he's doing," she said with a sharp smirk.

As Finn walked out of the statue staircase, she felt warmth building in her pocket. With quick hands, she pulled out the parchment and unfolded it.

Could you meet tonight to talk? Luka has set up a meeting with the Tattooed King for tomorrow night, and there's something else we could use your help with.

Finn was annoyed at the warmth pooling in her belly, at how she reread the note twice just to be sure. At how quickly her desire to keep her distance vanished.

She exhaled sharply through her nose. Since when did a stupid note from a stupid boy change her mood?

Since today, it seemed.

I'll be there, she wrote.

THE FAVOR

On the third night of the summit, Finn stood in front of Alfie's balcony doors for five minutes before finally willing herself to reach for the doorknob.

After her meeting with Emeraude, she'd sat through the members of la Familia telling her what they'd learned as they patrolled the city trying to find Los Toros.

They'd learned very little.

Anabeltilia confirmed that though they had located the *propio* seer's home, he was traveling and they had no idea when he would be back. It was the only lead Finn had come up with, but it seemed out of reach for the foreseeable future. Finn had even asked her for the man's local address so she could see for herself, and the place was empty, cleaned out with nothing to trace him by. Finn wondered if he'd run for the hills once he heard that Kol had died. Maybe he'd been waiting to escape Kol.

Finn told the girl to keep looking. Hopefully either Anabeltilia or Emeraude's people would find him. Maybe the vieja would have better luck.

And now she stood in front of Alfie's door, her palm still hovering over it.

She pulled her hand back at the final moment before the magic would register her presence.

"Mierda," she grumbled. When had she become afraid of opening a maldito door?

She and the prince had almost kissed. So what? There were bigger things happening. Murders, thief lords, general despair. Why couldn't she just focus on that?

"Just do it," she said to herself. She reached for the door again, only to have it wrenched inward, out of her grasp.

The prince stood before her, his eyes wide and hopeful.

"Hi," he said.

"Hi," she echoed.

"I heard a noise and thought it might be you," he said, rubbing the back of his neck. Finn felt hope catch alight inside her at the thought that he was excited to see her. Maybe he'd been waiting, staring at the door for just as long as she'd stood outside it. Then she felt annoyed at herself for that embarrassing thought.

Silence stretched between them.

Alfie stepped back, holding the door open. He cleared his throat. "Do you want to come in?"

Her confidence renewed, Finn lifted her chin and strode past him. Of course he was happy to see her. Why wouldn't he be?

But her cocky swagger wilted when she nearly stepped on the spot on the floor where Alfie had drawn the triangle. She stumbled back, keeping her feet away from it. The triangle had been erased, but it might as well still be there by the way Finn stared at the ground. Alfie came to stand beside her, and she knew he was thinking the same thing.

Yet another unbearable silence swept through the room. He was looking at her, she could feel it. The pull that turned her to face him was so seamless that it felt as if she hadn't moved at all, as if instead he'd stepped into her line of vision. He parted his lips to speak.

Then the bedroom doors burst open and Bathtub Boy walked through. Finn had never been so simultaneously glad and annoyed to see someone.

"Well, hello again, Madre." Luka grinned. He looked as if he'd just bathed and gotten dressed for something, but he was wearing oddly common clothes. Regular pantalones and a shirt drawn together with string as opposed to the usual shiny buttons.

"Don't call me that."

"Would you prefer Mamacita?"

"Honestly," Finn said, considering, "that is slightly bette " Finn stared at the bruises on Luka's knuckles, only visible when he tugged at his shirt strings. "What's with your hands?"

She'd expected Luka to make some kind of joke, but instead he fell silent. He and the prince looked pointedly away from each other. Something was up. But before she could question it, Luka had moved on.

"So we have our meeting with royalty tomorrow—Ernesto Puente, also known as the Tattooed King," Luka said. He quickly explained that his contact had secured them a meeting for tomorrow just after midnight. When he told Finn how much the meeting had cost, her eyes widened.

"Does the meeting come with a complimentary brick of gold?!" She knew money was no object to royals, but that price was ridículo.

"Let's just hope it's worth it," Alfie said with a frown. "He should have some answers on Los Toros, since he allegedly gave them their tattoos."

Finn nodded. It was a solid lead. "After that bounty you all offered, Los Toros might be even harder to find."

"You know about that?" Luka asked.

"It spread like wildfire. Now the guards are being very thorough during their patrols. They all want to earn a forehead kiss from the royal family." She rolled her eyes. "I'm not surprised that we haven't seen Los Toros make any moves in a day."

Alfie gave a sigh of relief at that. "That's what we're hoping, but even if they never attack again, we still need to find them. So tomorrow's meeting is paramount." He looked at her then, his gold eyes searching. "You'll come, won't you?"

Finn found herself nodding. "I'll be there."

Alfie smiled, and Finn knew that they'd been staring at each other too long when Luka half coughed, half laughed into his fist. "But we have more to discuss tonight besides tomorrow's date with the Tattooed King, don't we, Alfie?"

Alfie and Finn looked away from each other.

"Right," she said. "You asked for a favor?"

Alfie moved to speak, but Luka beat him to it. "Alfie and I are taking the Englassen royals out and we wanted to ask your help on disguising us so we won't be recognized."

Now it was Finn's turn to blink in surprise. "You're taking them for a night out?"

"Things have been tense and they're only going to get more so as we get deeper into the summit," Alfie said, his face pinched with worry. "We want to try to get to know them outside of the political pressure so that we can work together well in the future."

Luka cocked his head, smirking. "Princess Vesper seems to like Alfie quite a bit, but her brother is another story."

Finn stiffened. The Englassen princess *liked* Alfie. And now he wanted her to help him so that he could take her out? A silent fury rose in Finn like a wave, her shadow snapping like a whip at her feet.

"You want me to help you take some Englassens on a playdate?"

"It's not a playdate—" Alfie began.

"Aren't you excited by the prospect of doing something not life-threatening for one night?" Luka joked.

Finn glared at him and blew a stray curl out of her face. "No."

Luka grinned in an annoying way that told her he knew exactly why she was bothered. "Vesper will be disappointed if Alfie goes back on his word. She was so looking forward to going out with him."

Finn wanted to slap him.

"Finn," Alfie said, his honey eyes finding hers. He clearly hadn't noticed the game Luka was playing. "I know we're working together to look for Los Toros and learn more about what Kol had been up to, but the summit is a priority in my life too—it would mean the world to me if you could help us. Getting closer to Vesper and Marsden could help us make Dez's dream come true, continue his legacy. Please." His face dimmed in the way it always did when he mentioned his brother.

Finn hated when Alfie said please; it was oftentimes the last nail in the coffin of her resolve. Because when other people said please it was a game, a way of trying to manipulate what they wanted out of someone. But when the prince said please, it was a promise. A promise that he would catch you and offer his help before you even had the chance to ask.

Finn heaved a sigh. "Fine, fine. But I'm not doing this again."

"Thank you, Finn," Alfie said, a smile spreading on his face.

Finn looked away from him, her blood boiling. "Let's just get this over with."

After Finn had changed into the uniform of a palace servant that Alfie provided, the three snuck down the halls to the library just before the stroke of midnight. Even the scholars had abandoned their work at this hour. Gathered around one of the countless dark wood desks were two redheads. The girl was petite, almost dainty, with a delicate oval face. Finn could see Vesper brightening as they drew nearer, her light eyes on Alfie.

Finn felt her lip curling into a snarl.

Beside the girl was a tall, broad-shouldered boy, his back so stiff that Finn thought his spine might snap like a toothpick. He looked just as excited to see her as she was to see him.

"Well!" Luka said. "We're glad you made it."

"My sister wanted to come, so I obliged," the redheaded boy said, looking at Alfie with suspicion. Finn rolled her eyes. It was more than clear that he was only going because he didn't want the princess alone with them.

Good, Finn thought. It seemed she and an Englassen could agree on something.

"We're glad you're both here." Alfie offered a small smile to the Englassens.

"We are too," the princess said. Finn had a feeling that the girl didn't express herself much because her brother shot her a surprised look.

"Yeah, yeah, yeah," Finn said. "Let's get this show on the road."

After Alfie introduced her and her *propio*, Finn quickly moved to change the faces of the Englassen royals.

"Very nice to meet you," Princess Vesper said.

Finn eyed the girl. "Uh-huh. Anyway, how are we doing this? Am I only changing their faces slightly, or should I make them look Castallano so that they blend in more—"

"No thank you," Marsden said a little too quickly. "I'd like to stay Englassen."

Finn quirked an eyebrow, her jaw tensing. She didn't know as much history as Alfie did, but she knew that when Englass had colonized Castallan, they made it clear that fair skin and eyes and straight hair were to be coveted, while darker skin was a mark of inferiority. It sounded like the prince still felt that way. Well, he could keep his flammable, sunburn-prone skin if he liked it so much.

When Finn glanced at Alfie's and Luka's tense faces, she knew they were thinking the same thing.

"It'll just make the process easier for you," Marsden added. "We want to go out as soon as we can, yes?"

The princess nodded. "Yes, whatever is simplest is probably best." The Englassen prince was clearly a prejudiced jerk, but the sister was still a mystery. That bothered Finn even more.

"Very well," Alfie said tersely, nodding at Finn. "If you please, Finn?"

Finn blew a stray curl out of her face and stepped in front of Marsden. He looked as if he'd rather be touched by a pig than Finn. That made changing him all the more fun. She also made sure to accidentally step on his foot once or twice for good measure. Then she moved on to his sister, who thanked her profusely and annoyingly. Finally, with quick hands, Finn changed Luka's and Alfie's faces slightly too, making sure not to make eye contact with the prince or to let her hand linger. She'd wanted to look nonchalant, but every time she touched him for a moment too long, she lurched back as if she'd been burned.

While Luka only smirked knowingly, and the Englassen royals seemed oblivious, Alfie looked hurt. She forced herself to look unfazed, because if she didn't look unfazed she'd look angry instead, and if she got angry she'd have to think about why this pissed her off so much. And Luka would get too much amusement from that.

In a few minutes all four royals had faces that were similar to their own, but different enough to hide their identities. They each wore common clothes to further disguise themselves, though a royal's common clothes were still a lot nicer than what you'd find on regular people. Finn supposed it was the best they could do.

"Well," Finn said before rubbing her hands on her servant's skirt as if she'd touched something sticky. "My work is done for the night."

She moved to turn away, but the Englassen princess stepped forward.

"But you must come with us," she said. Finn glared at her. She didn't like people who were this nice this easily.

"I'd rather not," Finn said as Alfie looked at her in confusion. His gold eyes seemed to be asking, *Have I done something wrong?*

She hoped her glower told him, *Yes, absolutely.*

"I must return to my duties as a servant," Finn spat. "If you'll excuse me."

Finn turned on her heel and left the prince and his new friends to their night out.

She had more important things to do than babysit them.

THE MISSING PIECE

Finn stomped away from the library, anger burrowing into her bones.

The worst part was she didn't even know why she was angry. No one said Alfie couldn't go out with princesses with long red hair and pretty dresses. It wasn't as if she'd staked a claim on him. It wasn't as if he mattered—as if what had almost happened in that triangle had mattered.

Her shadow zigzagged angrily at her feet. The girl had seemed so at home in the library. She'd looked at the books the same way the prince did—with wonder. Of course Alfie wanted to take her out.

Why would he want Finn anyway? All she did was lose the vanishing cloak and find trouble. Now that he could have flame-haired, bookish princesses, he'd probably forgotten about that almost kiss in the bruxo triangle. Not that she cared.

Finn heard voices around the corner. She was wearing the face of a servant, but she didn't feel like putting on an act today. She dashed toward the nearest door and crept in, closing it quietly behind her. She waited for the footsteps to pass before she let out a breath. They were gone. Now she could go find one of the palace's many hidden passageways and go home. Maybe she'd go through the kitchens. No one would be confused to see a servant girl there. Why go back to the prince's rooms and climb down his balcony when she could grab herself a royal meal on her way out?

Finn was about to head back out the door when she took a moment to look around the room she was in. The parlor smelled strongly of incense, and at its center stood a small wooden table, in the middle of which sat a crystal ball. Finn rolled her eyes. In her years at the circus she'd seen her fair share of people spending their pesos to hear a fortune-teller's lies.

"Remember when I told you I didn't need one of those fake crystal balls to tell me the future?" Ignacio said, running a finger over the glass surface. "I already knew our fate was to be together, forever. And I was right, wasn't I?" he laughed. "Maybe I'm a fortune-teller."

"Shut up," Finn said, kneading her temples. "I'm tired of hearing you talk."

"Don't be upset because the prince found someone worthy of his pedigree," he tutted. "If you had listened to your papá you would've avoided that heartbreak. Pobrecita."

Finn couldn't take it any longer. She wanted to smash the crystal ball against his head.

Intending to do just that, she dashed to the table and grabbed the ball with both hands, but before she could swing it at Ignacio, a shock of cold poured down from her fingertips over her body. The crystal ball felt as if it was made of ice magicked to never melt.

Her mind was flooded with a slew of images. They moved so

fast she could hardly see them, but one image stuck out with sharp clarity.

The prince.

The vision was incomplete, the background simply blurred gray, so it looked as if he could be standing anywhere. Alfie's eyes went wide with fear as he was stabbed in the stomach. He crumpled to the ground, blood pouring from the wound, pain twisting his features.

Finn came to with a gasp, her fingers gripping the crystal ball tightly.

"What you touched is a globe of possibilities." At the sound of a woman's voice, Finn jumped, dropping the crystal ball. It hit the tiled floor with a loud *thwack* before rolling to a stop at a tall woman's feet. "It shows you the infinite paths of your future."

The woman didn't look annoyed or surprised to see Finn, and Finn was in no mind to make up an excuse, not with what she'd just seen.

"What if it showed me someone else's future? What then?"

The diviner tilted her head. "It is unusual to see someone else's future, but if you do, that means you are an integral part of why that future will come to pass."

Finn's throat went dry. The prince was going to die and it was her fault.

"What it showed me," she sputtered, pointing at the crystal ball. "How do I stop it?"

The willowy woman shrugged. "It may not come to pass at all. Or it will." She assessed Finn with her strangely light eyes. "Or perhaps it has already happened."

"*What?*" Finn said with a choking gasp, but before she could ask for clarification, the woman had crossed the room and was standing before her.

"You are what has changed. You are what is different," the woman said. "You're the missing piece."

"Qué?" Finn said again. This loca wasn't making any sense.

"I am Lucila, the palace diviner."

Finn blinked. This was the woman who'd told the prince that he didn't have a future. She could see why he didn't like her.

"I don't care who you are," Finn growled. "Can I change what it showed me?"

The diviner waved her hand dismissively. "No. The future will unfold as it should, when it should." Then, without a moment's hesitation, she raised a hand and plucked a hair straight out of Finn's head.

"Coño!" Finn shouted, rubbing her scalp. "Why the hell would you do that?!"

"Because you're the missing piece," she said.

"The what?"

"When the prince was a child, I was tasked with divining his future—"

"Yeah, yeah," Finn said, annoyed to hear a story that the whole kingdom already knew. "And you couldn't see anything. You said he didn't have a future."

"No," Lucila said. "That is not what I said. Not at all. I told him that he was missing a piece and without it I could not see his future." She stared at Finn. "I spent years traveling trying to find you, and now you stumble into my rooms."

Finn's mind overflowed with information. The vision of Alfie dying, of a blade sinking into his flesh, on its own was enough to overwhelm her, but now this?

"Your destinies are so intertwined that I could not see his future until I found you. And now, more than ten years later, here you are."

"You're wrong," Finn said. There was no way her destiny and the prince's were intertwined. He was a prince and she was . . . well, she was who—and what—she was. And if their destinies were intertwined, then would what she had seen come true? If the strange crystal ball showed it to her with such clarity, did that mean it would come to pass? "You're wrong and your stupid crystal ball is wrong."

The diviner watched her carefully, as if she could read something written under Finn's skin. "I don't know what you saw, muchacha, but know that telling the person what the vision was about may in fact make it come to pass. Or it may stop it. Or it may bring about something far worse." The diviner raised her hands as if offering options. "The choice is yours."

Finn's stomach dropped at the woman's words. Would telling him help or harm him? She shoved past the diviner and dashed out the doors. She needed to get out of the palace, needed to think. As she finally snuck out of the castle, Ignacio's voice echoed in her head, low and sure.

"Didn't I tell you, Mija?" he said. "You don't belong in his life, but if you do stick around you'll be the death of that poor boy."

THE STICKY SITUATION

The city was alive with music and energy.

Children ran about well past their bedtime as bachateros sang sweet ballads in the moonlight with guitars in their arms and food vendors sold freshly fried pastelitos.

When Alfie turned to look at Vesper and Marsden, he could see an awed surprise on their faces. They had only experienced a buttoned-up version of San Cristóbal, not the real city in all its glory.

Guardsmen were stationed at nearly every corner, their eyes scanning the crowds for Los Toros. The declaration of the holiday week this afternoon already seemed to be working to keep the people happy and content. The palace would supplement the people's pay, allowing work hours to be slashed for the week. People were wholly distracted from their anger over the summit. Thus far, there had been no more protests like there had been this morning.

Alfie could see that the initial tension between the Castallanos and the few Englassen commoners who explored the rings had lessened. He'd heard Maria and the guardsmen talking about it.

Castallanos had a hatred for Englassens, this was certain, but they couldn't help but pity the common Englassen folk who were not allowed to use magic. And though the Englassen commoners were taught to see Castallan as their enemy, they looked at the Castallanos with hope. After all, they had once been enslaved and now they were free. There were certainly still fights and moments of prejudice between the two groups, but things had calmed down. It seemed that most had found middle ground in their love of drinking and holiday festivities. Finn would love this.

A holiday means rum, rum means drunk people, and drunk people are the easiest ones to rob.

But Finn had refused to come. Was she still angry about when he'd tried to kiss her? Should he have apologized? He had been about to when Luka walked through the door. Alfie rubbed the back of his neck. How was he going to fix this?

He shook his head. He needed to focus on the tasks at hand, to break the tension between himself and Marsden. Vesper had been open and vulnerable with him this morning; he owed it to her and her people to try to find common ground with her brother.

But after Marsden's reaction to the prospect of looking Castallano, Alfie had a bad feeling about tonight. He was tired of seeing himself through Englassen eyes—a curly-haired oddity with cinnamon skin. If that was how Marsden saw them, there wasn't much hope to begin with.

"So!" Luka shouted, gesturing around him in a wide circle. "What do you two think?"

Vesper stared, awestruck. "It's magnificent."

"What?" Luka shouted.

"Magnificent!" Vesper shouted back.

"*Vesper*," Marsden chided her. "You're being far too loud. Just because we're surrounded by common folk does not mean you ought to behave like them."

Alfie clenched his jaw. Compared to Englassen culture, Castallan was loud and raucous. Marsden seemed to think louder meant inferior. The boisterous laughter echoing throughout the Pinch was just as Castallano as a bachata ballad. Marsden had no business calling it "common." Alfie wanted to correct him, but tonight wasn't about that. It was about making steps toward a peaceful future. That goal required a lot more biting of his tongue than he'd expected. It was infuriating that he should walk on eggshells for people who had stomped on the freedoms of his ancestors and made a profit from them. Yet here he was, biting his tongue and tiptoeing.

Marsden looked at Alfie with a frown. "Do excuse her."

Vesper looked down, chastened, and Alfie wished Marsden would leave her be. She was the one who had asked for this night out; the least he could do was let her have a little fun tonight.

"Let's get a drink, or maybe several," Luka chirped, cutting the tension as he led them through the throngs of people toward a nearby pub.

The pub was packed but Luka was able to claim a table just as a rollicking group was drunkenly stumbling out the doors. The table was wet with cerveza and Prince Marsden frowned as he sat, wrinkling his nose at the band playing bachata in the corner while couples danced.

The four of them sat awkwardly at the table. Luka beckoned a server and demanded a bottle of their finest rum, which, since they were in the Pinch, wouldn't be very fine.

"So this is the real Castallan," Marsden said. He kept his hands tightly clasped in his lap, as if trying his best to touch as little as possible. He shot Vesper a hard look, no doubt silently blaming her for dragging him out.

Before Alfie could respond, a rowdy cheer started on the other side of the bar. An Englassen man was being toasted by a trio of Castallanos. "Those pendejo royals took your magic from you, but at least we can buy you a drink!" They downed their cervezas.

Marsden stiffened, his face souring. Vesper looked at Alfie with a shine of panic in her eyes. Neither of them had anticipated this.

At that moment, Alfie had a feeling that tonight was going to be an absolute disaster.

"You know what the best part of Castallan is?" Luka shouted, pouring rum messily into the four shot glasses. "Castallano rum. It's the cornerstone of our culture. And I am so very excited to share it with you."

Marsden glowered at him, suspicion pulling his features tight. "Why is that?"

"Well," Luka said as he pushed the glass toward him, "I heard that Englassen citizens are so wonderfully proper and restrained that no amount of alcohol can cause them to lose their good manners. Is that true?"

Marsden raised his chin. "Englassen manners are impeccable. This is fact."

"Excellent!" Luka said. "Then let me have the cultural experience of witnessing it firsthand."

Marsden squinted at Luka, seeing through him, but at the sound of another shout about pendejo Englassen royals, Marsden snatched the glass and downed the contents in one fluid motion.

As Marsden gave a long, pained sigh at the burn of the cheap rum, Luka leaned close to Alfie. "Let me loosen him up a little and distract him from, well—" Luka tilted his head toward the loud, jeering Castallanos. "At the very least if he's tipsy he'll let Princess Vesper have some fun."

Alfie was not one for getting others drunk, but it might be exactly what Marsden needed to loosen up and not throw a punch at the people speaking ill of his family.

"Fine," Alfie hissed. "But don't get him too drunk."

"There's no such thing," Luka quipped back.

"Luka," Alfie said warningly.

"Fine, fine," he said with a wave of his hand before turning to Vesper. "Princess," he said, grinning. "Would you like to learn how to play exploding dominoes?"

Vesper nodded, looking desperate for distraction. "Yes, of course."

"I'll go grab a set from the bar," Alfie offered before disappearing into the crowd for a break.

By the time he came back with the dominoes, he'd heard another wave of anti-Englassen jeers, and according to Luka, Marsden had downed three more shots of rum.

As they began their fourth round of dominoes, Marsden was completely and utterly sauced.

"I told you to make sure he didn't get too borracho!" Alfie whispered at Luka while a worried Vesper tried to get Marsden to drink some water.

Luka threw his hands up. "He's a grown man! I can't slap the drinks out of his hand!"

Marsden hiccuped loudly, pushing away the glass of water Vesper was trying to coax him to drink. "E-veryone . . . E-veryone," he slurred.

Vesper leaned close to him. "What?"

He stared at her, glassy-eyed. "Everyone hates us here, Vesper. All of them." He waved his hand at the crowd. "Englassens and Castallanos. All of them." His face crumpled and he looked heartbreakingly young. "They all *hate* us."

Alfie stared at him uncomfortably, unsure of what to make of it. Did Marsden just have a melancholy personality when drunk? Or was he expressing what he secretly felt when sober?

Alfie pushed away any pity he had for the prince. Yes, everyone hated him—he treated his people like cattle. That was his own fault, his family's fault, his ancestors' fault. If he took the initiative to change his kingdom's ways, it would be different. But he wasn't. The main incentive for ending their caste system was the promise of economic opportunity with Castallan, not the hope of giving his own people a better life. Alfie could give him no sympathy.

For a moment, the Englassen prince looked as if he might even cry, but then he saw Alfie and his face broke into a slow smile.

"D-Did you know that your name is of Englassen origin?" he sputtered, his eyes hazy. "It comes from the name Alfred. Interesting, is it not?"

Alfie shook his head, not liking where this was going. "No. I grew up hearing that Alfehr was a family name."

"Marsden," Vesper said in quiet warning, but her brother ignored her.

"Oh, I bet it is," he said, throwing his head back with a laugh. "See, back during our occupation—" he said, then raised his hands to his mouth as if admitting a faux pas.

"You mean enslavement?" Luka added tersely, all the joy from exploding dominoes melting off his face.

"Uh-huh, yes, that," he said. "Back then, Castallanos tried to appear as Englassen as they could be, to ascend from their rank as servants. They didn't hate us like they do now, Vesper," he said to his sister, who stared at him in silent horror. "They wanted to *be* us. So they gave their children Englassen names to give them a b-better chance."

Alfie could feel his blood boiling, and he knew it showed on his face because Luka gripped his shoulder.

"He's drunk," Luka said, his voice tense.

"Marsden, please," Vesper said.

"Alfred is a classic, upstanding name back home," the Englassen prince went on as he tried to drink from an empty glass. "So many slave children were given the name, but they couldn't pronounce it properly. Which is how your name came about. Alfeh*rrr*, instead of Alfred." He emphasized the final letter of Alfie's name, rolling the *r* for a moment too long. "You people love to roll your *r*'s, don't you?" Marsden said as he knocked over the bottle.

Luka caught it, his jaw and his grip tight.

Alfie didn't care if Marsden was drunk—something in the way he said it made it feel as if he were reminding Alfie that his own culture didn't belong to him because Englass had indelibly changed it when they'd colonized them. He seemed to be telling Alfie that his culture wasn't his own, just as Englass had once claimed that magic was not for Castallanos to use. A knot tightened in Alfie's stomach.

"Marsden," Princess Vesper said, her eyes imploring.

"Vesper, I don't shy away from our kingdoms' history," he said, wiping his mouth with the back of his hand. "Don't be so childish."

Alfie couldn't stand this for a moment longer. "I don't shy away from it either, but I'd like to make one thing clear. Whatever origins my name carries, I can assure you that it is Castallano, just as I am Castallano and my ancestors before me were Castallano. How we fought to recover from your tyranny is embedded in our culture, that is true. But it still belongs to us. We look upon it with honor and celebrate it."

Marsden didn't seem to even hear him, which was just as well. When it came to talking to oppressors, they seldom listened. Hazy-eyed, Marsden turned to Luka. "Where'd the rum go?"

Alfie stood from his chair. "I need some air."

"I'll come with you," Vesper said.

More than anything, Alfie wanted to be alone. "That's not necessary."

"Please, I insist," Vesper said, looking desperate. "Please."

Alfie sighed and shot Luka a look. "Watch him."

Luka crossed his arms. "Don't be gone too long."

Alfie stormed out of the bar, Vesper following behind him. Remembering his manners, Alfie stopped and offered his arm. Then he grew angrier. Why should he remember his manners when Marsden could forget his own? Why was he doing so much work for a kingdom that had done nothing but harm his people? Why was he asking them for peace instead of them begging him for forgiveness?

Vesper took his arm, looking up at him apologetically, but Alfie was in no mood for apologies. He just wanted to be angry. With her arm wrapped tightly around his, Alfie led her through the throngs of people roaming the Pinch.

Children lit firecrackers on the side of the street, making Vesper jump and accidentally step on Alfie's foot.

"Sorry," she said sheepishly.

"It's fine," Alfie said without looking at her. He didn't want her to see the anger in his eyes.

"No, it's not fine," she said. "He shouldn't have said that. I'm so sorry."

"Why did you ask me to set up tonight if you knew he was like that?" Alfie said, all his decorum going out the window.

"Because he usually *isn't* like that," Vesper said.

"Oh, he *usually* isn't like that. So he's only like that sometimes?" Alfie asked, his eyes meeting hers.

She looked away from him, ashamed. "Can we walk this way?" she said, gesturing to the right. "It's quieter, so we'll be able to hear each other better."

They were silent for a long while and Alfie quietly fumed as he let her take the lead. He didn't care where he was going so long as his feet carried him away from Marsden.

"I never meant to put you in this position." She met his gaze, her face so genuinely contrite that Alfie felt guilty for nearly shouting at her. "To put you in a position where you would be hurt or insulted. But regardless of what he's like, he is the one who will need the most convincing when it comes to this peace treaty going through. He is the one you'll need to get through to, if you're to change Englass for good."

Alfie stared at her. "What do you mean, he'll be the hardest to convince?"

She opened her mouth to speak, but instead looked over Alfie's shoulder, her eyes alight. "What is this place?"

Alfie looked behind him and his stomach dropped. They were near the entrance to the Plaza of Peace—the plaza that had been made with the shattered pieces of the memorial Alfie had built to commemorate those who had died at Sombra's hands.

Of all the places for his feet to carry him, they had brought him here, to a reminder of his failings. The floor was inlaid with the stained glass from the memorial. At the center was a tall bubbling fountain—a statue of a woman kneeling in quiet grief. The plaza had been outfitted with benches so that people could sit in the quiet. Several families gathered here, dropping flowers into the fountain and praying. Alfie couldn't bear to meet any of their eyes.

He had been told that this was what would become of his destroyed memorial, but he himself had never come to see it. The sight of it reminded him of everything he wanted to forget. He'd spent the night so focused on Marsden's shortcomings that he'd ignored his own. He'd forgotten about those he'd failed. He'd failed to protect his own people from harm four months ago, but maybe, if he could keep his emotions in check, he could protect those in bondage in Englass and create a safer world for his own people, where magical bondage did not exist.

It was shocking to see that a project he'd spent months on had been so quickly rebuilt into something new. Now it was just a beautiful place devoid of the meaning he had intended. To him, it was as hollow as it was colorful.

"It's lovely," Vesper said, walking toward it so quickly that her arm slipped out of Alfie's.

"Wait," Alfie began, but the princess walked to the fountain. Guilt souring his stomach, Alfie followed her.

"What is this place?" she asked again quietly, her eyes on the statue's tearful face.

Alfie swallowed thickly. "It's a place to mourn those we've lost." That was the truth, in a way, but the omission of his hand in all of this sat like a stone in his throat.

"Ah," she said, looking about. "That's why it's so quiet. The floor is beautiful."

Alfie looked down at the stained glass and thought of how every color represented a life lost to his own foolishness. His eyes stung.

"You were going to tell me why Marsden is the person I have to convince," Alfie said, his voice rough with emotion. He cleared his throat and led her away from the fountain, feeling as if the statue's eyes watched him as they went. "Please, tell me what I need to know to make this work."

He needed to make it work. He needed to make *something* work.

"Marsden is . . . ," she began before stopping. "It's difficult to explain—"

Before Vesper could say another word, a great plume of blue smoke erupted around the fountain. A woman seated on the bench near Alfie and Vesper pointed and screamed, nearly falling as she leaped up.

When the smoke cleared, a limp body hung from the fountain statue's outstretched hand, the rope wrapped around its stone fingers. The corpse swung gently from side to side, the creak and groan of the rope keeping its rhythm while the man was silent with death. Alfie's heart sputtered in his chest. They'd only just been standing by the fountain a moment ago; how had this happened?

What had happened?

The answer was perched on the statue's shoulders. The man seemed to have appeared out of thin air. He wore a horned black mask, and though it clung to his face, the mask seemed to move as if it were made of a dark smoke. Alfie's throat went dry, fear pooling in his belly. It looked like Sombra's magic.

Snap out of it, Alfie thought. This was not the time to get lost in past fears when there was plenty to fear in the present. If that was Sombra's magic he would've sensed it; this was just Los Toros' tattooed masks of ink.

They'd been wrong. The bounty hadn't worked. Los Toros hadn't been hiding, only lying in wait. They were back. On the statue was the same message.

NO PEACE FOR COLONIZERS!
KEEP ENGLASSEN SCUM OUT OF CASTALLAN!

Alfie pushed Princess Vesper behind him as she gasped in fear.

"Stop!" he shouted at the masked assassin, but before Alfie could speak a word of magic, the man hurled something at the ground and another cloud of blue smoke spread through the area, making Alfie and Vesper choke. In the blink of an eye, the murderer was dashing down to the far end of the plaza, leaving only the corpse behind.

Those who had come to grieve screamed and ran from the square. Alfie was nearly knocked over by a man carrying his daughter away, his hand pressing her face into his shoulder.

Alfie's blood ran cold as pandemonium descended around him. He needed to stop the man, catch him before he escaped. This was his chance to catch Los Toros and put a stop to everything. "Princess Vesper, please stay safe. I have to stop this."

The princess reluctantly let his arm go, her face pale, and Alfie dashed after the man who was now climbing onto the hunched roofs of the Pinch and running across them.

Alfie followed, but the man was fast. He'd lose him if he didn't stop him soon. Hundreds of rooftops stretched out before him, leaning against one another like drunken friends. For the moment they were on the very same roof, the murderer not even caring to give Alfie a backward glance. That was fine for Alfie—that way the man wouldn't see the spell coming.

"*Paral*—" Before Alfie could finish uttering the paralyzing spell, the murderer turned and flung something at him. It zoomed toward Alfie's face so quickly that he hardly had time to block it.

With a wet slap something sticky slammed over his mouth, gluing his lips shut. Alfie clawed at the viscous substance, digging his nails into it, but no matter how much he pulled it wouldn't come off. He felt helpless. If he couldn't speak, he couldn't use spoken magic. It was his best line of defense. Now he was in a war without a weapon.

The masked man gave a little bow as if he were a stage magician who had just performed a successful trick.

Alfie glared at him. He wanted to rip the man's shifting mask off his face. If he'd learned anything from Finn, it was that spoken magic wasn't the only way to fight back. The fountain burbled in the square beneath them. Whipping his hands, Alfie pulled ribbons of water from it, and just as the masked man moved to sprint away, ice froze his feet to the adobe-brick roof.

Alfie dashed forward, pulling more water from the fountain. He pelted the man with frozen shards, but the stranger stepped forward into the barrage of ice, as if he welcomed it. Alfie's eyes widened; he had no desire to see or hear the ice penetrate his skin, but the man simply walked through it; the ice sailed through him as if he were made of air. He'd walked out of the ice constraints too. Alfie skidded to a halt, nearly tripping over his own feet. How had he done it? Then he remembered: the little boy whose father had been killed by Los Toros had said that his father was pulled through the wall. The murderer had the ability to move himself and others through matter. Was this the same man? Alfie stared at him and watched the magic move through the murderer, a chilling ice blue that moved erratically like lightning. The way the magic flowed made Alfie think this was a man who liked to play with his food before he killed it.

His heart pounding in his chest, Alfie forced himself to run forward again. He couldn't let this man get away.

Alfie took a page from Finn's book and froze a globe of ice around his fist. This man could make himself transparent, but Alfie did not know the other properties of his *propio*. Maybe he could only do it for so long—in which case, if Alfie kept attacking, a hit would eventually land. The man stood still as a statue, waiting for Alfie to strike.

Alfie swung his fist at the murderer's jaw, but it was as if his hand moved through thickened water. The man's head shifted as if it were made of smoke before snapping back into place. Hit after hit led to the same result until Alfie's shirt was soaked with sweat.

The masked man held his hands out as if asking, *Are you done yet?*

When Alfie tried to punch him again, the man just sank through the roof, as if it were water.

Alfie looked around, his eyes searching for the assailant. The man's *propio* let him sink through solid objects. This, without a doubt, must be the man who had killed Arturo Camacho and pulled his heart from his chest.

How would Alfie find him now? Panic surged through him and he tugged at the stubborn jelly on his mouth again as he moved in a slow circle. He felt naked without his spoken magic to help him.

Just as Alfie started to think the murderer had fled, the masked man shot up through the roof inches from Alfie's feet and hit Alfie's chin with an uppercut that left his vision spotted with pinpricks of light. Alfie swayed on his feet and fell forward. To his surprise, the masked man let the prince fall against him rather than step back to let Alfie crash to the ground, almost as if he wanted to help Alfie.

Alfie stared in shock at the ever-shifting mask before finding his senses and gripping the murderer by the forearm marked with the Los Toros tattoo. Wrenching himself free of Alfie's hold, the masked man shoved Alfie back with both hands until the prince was teetering on the edge of the roof, his arms windmilling to keep his balance. His mouth kept trying to open to speak some spellwork that would cushion his fall, but he couldn't utter a word.

The assailant dashed forward and kicked Alfie squarely in the chest, sending him sailing off the roof. The air whooshed around him as he fell, the pounding of his heart muted by the sounds of screams below. Were they screaming because of the corpse or because they'd seen him fall? He couldn't be sure. Alfie could feel the ground rushing up to meet him, to shatter him, and he couldn't speak a word.

"*Freeze!*" Vesper shouted in Englassen. Alfie's falling body came to a halt in midair. With another word of magic Alfie floated down to the ground into the princess's arms. "Are you all right?" she asked, her face shockingly pale against her dark red hair.

Alfie pointed to the jelly on his mouth. He wanted to tell her to use spoken magic to get rid of it, but all he could do was murmur desperately while pointing. He needed to get back up and follow the masked man, but he wouldn't be able to do much if he couldn't speak.

"What is it?" Vesper said, her eyes wide as she reached for the jelly, then pulled her hand back as if it'd been burned. "Erm, may I?" she asked.

Alfie had never encountered anyone so annoyingly polite. He gave a groan of exasperation and pointed more fervently at his mouth.

Vesper held her palm over his face and said, "*Dissolve.*" The jelly slowly began to melt off his face, but he still couldn't part his lips. "*Dissolve,*" she said again, her brow furrowing. She had to speak the spellwork three times for it to fully dissipate.

Alfie tried to get to his feet, but Vesper held his arm. "Prince Alfie, he's gone," she said. "Don't put yourself in danger again. Please."

"I'm so sorry," he gasped. He'd been upset because Marsden had said some prejudiced drivel while drunk, but he'd put her life in mortal danger. "This is not what Castallan stands for. We have tried to protect you from this—"

"This isn't the first time this has happened?" Vesper asked, her voice shaking.

Shame pooled in his belly. There was no point in lying any longer. "It isn't. It started just before you arrived. I'm so sorry. The memories of any Englassens in the areas of the murders were blurred with magic so that they couldn't report back to your family," Alfie admitted, not wanting to hold anything back any longer.

Vesper closed her eyes for a long moment, and Alfie wondered if she was going to start crying. Such public displays of emotion were unheard of in her culture, but a moment like this could test anyone's control. In the end, Vesper did no such thing. When she opened her eyes, her gaze was sharp with resolve—a cool, almost calculating look Alfie had never seen her wear before. For the first time since he'd met her, he could see her resemblance to Marsden.

"My brother can't know about this." Her eyes strayed to the corpse and the anti-Englass message written there. "Do you understand?" she asked, her eyes stony. "He cannot know anything about it—we need to get him back to the palace before he hears anything."

Alfie blinked. "What?"

"We can't let anything distract from the peace summit," she said, gripping Alfie by the arm. "We have to get my brother back to the palace now before he finds out."

Alfie nodded, his jaw still slack. He'd thought she would tell him that her family would hear about these incidents immediately, about how Alfie had endangered the lives of Englass's heirs, but instead she was willing to hide it for the sake of peace. He'd been skeptical, but now, for the first time, he truly trusted her commitment to peace. He didn't know how to repay her.

"Princess Vesper," he said, his voice thick. "Thank you."

She pulled him back toward the maze of pubs they'd walked through. "Thank me once we get my brother back without him seeing it."

With that, the two rushed through the panicked throngs of people who had closed in on the scene. By the time they got back to the bar, Marsden was still so drunk he could barely remember his own name. He sat slumped in his chair, his cheek pressed against the wet table he'd been so hesitant to touch before. Finn's magic was fading from his face now that he was too sauced.

"Took you long enough," Luka groused.

The bar was so loud that no one had heard the screams outside, but it was only a matter of time before they began clearing out the pubs, looking for suspects.

"We have to go," Alfie said. "Right now."

Luka stared at him for a long moment. "What happened?"

Alfie pulled the tether from his cloak pocket. "I'll tell you when we get home."

Together all four royals grabbed the tether, Vesper placing her drunken brother's hand on it, and returned to the library.

When they landed in the library with a stumble, Marsden slurred, "Why did we leave so fast? That was fun!" He gave a hiccup.

"Come on, Marsden," Vesper said, her face still pale from what she'd seen. She shot Alfie a look before guiding her brother out of the library, his arm draped over her shoulder. In her face Alfie saw disappointment, but also a spark of kinship. She wouldn't tell anyone about what had happened. She would keep her word.

"Alfie," Luka said once she was gone and the library was empty again. "What happened? And what's all over your shirt?"

Alfie looked down and saw that his shirt had a strange black footprint on it. He hadn't noticed until they were in the well-lit library. It was some sort of stain from where the assassin had kicked him in the chest, but a dirty shirt was the least of his worries right now.

"Another murder," Alfie said, his throat tight. "Los Toros weren't hiding—they were waiting."

THE REQUESTS

"Dez?" Alfie asked. He had the strange sense that he was too close to the ground. His legs were so much shorter now. He was twelve years old again.

"Hmmm?" Dez didn't look up from the book he was reading. There was a cut on his face from shaving, and Alfie rubbed at his own jaw, annoyed at how smooth it was.

"When you grow up, you'll be king," Alfie said as he walked the perimeter of the library, running his small hands over the spines of leather tomes that were older than he was.

Dez laughed. If sunlight made a sound, it would be Dez's laugh. "That's what everyone keeps telling me, hermanito."

"But what will I be?" Alfie asked, his hand dropping from the books.

Dez looked up this time, closing the book but using his thumb to keep his place. "What do you mean?"

"Right now we're both princes," Alfie said with a shrug. "We're the same. But in a little while you'll become king. What will I become?"

Dez tilted his head, thinking for a long moment, and Alfie knew that he'd asked a difficult question, otherwise Dez would've just laughed it off or magicked some books to chase Alfie around the library.

"You're right, Alfie, I will become king," Dez admitted. "But you will have the freedom to become anything you want. Anything in the whole wide mundo. It's yours to decide." Dez motioned to the piles of books on the table, books he was tasked with reviewing as he prepared to become king. Dez was always surrounded by books, by things to learn. "I wish I had what you had, Alfie. I wish I had that freedom. Instead, I have books."

Alfie looked away from Dezmin, ignoring the joke. He wished that the diviner had told him something, anything that would assure him of what to expect from his life. Dez knew he was going to be king, that his legacy would be eternal, but Alfie knew nothing.

"Alfie," Dez said gently. He tapped Alfie under the chin. "Look at me."

Alfie turned to his big brother, his pulse jumping at the sight. Dez's face was so still that it looked like a statue, as if it had died long ago but had been frozen in time before it could fester and rot.

"Help me," Dez whispered, his face still frozen aside from his lips. "Don't let me go." And then he was screaming so loudly that Alfie had to cover his ears. He tried to run but Dez gripped him by the jaw, holding him painfully tight, forcing him to watch as his face crumbled away into nothing.

Alfie sat up in his bed, his head pounding.

He gasped for breath, but the air didn't seem to find him. Kicking the tangled sheets off his legs, Alfie shakily stood before walking out onto his balcony. The morning chill dried his sweat as he gripped the railing and took in the fresh air.

Finn's voice found him then, telling him to count just as she had when he'd spiraled into panic at the Clock Tower. She'd taken his hand and held it to her chest, her heart beating steady beneath his palm, so controlled compared with his own.

Slow yours down, she'd said. *Meet me in the middle.*

Alfie counted down from ten twice over, feeling his heart begin to calm. The sun hadn't even begun to rise yet. Why was he having so many dreams of Dez lately? It hadn't been this bad since just after Dezmin had died.

"It's just stress," he mumbled to himself. "Nothing more, nothing less." His mind was conjuring his brother because while Dez had worked so hard to orchestrate this summit, Alfie was the one participating. Guilt sat heavy in his chest at the thought of what this summit could have been if Dez were alive—that guilt had built up into a few nightmares. That and his anxiety about Los Toros was getting to him, that was all.

Last night he'd seen the power of Los Toros face-to-face. He had never encountered such a powerful *propio*. Thus far he knew they had members who could manipulate bones and move through matter. What more would Alfie find if he kept pursuing them? He had been lucky to make it out alive last night. And what would happen if Vesper changed her mind and told her parents what she'd seen?

Los Toros threatening the lives of the delegados was bad enough, but they also threatened this summit and all they hoped to accomplish through it. If the rest of the Englassen royals found out what was going on, they'd likely end the summit, and a caste system that destroyed the lives of thousands—just as it had destroyed the lives of his ancestors generations ago—would stay firmly in place. He had to hope that she would keep her word and not tell them, and that they'd at least keep Los Toros at bay until the summit ended.

Breakfast would be served in a few hours. Alfie grimaced, thinking of how little sleep he'd gotten. His chest ached from the assassin's kick, which would have sent him falling to his death had Vesper not caught him with her spellwork.

After he and Luka had returned home last night, with Vesper and a very drunk Marsden in tow, they had been brought into another late-night meeting with his parents about the murder. There was nothing to be done at this point but to increase security even further and hope that they could finish the last four days of the summit. The guardsmen were now tasked with inspecting any and all citizens for bull tattoos.

Marsden's words still rubbed Alfie raw, but Vesper's promise to keep the murder a secret fell over him like a salve. She was so committed to peace and helping her people that she was willing to hide such immediate danger from her own family. It was admirable beyond words. Yet last night he'd yelled at her. It wasn't her fault that her brother was who he was. In her own way, she'd been trying to help. It was disastrous, but she was trying.

Alfie massaged his temples. Today was the fourth day of the summit, which meant they would finally begin discussing the deconstruction of Englass's caste system. He had to hope that things would go well, but after last night, hope was in short supply. Even though Marsden had been drunk, Alfie was sure he'd remember their argument at the pub.

Alfie walked back into his rooms, stepping over his clothes from the night before. His shirt was still covered in the strange residue from the assassin's shoe. Usually the servants would clean his room and take his clothes to be washed daily, but he'd asked them to keep out for now. The last thing he wanted was for the servants to walk in on Finn waiting for him.

Alfie stared at the shirt, thinking of the panic that had surged through him as his hand sailed through the assassin's head, as if the man were a ghost. Of the look of pure fear on Vesper's face. Alfie balled up the shirt and threw it in his overflowing hamper.

With shaking hands, he opened his bedside drawer. Inside was the parchment that connected him to Finn. He'd written a long, messy paragraph about what had happened, but she hadn't responded. Did she not want to help him investigate Los Toros anymore? Was that why she was ignoring him now? His shadow wriggled nervously on the floor.

A knock sounded on Alfie's door, loud and insistent. Alfie squinted at the clock. It was still far too early for breakfast. Everyone should still be asleep.

Alfie opened the door to see Paloma standing before him. She looked haggard, her face drawn tight with stress. "The royal families are having a meeting. Get dressed and come to the throne room immediately."

"What's happened?" Alfie asked.

"The Englassen royals know about the murders."

Alfie's heart froze in his chest as Paloma left him to get dressed.

When Alfie got to the throne room, it was as if he'd stepped into a different world.

His parents sat on their thrones, surrounded by guards, Luka hovering just beside them. The Englassen royals stood before them with a retinue of their own guardsmen. It looked as if a small war was about to take place in the throne room.

Alfie moved to stand at his parents' side and watched Marsden's eyes land on him before narrowing into slits. Had Vesper told them what had happened the night before? Was that how they'd found out?

But when Alfie met Vesper's gaze, he could see the answer in her eyes. She hadn't told them.

"Several of our guardsmen were exploring the city last night only to find themselves in the midst of an anti-Englass murder scene," King Alistair said, his face pinched with anger. "And, what is more, it appears that this was not the first anti-Englassen murder there has been in the city, but the third. The *third*," he seethed.

"We meant you no harm," said Queen Amada. "We thought we had the situation under control—"

"You had no such thing," the Englassen king interrupted. "You had no control, only chaos. Chaos that is a danger to my family."

"We have half a mind to leave this very instant. How are we to trust you, make peace with you, when you hide such significant information from us?" Queen Elinore asked.

"Please," Alfie said, stepping forward. The Englassen king and queen stared at him as if he were a toddler trying to speak his first words. "Let me explain. The anti-Englassen threat only started the night before the summit was to begin. We have waited so long for this summit and were afraid to postpone it in fear that it would never come to pass. We were foolish not to tell you the truth about what has been happening in the city, but know that our poor decision was made with good intentions—the intention to make peace with you regardless of the risk. We have seen our own people be slaughtered and yet we are still here, hoping to make peace with you above all else. We are so close to meeting that goal."

The Englassen king stared at Alfie, his eyes assessing. Alfie couldn't tell if he had saved the summit or doomed it. Marsden's heated glare made him feel as if he'd accomplished the latter. His mother squeezed his forearm, her eyes hopeful.

King Alistair and Queen Elinore spoke to each other in hushed tones before finally turning their attention back to Alfie and his family.

"We understand that this summit is of great importance to you. We came here because it is important for our kingdom as well," Alistair said, his voice level but still edged with anger. "And, of course, we knew that our shared history would breed anger among your people. That much was expected, but not to the level of murder. We cannot stay here without knowing the full extent of the dangers that exist and implementing precautions to protect my family and my dignitaries should we continue this summit."

"Speak your mind," King Bolivar said. "What can we do to ensure that we may finish our great work at this summit?"

"All remaining events must be relocated onto palace grounds for our safety. Now that we know there is a threat, we will not gallivant through your kingdom," Alistair said.

"Very well," King Bolivar said. All things considered, that was an easy demand. "It will be done."

"From here on out we must know about any anti-Englassen

behavior," Queen Elinore said, her chin held high. "If we are to be targeted, then at least arm us with that knowledge."

"Of course," Queen Amada said, though Alfie could feel the tension emanating from her. "It will be done."

"And we require protection," King Alistair continued.

"We are happy to have our trained guardsmen protect—"

"No," King Alistair said. "No, you must understand that there is an anti-Englassen threat here in this city and we cannot know which Castallanos are for or against it. To naively trust any Castallano guard would be foolish."

Tension stretched between the families.

Alistair met Bolivar's gaze. "We will triple our own guards in the palace and station guards in the city."

Luka's eyebrows shot up his forehead at that. Alfie had to stop his jaw from dropping. Posting armed Englassen guardsmen around the city was asking for more trouble. The people would riot. It would look as if Englass had taken over once more.

"With all due respect," Queen Amada said, "our city is our own and we cannot have foreign guards monitoring our people."

"If we cannot have our guards patrolling the city and assisting in catching those who threaten us, then we cannot stay," Prince Marsden said, his eyes falling on Alfie. "We are in danger every moment we remain here. Imagine if Vesper and I had decided to explore the city last night." He shot Alfie a pointed look, clearly aware that Alfie had decided to take them out knowing that the threat was out there. Alfie held little respect for Marsden, but he knew the other prince was right to be angry. "Our economy is not in such dire straits that we're willing to be slaughtered. Should you want us to stay, you will have to do what we ask so that we may feel safe."

Vesper stood behind him, looking at Alfie beseechingly. He could tell from her face that this was the only way that they would stay. And could he blame them for wanting to protect themselves when they'd learned of the murders done in the name of ousting them from the kingdom?

Alfie's parents looked at one another, words passing between them silently. They always knew what the other was thinking without speaking a word. The king gripped the arms of his throne tightly, loosening his grip only after Queen Amada took his hand. She nodded at him before turning back to the Englassen royals.

"We agree to your requests," she said. "For these final four days of the summit, your guards will help patrol our streets and end this threat once and for all."

Alfie could hear how difficult this was in her voice, and he knew that this summit would become rougher still.

"Then we will adjourn until our meeting this morning," King Alistair said.

With that, the Englassen royals left the throne room, their retinue of guards close behind.

King Bolivar sagged in his chair. "This is an absolute disaster."

"We salvaged it the best way we could," Queen Amada said.

"But at what cost?" the king asked. "How do you think the people will feel being watched by Englassen guardsmen? They will think we've sold ourselves right back into slavery."

"But we aren't; we are doing this to establish peace and end Englass's history of slavery. In the end, it will be worth it," the queen said, and Alfie had to believe that this was true. Dez had believed it, and he knew that peace wouldn't come easily. Four days of Englassen guards roaming the streets was a steep price, but worth it if it put an end to their caste system. When magical enslavement existed anywhere, it was a danger to everyone. They were doing this for the suffering Englassens just as much as they were doing it for themselves. "We're five generations free and we still know too well the damage that enslavement does to a people. We must free them."

"That's not how the Castallano people will feel," Luka said somberly. "They will hate us even more for this."

"Their hatred will be temporary," Paloma said, but she looked uncharacteristically worried. "The end of the practice of magical enslavement will be eternal if we can do this right."

Queen Amada nodded. "We weather the storm for these remaining four days, but we keep our eyes on the horizon."

Alfie couldn't help but feel as if the horizon had all but disappeared and they were sailing blindly into oblivion.

The sun was only just beginning to rise on the fourth morning of the summit when his family parted ways to prepare for today's meeting. On this of all days, they would be discussing the deconstruction of Englass's caste system. Alfie rubbed the back of his neck warily. That meeting would have been tense no matter what, but now it would be almost unbearable.

When Alfie turned the corner to get to his rooms, he was surprised to find Prince Marsden in front of his door, two Englassen guards accompanying him.

The Castallano guards stationed throughout the hall and at Alfie's doors stood at attention, their hands twitching to reach for their machetes should anything untoward happen.

Alfie swallowed a lump in his throat. "Prince Marsden, I—"

"Let me make this abundantly clear," Marsden hissed quietly, stepping forward so that he was closer to Alfie, but not so close as to anger the Castallano guards, though Alfie could feel them shifting behind him, moving closer to protect him. "I did not tell my parents about you and that fool taking us into town because Vesper begged me not to. Since she foolishly insisted that we go, she would be partly blamed, so I will keep it to myself. But know this: after learning that you dared to take my sister gallivanting in the streets when you *knew* there was danger, I will never trust you again. Not unless you earn it."

His eyes blazing, Marsden turned on his heel, his hand curling into a fist as he walked.

"Are you all right, Your Highness?" a guardswoman asked. Alfie turned to see that two had moved to flank him while Marsden had spoken. He'd never felt more grateful.

"I'm fine, thank you," Alfie lied. The worst part was that he couldn't blame Marsden for being angry. He had put Vesper in danger, and now he was paying the price.

THE ABANDONED DOG

Finn woke up late on the fourth day of the summit, her mind hazy from the long swigs of rum she'd drunk before falling into bed.

She'd hoped that chasing the diviner's words with liquor would help, but it only gave her a headache when Anabeltilia forced her out of bed just before noon.

"Levántate!" Anabeltilia grunted, tugging the sheets off Finn in one quick motion. "We need to talk."

"Go away," Finn groused, folding the pillow around her head so that it covered both ears. "Unless you found the maldito *propio* seer, leave me be." That was the only lead they had left anyway.

"It cannot wait," she argued.

"I already know everything about the murder, Los Toros, blah blah blah," Finn groaned. "Let me sleep."

Anabeltilia crossed her arms. "Englassen guards are patrolling the streets."

That was enough to jolt Finn out of her drowsiness. "*Qué?!*"

"As of this morning," she said. "Now get up and meet me in

Kol's"—she paused for a long moment—"your office."

When Finn finally stumbled in, Anabeltilia was staring at the map of San Cristóbal hanging above the desk. A new red tack had found its place on the eastern side of the Pinch to mirror the third murder on the right side. Finn grimaced. The prince had written to her about what had happened after he took the Englassen princess and prince out for the night, but by the time she'd read it, she was already half-drunk, her mind still rattled by the diviner's words.

Your destinies are so intertwined that I could not see his future until I found you. And now, more than ten years later, here you are.

Finn went cold at the memory of her vision—the prince knifed in the stomach and left to die.

It is unusual to see someone else's future, but if you do, that means you are an integral part of why that future will come to pass.

The diviner had all but told her that she was the one responsible for Alfie's death.

"If that's his fate, it must be because you're here," Ignacio said, sitting on the edge of her desk as if he owned it. "You know that."

"Shut your mouth."

"I didn't even say anything." Anabeltilia turned around, looking offended. "Are you still drunk?"

Finn pinched the bridge of her nose. "No, I'm just . . ." She sighed. "Just tell me what we need to talk about."

Anabeltilia stared at her, expectant. "Los Toros murdered a third delegado last night, and now there are Englassen soldiers marching around. You think that's a coincidence?"

Even though she was still a bit tipsy, Finn could see the logic there. Had the Englassen royals found out about the murders? A thought sparked to life in her mind. Of course they'd found out. Alfie had written that the princess had witnessed the murder. She'd probably told them.

Finn smirked. The princess probably had gone crying to Mamí and Papí about it. She'd had a bad feeling about her and now it was confirmed.

Finn scowled. Why did she care if the princess had a spine or not?

She remembered the look on the girl's face when Alfie had walked into the library last night. Finn's scowl deepened, her shadow twisting at her feet.

It didn't matter.

"But it does matter," Ignacio crooned. "Because we all know who the prince would pick if given the choice between a little murderess who lost the vanishing cloak, his greatest possession, and a princess with her nose in a book."

Finn bit her lip and willed herself not to shout another insult at him.

"Do you know how much harder it's going to be for la Familia to do any thieving with not only Castallano guards all over the place but Englassen ones too?"

"You've got a point." Finn rubbed her temples. "Maybe you should be running this stupid family instead of me."

Anabeltilia squinted at her. "Are you being serious and complimenting me or are you being sarcastic and insulting me?"

"Yes," Finn answered, standing.

"I'm trying to help you," Anabeltilia said through gritted teeth. "And all you do is drink and make stupid jokes and disappear."

"She's not wrong, Mija," Ignacio chimed in. Finn could feel a devastating headache blooming just behind her forehead. "Look at her, protecting the legacy of the one who raised her," Ignacio said. "You could learn a thing or two from her."

Anabeltilia glowered at her. "I'm trying to save this maldito gang—"

"No," Finn shouted. She didn't know if she was shouting at Ignacio or Anabeltilia, but at this point she'd settle for both. "You are working yourself into the ground to serve the memory of a monster who put you on your knees and scars on your back! It's pathetic. It makes me sick to my damn stomach." Finn's chest heaved, her breaths ragged.

Anabeltilia took a step back as Finn advanced. "You don't know what you're talking about."

"I know exactly what I'm talking about!" Finn shouted. "Kol's dead—dead and gone and you could've left this place! Could've been free! Instead you're still here, chained here like an abandoned dog."

Anabeltilia stared at her for a long moment. The look on the girl's face was so broken that Finn had to look away.

Finn heard Anabeltilia walk out the door.

Ignacio began to clap his hands in polite applause as if he were watching a play. "Muy bien."

THE SINS OF OUR FATHERS

Today was not the ideal day to have this meeting.

If Alfie had been asked about this a week ago, he probably would've said that there would be no right day to have this meeting with the Englassens, but after this morning's events, today of all days, past, present, and future, felt like the worst possible option. On top of that, he could hardly focus because he, Finn, and Luka would be meeting with the Tattooed King tonight.

The enormous meeting room had been comfortable before, but now it felt claustrophobic as they all took their seats, shoulders tense. The progress made thus far would only be worth it if today went well—if Englass finally agreed to dismantle their caste system in exchange for reopening trade relations. Englass had come into this summit knowing that this was what would be asked of them. Alfie could only hope that they would be able to come to an agreement quickly—but after this morning, he doubted it.

Vesper had already warned him that Marsden would be hardest to sway, and now that he knew about Los Toros he had all the more reason to sabotage this meeting.

The Englassen royal family and their many advisors took one side of the table and the Castallanos took the other. When everyone was settled into their seats, Alfie's father cleared his throat.

"Buenos días to all," King Bolivar began. "We have discussed, at length, how a partnership would benefit both our kingdoms. Now it is time to discuss the great compromise that must be made for us to reap those benefits. In the interest of reestablishing our economic relationship, we request that you immediately dissolve the Englassen caste system that enslaves your people, and allow your newly freed population the opportunity to use magic and work for fair pay," he said, his voice confident despite the morning's tension. Alfie didn't know how he did it. "Only then can we reopen trade and truly consider ourselves allies. We have prepared a proposal for how this might be achieved."

With that, a trio of delegados stood and outlined Castallan's proposal to immediately free the magically enslaved Englassens, with Castallan loaning Englass the funds to provide reparations and basic magical education to them all. The loan would also help Englass transition to an economy that did not rely on the cheap labor of the enslaved and would give them the means to properly integrate the freed people into a new way of life. Englass would have to pay Castallan back with interest for decades, but they would have the help they needed to end the practice of magical bondage.

As the delegados spoke about educating the newly freed Englassens, it occurred to Alfie that even his own kingdom didn't provide basic magical education to the lower classes. While the wealthy could afford tutors for their children, the poor learned what they could from each other.

Finn's voice sounded in his head, *The rich are born rich and die richer, the rest of us die early.*

He swallowed the lump in his throat. Her words were as poignant now as they had been four months ago. It was easy to pretend Castallan was perfect compared to Englass, but it was far from it. This was something he would have to change when he became king. At that thought, Alfie could swear that he felt Dezmin with him, nodding along.

When the delegados finished their presentation, Bolivar nodded at the Englassen king, waiting for him to respond.

"We are humbled by the detailed plan you have so eloquently described and we have considered your demands with great care," Alistair said, his light eyes nearly hidden by his bushy brows.

"We look forward to hearing your thoughts on our proposal," Queen Amada said magnanimously, but Alfie could read between the lines. His mother was telling the Englassen king that she was looking forward to his concessions.

King Alistair cleared his throat. "We understand your request that we end our caste system immediately with the help of your aid. But that would necessitate Englass being indebted to Castallan for so long," he said. Alfie could feel his jaw beginning to clench. The man might as well have been speaking about the weather, not the lives of thousands of Englassen people who'd been robbed of their magic, robbed of themselves. "Our preference is to forgo the loan and end the caste system slowly over time, with the promise of dissolving it entirely within fifty years."

Alfie shot his mother and father a look of barely veiled horror. Fifty years?

"A single decade would allow far too much suffering, let alone five," King Bolivar said. Alfie could hear his father trying to stay poised, but it was clear he was disturbed.

"I have brought my council to explain our plan to end the caste system gradually," King Alistair said, unfazed by their reaction as he gestured at a group of older Englassens, who stood and began to explain the plan.

"To accept such a loan from Castallan is out of the question, as it would be nearly impossible to repay. So we must end the caste system slowly. As your plan pointed out, much of our economic strength relies on the inexpensive labor of the lower classes. To create a system of magical equality at all, let alone that quickly, would upend our economy," one of the advisors began.

Fury singed Alfie from the inside out. Fifty years. Fifty more years of magical enslavement—*that* was their great compromise.

When the Englassens finished their proposal, the Castallano advisors murmured among themselves and Alfie's parents listened intently, nodding.

Queen Amada stood, and the room fell silent. "We appreciate the thought you have put into this plan, but we cannot help but think that fifty years is far too gradual while your people continue to suffer as our ancestors did. To support that practice is not something we can in good conscience do."

Before Queen Amada could continue, Marsden stood, his face reddening to match his hair. "You are already asking us to dismantle a huge part of our culture," he said, and Alfie could see anger from this morning lingering on his face. Marsden already knew that this was going to be asked of them, yet he was fighting it as if he'd been blindsided. "The least you could do is give us enough time to do so properly. Instead you ask us to take a loan so that we'll be filling your coffers for generations trying to pay it back. You wish to hobble Englass permanently!"

"Marsden," Queen Elinore said tersely from her seat, but the prince waved a dismissive hand at his mother as if he were waving away a fly. Alfie raised his eyebrows. He couldn't imagine what his mother would say if he'd waved her off like that.

Marsden ignored his father's warning look and stood his ground, his wide chin raised high. Though Alfie still felt bad for endangering him and Vesper the night before, he wanted nothing more than to make the arrogant prince bow his head in shame. But he didn't know how to speak without losing himself to anger or seeming too meek.

What would Finn do? he wondered.

Throw a dagger at Marsden's face, his mind supplied. Alfie shook his head. He missed her, but she was not the one he should be taking a cue from in this situation.

Dezmin. What would Dezmin do?

The answer came so swiftly that he barely had to think.

Dez would fight. For Castallan and for anyone who needed him. The people of Englass were not Alfie's kin, but they needed his voice all the same. He had to use it. He had to try.

Shooting his parents a silent look asking for permission, Alfie cleared his throat. "With all due respect," he said, rising. "You speak of your people as if they are cattle. You speak of them in terms of numbers, economic growth and decline. But they are not simply pesos in your coffers. They are people—people who have suffered greatly under this caste system. You ask for three generations as if you're simply asking for time, and not their children and their children's children. Their lives. Their well-being. To accept anything less than an immediate end of the caste system would be a disrespect to your own people as well as our ancestors."

Ignoring a quelling look from his father, the Englassen prince responded. "You are punishing us for a past that we did not orchestrate." His nostrils flared. "What of Queen Amada's words at our first meeting? I thought you held no one responsible for the sins of their forefathers?"

Alfie took a deep breath, smoothing the anxiety from his voice. "We do not hold you accountable for the past, Prince Marsden, but we do hold you accountable for the present and the future. You did not create the system that enslaved my people or your own, but you benefit from it today and choose to continue it. Until you agree to stop receiving those benefits, we cannot become allies and we will not resume trade or encourage our allies to do so."

"You don't seek peace between our kingdoms, you seek vengeance. You want to enslave Englass with that loan!"

Alfie leaned forward across the table, anger singing in his blood. "You speak as if paying back a loan is the same as enslaving a whole kingdom."

"It may as well be!" Marsden shot back, and Alfie was stunned by how insensitive the prince was, how bold he was to equate anything to the horrors of enslavement. "All this after your family lied to us—"

"Prince Marsden," his father said, thunder in his voice. Marsden started and looked at his fuming father. "Sit. Down."

Still glaring at Alfie, Marsden finally sat.

The Englassen advisors were whispering now too as the king admonished Marsden quietly until the prince crossed his arms and huffed.

King Bolivar squeezed Alfie's shoulder. "Well done, Mijo," he said quietly, keeping his face calm and unreadable to the Englassens across the table, but Alfie could see the spark of pride in his eyes.

The Englassen royals and advisors conferred for several long minutes. Alfie waited, wringing his hands.

Alfie had never been aggressive in any sense of the word, but it was as if for a moment he was a king, and he was surprised to realize that it felt good.

When Alfie looked across the table, he expected glares of disapproval from the Englassens, but instead he caught Princess Vesper's eye. He could've sworn she looked impressed.

King Alistair cleared his throat and stood, silencing his advisors. "We ask that we have time to deliberate so that we can discuss the issue in more depth at tomorrow's meeting."

"Very well." King Bolivar nodded, his voice tense. "We look forward to it. We will reconvene tomorrow morning."

THE NEW DESTINY

Finn wished she were asleep, or at least drunker, but instead she had to be here at yet another meeting with the thief lords.

She was hungover, stressed, and guilty. Hungover from all the rum she'd drunk. Stressed over what she'd seen in the diviner's crystal ball last night and what that kooky woman had said to her. And guilty for yelling at Anabeltilia and ignoring Alfie.

She knew he'd sent her messages in the parchment, but she left it at home, refusing to look at it. He'd told her before that today would be the first meetings about ending the caste system with Englass. He was probably nervous, but still she couldn't bear to look at the parchment.

She, Elian, and Rodrigo sat at the table waiting for Emeraude. She'd said she needed a moment to talk to her underlings, and Finn was grateful for the silence for the sake of her headache, but angry about it for the sake of her thoughts. There was nothing to distract her from remembering what she'd seen in the diviner's rooms.

"New Kol," Rodrigo said.

Finn raised her head, scowling. "What?" She didn't have the energy to fight him on that stupid nickname anymore.

"Looks like you and Emeraude have a special bond, all that extra talking after Elian and I leave. . . ."

Elian nodded.

"What can I say," Finn groused, rubbing away the crust at the corners of her mouth. "I'm all about girl power."

"Just because she's the eldest among us doesn't mean you should trust her," Rodrigo continued, unamused. From the brief interactions Finn had seen between him and Emeraude, it was clear that they had a tense relationship. She wondered what made him hate the older woman so much.

Finn scoffed. "Are you saying I should trust you instead?"

"Oh no," he laughed, his face turning a shade more serious. "You shouldn't trust a single one of us."

She couldn't tell if he was joking or warning her. Before Finn could speak, Emeraude walked into the room and sat in her chair.

"Thank you all for coming," she said, her eyes staying on Finn's tired face for a moment too long. "We have much to discuss."

"Should we start with the fact that Englassen guards are now patrolling this city?" Rodrigo said, crossing his arms. "This so-called peace summit feels more like an invitation for those pendejos to run our kingdom again."

Finn had seen the Englassen guards posted on corners throughout the rings as she came to this meeting. Even though Anabeltilia had warned her about it, at first she thought she was just so drunk that she thought she was imagining things, but upon realizing it was real, she was shocked.

She could feel the tension rising with every Englassen guard she passed. To give Englass the power to station their guards felt like a violation, a step backward toward the years of their occupation in Castallan. Whatever had happened for the Castallano royals to allow that must've been big. Maybe Anabeltilia was right; maybe the Englassens had discovered the anti-Englassen murders.

A knot of guilt formed in Finn's stomach at the thought of the girl. Of how she'd yelled at her when she'd really wanted to yell at herself. Finn crossed her arms. Why should she care about hurting Anabeltilia's feelings? When had she started caring about anyone's feelings?

"Trust me, I'm not a fan of the Englassen guards either." Emeraude frowned. "Finn, did your connections in the palace tell you why this is happening?"

At the sound of her name, Finn straightened in her seat. "Nothing yet," she lied. Alfie had probably explained on the parchment, but she'd tucked that away into her desk.

"Shame." Rodrigo drummed his fingers on the table.

"My guess is that Englass learned about the murders and about Los Toros, and they demanded this for the rest of the summit," Emeraude said.

"Disgusting," Rodrigo groused, his eyes on Emeraude. "You wanted our forces to protect the summit, but Castallan has that covered with Englassen soldiers. Our job is done; they've got all the help they need."

Emeraude shot him a hard look. "I still think we ought to consider it—"

Rodrigo gave a bark of laughter, a sharp, angry sound that spoke of nothing funny. "They let Englass station guards all over our city like they own us again, and you still want us to send our people to help them?! Have you gone senile in your old age?"

"Rodrigo, we have never faced a threat like this!" Emeraude shouted. "A gang with so much power that they kill delegados and destroy our own connections with impunity! You think we should just sit and wait? Hope that the royals handle it when they can barely handle this summit as is? For all we know Los Toros are coming for us next."

"I would rather let them take me than help the royals in any way," Rodrigo huffed.

With that, an argument erupted between the two, as Rodrigo shouted at Emeraude for even suggesting that they protect the royals and Emeraude defended her position. Finn buried her head in her arms, the headache pounding against the inside of her skull. When all was said and done, Rodrigo had stormed off in anger and Elian had simply shrugged and left.

With an exasperated sigh, Emeraude flexed her fingers and the swords in the wall behind her quivered.

"Perhaps he was right," she said as Finn raised her head. "Perhaps it was the wrong thing to suggest."

Finn leaned her cheek on her palm. "I don't know," she admitted, which was the truth. They both made good points. "What I do know is that he's annoying and loud."

Emeraude stared at her before saying, "My people haven't gotten to looking for the *propio* seer yet, but it's on the agenda. I'll let you know what they find."

"Sure."

"What's the matter, muchacha?" Emeraude asked. "You've got no spark today."

Finn kneaded her sore temples, her headache pounding steadily behind her eyes. "I can't have spark *and* solve this Kol mystery for you too." Her shadow slogged on the floor at her feet.

When Emeraude only watched her, waiting for an update, Finn spoke again. "I'll be exploring the Tattooed King lead tonight." She didn't know how she would face the prince after what she'd seen in the Diviner's quarters, but she'd already agreed to go with him and Bathtub Boy yesterday.

"Good," Emeraude said.

"That's all I've got," Finn said. She stood, eager to go back to bed.

"Wait," Emeraude said, her concerned eyes sweeping over Finn. She seemed to barely pay attention to the update. "What's going on with you?"

Finn sank back into her seat and gave up on holding it all back. "I'm working with someone to figure out what Kol was up to," Finn finally said.

Emeraude narrowed her eyes. "Are they trustworthy?"

"He is," Finn said, and the way she said it must have revealed something because the old woman tilted her head, her scowl melting away.

"Do you love him?"

Finn jolted in her seat. "That's a stupid question," she said, her voice sounding clunky and wrong. "That has nothing to do with what I'm here to talk to you about."

Emeraude folded her hands on her lap. "All right, I'm sorry," she said delicately, but Finn could spot a smile trying to worm its way across her lips. "What did you want to ask me about him?"

"Do you believe in diviners?" Finn blurted out.

Emeraude squinted at Finn. "The boy is a diviner?"

"No, no," Finn said, frustrated. "It's related, but he isn't a diviner."

"How is it related?"

Finn mashed her lips tightly together, not wanting to speak any longer, but thinking about what she'd seen in the vision made her eyes sting and Ignacio's voice rise within her like a tidal wave.

"Finn," Emeraude said gently. "Tell me, what does a diviner have to do with this boy?"

Finn wrung her hands in her lap. "What if you went to a diviner and you saw a vision of someone you . . . your friend getting hurt."

Emeraude looked at Finn as if she were a sheet of pristine ice and she could see all that lay beneath. "You mean you saw him die, don't you?"

Finn bit the inside of her cheek so hard she feared she would cut the skin. She nodded, her eyes pointedly looking away from Emeraude. "The diviner told me that our destinies are intertwined, that we affect each other's futures. She told me that I saw him get hurt because I am part of the reason it happens. And I know, I just *know* that she's right. I bring trouble wherever I go." The words rushed out of her so fast that she was left breathless. Her face felt hot. She'd let her panic show so easily, but that's what always happened when it came to the prince—things she wanted to hide began to reveal themselves.

Emeraude tapped her chin with her finger. "It is very rare for a diviner to find two people whose destinies are so tightly woven together."

Finn stared at her. "How do you know that?"

"My abuela was our pueblo's diviner. Not a famously talented one, but a diviner all the same," Emeraude said with a wistful smile. "She would read my mamá's café grounds every morning to see what the day had in store."

"Nice story, but it doesn't help me," Finn groused.

"Listen, muchacha, I cannot tell you if what the diviner showed you was real. Diviners can be wrong, but I can tell you what my abuela would tell you if she were here."

"What?" Finn asked, annoyed by the hope in her voice.

"She would tell you to accept your fate as it is. To not fight it. But my abuela was a traditionalist and I'm very different than her. So I will also tell you something else: if you think the future you saw is a product of your destinies being intertwined, then maybe you can create a new destiny. Change it."

"Qué?"

"The future is fluid as water, never set in stone. If you think being close to him will bring about that fate, then untangle your destinies. Pull away, and maybe that will birth a new destiny for him. One in which he doesn't get hurt. There are no guarantees, no promises that it will work, but it's something."

Finn chewed her lip. She hadn't thought of that. If she left the prince alone, then maybe that would create a different future, a safer one.

One where they never saw each other again.

"It would be hard," Finn said, so quietly she could barely hear herself.

"It would be," Emeraude said with a nod, her eyes soft with compassion. "But if you . . ." She paused. "If you, hypothetically, love this boy."

"Hypothetically," Finn agreed.

"Then you will do anything, no matter how difficult, to save him."

Finn closed her eyes. It wasn't what she wanted to hear, not in the least, but it was what she needed to hear. Funny how those two things tended to intersect.

She would keep her distance from the prince and ignore the parchment. She couldn't be the reason he took a knife to the belly. He and Bathtub Boy would have to meet the Tattooed King by themselves tonight.

"Gracias, Abuela," Finn muttered, scrubbing at her eyes with the back of her hand. Before Emeraude could say another word, Finn rose from her seat and walked away.

THE TATTOOED KING

Alfie looked at the clock, his annoyance growing with each tick and tock.

Finn still hadn't responded to Alfie's messages in the parchment. She'd promised to come with him and Luka to see the Tattooed King, but now it seemed that she wouldn't. It was unlike her to break a promise like this. Alfie chewed his lip. She'd seemed so upset with him after she'd disguised Marsden and Vesper for their outing. Was that why she wasn't coming? It had to be. Doing that favor had offended her somehow. Alfie wasn't exactly sure of what to make of her absence, but at least Luka would be going with him—except, of course, Luka was nowhere to be found.

Alfie ran a hand through his hair as the clock ticked. Should he just leave? Luka himself had said that the Tattooed King didn't appreciate tardiness, and they'd paid a large sum for this meeting. If the Tattooed King had created Los Toros' tattoos, tonight was too important to miss, especially after how angry the Englassens had been this morning upon discovering the murders. He needed to put an end to Los Toros to save the summit and any innocents who might become their victims. He couldn't risk it by waiting for Luka and Finn.

His eyes darting to the clock again, Alfie grabbed the tether. "The meeting is set for tonight, with or without them."

Alfie held the tether in his hand and spoke the word of magic he'd assigned to it, then vanished out of sight.

"Right this way, pretty boy," the heavily tattooed man snickered as he shoved Alfie through the double doors of the parlor. Without Finn to help him disguise himself, he hoped his hood and common clothes would be enough to hide his identity.

The scent of paints stung his nostrils, as if he'd walked through a waterfall of them. He may as well have dipped his clothes in them. Alongside the stench of paints was the smell of sweat from squirming clients, and underneath it all, blood from freshly cut skin.

The tattoo parlor was surprisingly large, with countless tables equipped with paint palettes built into the wood. Alfie watched a tattoo artist spin a palette before dipping a sharp pointed quill into a well of cerulean paint, the feather changing from white to blue as it drew the paint in. The man pressed the needle-pointed quill into his client's quivering forearm. The skin welled with blood before the paint overtook it, leaving nothing but swaths of blue. The customer winced, his fingers twitching in pain as he took a long swig of rum.

The honeycombed walls were stocked with long-necked bottled paints, like a colorful wine cellar. Tattoo artists spoke words of magic that drew streams of paint from particular bottles and into their spinning table palettes.

A loud pop sounded to his left and Alfie jumped. Beside the front doors, two clients were playing a game of exploding dominoes as they waited their turn.

"Coño!" the losing man shouted, patting the small flames on his singed eyebrows.

The other player laughed before glancing at Alfie, his eyes sweeping over him from head to toe. Alfie could see him taking notice of how clean and polished he looked in this parlor of men and women who were patchworks of scars and tattoos. "A little jumpy, aren't you, chico? What's a rich boy like you doing in a place like this?"

"Hands off," the man leading Alfie said. "He's paid for an appointment with the King."

The other man raised his eyebrows and looked away. As the parlor's intimidating clientele sized Alfie up, he wished Luka and Finn had come with him like he'd promised. There was strength in numbers. Without them, not only did he stand out, but he looked weak and easy to pick on.

Alfie was led clear across the parlor and down a hall where a single red door stood.

"In you go, muchacho," the man snarled. "You've got ten minutes."

Alfie squinted at him. "Ten minutes? I paid—"

"You paid for ten minutes," the man interjected, leaning so close that Alfie could smell the rot in his teeth. Though Alfie was tall, the man towered over him; his chin was inches higher than the crown of Alfie's head. "Time with a legend is expensive. And now you're down to nine and a half." He looked down at Alfie as if telling him to keep pressing his luck.

Alfie glared up at the man. His magic was a mud brown, not the deep chocolate of Alfie's mother's magic, but the color of the slurry from a horse stable dribbling down the street after a rain shower.

"Very well," Alfie relented.

The man snorted, but before he could make fun of Alfie for his choice of words, Alfie opened the door and stepped into the room. As soon as he shut the door behind him, the room fell eerily silent, as if it was detached from the rest of the world, floating through an empty void.

Alfie shuddered and stopped that path of thinking before it took him places he desperately did not want to go.

There must have been a silencing charm placed on the room to stop any sound from coming in or out, that's all. Nothing out of the ordinary. If he shouted for help, if he screamed, no one would hear him.

Alfie's shadow skittered back toward the door.

The parlor, with its tattood workers and bottled paints jutting out of the walls, had seemed like a riot of color, but it was nothing compared to the room Alfie stood in now. The walls were painted like a jungle, all swaying trees and leaves with none of the sound. Something about the silence of the lively scene made goose bumps rise on his skin.

The trees had every shade of bark Alfie could imagine. Flowers bloomed against the scene before budding once more. But the leaves were not green as they should be; they were a dripping explosion of color. Some were blue with silvered veins. Others couldn't seem to decide on a single color and shifted from shade to shade.

He reached for the wall with careful fingers. Alfie started at the texture of it. It didn't feel like a normal wall—cold and hard. This wall had give to it—it was almost warm. He could feel small bumps rising upon it at his touch. Strange. Alfie wondered if water had pooled in the wall to make it feel so or if it'd been magicked to have a spongy quality. But then the sight of a figure slinking between the trees made Alfie draw his hand back with a start, erasing his thoughts of the wall's strange texture.

Brightly painted creatures crept through the painted jungle, their tails curling around the tree trunks as they moved, their eyes watching him as they crept in and out of sight.

Alfie trembled where he stood. Regardless of the wild use of color, the scene looked so real that he expected to hear the sound of leaves rustling in the wind, of animals growling as they stalked their prey, but the room was still silent.

Alfie spun in a slow circle. There was nothing in the room aside from a single table with two chairs. On it was a messy palette of paints and a set of sharp tattooing quills.

Alfie thought again of the silencing charm on the room and how its limits might have been tested when those needled quills cut through warm flesh. He'd heard that Ernesto Puente's tattoos were exquisite, but that the pain was nearly unbearable. Everything always came with a price.

Then the dark magic's voice came once more, slithering into his mind, sinuous as a snake. *Yes, a price. Set us free and we will save your friend. A small price to pay, don't you think?*

Alfie rubbed the back of his neck to calm the goose bumps

sprouting there as he pushed that voice away and stared at the living art on the room's walls and ceiling. It seemed that the man was called the Tattooed King for good reason. His tattoos were far from normal. He made exquisite works of art. He could draw tattoos that connected one person to another, tattoos that pulsed with the heartbeat of a lover, matching sets of tattoos that, when touched by one, could be felt by the other. Art that lived on the flesh just as Alfie lived within his own skin. While other artists carved tattoos that were stagnant or, at best, moved in set patterns, Ernesto's tattoos moved with a will of their own. He breathed life into his art the way Dez had breathed life into his wooden figurines. Alfie's throat thickened at the thought of the cabinet in Dez's empty room, where the figures now sat still as death.

But he couldn't dwell on that now. Dez was gone; the portal he'd been spirited into was forever closed now that Xiomara was dead. The best he could do was find out why it had happened, which was exactly why he was here to see the Tattooed King in the first place.

Now Alfie need only wait for the man to arrive.

"Alfie is going to murder me," Luka muttered as he raced down the halls. If he didn't hurry, he would make them late to their meeting with the Tattooed King.

Luka raced toward the stairs to Alfie's floor, only to stop in his tracks as he heard the most wondrous sound in the world.

A puppy's bark.

Luka whirled around and there stood James, the puppies rolling and playing at his feet and nibbling on their leashes. Luka hadn't seen James or the puppies for a few days. Marsden had said he'd been ill, and from the looks of it, he still was.

Luka's eyes moved back and forth between the puppies and the stairs to Alfie's rooms.

Alfie would forgive him for being just a little late, wouldn't he?

"James!" Luka called as he walked toward him. The puppies seemed to recognize him from the night in the palace gardens. At the sight of him they ran in circles, entangling James's legs with their leashes.

Luka caught him by the shoulders as he nearly fell. "You're all right," Luka said as he righted James.

"Gracias," James said quietly as the puppies began jumping on Luka's legs. "They're still not properly trained yet, I'm sorry."

"No one ever has to apologize for puppies being puppies," Luka said, turning his face comically serious. "I shall ask Alfie to write that into law when he becomes king."

James only looked at him, his expression controlled in a way that made Luka's heart ache. When was the last time this boy had truly laughed?

Luka could hear a male voice speaking Englassen from around the corner of the hall and James startled, looking over his shoulder before composing himself when he saw that it was two Englassen servants.

Luka remembered the same look of fear on James's face when Marsden had made him remove the chorizo from his plate. When the servants were a safe distance away, Luka said, "You jumped because you thought it was Marsden coming, didn't you?"

James's green eyes widened for a fraction of a second before he turned his attention to the puppies.

When Vesper and Alfie had left Luka and Marsden in the bar together, Luka hadn't been able to resist taking advantage of Marsden's overly honest nature while drunk and asking about James.

"Why do you care about my little servant?" Marsden had slurred with a grin.

"Because he always looks afraid of you," Luka snapped, his hand gripping the lip of the table.

"You know why James is afraid of me?" Marsden had said, leaning across the table until Luka could smell the rum on his breath. "Because he's a very smart boy."

Now, standing before James, it took all Luka's strength not to ask what was wrong. After Marsden had exploded at this morning's meeting in front of other royals, Luka couldn't imagine how badly he would behave when it came to his servants. "I haven't seen you for the last couple of days," Luka said, eyeing James's tired face. He looked like he was fighting a battle with every breath. "Are you all right?"

"The dogs need to be walked, Master Luka. If you will excuse me." He bowed low before tugging the yipping puppies away.

Luka jogged to keep pace with him. "Wait, wait." He sped up so that he was in front of James, walking backward to keep facing him. "I just want to talk to you—"

The puppies had whizzed forward at the sight of him, tangling in his legs until Luka fell backward with a yelp. The puppies leaped onto him, licking his face and biting his clothes. Luka couldn't stop himself from laughing in delight.

"See what you've done," Luka joked. "You've made me make a fool of myself."

Pure panic twisted James's face. He dropped to his knees, pressing his forehead to the floor in a bow. "I'm sorry, it wasn't my intention. I would never choose to embarrass a royal."

The sight was so heartbreaking that not even the puppies could salvage it.

"I was only joking," Luka said gently. He rose from the ground and offered James a hand. "Please, I insist."

His fingers shaking, James took his hand and let him pull him to his feet. The boy looked like a child living in a nightmare. Luka couldn't stop himself from asking, "What has Marsden done to you?"

James closed his eyes, his jaw tight. "Please don't ask me questions I am not permitted to answer, Master Luka."

"But—"

"Please, Master Luka," James said, his voice beseeching.

Luka hung his head, guilty for making James look even more afraid. "All right." If James didn't want to tell him, he couldn't force him, but something was eating away at him, Luka could tell. Each day he looked more and more frail. As the boy tugged the puppies around the corner, Luka wondered how long he would last.

As Alfie waited alone in the colorful chamber of the tattoo parlor, a sudden cough sounded from the other end of the room.

Alfie jolted as a man stepped forward. He'd somehow blended in with the kaleidoscope of colors painted on the walls.

Alfie had no idea what shade of brown the man's skin was. Every inch was covered in moving tattoos. Flowers bloomed and budded, trees swayed in the breeze, dropping their mangoes from his upper shoulder down to his elbow before blossoming on their branches once again. Pájaros flew and perched on his collarbone. Iguanas raised their lolling heads as if searching for a patch of sunlight to stretch on. Alfie stared, his eyes overstimulated. Ernesto's skin was so alive with movement, it was difficult to know where to look.

"Who are you, chico?" the man asked, his voice weathered and low. Now Alfie could see that Ernesto's eyes were milky white. The way he moved, a hand stretched before him to find the chair, confirmed Alfie's guess—the man was blind or at least had difficulty seeing. Ernesto slowly sat in the chair. When he blinked, Alfie could see tattoos of butterflies fluttering on his eyelids.

"Just a boy looking for answers, Señor Puente," Alfie said. "I thank you for your time."

"Señor, eh? So respectful. You must be a rich boy, then. Un chico affluente."

Alfie didn't know what to say to that. He'd paid a hefty sum for this meeting, there was no point in denying his wealth. Ernesto only smiled at his silence.

"I hear you've paid dearly for answers." He laughed and motioned at the seat before him. "Siéntate, Mijo. For the price you paid for this meeting, you deserve to sit."

Alfie stepped forward and carefully took a seat. Something about the man made him uneasy, made him want to perch on the very edge of the chair in case he needed to run. He wished he could leave and come back with Finn and Luka, but he needed to be here. If he wanted to stop Los Toros from endangering the summit, he needed to learn what he could from this man.

"Very few people are willing to pay the price for a tattoo from me, and you pay it in full three times over just to ask a question." The man laughed, his smile unearthing a new maze of wrinkles on his face. "I look forward to hearing it."

Alfie shifted in his chair, willing the goose bumps rising on his chest to calm. The overwhelming feeling of being close to the truth had overtaken him, dusting him with a hope so fragile that he was afraid to even ask his question. "I have a tattoo that I want to know the origin of. I hear you know every tattoo to grace Castallano skin."

"Dimelo. I haven't met a tattoo I didn't know yet," he said. "Show me."

Alfie looked at him uneasily, the man's cloudy eyes giving him pause. "How?"

The old man shrugged. "I'm sure you'll find a way, muchacho."

Alfie took out the roll of parchment and unfolded it. On it was Finn's fine sketch of the bull tattoo he'd seen when he'd stood before Marco Zelas's cold corpse. The very same tattoo that Finn had seen on Kol's arm. The tattoo that would lead him to who was behind his brother's death and why. He couldn't be blocked from his answer now. He didn't want to simply describe the tattoo. He wanted to be sure that Ernesto could really see it as if it were a picture in Ernesto's own mind.

"I made the mistake of hunting down the runaway wife of a powerful man in return for that man funding my tattoo parlor. After she killed him, she took her vengeance upon me by taking my sight. Take it from me, muchacho, don't mess with other people's marriages. But her actions didn't end my career as she'd hoped. I'm smart enough to know that there are other ways to see." Ernesto cocked his head at Alfie, like a teacher patiently waiting for his student's answer.

Alfie looked down at the drawing, an idea sparking in his mind. He moved the color palette and the sharp set of needled quills before smoothing the sketch flat on the table. The words of magic blooming in his mind, Alfie placed his palm over it. He held the image of the tattoo in his mind, but not as if it were flatly drawn on skin; it was as if it had risen off the flesh it'd been drawn against and given dimensions, a living form of its own.

"*Tomar forma*," he said. Slowly, the paper began to rise and bend itself into the tattoo—the angry-faced bull with its curled lips and its horns thrust upward. Alfie carefully placed the paper in the old man's hands.

The man ran his fingers over it gently, turning it this way and that. "Ay sí, I know this tattoo. I know it well. Some of my best work. Not many can say that they made a tattoo that turns into a mask."

Alfie couldn't stop himself from putting his hands on the table and leaning forward. He hissed in pain when his finger fell on the sharp edge of one of the needled quills; a bead of blood welled on his finger, dropping to mingle with the paints staining the table.

"Can you tell me about the gang you created this tattoo for?" Alfie asked, too hopeful to delay the question any longer. "Please, it's important."

"You seem like a good boy, muchacho," the colorful man said before laying a weathered hand on Alfie's cheek. "I don't see many of those here."

Alfie made to pull away, but Ernesto gripped him tight by the jaw, surprising strength in his wrinkled fingers.

"Señor," Alfie said, his jaw clenching. "Let go. Please."

The old man's grip tightened, his thumb and index finger digging into Alfie's cheeks. "I've been given very specific instructions should anyone ask about that tattoo. I can't let you go, Mijo. The consequences would be too high."

The moving etchings of swaying trees and leaves on the walls fell painfully still, as if the flowing breeze through the painted jungle had been trapped and bottled. Alfie could feel his blood pulsing through him around Ernesto's fierce grip.

He grabbed Ernesto by the wrist and pulled himself free, his jaw stinging. Alfie stood and staggered backward, his chair clattering to the ground behind him, but the old man only smiled up at him from his seat.

"What do you mean you can't let me go?"

"Anyone who asks that question doesn't leave this room."

Alfie froze where he stood. He didn't care if the price of the information was his life, he needed answers to save the summit and finally learn the truth about Dezmin's murder. "I paid to ask my question. Tell me about the gang. Who are they? Where are they hiding?"

"I'm afraid you won't be finding out, muchacho."

The man raised his gnarled hands and the creatures moving in and out of the painted trees dashed forward, bursting free of the walls in surges of flowing paint, somehow both solid and liquid. In the blink of an eye, Alfie was surrounded by the beasts of Ernesto's mind. Purple-striped tigers with unimaginably sharp claws, silver-backed apes with gnashing red teeth, long, sinuous boa constrictors with their venomous fangs bared.

Alfie looked at Ernesto beseechingly. "Don't—" But before Alfie could finish his sentence, a tiger sprang from behind Ernesto and lunged at him, its teeth clamping around his wrist with actual flesh-and-bone force. Alfie shouted as the tiger wrenched his arm back and forth, its painted teeth digging into his skin. With a cry, he jerked his arm free of the beast's hold. As he fell to the ground, the tiger's jaw exploded into streams of paint before slowly oozing back into place and re-forming, just like Finn had said had happened when she'd tried to snatch the mask off the member of Los Toros who'd stolen the vanishing cloak from her, but Alfie had no time to marvel at the mechanics of Ernesto's magic. The tigers were made of paint, but they somehow had will and strength, and from the look in their eyes, Alfie knew they were hungry.

"I told you," Ernesto said where he still sat at the table. "There's more than one way to see. They took my eyes, but my beasts see for me just fine." Creatures slunk out of the scene from every which way, baring their teeth. "You won't be leaving this room. But don't worry, I won't kill you. I would never be so cruel as to take a young life. You'll be very much alive. More than just alive—you'll become art, muchacho."

Alfie skittered backward on the floor like a crab, away from the creatures that stalked toward him, teeth bared. He stretched his arms forward and felt for the water in each creature. After all, paint had a high water content. He could stop them. He had to. One by one Alfie disrupted the creatures into puddles of paint, leaving splatters every which way. But each time, they re-formed in the blink of an eye, advancing on him once more until Alfie's back was against the wall.

"Why are you doing this?" Alfie asked, breathless with fear.

"Ay, Mijo," Ernesto said. "There's no point in telling you when you won't be able to tell a soul."

Before Alfie could speak, something snaked out of the wall behind him and covered his mouth, a cold long-fingered hand made of scarlet-red paint. Then other hands oozed from the wall, pulling him flush against it until his feet were off the ground. Only then did Alfie realize what the wall was made of.

Skin.

He could feel goose bumps rising on the wall, pressing against the back of his neck. It was excited to have him so close, eager for another addition to this repulsive room.

"You'll be part of my canvas." Ernesto brandished the sharp machete in his hand. "When I put art on flesh, it never dies. My art, my *propio*, keeps it alive." He gestured at the walls, a smile of disturbing pride unfurling on his face. "Forever beautiful, so long as I will it. I just need to free you from that pesky body of yours and make you part of my canvas."

The painted hand still clamped over his mouth, Alfie screamed into its cold palm, wrenching his head back and forth, but it was no use. More hands snaked out of the walls to hold him down, pinioning him to the wall like a mortician's subject.

"You'll see that those bones are nothing but a cage. I promise." Ernesto advanced with his blade, his gait slow but sure, and Alfie wondered how many times the blood of his victims had mingled with his paints. His heart pounding in his chest, Alfie tilted his head and bit at the palm covering his mouth. It exploded into paint, clogging his throat.

"*Fuerza!*" Alfie shouted as paint dripped down his lips.

Ernesto was thrown backward against the opposite wall. With their master so close to losing consciousness, the paint creatures and the hands holding Alfie hostage paused, not knowing what to do.

Alfie squirmed free and fell to his knees. He thought of subduing Ernesto and trying again to make him talk, but there was only so much time before Ernesto's minions would return. They would leap to Ernesto's aid, and then what would happen to Alfie? How long before he was just a swath of flesh in this painted room?

Still, he wanted the answer so badly.

Then Finn's voice bloomed in his head. In the last four months his mind seemed to have become a garden where she grew in fields.

We all want the truth, but is it worth your damned life?

With shaking hands, Alfie dug in his pocket for his tether, but it was gone. It must've fallen out during the fight. Left with no other choice, he pulled the doorknob from his pocket and dropped it onto the floor. He didn't want to enter the magic again to hear those terrible sounds, but he didn't have a choice. Ernesto was grunting on the ground, raising his weathered hands. The painted beasts heard his command. They sped toward Alfie, their teeth flashing.

With his magic its natural royal blue, Alfie hurriedly thought of home and turned the knob once to the right. The floor opened just as the tiger leaped for him. Alfie sank into the channels of magic, the tiger leaping through just before the portal could close.

Falling into the magic was like plunging into a pool, but instead of calm silence, all he could hear were those haunting cries, the sound of magic rejecting him with all its strength.

His hands clapped over his ears, he whispered, "Stop, no, no.

Please. I'm sorry, I'm so sorry."

The terrible, bone-chilling sound did not stop.

The transport back home felt like years instead of moments.

Alfie was spat back into his bedroom through the wall, landing on the tiled floor just as he was hit with a wave of purple and orange paint that had once been the tiger—too far from its master to keep its shape.

Alfie was lying on his back, spitting and sputtering paint, when his bedroom doors burst open.

"Sorry I'm late! I got caught up—" Luka stopped in his tracks at the sight of a splattered Alfie lying in a puddle of paints. "You know," Luka said. "When I told you to diversify the color palette of your wardrobe, this is not what I meant."

Alfie scraped the paint off his tongue with his fingers. "I hate you so much."

"Love you too," Luka said.

THE PROPOSAL

"Walls of skin?" Luka said, his mouth tightening in disgust. "Literal walls of skin?"

"Yes," Alfie said after he'd finally finished washing the paint off. "Walls of skin that I almost got sucked into. I would have become a human canvas."

"Dioses," Luka said, his voice hushed.

"He confirmed that he did create the tattoos for Los Toros, but told me that anyone who asks about them isn't allowed to leave." Alfie shuddered at the memory of the hands pulling him against the flesh wall. "I got away as fast as I could."

Part of Alfie wanted to finally tell Luka about the screams he kept hearing in the magic, but that topic paled when he thought of how he'd been left to handle the Tattooed King by himself. Where had Luka been?

"I really could have used your help," Alfie said, his voice more brusque than he'd intended. "He clearly has information on Los Toros, but I couldn't handle him alone."

"I'm sorry," Luka said, looking apologetic. "We can try to go back together. I didn't mean to be late. I ran into that servant, James, and—"

Alfie stared at him, incredulous. "You left me to handle that alone because you were off chasing a guy?"

Luka recoiled. "I wasn't *chasing* anyone. We bumped into each other. He seems to have a weird relationship with Marsden. I think he's truly afraid of him."

"Seriously?" Alfie snapped. He agreed that James did seem particularly skittish around Marsden, but that was hardly a reason to leave Alfie to fend for himself. "Marsden is a terrible jerk, so it's no wonder James is uncomfortable around him, but you should've shown up for me. I needed you and you weren't there. Whatever James is worried about can't be as important as this."

"Well, you don't look half as mad about Finn leaving you hanging," Luka huffed. "Do you need to have a crush on someone for them to catch a break?"

Alfie flinched. "I'm just surprised you were in the palace instead of out at a fight club acting stupid and reckless for absolutely no reason."

They stared at each other, their eyes hard.

"I'm going to leave before you say something you'll regret," Luka said.

"Avoiding me seems to be what you're best at now," Alfie sniped.

Luka paused at the door, his shoulders tensing, then walked out.

Guilt formed a pit in Alfie's stomach. Why was he picking a fight? But then why couldn't Luka just focus for a moment? And why hadn't Finn come? He gave an aggravated sigh, his eyes drifting to his balcony doors.

Luka was right—Finn was just as responsible for leaving him alone with the terrifying tattoo artist, but he couldn't bring himself to be mad at her as easily. She'd looked so upset with him when she'd helped with changing Vesper and Marsden. Maybe he'd made her feel used by asking her for that favor. Maybe she was still upset about the almost-kiss too.

Alfie flopped onto his bed.

She still hadn't responded to any of his messages, even the one about witnessing the murder with Vesper last night, but he still picked up his quill and detailed the things he'd seen in the Tattooed King's parlor. Now he just had to wait.

Alfie rubbed the back of his neck and threw open his balcony doors, hoping she would still come by.

A knock sounded at his door.

It was so quiet that at first he thought he'd imagined it. It certainly wasn't Luka. When he opened the doors, Princess Vesper stood there, between the two men who guarded his doors.

Alfie started, his tongue heavy in his mouth. "Princess Vesper," he said, his hand gripping his door. "What are you doing here?" And what guards had she bribed to let her come to his room without a chaperone?

"I'll explain. Can we speak?" she asked. He could see the panic behind her eyes. She'd taken a risk coming here. It must be for something important. "In private. Please."

Alfie turned to the two guards. "No one is to speak of this, is that clear?"

The guards bowed in a soundless affirmation as Alfie ushered the princess into his rooms.

"I'm sorry for barging into your room like this," she said as she paced back and forth in front of his desk. "This is madness; I should go." She turned toward the door Alfie leaned against.

"Wait, wait," he said, though part of him wanted the princess to leave as quickly as possible before their families had yet another reason to argue. "You're already here, and you look as if you have something important to say."

Vesper swallowed thickly. "I do."

"Does this have to do with today's meeting?" he asked.

Vesper wrung her hands. "Yes."

"Then tell me," Alfie said. Whatever she was going to say clearly needed to be said, based on the way she was pacing and fidgeting.

"Negotiations were never going to be smooth between our families," she began, her green eyes intent on him. "But things have gotten messier because of the anti-Englassen violence."

Alfie couldn't disagree. The summit had been on thin ice from the moment it started and now it was only getting worse.

"I don't have much time before Marsden comes to check on me," she said, her voice urgent. "Maybe I should just go."

"Princess Vesper," Alfie insisted. "Please say what you've come to say."

Vesper blurted, "I think we should get married."

Alfie stared, certain he'd heard her wrong. "*Qué?*"

"The summit is falling apart," she said, her voice shaking. "But we can mend it. If we get married, we heal the divide between our kingdoms. It would make the dismantling of the caste system easier to negotiate since our families would be joined. All would be forgiven—the lying about the murders, everything. Our kingdoms could finally start over."

Alfie was too shocked to say a word, but she was right. If they married, they would become more than just economic allies. Their interests, economic and otherwise, would become shared. The transition would happen more smoothly.

But *marriage*?

"I . . ." Alfie flopped onto the edge of his bed, his limbs suddenly feeling too heavy to hold him upright. "Isn't . . . isn't that drastic? The summit hasn't ended yet. It is still possible to broker a peace between our nations without us marrying."

Vesper shook her head. "You don't understand."

"Then explain it to me," Alfie said, desperate to find a way out. "Please."

"Marsden has always had war on his mind when it comes to Castallan," she finally said. "Always. That's why I wanted to make sure he didn't hear anything about the murder. I knew it would be the excuse he needed to start a war."

Alfie's stomach dropped. When had war been put on the table? Was she just so panicked that she was jumping to extreme conclusions?

"Vesper," he said. "What do you mean *war*?" Alfie had thought the worst-case scenario was that no peace treaty was signed and the caste system continued, not *war*. He had a feeling that this was what she'd wanted to tell him when they were in the Plaza of Peace.

She took a deep breath. "Back in Englass, there's an obsession among the nobles with the way things were before. The 'good old days' or a 'return to traditional Englassen values' is what they call it. They're intoxicated by nostalgia for a time when we were a world power, our coffers made fat off the gold gained from the colonies we owned. And now all anyone wants to do is complain about how we lost that status instead of finding a new way to improve our circumstances." She kneaded her temples. "Frankly, it's exhausting."

"The *people* you owned," Alfie corrected her tersely.

"What?" she asked, confusion on her face.

Alfie's jaw clenched. Vesper seemed so thoughtful at times that he didn't know how she could suddenly be so insensitive, but she was still Englassen. She would never understand. "You said the colonies you owned. What you owned were people. *My people.* You would do well to remember that distinction."

This was why Los Toros had stolen the cloak and deemed him unworthy of the throne for wanting peace with Englass. This was why protests had broken out in his kingdom—because Englass would never truly understand what they'd done to this kingdom. It was impossible for the oppressor to fathom the damage they'd done to the oppressed. Maybe Los Toros were right. Maybe this was all a mistake.

Her mouth opened and closed soundlessly, her eyes darting away from his. "Yes, the people. Excuse my mistake."

"Why are we all defined by this?" Alfie asked in frustration as he ran a shaking hand through his hair. "Defined by the past. Your people trying to return to it, and my people trying to escape it."

"I don't know," she said. "But I do know that we can change things, make things better."

"I still don't understand," Alfie said. "What would our marriage solve? How would that stop your brother?"

"Marsden is obsessed with returning to the way things were in order to repair our economy and restore our kingdom to greatness. He has always believed that the best solution is to go to war and regain control of Castallan and its assets. But he knows that it's risky, and that it would cost the lives of his people, so he conceded to coming to this summit and making peace instead. But now that your family has put us all in danger, he's changing his mind. Regardless of what my parents want, it's he who will be king in a few years. They won't be able to stop him if he chooses to go to war with you."

Alfie felt ill. Marsden wasn't just prejudiced; he wanted to own Castallan again. He wanted to own Alfie, his family, and every person he held dear.

Alfie rubbed his temples with shaking fingers. "You're certain?"

She nodded. "I wanted you two to get to know one another. I thought that would stop it." She shook her head. "But all it did was make things worse."

Alfie cradled his head in his hands. He knew that her proposal came from a place of sacrifice, to prevent a war and ensure that her people were finally freed, but he couldn't make this decision on his own. His parents had to know that war was at stake.

"I appreciate you telling me this, but I have to tell my parents," Alfie said, his mind racing. "If Marsden truly wants to conquer Castallan, they need to know now."

"But if you tell them, it could end the summit," Vesper argued, desperation in her voice. "And my people will never be freed. I came to you because I knew you'd think it through, that you'd be kind enough to take pity on my people instead of ending the summit."

She wasn't wrong. His parents would end the summit, full stop, if they knew what Marsden was plotting. There would be no chance of reconciliation between their kingdoms. He shook his head at her, hopeless. "I still have to tell them. I'm sorry." Even if telling them destroyed the chance of the Englassens being freed, his parents had to know. He wasn't ready to solve a problem like this.

"Wait!" Vesper cried out as Alfie made his way to the door. "If you tell your parents, then this summit will come to an end and there will be no peace treaty to stop Marsden. And if we do go to war, you will win," Vesper admitted, her face ashen. "You have the numbers and the financial stability in your favor. You would lose some soldiers, but you would win the war. For Englass . . ." She shook her head. "War would be catastrophic. The magically bound would be the first to be killed on the front lines. You'd be signing their death warrant."

The blood drained from his face. "Why?" he gasped, unable to say anything else.

"It's Englass's way," she said, looking away from him, shame in her eyes. "The lower classes will always be used as shields, as less than human, unless we change it."

"Your brother would fight an unwinnable war?" Alfie asked, but even after knowing Marsden for a few days he already knew the answer to that question.

"He would," Vesper said. "He would rather die with his pride than live without it."

Alfie felt sick to his stomach. If he told his parents and they ended the summit, the people he wanted to save and protect would not only live the rest of their lives magically enslaved, they'd be slaughtered by Alfie's own soldiers.

He couldn't tell them. He had to try to fix this and make the summit successful. He wasn't ready to give up on Dezmin's dream and the hope of freeing innocent people from magical bondage. But there had to be a way to do that without marrying Vesper. He barely knew her. He didn't love her. How could they buy time to figure out a new solution?

"If we get married, Marsden would see this kingdom as mine and, by extension, his. He would not conquer what would belong to me and his future nieces and nephews."

Alfie's stomach twisted, her words making him feel sick. "What would belong to you and your children?"

"It's the way he would think of it," she said hurriedly. "It's not what I believe."

Alfie looked at her for a long moment. She was right. That was certainly how Marsden would see it. But there had to be a way out of this that didn't end with him getting married to a girl he'd met four days ago.

"If we do this then he would never send a single soldier to your shores. Neither Castallano nor Englassen blood would be spilled. We can free Englass too. It's the only way to help both kingdoms."

Alfie wanted to clap his hands over his ears to stop her logic from reaching his mind, but it was already there, making a home between his ears.

"Prince Alfehr." Vesper closed the distance between them, taking his hands in hers. Englassens were not fond of displays of affection, so that simple touch felt pregnant with meaning. "Will you marry me? Will you join blood with me?"

Alfie startled at her phrasing before remembering that in Englass, betrothal ceremonies included the literal joining of blood between families. Both families would cut themselves and mix their blood together to represent the union and the future children to come from the marriage. It was so literal and unromantic compared to Castallan's ceremonies.

Alfie closed his eyes for a long moment before finally speaking, his heart in his throat. "If you'd asked a few months ago, then I would have thought about it, to get our kingdoms to end this. But now . . ." His voice petered out into nothing.

Her eyes swept over him, a hint of sympathy lighting her face. "You love someone."

A long breath escaped from his lips. He felt as if he'd just put down something very heavy. He himself had never said it out loud, but just hearing someone else say it had set him free. "I do." Finn was avoiding him, and he'd ruined things with that near-kiss, but his feelings were still clear.

"Some things are more important than love." The way she said it made Alfie feel that she was thinking of someone else too. She was willing to sacrifice so much, Alfie could at least meet her halfway.

"I'll need time to consider it," he said. "You have to understand that not only would this be a huge sacrifice on both our parts, but also our marriage would not be taken well in Castallan. I would risk losing the people's already-shaky faith in me." Alfie could already see the endless protests that would plague the kingdom if they were to announce an engagement. It would be chaos. "Marriage must be our last resort. Give me time to try to fix it first."

Vesper nodded. "I understand. But it may be our only hope."

It occurred to him that her people wouldn't want this either. While Castallanos would see it as a betrayal on Alfie's part—wedding the enemy—her people would see it as her marrying into an inferior family, a family unworthy of magic. There was no winning on either side.

With nothing left to say, Vesper made her way to the door. Grasping the knob, she turned to him one final time. "Prince Alfehr," she said, her eyes softening. "Thank you for considering my proposal."

Before he could say anything more, the princess departed from his rooms, shutting the door behind her.

He could hardly breathe. This wasn't how his life was supposed to go. He wasn't meant to marry Vesper. Her shoulders weren't the ones he was supposed to wrap the vanishing cloak in. Alfie's stomach lurched as he remembered once again that he didn't even have the cloak anymore.

He needed fresh air. Alfie walked out onto his balcony, and if he'd looked down at that moment, he would've noticed the girl whose shoulders he *had* wrapped the cloak around climbing down the side of the palace, her shadow whipping around her in angry zigzags.

Finn walked through the Brim, aimless and furious.

After her talk with Emeraude, she'd decided to put some distance between her and the prince, to give him a chance at a new destiny. But once she'd read about his brush with Los Toros last night and the flesh walls at the Tattooed King's parlor, she'd caved and gone to check on him. She wasn't going to talk to him, only peek into his rooms to make sure he was still in one tall skinny piece. When she'd found him, he'd seemed more than all right. He'd looked downright cozy with the Englassen princess, holding her hands as she'd asked him to marry her. Finn hadn't even needed to sneak a look. He'd left his balcony doors open, as if he'd wanted her to see it. As if he knew she'd be coming.

Clearly, the prince didn't need her. He was getting on just fine with his new friend. Finn had left the tower before she heard him give the answer she knew he would say. Of course he would marry a princess. Why wouldn't he? It wasn't as if she mattered to him.

Finn shouldered her way past a pair of Englassen guards. "Go choke on your tea and crumpets," she spat, leaving the guards to stare at her. "Maldito colonizers."

Now she couldn't help but feel a little glad that the vanishing cloak was gone. The prince had said he'd need it for his wedding ceremony. He could wrap himself and the princess in a prickly quilbear-skin rug for all she cared.

When Finn finally arrived at the pub, Anabeltilia was organizing her office. The girl froze at the sight of her, a flash of fear on her face.

Finn's stomach tightened at the memory of how she'd yelled at Anabeltilia this morning. It wasn't right. She knew that much, but she also knew that she had never been one to apologize, and she wasn't going to start tonight.

"You said you want to help me run this gang, right?" Finn asked.

The girl nodded. "That's all I've ever wanted."

"Then help me figure out how to track down Los Toros. We'll start with the Tattooed King." The prince hadn't been able to get any information out of the man, but Finn would. She didn't need the prince's help to do it. "You're gonna help me come up with a strategy that won't get me turned into living art."

Anabeltilia blinked at her. "What?"

Finn rolled her eyes. "I'll explain."

The sooner she found Los Toros, the sooner she could leave, and the sooner the prince could start a new destiny with his tomato-haired princess.

THE ONLY OPTION

Finn had stayed up all night with Anabeltilia strategizing on how to storm into the tattoo parlor and interrogate the Tattooed King to learn the truth about Los Toros.

They'd come up with a good plan, if Finn said so herself. Well, a decent enough plan on a couple of hours' notice.

Anabeltilia had run around town, waking up her connections to get as much information on the king as they could find. They'd learned that the shop opened early, before the sun properly rose, during which time the Tattooed King and some of his associates would mix new paints. This was when the parlor was at it emptiest—the best time to attack.

"Do you want to take a team with you?" Anabeltilia had asked her.

"And have them mess it up?" Finn said, bleary-eyed from lack of sleep. "Absolutely not."

"You should take someone you trust," Anabeltilia insisted. Finn had told her about the skin walls. "This guy is no joke."

Finn thought of the prince's note and shuddered. Anabeltilia was right. She probably shouldn't go alone, but she didn't want to take Alfie. She didn't want to see him. Not now, maybe not ever.

She sighed. There was only one option, then.

"I'll handle it. I'm off," Finn said when her daggers were secure in their holsters.

Looking as if she was about to fall asleep on her feet, Anabeltilia plopped into a chair. "Good luck not getting turned into a painting or a thief-skin rug."

"Yeah, yeah, yeah." Finn walked out the door, her shadow dragging sleepily behind her. The fifth morning of this stupid summit was already her least favorite.

"Wake up." Finn slapped Luka's face gently. "Levántate, Bathtub Boy."

When Luka finally opened his eyes and saw Finn standing over him, he screamed so loud that she put her hand over his mouth. "Calm down," she sighed before pulling her hand back.

"Finn?" he said. "What the hell are you doing here?" He looked around for Alfie.

"The prince isn't here," she said, her voice short. "I'm here for you."

Luka cocked his head. "What?" He sniffed loudly. "And why do you smell like adobo?"

"I snuck in through the kitchens again," Finn snapped. "But that's not important. You and I are going to investigate the Tattooed King this morning."

Luka's eyes drifted to the clock ticking at the corner of his room. "But it's so *early*."

Finn ripped his sheets off him and Luka groaned but got up.

"Have you told Alfie about this?" Luka asked with a yawn.

Finn crossed her arms. "No, just you and me today."

"Why?"

"I just don't want to see him," she said. Luka clearly didn't know about last night's proposal or he would've been talking about it nonstop, and Finn wasn't going to tell him. She didn't want to think about it. She just needed backup for today. The faster she found Los Toros, the sooner she could leave the prince and his little girlfriend to their lovely future. A future where he didn't get stabbed to death.

Luka raised his eyebrows. "That makes two of us, then."

Finn squinted at him. "What's been going on with you two anyway?" She'd noticed an odd tension between them two nights ago before they took the Englassen royals out. And in his note Alfie had mentioned that Luka hadn't gone with him to see the Tattooed King last night, which seemed out of character.

"You don't have to tell me why you don't want to see Alfie, but I do?" Luka asked as he pulled on a shirt.

Finn chewed the inside of her cheek. She was curious, but she couldn't argue with that. "Fine. Let's deal with this now, together. You and I both missed the meeting last night and things went bad."

"To say the least," Luka said, guilt tightening his features.

"So let the prince sleep while you and I take down the tattooed creep on our own." She looked away from Luka, remembering how panicked and messy Alfie's script looked when describing what had happened. "It's the least we can do."

Luka nodded. "Agreed. I just need to get back in time for the final exhibition."

"Fine," Finn said, pulling the tether that Anabeltılıa had provided from her pocket. "Let's go."

When Luka and Finn were still a few blocks away from the tattoo parlor, the stench of decay hit her like a physical blow.

Luka gagged. "What is that?"

Finn pressed her hand over her nose and mouth. "I don't know."

She knew her luck was bad, but she was still hoping that maybe there was a butcher shop full of rancid meat somewhere and the stench had nothing to do with the tattoo parlor. But, of course, that wasn't to be. The smell grew stronger and stronger the closer she got to the colorful building. The parlor was dark even though Finn knew they were supposed to be mixing paints at this time.

"Mierda," she bit out.

"You ready?" Luka asked as they stood before the door.

Annoyed and on the verge of vomiting, Finn kicked open the door. The inside of the tattoo shop was completely empty. No furniture, no paints, nothing. Only that terrible smell. The honeycombed walls where Finn was sure bottles of paints had once been stored were empty.

Her only chance of finding anyone was a door at the back of the parlor, but the closer she got the more powerful the smell became. Finn threw open the door and the scent attacked her senses. This must've been the room the prince was talking about. The walls where Ernesto had kept his victims. The warm flesh walls that Alfie had so eerily described on the parchment. But the walls weren't vibrant with moving art the way he'd said. They were rotting. Purpling, decaying skin sloughed off the walls. At first, it looked as if the walls were moving, twitching almost. Then Finn saw that maggots were worming their way out, feasting on the decay.

Luka vomited.

This was not how she'd wanted to start the day.

In his note Alfie had written that the Tattooed King said no one could leave after asking about Los Toros or he would pay the price. Clearly he'd left before he was made to pay the price himself. Just like how Alfie traced Finn using her journal of faces, if he'd left something behind, Finn might've been able to ask a bruxo to use something to trace him, but he'd left nothing behind.

Finn heard a sound from behind them, outside the flesh-walled room.

Someone was there.

Vomit crawling up her throat, she stumbled out of the room, leaving Luka to retch again behind her.

A man stood in the entrance to the parlor, looking just as confused as Finn. Maybe he could tell her where the Tattooed King had gone.

"You!" Finn said as the man backpedaled at the sight of her. "Don't move." She pulled a dagger from her belt. "I have great aim, don't test me."

The man stopped, his nose curling in disgust at the smell.

"I'm only here to pick up my things," he said, his voice shaking.

Finn walked to him, the dagger in hand. "You worked here?"

He nodded, sweat pooling on his upper lip.

"Then tell me where the Tattooed King went," she snarled,

tapping the man's chin with the point of her dagger. She could hear Luka approaching from behind. He stood beside her, wiping a film of vomit from his lips.

"Tell us the truth and no harm will come to you," he said. "We just want information, not your life."

The man swallowed, his eyes on Finn's dagger. "I don't know anything. I'm just an apprentice. I came back to get my tools, that's all!"

"Why are the walls rotting?" Finn asked him, her nose burning. "Did all of his tattoos fall apart like this?" Did the Tattooed King leaving make it so that Los Toros couldn't wear their masks anymore?

The man shook his head, his face glimmering with flop sweat. "When he makes tattoos for people, the tattoo is connected to them specifically. All their tattoos would be fine. The walls were his; they would only rot like this if he disconnected himself from it when he left. Can I go now? Please?" he begged. "I'll leave my tool. I just want to go home."

But Finn wasn't ready to let it go. She'd lost the damn cloak to Los Toros, lost her sanity to Ignacio, and lost the prince to a tomato-haired fiend. She wasn't going to leave this place empty-handed. She needed information on Los Toros so that she could get out of this stupid thief lord job and leave before she got Alfie killed like she'd seen in that crystal ball. This man had to know something. Without the prince, there was no sure way to tell if he was lying.

"You know," Ignacio said from her other side. "There are simpler ways to tell if someone's lying. Pain is an easy motivator."

Finn didn't dare look at him but she knew he was right.

"Finn?" Luka said uneasily. "I don't think he knows anything."

"Use the new piece of your *propio*," Ignacio said, his voice low as if he were telling her a secret. "I'm sure you'll find a way to get creative."

Finn pulled the dagger back and the man sighed in relief. But before he could run, Finn transformed into him, her body stretching taller, a short beard sprouting on her chin.

The man stared at her, too surprised to move.

"Finn?" Luka said, confusion on his face.

The connection between her and the man solidified until he couldn't move unless she moved him. "Are you telling me the truth?"

The man seemed to realize he no longer controlled his own body. She could feel the fear thrumming through him. "What have you done to me? What is this?"

"Are you telling me the truth?" Finn shouted.

"I am," he said, his breaths coming out in gasps. "Please just let me go."

Luka gripped her shoulder. "Finn—"

"Make sure you know he's telling the truth before you let him go," Ignacio whispered.

Now that she had him under her control, anything her body did, he would have to mimic. But what if she did something his body couldn't? She could stretch her bones, transform, but he couldn't.

Finn willed her left arm to lengthen. The man cried out in pain as his own arm began to shift. "Stop it!"

"Tell me the truth," Finn pressed.

"Finn!" Luka shouted, shaking her by the shoulder, but it was too late. Finn lengthened her arm a few more inches and she could hear the dry snap of a bone. She felt the pain of it ring through her.

With a gasp she let him go, severing the connection and transforming back into herself.

Clutching his arm, the man ran from the parlor, sobs parting his lips.

"Muy bien," Ignacio said. "Very well done."

As she looked at Luka's frightened face, shame pooled in her stomach. "I didn't mean to—" Her voice sounded pathetic to her own ears. This was why her sticking around would lead the prince to his death. Because she was nothing but a monster, an extension of Ignacio who would carry his legacy. Her stomach lurched and her mouth filled with saliva. "Don't tell Alfie."

Finn vomited, and it had nothing to do with the smell.

THE CULTURAL EXPLOSION

Alfie didn't need to wake up on the fifth morning of the summit, because he'd never slept in the first place. With the thought of Vesper's proposal on his mind, his eyes simply wouldn't drift closed. Likewise, he feared having yet another dream of the screams he'd heard in the realm of magic or of Dezmin. Sleep was no longer an option.

How would he fix everything without marrying Vesper?

Finn still hadn't gotten back to him about what had happened when he'd met with the Tattooed King last night. He didn't write to her about the proposal. Writing it down would make it seem real. He couldn't bear that.

Long before the sun had even risen, he'd worked up the nerve to go to talk to Luka about the proposal, but his cousin was nowhere to be found. Maybe it was for the best given that they'd had yet another argument before they parted ways last night. So Alfie could do nothing but stew in his own thoughts until it was time to dress for the morning's summit events. The second cultural exhibition was supposed to take place on a Castallano mountainside, but, in adherence to the Englassens' wishes, it now would be on the vast greenery of the palace grounds.

Even though there had been no murder last night, thank goodness, his parents were understandably stressed about how badly yesterday's meeting with Englass had gone. And tension was rising in the city now that Englassen guards were stationed throughout.

The grounds were covered with tents of brilliant colors depending on the nationality of the merchant. There were stalls of foods from the two kingdoms—he spotted vendors selling the gargantuan turkey legs that Englass was known for and, of course, tender strips of pernil and sweet plantains from Castallan.

It should have been a joyous event, but Alfie couldn't stop thinking about Vesper's proposal. He kept his distance, sticking close to his parents so that she wouldn't have the opportunity to talk to him about it again. He still didn't have a plan to fix everything, and he didn't want her to know that. Likewise he worried about the threat of Los Toros. His eyes scanned the crowd for any threat while pointedly avoiding Vesper's gaze from where she stood beside her family a few paces away.

When Luka finally appeared, slightly late, he was oddly quiet. Even though they'd had a fight last night, an argument never stopped Luka from making his usual jokes the next day.

"Are you all right?" Alfie finally asked him after they'd arrived at the beach.

Luka shook his head. "We've got to talk later. This morning—"

"I tried to talk to you this morning but you were gone," Alfie interrupted. "No clue what you were up to but I can make a guess—"

"That's not what I was doing!" Luka shouted, fury in his eyes.

"Stop acting like fight clubs and drinking are all I do. And stop saying that I'm doing it just to be reckless."

"How am I supposed to think otherwise when you won't tell me why?" Alfie sniped back.

Luka was silent for a long moment, still glowering at Alfie when he finally spoke again. "It's about the Tattooed King. We need to talk when we've got some space." Luka looked around at the mingling dignitaries and royals.

Alfie straightened. What could Luka have to tell him about that? "I have to tell you something too." Even though he and Luka weren't in the best place at the moment, he needed to talk to someone about the proposal, though now, surrounded as they were by dignitaries and foreign guests, was not the time. "After the exhibition?"

Luka only nodded.

The royal families moved through the palace grounds in a mob of opulence, tailed by a retinue of both Englassen and Castallano guards. After the disastrous meeting on ending the caste system, no one was speaking to each other. Each royal just pointedly looked ahead as they moved through the exhibition.

The nobles invited to attend the exhibition whispered behind their hands as they passed. At least there were no protestors this time, wearing bull masks or otherwise.

"Perhaps we could split up," Princess Vesper said, pushing her waist-length tresses over her shoulder. Alfie was so used to the silence among their group that he almost jumped at her voice. "Certainly it will be easier to explore everything the exhibition has to offer in smaller, more private groups."

"Splendid idea," King Bolivar said, though Alfie wanted to

protest. The last thing he wanted was to be alone with Vesper, but he had a feeling that was exactly what Vesper intended.

The Englassen queen nodded at Vesper. "Very well."

Without pause, Luka took to Bolivar and Amada's side, and Marsden stuck close to his parents. After yesterday's tense meeting it was clear everyone wanted to stay with their own family and take a break from the mounting tension.

That left just Vesper and Alfie.

"Prince Alfie," his mother said. "Perhaps you'd like to show Princess Vesper around the grounds?"

Amada held his gaze and he knew what she was trying to tell him.

You and Prince Marsden had a fight during yesterday's meeting. Please have better luck with his sister.

"Of course." Alfie nodded, conjuring a tight smile though this was his worst nightmare. "It would be an honor." His mother had no idea that Vesper had told him the truth of Marsden's intentions and nearly begged him to marry her yesterday to prevent a war. If Amada knew that, they probably wouldn't even be having this exhibition. But Alfie hadn't told them and now he wondered if that was a mistake.

The Englassen princess looked at him, not smiling, but not frowning either. She seemed nervous. He knew the proposal must be on her mind too, and he couldn't help but think of how hard it must've been for her to ask him in the first place. But it wasn't a decision he could make lightly, no matter how much he wanted to fix this mess they were in.

Her parents shot her a look and she tacitly moved to stand beside Alfie. They seemed to want them to get along as well, though Alfie didn't know why. Maybe they also wanted him and Vesper to have a good relationship in the face of his argument with Marsden. At least he wasn't the only one stressed by his parents today.

Princess Vesper drifted to the lane of tents on the right and Alfie walked beside her, feeling far too awkward to say anything.

They walked on in silence. Alfie had no idea what he was supposed to say to her.

"I—" he said.

At the same time she said, "Could I—"

"Sorry," they said in unison.

"I'm sorry for . . ." Her eyes darted to the guards standing a short distance from them. "For what I asked of you last night."

Alfie stared, surprised. "You are?"

"I may have jumped to conclusions. There's a small possibility that we can make this work without . . . doing that. We should explore other options as much as possible before considering it," she said furtively, avoiding the word *marriage* when the guards and other foreign guests were so close. "I'm so sorry for making you feel pressured. Please forgive me."

Alfie held back a sigh of relief. Thank the dioses. "It's all right," he said. "I admire your commitment to making sure this summit ends well, but I'm glad we don't have to do something so extreme so soon."

They would figure out a way to end the caste system without marriage. Alfie just needed to make sure that he and Finn stopped Los Toros soon before they could do any more damage.

A vendor bowed and held out samples of chorizo. For now maybe it'd be easier if they just ate and enjoyed the exhibition instead of talking about yesterday. To think he'd panicked about not having the cloak for a betrothal ceremony that wouldn't even happen! Alfie grabbed two and handed one to Vesper. With a small smile, she took it.

Together they approached a corner of the exhibition where a raised platform stood. Dancers from Englass and Castallan kingdoms took turns throughout the day performing dances and music. Now it was Castallan's turn.

The dancers began on the raised platform, then leaped gracefully onto the ground to dance with the crowds. They wound about Alfie and Princess Vesper in a circle. The women wore long, brightly colored ruffled skirts that unfurled as they twirled. Vesper looked at Alfie with embarrassed discomfort but tried, unsuccessfully, to clap along to the beat.

Then, in the whirl of dancers moving this way and that, Alfie saw something strange, a blotch of black marring the colorful scene. His eyes followed it as it ducked between the performers, emerging before disappearing like a whale breaching only to sink beneath the waves once more. When it was closing in, when it was too late, Alfie finally realized what it was—a horned mask.

He heard the wet thunk of a blade sinking into flesh.

Luka had been content to distract himself from this morning's gruesome trip to the Tattooed King's parlor by tagging along with King Bolivar and Queen Amada, until they both started pressing him about why he was so quiet. Luka didn't have the energy to field their questions and slipped away with his own pair of guards to protect him.

Everyone seemed to be in his business today. First, Alfie assuming that he was off being "reckless" at a fight club when he'd been putting his life in danger to help Alfie figure out what Los Toros were up to. It seemed like nothing he did was right when it came to Alfie lately.

Even with the exhibition surrounding him, he couldn't get this morning out of his head. The scent of the walls. The way Finn had made that man's arm twist and snap. He shuddered. She'd begged him to keep it to himself and Luka couldn't help but oblige. *Propios* were personal things, and he had no business revealing anything about it to Alfie without her consent. But still, he'd never seen her behave like that. She'd looked so painfully desperate for the information. They all were anxious to solve the mystery of Los Toros, but something was pushing Finn to the limit. He couldn't tell Alfie about it, but he hoped she would, for her own sake.

He himself still needed to talk to Alfie about how the Tattooed King had fled, leaving no trace behind. Would he be upset that Luka had gone with Finn without him? Or about how the Tattooed King, their one solid lead, was gone? Luka sighed through his nose. If he'd been with Alfie when he'd gone to meet the Tattooed King, maybe things would've turned out differently. Luka ran a hand through his curls. No use in agonizing over it now; it would have to wait until they got home.

Eyes followed him as he moved through the venue. They always did. After all, he was considered extremely lucky—a minor royal who got to live like a prince. Literally. When people approached him it was as if they couldn't decide whether he was important enough to warrant a fuss or not. He was no prince, but was close to *the* prince.

A royal but not very high up—it'd take an unholy slaughter for him to sit on the throne. He seemed to always be in between.

He winked at a young girl who tugged on her mother's skirt and pointed at him. Being in between could be quite nice.

Until it came to being in between living and dying one too many times.

Luka grimaced as he rubbed a knuckle that was still a bit bruised from his last foray into a fight club two nights ago. Alfie had looked upset and disappointed when he'd noticed it.

He would never understand why Luka needed that searing adrenaline rush. Then again, Luka didn't fully understand it either.

Before he could slip deeper into his thoughts, he spotted a familiar face. James. He was nervously lingering around a food stall that had samples of flan, looking as if he didn't know what to do at an event that invited its guests to have fun. He still looked oddly pale to Luka, but maybe that was just the Englassen complexion.

He still didn't know why James was so afraid of Marsden, but the look of fear on his face whenever Marsden was near him had been haunting Luka. Luka wanted to talk to Alfie about it, but then he remembered Alfie's words when Luka had come too late for the meeting with the Tattooed King because he'd been trying to understand why James was so afraid of Marsden.

You left me to handle that alone because you were off chasing a guy?

Alfie hadn't even listened to him. He just assumed that Luka's interest was romantic, when it wasn't. Not that James wasn't attractive. He was. Why did that even matter?

Luka moved away from that train of thought. He wanted to help

James, but he doubted that the boy would tell him the truth about Marsden if he asked him. The least Luka could do was show him a bit of kindness.

Luka walked to him and waved. James turned and looked behind him to make sure Luka was waving at him before awkwardly returning the gesture.

"Good morning, James," Luka said with a grin. "Are you enjoying the festivities?"

James nodded, his eyes shifting toward Luka's guards.

"Give us some space," Luka said to them. When they both shot him a look, Luka rolled his eyes. "I promise I won't be maimed if you take five steps away from me."

The guards begrudgingly stepped away and Luka watched James's shoulders relax. His green eyes caught on Luka's hand. He was staring at the bruise on his knuckle.

"You hurt yourself," he said, and Luka was struck by the gentleness in his voice. Thus far James had always been so nervous around Luka that he couldn't quite get a read on him, but now he could see that beneath that anxious energy was someone who looked after others.

"It's nothing much," Luka said with a debonair smile. "I went looking for a fight and found just that." Usually when he said something like that, boys would fall into the palm of his hand, excited to hear a story about a reckless royal and his battle scars. It was a surefire way to at least earn some platonic admirers and at most earn a kiss or two. Or more. Depending on his mood.

But James just looked at Luka in confusion. "Why? You live such a charmed life, why would you choose to fight?"

Luka stared at him. This was the strongest reaction he'd seen from James since they'd met. James seemed to realize it too.

"I'm sorry," he said, his gaze dropping to his feet. "I shouldn't have said that."

"No, no," Luka said. "It's quite all right. You're not wrong. I seek trouble when I know I shouldn't, when I know I'm lucky to live a safe life."

James's eyes found his again. "Why?"

Luka opened his mouth to speak before thinking better of it. What business did he have burdening James with his sad little story? But, then again, he couldn't talk to Alfie about it. It would make his cousin too sad to know that saving him from Sombra had left parts of him broken, the shattered bones healing at odd, painful angles. And James would be gone soon anyway. Maybe telling him would help Luka move on.

"Something happened to me recently," Luka began slowly. He could tell James the gist but certainly not the whole story. "My life was saved but many others were lost." Luka had to stop for a moment, thinking of the dead that littered the city after Sombra had finally been banished to the void. "And I can't understand why I was allowed to live and they were left to die. It doesn't feel right that they suffered and I didn't."

James watched him, his eyes softening, and Luka looked away, embarrassment welling in his stomach. "I sound loco, don't I?"

James shook his head. "You punish yourself because you feel you deserve it. You look for trouble because you don't understand why you've been spared it for so long. I can understand that. Sometimes punishing yourself feels like the only way you can gain some control. But that is an illusion," James said gently. "It feels like control because you chose this chaos instead of life dealing it to you. But chaos is chaos. In the end it'll get you hurt. The results are the same." Their eyes met and it felt like James could see through the charming smiles to the broken pieces beneath. "Be careful."

He didn't know why, but James's words made his eyes sting. Luka coughed into his fist, clearing his throat. "Well, now I've told you something, so you must tell me something too."

James stiffened.

"It's not a command," Luka corrected. It was heartbreaking to see how afraid he was. "You don't have to tell me if you don't want to." James looked away from him, and Luka knew he had overstepped. "I'm sorry, we can talk about something else. Something fun," Luka said, thinking of a new topic. "Like the puppies or—"

"I wasn't always a servant," James finally said. His voice was so quiet that Luka had to lean forward to hear him. "I came from a fine family that was favored by the royals, but I angered the royal family. I was asked to do something and I refused. Marsden chose to make an example of me to show that even noble families can be stripped of everything if it is his will. Now I am Marsden's servant until he sees fit. Until he feels that I've served my time."

Luka watched him wring his hands as a nearby flame caster blew a stream of fire over his skewers of meat.

"Unlike the rest of the servants, I can still use magic. Marsden never had the spellwork performed on me to stop me from being able to use magic. Instead, I have been forbidden to use it—a punishment that Marsden loves. He understands that it is all the more torturous, to know magic is at my fingertips but I'm not allowed to call upon it."

Luka jolted in surprise. "You can use magic?"

James looked around him first before nodding and gesturing at the ground. For a quick moment his shadow moved about erratically, almost violently. As if fighting to be free. Then, with a grunt of effort, James forced it still.

"You have a *propio*?" Luka whispered, his eyes wide.

James nodded. "But I cannot use it without consequences. Marsden has used spellwork to keep me in line. If I use magic, he'll know and he'll punish me however he likes."

Luka could only stare at him. He couldn't imagine what it would be like to grow up with magic only to have it stolen away from him.

"What did you do?" Luka asked. "What crime could you have committed to warrant this?"

James shook his head. "You kept some details of your story to yourself, and so will I."

Luka wanted to argue, but James wasn't wrong. Luka had kept the biggest details out of his story. He would allow James the same privacy for now.

For a long moment, they only stared at each other. It was strange to share such personal stories with a stranger, even if the details were vague, but Luka could see the relief on his face. Luka felt it too. Maybe a stranger was the exact right kind of person to share your secrets with.

"Now that we have exchanged stories, perhaps we should speak of lighter topics."

Luka grinned. "I specialize in light topics. What shall we discuss?"

"What will you name the dogs?" James asked.

"Alfie said I could name one, and he gets the other," Luka said. "Which means one of those dogs will have a great name and the other will have a boring one."

James chuckled, his usually timid face filling with light, and Luka felt accomplished to have caused it.

"I've chosen a brilliant name," Luka said. "One of the puppies shall be forever known, from this day on, as Concón."

James stared at him blankly.

"You don't know what concón is?"

He shook his head. "My Castallano is not perfect. I've never heard that word."

"Well, allow me to educate you," Luka said with a smile. "When we make rice, there's this layer that's kind of burnt and stuck to the bottom of the pot. That is the popular Castallano dish known as concón."

James stared at him again. "You eat burnt rice?"

"It's not burnt. Well, not burnt-burnt. It's . . ." Luka waved a hand, unable to grasp the words. "It's a delicacy. It's like crunchy, starchy fireworks going off in your mouth!"

James's lips curved into a small, nearly imperceptible smile. "I will have to take your word for it."

"You will," Luka agreed, deciding he would have the palace cook send a bowl of perfectly crispy concón to James sometime soon. But there was no time to dwell any longer on his love for all forms of rice as the sounds of screams erupted on the far side of the exhibition.

Luka watched as the guardsmen dashed away to follow the sound, his own pair moving to flank him. Was it Los Toros attacking? Where was Alfie?

"Whatever that is," Luka said, his heart pounding, "we've got to help."

"Master Luka—" the guard to his left began, but Luka raised a silencing hand, his eyes still on James.

"You know very well that I can defend myself. I'm no prince, so no need to treat me preciously."

James shifted anxiously on his feet. "Luka, maybe you shouldn't—"

"You will address him as Master Luka," the other guard said, his eyes narrowed. James looked like a turtle pulling back into his shell. Luka was so tired of watching him open up for a small moment before collapsing in on himself once more.

"He will call me whatever he pleases," Luka said to the guard before looking him up and down. "*You*, on the other hand, can continue to call me Master Luka."

James's smile was so bright that Luka almost forgot that an emergency was happening. Almost.

"I'm going to go help," Luka said. "Do you want to come with me?"

James looked hesitant, as if he were warring with himself, but courage won out in the end. "Yes," he said. "Yes, I would."

After this morning's awful, vomit-inducing trip to see the Tattooed King, the last place Finn wanted to be was at this maldito cultural exhibition.

Yet here she was, watching nobles stroll the sprawling palace grounds, enjoying food and drink when all she wanted to do was throw up again.

After she'd returned from the tattoo parlor this morning, she and Anabeltilia agreed that attending the exhibition was the smartest move. The only other option was the *propio* seer, but Anabeltilia still couldn't find him. It seemed that he was a lost cause. And, after all, if Los Toros planned on killing more delegados, the summit was the place to be. The exhibition was crawling with delegados and political players, so she had no choice.

Her mouth still tasting of bile, Finn wished she were in bed. She didn't want to spot Alfie and the tomato-haired princess strolling arm in arm after she'd proposed to him last night. Finn had arrived just in time to hear the princess ask him to marry her and couldn't stand to hear what came next. She'd pulled away, making her way down the prince's tower. She'd had to climb down pathetically slow because her shaking hands made it impossible to speed down like she usually would.

"You should be happy for him," Ignacio chimed in. "She's quite pretty, isn't she?"

Finn ground her teeth.

She ignored his lilting voice and scanned the crowds, hoping to happen upon a clue or spot a member of Los Toros somewhere in the endless throng of people. She'd even enlisted members of la Familia to search the area as well.

She should be focusing, but all she could think of was what had happened this morning and the Englassen princess in Alfie's rooms last night.

And would Luka tell Alfie what she'd done? The thought of that made her stomach clench. After she'd hurt that man, Luka had looked terrified. He'd looked at her the way Finn used to look at *him*.

"Me?" Ignacio asked from beside her. "No need to avoid it. One should always try to be specific."

"Shut up," she growled.

She'd let her desperation get the best of her. She just wanted to solve the mystery of Los Toros so she could leave and make sure Alfie would be safe from the bloody destiny she was bound to deliver upon him. So she'd done exactly what Ignacio would've done—she'd tortured a man.

"If it's any consolation, I'm very proud of you, Mija."

Finn spat out the chorizo. It might as well be as full of maggots like the Tattooed King's walls.

She was the monster that Ignacio had always told her she would be. She was so stupid to think that anything could change that. Her eyes stinging, she forced herself to focus. She was here to find Los Toros. Then she could leave. Then the prince would be safe from that knife to the stomach. Just because she was a monster didn't mean she was going to bring him down with her.

Finn leaned against an empty stall and watched the crowd ebb and flow. If she were an annoying murderous gang, where would she be?

"Come now, Delegado Culebra," a man said to another as they passed Finn. "You could crack a smile, no? This is supposed to be a fun occasion." Finn could see that both men were wearing golden pins with the Castallano crest of a bird breaking free of its chains. They were both delegados. "The summit's been on for five days now, you've got to let it go."

"Veras, this is a maldito travesty and you know it," Culebra sniped back. He was a thin angry man who looked like he'd be no fun at a party. "Fools like you are why our former slavers are currently making themselves at home in our kingdom, their guards patrolling our streets. Do they really think that some cultural exhibition will solve the problems between us? We are walking into the lion's den."

Veras gave a laugh. "No, we are walking into the future. I wish you could see that."

"And I wish that you would keep your foolish opinions to yourself," Culebra spat back.

Finn raised a brow as the two men stepped a little closer to each other. This might end in a fight. She leaned forward to watch. Honestly, she could use a good fight to distract her today.

But the fight never began because a chorus of screams and panic sounded from the far end of the exhibition.

The guard to Alfie's left was clutching his neck, blood bursting from between his shaking fingers as he fell to the ground.

A masked flame caster gripped Vesper by the neck and Alfie could swear he heard the sizzle of flesh before he heard the princess scream.

The circle of guards around him fell so quickly that Alfie barely had time to process how they'd died—a dagger to the chest, a slashed throat, a blast of rock to the head leaving nothing but a crushed skull in its wake. It had all happened so fast that the world had slowed around it, the sounds muffled beneath the pounding rhythm of his heart.

But Vesper's scream of pain and the smell of burning flesh brought him careening back into the present.

Alfie's body moved before his mind could process.

He pulled water from the air, dousing Vesper in water before shouting *"Fuerza!"* at her masked attacker.

The assailant flew back, barreling into the crowds that had begun to run and scream, but more and more masked figures were pushing through the panicking throngs. They slipped through easily, flowing like water around the chaos.

Beside him Vesper groaned in pain, her hand clamped around the burnt skin at her neck. Alfie pushed her behind him as five people in horned black masks crept forward, their movements practiced and silent.

"Princess Vesper," Alfie said, his eyes wide. "Stay behind me. Heal yourself."

But Vesper just whimpered, her eyes lost. Alfie knew shock when he saw it. It had swept over his mother like a wave after Dez was taken.

"Vesper!" he shouted, dropping the formality of titles. "Vesper, snap out of it!"

The princess said nothing; she only shook behind him.

"Mierda," Alfie cursed. Was this how Dez had felt when he'd faced Xiomara—this creeping dread that his life was about to be snatched away from him?

Alfie held his hands out in warning and mustered every ounce of courage he could find before he spoke. "Let her go and you can do whatever you want with me."

"We're not here for you, Your Highness," the masked woman to his left said. Alfie was surprised at the deference with which she addressed him. "We're here for her. Step aside."

"I won't let you do this!"

The masked woman tilted her head. "We thought you'd say that." She snapped her fingers and another masked villain strode forward, dragging a child roughly by the arm.

"If you don't surrender the Englassen scum, if you try to utter a word of magic to protect her, a child of your own kingdom dies."

Alfie felt the blood drain from his face. The child was staring at him with weepy brown eyes, mucus running down his face as he sobbed. The masked man shook him by the arm, as if trying to quiet him, but it only made the child cry louder.

Alfie didn't know what to do. There was no magic he could use that would stop all of them before they had time to hurt the child. He swallowed thickly.

There was no winning here.

"Por favor," Alfie said. "I'm begging you, as your future king, please—"

"Make your choice!" the woman said. "Castallan or Englass?"

Anguish on his face, Alfie stared at the little boy. He couldn't let this child be killed, no matter the consequences. Alfie took a step away from Vesper.

"Then let the child g—" Alfie's words were cut short as a jet of flame erupted behind the woman.

"Alfie!" Luka barreled through the crowd, knocking down three masked men. Los Toros may have incapacitated the guardsmen, but they didn't know about Luka's strength. James was behind him. As Luka knocked out the man holding the child, James snatched up the boy and carried him away to safety.

Luka summoned a ring of fire, trapping the two other masked figures. Alfie stepped forward and made to speak a paralyzing spell at the woman, but she was already prepared. At the sight of the guardsmen—Castallano and Englassen alike—closing in, and Alfie moving toward her, the woman put her hand on her chest and shouted. *"You know what you must do!"*

Without fail each of her comrades put their hands on their chests, and Alfie could see her mouth form the word of magic.

"No!" Alfie shouted.

But the woman spoke the self-killing spell and fell to the ground, the others immediately following suit. The tattooed masks dripped down their faces—the ink had changed into some kind of acid that melted their faces down to nothing but raw muscle and bone. Now there would be no members of Los Toros to interrogate, no one to question. They wouldn't even be able to identify the corpses. These people were so loyal to their cause that they would rather die than give up any information.

Alfie could do nothing but stand among the corpses as, behind him, Vesper gripped her neck in pain and the guardsmen rushed forward.

THE BRINK OF WAR

"You brought us here for revenge, not peace!" the Englassen king shouted when they'd returned to the throne room, spittle flying from his mouth.

"That isn't true," Alfie couldn't stop himself from responding.

"Father," Vesper said, her voice drawing the Englassen king's gaze. "Prince Alfehr protected me. He saved me."

Prince Marsden raised a silencing hand before stepping in front of his sister. "How are we to know that this wasn't your intent all along? You've already lied to us once; why not again? You brought us here to murder us in vengeance for the transgressions of our ancestors."

Alfie's stomach tightened. Marsden was trying to use Los Toros' attack to frame the Castallano royals, to give him yet another reason to go to war.

"That is far from the truth," Queen Amada began before she was interrupted by the Englassen queen.

"And why should we believe that?" Queen Elinore demanded. "How are we to know that this peace summit wasn't a setup for you to exact the revenge you've been waiting on for generations?"

"*Because we're not like you!*" Alfie shouted. The room fell quiet as all eyes moved to him. Alfie's face grew hot. "That," he corrected himself. "We are not like *that*."

But the damage had been done. With one sentence, Alfie had made his views on Englass clear and he'd made his family look even more guilty of planning the assassination.

The Englassen king was smiling now, a cruel pantomime of a grin. "And there we have it. The truth straight from the prince's mouth." He looked at King Bolivar. "You spoke of peace, of the sins of our ancestors not falling on their children. You spoke of new beginnings, but now I am not so certain. Your crown prince seems to think we are bloodthirsty, desirous of seeking vengeance because of the past, but we came here seeking peace. I thought your family felt the same. But it seems I was wrong."

"You speak as if war is imminent."

The Englassen king shot them a look, his face twisted with rage. "Then I'm glad to know I am speaking clearly."

Alfie looked at Vesper in panic. She'd told him that her parents might be able to curb Marsden's lust for war, but now it seemed that they wholly agreed with him. Vesper's face was so pale that her hair looked shockingly red in comparison.

"The moment we learned that you people couldn't even protect your own crown prince, we should have known not to come here," Marsden sniped. "Whether you planned this or not, you're clearly incapable of protecting yourselves, let alone anyone else."

At the mention of Dezmin, Alfie was so full of rage that he could barely stop himself from silencing Marsden with a fist. "Keep my brother's name out of your *maldito* mouth," Alfie seethed through a clenched jaw.

"Control your beast of a son," Queen Elinore snapped as she gripped a sneering Marsden by the shoulder.

"I will the moment you control yours," Queen Amada said, moving to stand at Alfie's side.

"Your son was willing to sacrifice our daughter today," the Englassen king shouted. "He stepped away from her in favor of saving a common child! How can you expect us to trust you in the face of that?"

Alfie looked away from Alistair's glower. The child being threatened was his citizen, his to take care of. He couldn't simply watch him be hurt. By the look on Vesper's face, Alfie knew she understood.

"Father—" Vesper began.

"Be quiet, Vesper." Marsden rounded on her. "You've been wounded, you're not thinking properly."

"You expected me not to even flinch at the thought of a child being murdered before my eyes?" Alfie said, frustration bubbling within him.

King Alistair's face reddened with fury. "It was a common child. They are nothing compared to my daughter! This is why your kingdom is full of protestors and murderers; you do not keep them in their place."

Alfie clenched his jaw. He had spent most of his life hating himself for the decisions he made, the thoughts he had, and the feelings he felt. But wanting to save a child was not one he would shame himself for. "And that kind of thinking is exactly why your kingdom relies on slave labor to get by," Alfie sniped back, unable to stop himself

A tense silence swept the room as the Englassen king glowered at him, momentarily stunned.

"You have done nothing to prove your commitment to this alliance," Alistair finally said, his voice thunderous. "Nothing to make us truly believe that you are not part of this mob seeking to kill us. My family and I will retire and discuss whether we will stay for even a single day more in this sham of a summit. Until we make a decision, the summit is on hold."

Alfie's eyes widened. They were threatening to leave, to end the summit now. Vesper met his gaze, fear pinching her face. This was what she'd warned him about.

"King Alistair," Bolivar said, a hint of desperation in his voice that Alfie never thought he'd hear in public. "Please. Our son dreamed of this summit. He knew that if we did not work through our pasts, we would never truly be able to move forward. Please let us continue negotiations; let us make peace with each other once and for all and move into the age of a world without magical enslavement."

"Your son is dead," Alistair spat, and the words felt like a slap. "And because of your foolishness my daughter almost joined him. You are lucky that I am even considering staying one more night. Tomorrow we will inform you of our decision."

With that, the Englassens took their leave, sweeping out of the room with their guards in tow, around the corner and out of sight.

THE PAPER BIRD

Alfie and Luka stood in his rooms, still shaken by what had just transpired.

Luka perched on the bed, watching as Alfie paced.

"Burning a hole into the tiles isn't going to fix this," Luka said gently. "Sit down, take a moment."

Alfie could barely hear him. He could only remember what his parents had said when the Englassens had stormed off.

"If they decide to leave, we must accept it," Bolivar had said, his face drawn and tired. "We can do nothing more."

"We took a risk when we continued the summit in the middle of this crisis," Amada added, taking her husband's hand. "We will handle the consequences with grace."

But Alfie could not sit still and wait for Englass's verdict. Not when the Englassen king had all but threatened war to their faces. Vesper had said her parents were the only ones who could possibly curb Marsden's lust for war, but now they were on his side. There was so much at stake now. If Marsden truly believed that they'd brought them here to kill them, he had all he needed to start the war that Vesper so feared.

A tapping sounded at his balcony doors. Alfie's heart sputtered in his chest. He'd written Finn to come quick, but he hadn't expected her to come at all let alone to get here so fast. Especially since she had been nowhere to be found since she'd helped transform Vesper and Marsden for their night out. Alfie dashed over, hoping it was Finn, but it wasn't.

It was a paper bird.

The bird landed weightlessly in his palms before unfolding into a letter.

"What is it?" Luka asked.

"It's from Vesper," Alfie said, his eyes scanning her neat script.

"You and Vesper write to each other?" Luka squinted at him.

Alfie,

I am doing my best to convince my parents to stay, to work toward peace, but today has given my brother the ammunition he needs. Though I know the truth, that you and your family had nothing to do with the attempt on my life, my family doesn't, and I have no proof to convince them otherwise.

I know it isn't what you want. It isn't what I want either, but we may have to make the sacrifice that we discussed. It could be the show of commitment and good faith that gets my parents to reconsider.

Tomorrow may be our last chance to try. Please think
about it. I would not ask this of you if we had any other
choice.

Your friend,
Vesper

For a moment, Alfie wondered why the parchment was shaking. Then he realized it was not the paper quivering, but his hands.

"What is she talking about, Alfie?" Luka asked. "What sacrifice?"

Alfie folded the letter. He hadn't told Luka about Vesper's proposal. Somehow that would make it more real. More possible. But he couldn't hold it back any longer.

"Vesper proposed that we get married to create a peace between our kingdoms."

Luka gaped. "What? When?"

Alfie quickly explained.

Hurt flashed in Luka's eyes. "Why didn't you tell me?"

Alfie didn't know what to say. "I didn't want to tell anyone. Just the possibility of it was too much to handle without saying it out loud."

Luka squinted at him. "You didn't tell Finn, then?"

"No," Alfie said. "I didn't tell a soul."

"But you only haven't told her yet because she hasn't been around," Luka said. "I've been here with you the whole maldito time."

Fury burned in Alfie. "*Have* you been here with me the whole time?"

"Yes," Luka bit out.

"Well, I went to your rooms to tell you this morning," Alfie sniped. "But you were gone, as usual."

"I was out with Finn trying to make up for missing our meeting with the Tattooed King!"

Alfie's jaw went slack. "Qué?"

"Finn woke me up early this morning and had me go with her to see if we could get some answers," Luka said, sheepish. "She needed backup in case things got too dangerous."

Alfie felt a pang of hurt in his chest. Why hadn't she taken him too?

"Why didn't you tell me?" Alfie demanded.

"I don't know if you noticed," Luka shouted, "but things got a little busy! It was hard to find a moment to explain."

"What happened?" Alfie asked, angry and hurt. Why had they abandoned him for the first meeting only to leave him out of the second?

"He'd packed up the shop and left," Luka said. "Finn interrogated a guy there." Luka looked away from Alfie. "All he knew was that the Tattooed King is gone."

Alfie blinked. Ernesto had said that if anyone asked about Los Toros and left the tattoo parlor alive, he would be responsible. Alfie's escape had driven him away and into hiding.

He plopped onto the edge of his bed, his head in his hands. "We need to talk to Finn."

"Did someone say my name?" Finn said, walking through the balcony doors, flushed from her climb. "I got here as quick as I could. I had a meeting with Emeraude to talk about what happened today with Los Toros."

Alfie was both so happy and so angry to see her that he didn't know how to react. Why had she gone behind his back with Luka? Why had she left him to handle the Tattooed King alone in the first place? Why had she been avoiding his messages?

"We need to talk" was all Alfie could muster.

"We do," she agreed, her expression oddly cold. "I was there today when Tomato Head almost got killed."

Luka snorted at the nickname.

"Vesper," Alfie corrected her, making Finn frown, "was nearly killed by Los Toros. It's not a joke."

Finn nodded, looking more and more annoyed each time Alfie mentioned her. "But I saw the guards swarm them. Didn't they catch any of Los Toros to interrogate?"

Alfie shook his head, his stomach souring at the memory. "The members of Los Toros performed a self-killing spell before they could be captured. The tattoo masks turned to acid. Their bodies disintegrated before we could identify them."

Finn's spine straightened. "Coño. We're back to square one."

Luka crossed his arms. "I feel like we never even got to a square at all. We're still on circle."

"The Englassen royals have threatened to end the summit and leave tomorrow. They think we are secretly in support of Los Toros and that we brought them here to be killed. Now we're being forced to prove otherwise. We only have tonight to try to figure this out." Alfie paced in his rooms, wringing his hands. "I have no idea what to do next."

"You could start by explaining why the tomato princess was in your rooms last night," Finn said as she perched on the edge of his desk, her eyes narrowed.

"Vesper was in your rooms?" Luka gasped.

Alfie gritted his teeth, his shadow snapping like a whip. "How did you know that?"

"I came for a visit and you were busy." Finn shrugged. "So I left." She looked at Luka. "They were holding hands and everything," Finn went on as she picked her fingernails with a dagger.

"Qué?"

"She asked me to marry her," Alfie blurted. "So that we can stop a war between our kingdoms. And if we don't figure out how to prove that my family is not part of Los Toros, I will have to do it. Making Vesper queen here would be the only way to stop her brother from trying to destroy this kingdom. He's wanted to go to war with us and reconquer Castallan from the beginning, but now he has a reason to do it."

Luka's jaw tightened. "That makes sense based on the colonialist mierda he was spouting when we took him and Vesper ou ."

"If we go to war with them we will win, but they will put their magicless lower classes on the front lines to be killed," Alfie said, the words rushing past his lips like vomit. "I can't have that on my conscience, not if I can stop it. Even if it means marrying someone I don't love."

Finn stared at him, her face frozen, her dagger gripped tight in her hand. Alfie searched her face for something, something he didn't want to admit he hoped to find, but Finn simply tucked her dagger away.

"Then it's good you have a backup plan," she said.

Something in Alfie wilted.

"And the king and queen don't know about this?" Luka asked.

Alfie shook his head. "I knew that if I told them they would end the summit, and leaving this summit without an official peace all but guarantees Marsden's war."

"There has to be some way to prove that we're not in league with Los Toros so they'll stay," Luka said before Alfie could speak again. "Anything."

He was right. Finn's reaction to his impending marriage was hardly as important as solving the mystery of Los Toros tonight. Yet he still searched Finn's stiff face for a sign of . . . something. Anything.

"What's left to investigate?" Alfie said, rubbing his temples. "The Tattooed King was the only one who seemed to have any information, and I let him go."

"You didn't let him go," Luka said, standing from his perch on Alfie's desk. "You escaped with your life. It wasn't your fault."

"Countless Englassen people are going to stay enslaved because I couldn't figure this out," Alfie said, his voice breaking. "Dez's dream is dead because I couldn't handle this. It *is* my fault." Alfie couldn't help but think of the two Englassen servants carrying that heavy chest to him, of the shock and confusion on their faces when Alfie had treated them with common courtesy. They and thousands more would live their lives without dignity because he couldn't fix this.

Finn was still perched on the desk, her brow furrowed in thought.

"How does beating yourself up help?" Luka said, taking Alfie by the shoulders. "Maybe there is a solution, but we won't find it with you tearing yourself apart."

"What do you want me to do?" Alfie shouted, shaking off

Luka's hands. He was tired of being told to calm down. If his parents had listened to him in the first place instead of telling him to calm down, then they could have postponed the summit and stopped all this from happening. "Make a joke like you? I don't have time to play maldito games. If you'd come with me to see the Tattooed King instead of getting distracted by a boy, then maybe we wouldn't be here!" As soon as the words passed his lips, he wished he could take them back.

A tense silence swept through the room. Finn looked up, a wince curling her lips.

Luka stepped away from him, a flash of hurt in his eyes. But that hurt was quickly smothered by anger. "It's my fault, then? I'm the one who ruins everything, huh?"

Alfie shook his head, already regretting his words. The fear of what tomorrow would bring had given way to anger. "Luka, I didn't mean—"

"No, no, you're right. Maybe you should've let the poison kill me that night," Luka spat. "It would've saved us all the damn trouble."

Before Alfie could apologize, Luka stormed out of the room, Alfie's shadow chasing after him until the door slammed shut. The words struck Alfie like a slap. This was why Luka had gotten that gravehopper tattoo. Because he thought he should've been left to die when he'd been poisoned. And Alfie had made it worse.

Why did he always ruin everything?

Why couldn't he be the prince everyone needed? Why couldn't he be like Dez?

Alfie snatched an inkwell off his desk and threw it at the wall, black ink splattering the tiles as he took in ragged breaths.

THE KITCHENS

Luka stormed down the hall, anger clouding his thoughts.

All he'd done was try to help and Alfie had to throw it all in his face. Sure, he'd gotten distracted, but he'd never meant to hurt him.

Luka ran a hand over his curls, his eyes stinging.

Alfie and he needed their space from each other. Even though he wanted to help, his presence would just cause more problems. So Luka went to the place he always escaped to when he felt hopeless and alone—the kitchens.

At any given moment, there would always be a tray of flan waiting for him. He'd have some, clear his head, and try to talk to Alfie again afterward.

As soon as Luka stepped into the kitchens, he heard a familiar sound.

Crunch.

He peeked around the corner to the counter where the chefs cooked, and there was James eating a bowl of concón.

Luka had never been so excited to see someone he barely knew.

"Well, well, well," he said, startling James. "Looks like some-one finally saw the light."

James smiled shyly, putting his spoon down. "You scared me."

"I didn't mean to," Luka said before walking past him to the pantry that was magicked to stay cold. His teeth chattering, he dashed in, grabbed the nearest pan of flan, and ran back out.

"You're upset?" he asked as Luka aggressively tucked into the dessert.

"It's how I know I'm alive," Luka retorted.

"My sister used to eat sweets when she was upset," James said quietly. Luka was struck by the twinge of pain in his voice. It was the same way Alfie sounded when he spoke of Dezmin.

"What's her name?" Luka asked.

"Kiera." He spoke it as if there was a candle in front of his lips and if he spoke too forcefully the light would go out.

"What happened to her?" Luka finally asked. When James said nothing, he continued, "It has to do with Marsden, doesn't it?"

James gave him a sad sliver of a smile. "You're not going to give up, are you?"

Luka shook his head. "Nope. And maybe I can help."

"You can't."

"What happened to her?" Luka asked again, putting his fork down.

"I don't know," James finally said. "And there's nothing to be done about it. I never got to say goodbye to her or any of my family. I suppose most don't get the chance."

Luka's hand found his shoulder, and James startled. Luka wondered when the last time he'd felt a gentle touch was. "If I can't help by doing something, I can at least help by listening."

James chewed the inside of his cheek. "I come from a family of merchants. Our business was transporting goods throughout Englass. We usually worked moving cloth, food goods, and the like. But then we were asked to transport a different kind of cargo." James looked at him for a long moment before speaking. "We were asked to transport children."

Luka's eyes widened. When the lower caste in Englass were made impotent at a young age, a small percentage were sent to work for the upper-class families, while others took on menial jobs. James had been asked to take them from their families to become servants.

"You must understand," James said, his eyes shining. "I grew up with magicless servants in my own home. Servants who raised me. I didn't understand that it was wrong until I saw them being pushed about like cattle. I couldn't do it. I refused. To defy the caste system is to defy the royal family's will. So now I am made to serve Prince Marsden in any way he asks until he deems me worthy of freedom, all with my family hanging in the balance as collateral for my obedience. I don't know where he's keeping my family, but he said he can only guarantee their safety if I do as he asks. We were made an example of how no one, regardless of class, is safe from the royal family's wrath."

Luka was angry at James for not realizing how wrong the caste system was for so long, but it was also refreshing to see an Englassen seeming to understand what Castallan was fighting for at this summit. It was a low bar, but maybe there was reason to hope after all.

James shook his head. "I'm sorry that it took that moment for me to understand why your kingdom hates us so much. At home, we're taught that we shared our greatness with the world through colonization and that your people had rebelled against us like ungrateful children. But the truth is so clear to me now—I'm here and I see all children and families drawing upon magic as easily as we draw breath. It shouldn't have taken me so long to understand."

Luka put his fork down, hope and anger blooming in him simultaneously at James's words. "No, it shouldn't have."

Silence swept between them.

"Now I've told you my story," James said, putting his fork down. "Will you tell me yours? What happened that makes you want to fight?"

Luka bit his lip. He couldn't tell him about what had happened with Sombra, but he could tell him about the first time he'd cheated death.

About the little tombstones beside the larger ones.

Luka swallowed thickly, his appetite gone. "I wasn't raised in the palace. My family and I lived at our estate up north. I came from a big family," Luka said, a smile tugging at his lips. "Four little sisters and brothers following me around all day. I'd always complain that I wanted them to leave me alone so I could have some peace and quiet." His smile fell away then, a tear sliding down his nose. "And I got my wish."

"What happened to them?" James asked gently.

"A sickness swept through the north," Luka said, recalling the nights of feverish dreams, the smell of sick. "It took my whole family. Everyone but me."

Luka remembered the funeral service. Watching the bodies of

his family burned as was Castallano tradition, visiting the line of tombstones built in their names. Alfie and Dez being there, insisting that Luka come stay with them.

"You feel like you shouldn't be here because they are not," James said, understanding in his eyes.

Luka nodded, his throat burning. "Please don't say it all happened for a reason. I'm tired of hearing every version of that stupid phrase."

It was something that he and Alfie both understood after the family members they'd lost. Luka suddenly missed his best friend and their relationship before Sombra so badly that the tears slipped out quicker, heavier.

"I would never say that," James said. "I don't think there's a reason that they are gone and you are not, but I do think there is something you can do with this life while you have it. And I don't think that thing is fighting."

Luka took in a deep, shuddering breath, a strange relief passing over him.

The two met each other's gazes, and Luka couldn't help but wonder if maybe there was something besides dying to live for.

THE OLD FRIEND

"Prince," Finn said, standing up and walking to him. Alfie could barely hear her. "Breathe. You're all right. Inhala, exhala."

Alfie's eyes stung. "I don't know what to do, Finn. I've messed up everything and there's no time to fix it."

Finn shook her head. "We've got all night. If I remember correctly, we saved the whole mundo in less time. We've just got to think. After reading all those books, you're good at that."

Alfie breathed a long sigh through his nose, his shadow calming at his feet. Then he turned to the door, guilt still knotting in his stomach. "I should find Luka. Apologize."

As he made his way toward the door, Finn gripped his shoulder. "Listen, I don't know exactly what's going on between you two, but it sounds like Bathtub Boy needs some time. And we need to figure this out."

Alfie opened his mouth to argue but thought better of it. They had no time tonight. He needed to handle Los Toros first so that he could save this summit, save his people from a future war, and save himself from a marriage he did not want. His shadow moved away from the door and curled back around his feet. And though he hoped he wouldn't need it for a betrothal ceremony, maybe he could still get the cloak back from Los Toros. "All right, let's think."

Together they went over all that had happened from start to finish. From Alfie and Luka's discovery of the first murder, to Alfie's encounter with the Tattooed King, onward. Only when he got to the part about the night he'd fought a member of Los Toros in the Pinch did Finn think of something.

"Wait, so when you were out with Tomato Head—"

"Vesper," Alfie corrected her.

"—you fought a member of Los Toros on the roof and he kicked you in the chest? Left something on your shirt?"

Alfie nodded, not sure of why this was of interest to her. "Yes, dirt from his boot, I think."

Finn chewed the inside of her cheek. "Let me see it."

Alfie pulled the shirt out of the overflowing hamper he'd tossed it in. The footprint was still visible on the white fabric.

Finn inspected the shirt and raised a brow. "Can you use magic to track him?"

"From the dirt he left on my shirt?" Alfie shook his head. "It doesn't work that way. You need something personal to track someone down. It can't just be whatever dirt they stepped in."

Finn ran a finger over the fragmented footprint and sniffed. "This isn't dirt. Smells raro."

Alfie squinted at the dirty shirt before giving it a sniff himself. The scent was strong enough to make his nose twitch and his eyes tear. Finn was right; it couldn't be dirt. He hadn't really thought about what his shirt had been stained with. If not for the fact that he'd asked the servants to leave his rooms be, they would've just taken it and washed it.

"Whatever this is," Finn said, "it isn't found just anywhere. I've never smelled anything like it."

Alfie nodded. "Maybe if we figure out what it is and track it down—"

"We'll find out where Los Toros are hiding!" Finn finished, a spark in her eyes.

"We just need to find someone who can tell us exactly what this is." Alfie's eyes strayed to the clock in his rooms. It was already nearly midnight. They needed to figure this out quickly before the Englassen royals announced their decision tomorrow morning. If Vesper's letter told him anything, it was clear that they were already on the verge of ending the summit and returning to Englass.

A smirk tugged at her lips. "Easy," she said. "We already know someone with knowledge of weird substances, Prince. We're gonna have to go visit an old friend."

"Who?"

"Here's a hint," Finn said, her smirk tightening. "You really don't like him."

Alfie blinked. "The poison master." She was right. Even if Alfie despised him, the poison master was their best bet at learning more about the substance on his shirt.

"Muy bien," Finn said, like a teacher praising a student.

"I have a tether that'll get us to the Pinch," Alfie said, rushing to his desk drawer to get it. It was the same one he'd used to sneak Marsden and Vesper out of the palace. Alfie found himself creating more and more tethers now that he was avoiding transporting with his *propio* because of the awful sound.

As he gripped the tether and walked back to Finn, Alfie's eyes went to the door that Luka had stormed out of. He couldn't apologize to Luka now, but he could apologize to Finn.

"Before we go," Alfie said to her, clasping his hands behind his back. "I want to apologize for what happened before . . ." He paused uneasily. "In the triangle."

When Finn only looked away from him, Alfie felt even worse. He must have made her so uncomfortable that she couldn't even acknowledge it.

"I overstepped. I shouldn't have tried to kiss you," Alfie said, his head hanging in shame. "I was afraid to talk to you about it because I was so ashamed of what I'd done. I took your lead in acting like it didn't happen because I was weak. I should've apologized days ago. Despite all that you're still here, helping me." Alfie bowed low. "Please accept my apology. I am truly sorry. It won't happen again."

Finn shook her head. "You didn't do anything."

Alfie stared at her. Why was she letting him off the hook? "You don't have to pretend that I didn't do anything wrong when I—"

"You didn't," Finn blurted out. "I wanted you to kiss me."

Alfie recoiled as if he'd been slapped, but those words were the opposite of a slap. They were a caress. They were an embrace.

A kiss.

He couldn't understand it. She'd disappeared afterward and avoided him. Why would she do that if it was what she wanted? "*Qué?*" he breathed.

Finn fiddled with a dagger so sloppily that it flew out of her hand and clattered on the tiled floor. She threw her hands up in the air. "There's nothing else to say about it!"

"Wait," Alfie said, his mouth forming an O of surprise as it finally dawned on him. "That's why you were so upset about Vesper being in my rooms. You were jealous!"

"I never said that," Finn snapped.

"Why would you think I liked her?" Alfie asked, bewildered.

Finn crossed her arms. "She's a princess," she finally said. "She likes books—I don't know. I figured if you had the chance to marry someone like her you'd expect me to tell you congratulations."

When he opened his mouth to speak, Finn beat him to it.

"We've got things to do tonight. Say the maldito word so we can use the tether to get to the Pinch."

Alfie's eyes softened, his shadow moving toward her while her own skittered away. "Finn . . ."

"Just say the word, Prince," she demanded, her face growing hot.

With the stained shirt tucked under his arm, Alfie cocked his head. "You have to take my hand first."

Finn blew a stray curl out of her face, looking so flustered that Alfie couldn't stop himself from smiling. She took his hand, wrapping her fingers around the tether in his palm.

Alfie spoke the word of magic, and as the world fell away, he pulled her closer.

When the prince and Finn landed in an alleyway in the Pinch, she was still reeling.

Not from using a tether, though it always did turn her stomach a bit, but from everything she'd just learned. And everything she'd just admitted.

First, there was the shock of hearing *why* that tomato head had asked for Alfie's hand in marriage and that unless they found proof to exonerate Alfie's family from all things Los Toros–related, Alfie would have to take her up on her offer. Finn had watched the princess take Alfie's hands and ask her to marry him. She hadn't stuck around to hear his response or the reasoning afterward. She'd left before she could hear the truth. And there was so much comfort in how afraid Alfie looked at the prospect of marrying the princess. It cheered Finn up so much that she nearly forgot the small fact that she'd just admitted that she'd wanted Alfie to kiss her that night.

She didn't know why she'd said it. Maybe it was the inconsolable guilt on his face. Or maybe it was because she knew she would be walking out of his life soon and she didn't want anything left unsaid.

It didn't matter why she'd said it; it was a very stupid move. She'd seen his bloody fate in the diviner's parlor and she knew that leaving Alfie might just give him a new one. Why would she tell him that now? It would only make it harder to leave later. And after she'd hurt that man in the tattoo parlor this morning she'd proven to herself that she was exactly what Ignacio said she was—a monster. And princes didn't kiss monsters—they slayed them.

Finn looked up to see Alfie smiling down at her. She hoped they would land near the poison master's place so the prince wouldn't have time to ask her any more questions, but now she could see that they would have a short walk before they got there.

"Come on, then," she groused, wrenching her hand away from Alfie's. "Let's go."

Alfie followed closely after her, still smiling. "We should talk about this."

"We should focus on what we need to get done tonight," Finn fired back as she weaved between drunkards pouring out of pubs.

"I'm just confused," he said, sounding breathless beside her. "Before when we were standing in the bruxo's triangle. You said you didn't want—"

"I didn't say anything," Finn interrupted.

"Yes, well, your behavior spoke volumes," Alfie sputtered. "You all but ran away from me!"

"Maybe," Finn retorted, refusing to look at him. On the ground their shadows played tag, Finn's hurrying away as Alfie's edged closer. "But I still never said anything to confirm or deny whatever you're thinking right now."

Alfie quirked a brow as Finn turned a corner. "And what am I thinking now?"

She was thinking that now he knew that she loved him.

"Cállate," Finn growled. She didn't have to admit that out loud. Saying that she'd wanted him to kiss her did not confirm that. She could still talk her way out of this.

"So you're *still* not saying anything to confirm or deny what I'm thinking."

"It doesn't matter," Finn huffed.

"It matters." Alfie took her hand, stopping her mid-step. "Finn, look at me." His gold eyes regarded her as if the world had emptied aside from the two of them. "It matters to me."

Finn's face warmed. But she knew the truth. *It didn't matter,* because she was leaving him behind after they solved his mystery so the fate she saw in the diviner's parlor wouldn't come true.

"We're here," Finn said, gesturing to the poison master's lab. "That's what matters."

Alfie's eyes darted to the door, then back to her. She could see him fighting an internal battle of wanting to talk more about this and dealing with Los Toros. She sincerely hoped for the latter.

"Last time we met with this payaso we didn't know what to expect," Finn said, remembering meeting the man at the pub and watching the prince slam his head against the bar. "But now we know he's a coward. So let's scare the information out of him fast. We don't need to hurt him," she said hurriedly, thinking again of the man she'd tortured in the tattoo shop. Her stomach soured. She would never do that again, but intimidation was still fair play. "We just need him to think we might."

Alfie looked as if he wanted to argue, but he was smart enough to know it wasn't worth it. They didn't have any time to waste. The prince stepped away from the door and waved her forward, disapproval in his honey eyes. "After you, then."

Finn had to hold back her laughter at that. He was always so formal. Well, that made one of them. After cloaking her foot in stone, she stepped forward to kick in the door.

But just before her foot made contact he spoke again. "Esperate."

Finn stopped and forced herself to look at him. The prince was silent for a long moment, and the longer she waited the more she wished she'd just kicked open the door and ignored him.

"For the record," Alfie said, his eyes on hers, "if I were to get married to Vesper I would never expect to hear congratulations from you." He shook his head, as if the idea of it was absurd. "Instead I would apologize."

"Why?" As soon as she said it, she wished she hadn't asked, because his gaze had gone soft and she knew that what he would say next would make things more difficult.

He reached for the sleeve of her shirt, rolling the fabric between his fingers. "Because if I married Vesper, I would be giving her something that already belonged to you."

Finn stared at him, warmth spreading from her head to her toes, as if her veins carried light instead of blood, but before his words could truly land, before she could feel their soft weight on her skin, on her heart, Finn kicked the door. It took three good hits before the door fell inward off its hinges. The poison master stood frozen at his worktable, his eyes wide with fear.

Finn leaped into the doorway, her arms spread wide. "Honey, I'm home!"

At the sight of her, Hidalgo shrieked in pure terror. If she'd had her eyes closed she would've thought it was a pig squealing. Hidalgo dropped the clothes he was folding into his luggage and ran away from the door, deeper into his lab.

"You said you'd leave me alone!" He haphazardly grabbed a handful of vials and tossed them at the pair. "You said you'd give me a week to leave!"

Finn rolled her eyes, more annoyed than anything else. Men were such babies.

"This is why we should've just knocked and been civil," Alfie said.

"Come on now, that would be boring. That's your style, not

mine." Before Alfie could give another retort a vial of yellow liquid flew over their heads, shattering against the wall behind them.

"Get out of my house!" the poison master said as he grabbed more bottles to throw. "This is trespassing! It's illegal!"

Finn dashed forward, unafraid. "Oh, by all means, call the guards. I'm sure they'd love to protect the man who had a hand in trying to poison the maldito prince!"

Alfie gripped her by the shoulder and pulled her out of the way right as a vial of bubbling green liquid whizzed past them. The vial shattered on a wooden table. It sizzled and popped, eating its way through the wood in mere moments before dripping on the ground.

Alfie shot her a withering look. "Ten cuidado. That could have been your face."

"I would've dodged it," Finn shot back as she ran after the poison master.

He dashed through a doorway and slammed it closed.

"Ridiculous." Alfie stared at the door. "Haven't you already proven that doors are optional for you? Let me," he said as Finn readied to kick it in again.

He stretched out his hand. "*Desintegrar!*"

The door melted off its very hinge, collapsing into dust.

Finn and Alfie dashed into the room to find the man trying to squeeze out of a window, but his hips were too wide. He wriggled like a fish on a hook but got nowhere.

Finn rolled her eyes before gripping him by the feet and pulling.

"No, no!" he cried, trying to kick her in the face. "Dejame! Let me go!"

She pulled so hard that she was leaning back on her heels. Alfie gripped her around the waist and pulled. As Finn and Alfie pulled him in, he grabbed the window frame, fighting against the pull.

"This is absurd." Alfie let go of Finn with a groan of annoyance. "*Golpear!*"

The poison master yelped as if he'd been struck and fell from the window onto the floor. Finn stumbled back and would have landed on her backside if Alfie hadn't gripped her shoulder and righted her.

"I have children!" he shouted. "Por favor!"

Finn stared at the man. She'd impersonated enough people to be able to read them, and this man wasn't a father. "No, you don't."

"Yet," he said as he scuttled backward like a crab until he was against the wall. "I don't have children *yet*, but I might if you let me live."

Finn flexed her hand and a dagger shot into it. "The prospect of you procreating is enough reason to kill you where you stand."

The man began sobbing again, tucking his head between his knees.

"Dioses," Alfie said, pinching his nose. "We're not here to hurt you."

Finn sucked her teeth as the man looked up and whimpered. "Stop crying."

Snot ran down the man's round face. "Then wh-what do you want?"

Alfie pulled the shirt from his cloak and held it out to the man, a look of distaste on his face. "We need you to tell us everything you know about this substance."

"And if you don't . . . ," Finn began, pulling stone from the ground and encasing her fist in it. "Who knows what'll happen?"

"I thought you weren't here to hurt me!?" the man blubbered, his gaze jumping from Finn's fist to the prince's stoic face.

"Yeah, we didn't come here to hurt you, but that doesn't mean I won't. After all . . ." Finn rolled her shoulders back. "I haven't gotten much exercise today. Making you my personal piñata could be a good way to pass the time."

The man scuttled away from Finn and toward Alfie. He gripped the prince's pant leg, his eyes wide, his glasses askew on his nose. "Please don't let her hurt me. *Please*."

The prince's stone face only lasted for a moment before he relented and rolled his eyes. "Finn, put your fist down. Please." He shook the man's hand off his leg with a look of disgust. "Just tell us about the substance and we'll leave you alone. You have my word."

The man clumsily stood and wiped his nose on his sleeve. He watched Finn with the eyes of cornered prey as he took a whiff of the shirt. He closed his eyes and rocked on his heels, elation on his face. Finn grimaced. She liked him better when he was scared. Seeing someone so awful look so happy made her skin crawl.

"By scent alone I can tell it's a combustible substance." He looked at Finn pointedly, seeming to have gained confidence now that they needed his help. "That means it's explosive, in case you didn't know."

Finn's fingers tightened around the hilt of her dagger. "You know what else is explosive—"

"Finn," Alfie said, warning in his tone.

After a long look, Finn finally relented and tucked her dagger back up her sleeve. "Fine," she growled.

"Go on," Alfie said, watching the man with narrowed eyes.

"To figure out what exactly it is, I need to get back to my lab," he said, shooting a wary look at Finn.

"Go on, then," Finn said. "We don't have all noche."

He scurried out of the room and back to the table, where different substances boiled and fussed. The walls were lined with jars and vials of oddly colored liquids and pickled plants. While the prince watched the man perform his strange tests, Finn walked around the room, gazing into each strange jar. There was a section of shelves holding jars of pickled animals. Pygmy monkeys with their jaws stretched wide in terror, insects caught mid-flight. Finn grimaced at the sight of a jar with a large heart in it.

"What beast did you come from?" she murmured, leaning so close that her breath fogged the glass. Suddenly, the heart began to beat, sloshing in the viscous liquid.

Finn jumped and strode back to the prince and the poison master. The squat man was wearing a strange monocle over his eye. It had tiny, uncountable panes of glass through which he stared at the black powder he'd scraped off the shirt.

He rolled it between his fingers, muttering to himself and tapping his chin thoughtfully.

Finn shot Alfie a questioning glance, but he only shrugged, looking just as curious as she did.

The man took a vial from his cabinets and let a bit of its purple fluid drip on the powder. Finn raised her brows as nothing happened. Then, after a long moment of silence, the powder erupted in a spurt of flame.

Turning away from the explosion Alfie gripped Finn by the shoulders and pulled her close, shielding her from it with his back.

He molded himself around her, ducking down so that her face was tucked into the crook of his neck. She could smell the same clean scent she'd caught when they'd reunited. When he'd embraced her, fresh from the bath.

When he was naked.

Finn shoved that thought away. It was the smell of his bath soap. That's all. Nothing more to think about.

The poison master spoke a word of magic and the flames were smothered, leaving nothing but smoke.

"Are you all right?" the prince asked as he pulled back. They were close enough that she could feel his breath ghost over her face. His eyes were scanning her for injury.

Finn ducked out from under his arms. "I'm fine. You're so damn jumpy." Finn felt a sudden, potent need to look anywhere but at the prince's face.

"It's ráfaga powder!" the poison master chirped as he cleaned the soot off his microscope monocle. He was so excited that he seemed to forget to be afraid of them anymore.

"The powder used for mining?" Alfie asked, and Finn was glad to see his focus shift elsewhere.

Of course he would know what it was.

"Precisely!" Hidalgo said. "It's used in underground mining to more quickly break down walls of rock as well as bombs, explosives," he said, a look of cheer on his face.

"Can you trace where this was packaged?" Finn said, pointing at the black powder.

"Of course," the poison master said with a snort. "Ráfaga powder is mixed with different components based on where it's produced." He took another sniff of it. "This one is mixed with red palm bark."

"And that is helpful to us how?" Finn groused.

"Those trees are native to the northeast of the continent, which is here. It was likely made in the city. There's a ráfaga processing warehouse on the outskirts of the Pinch."

Finn need only look at Alfie to know that that was where they were going next.

"Does this mean I don't have to leave the city anymore?" Hidalgo asked.

Alfie glared at the man as Finn flexed her fingers, pulling a dagger from her sleeve.

"Okay, okay!" he huffed. "I was just checking."

THE PROOF

Finn didn't know what to expect when they broke into the ráfaga warehouse, but she had high hopes. After all, this was the only lead they'd pursued that was actually leading them somewhere. If there was a time to hope, it was now.

What they found was an empty, cavernous building full of barrels of strong-smelling powder. The dirt floor was covered in trails of endless footprints from the workers who had been preparing the product.

"Where should we start?" Finn asked, kicking a pebble in the dirt.

"There should be an office where whoever runs this place keeps documents. That would be the place to start."

"You mean like that?" Finn pointed above. There was a rickety wooden flight of stairs up to a second floor, where an office sat with glass windows so that whoever was in there could watch the workers work.

Alfie nodded. "Just like that."

Together they raced up the stairs to the office. There was a desk and a cushy chair, as well as file cabinets that Alfie immediately darted to while Finn inspected the desk drawers. They just had to hope this person was careless enough to leave proof of his connection to Los Toros in this office. But Finn found nothing but a wax seal kit and some boring letters from suppliers.

After a few long minutes she asked, "Find anything?"

"Not yet," the prince said, disappointment in his voice.

"Don't give up," Finn said, her words sharper than she'd intended. She wouldn't let this wedding happen. She couldn't. But at the same time Finn didn't know why she was fighting it. Emeraude had told her herself that if she wanted to give the prince a new destiny then she needed to stay away from him. It wasn't as if stopping this wedding would let them be together. He was lost to her anyway.

Pressing the heels of her hands into her eyes, Finn slumped into the desk chair. There was nothing that could be done now. The Englassen royals were likely going to leave in the morning and a war would follow if Alfie didn't convince them to stay by marrying the princess. Anger flared in her, hot and wild.

"It's adorable that you thought it'd be that easy," Ignacio crooned from where he perched at the edge of the desk. "Did you really think someone like you could be smart enough to figure this out?"

Finn glared at him as Alfie continued his search behind her. If she were alone she would shout every curse she knew at him, but not when the prince was here. Not when he himself was so close to breaking.

But Ignacio sat there, looking so damn smug. Finn wanted to swipe all the stupid little trinkets off the desk, and she almost did until her eyes clung to the teacup on the table.

She hadn't really looked at it until just now. The design around its rim and on the saucer was elephants.

Finn's eyes widened. This was the same teacup she'd seen in Kol's office.

The voice of Kol's teacup maker sounded in her mind.

She often asked them to be made in pairs so that she could gift the teacups to her associates. Sometimes she'd have me inscribe little messages or images on them for colleagues . . .

"Wait. I think I found something." She picked it up, staring at the design just to be sure it wasn't some other random elephant cup, but no, it was the exact one she'd seen.

Alfie turned away from the ledger he was tearing through, his face alive with hope. "What is it?"

"This teacup," she said, standing up from the chair so fast that the cold tea inside it sloshed over the rim.

She held it under his nose and the prince stared at her for a moment, then put his hands on her shoulders, concern in his eyes. "Maybe you should sit down for a moment." Clearly he thought she'd lost her mind. She couldn't blame him.

"No, listen," she said. "Kol collected teacups."

Alfie's face grew more worried. "Finn, I don't think that's enough. Some people just . . . like teacups?" he said.

"Ugh," Finn groaned. "You're not listening." She quickly explained the collection that Kol had and what the man had told her.

"He said she even had messages inscribed in them—" Her eyes went wide. Finn dumped the tea onto the ground and held the cup close to her face. "Give me some light, Prince."

Still looking concerned, Alfie held out his palm. "*Luz.*" A globe of light floated above his hand. Finn rotated the teacup this way and that, her eyes searching. Nothing on the outside.

"Finn," Alfie said tentatively. "I think—"

"Shhh!" she said as she began checking the inside, where the cup was stained with a brown rim. She turned it sideways—there it was! "Look," she said to him. When she tilted it just so and the light hit it at the right angle, you could see the symbol of Los Toros engraved into the bottom in silver.

"The person running this place is in league with Los Toros. If we find them, maybe we can get the information we need to get you out of this mess."

Alfie's eyes found the wax seal. "I know who runs this place." He turned it over in his hands and Finn spotted the insignia of a snake. "Delegado Culebra."

"Who?" Finn asked, but then she remembered the two delegados who were arguing at the last cultural exhibition. Delegado Culebra was one of them. "Wait, is he a skinny, surly-looking delegado?" she asked. Alfie nodded, surprised that she knew. "I saw him at the exhibition arguing about how he hates Englass."

"That sounds more than accurate. He's been against the summit since Dez first suggested it. He has to be the key to figuring this out. I can't believe it," Alfie gasped. "We might actually be able to save the summit."

"And maybe we'll save you too," she said before she could stop herself. Maybe they could stop this betrothal and the prince wouldn't need to find the cloak to wrap around Vesper's shoulders after all.

Alfie looked at her, his eyes warm and soft. He took her hand in his, marveling at it as if it were the key to fixing everything, not the teacup. He looked up at her, smiling softly. "No, we'll save *us*."

But the prince was wrong. There would be no "us" after this. He would be free to marry someone he chose and she would be free to leave him forever and spare him from the fate she'd seen in the diviner's quarters.

She pulled her hand free of his, and for a moment, he looked lost, as if he were about to ask her what was wrong. But she shot him a telltale smirk to stop him from worrying. "Let's go; this summit isn't going to save itself."

Before Finn knew it, she was inside the king of Castallan's study.

"Alfehr," his mother said, her eyes blazing. "After everything that has happened today, you leave the palace, sneak this girl in, and wake us in the middle of the night?"

"Mamá," Alfie said. "It's urgent. It's good news."

"How are you smiling right now?" She shot a hard look at Finn. "And how is it that every time this kingdom falls into great peril, this girl is with you?"

Finn inclined her head. "Thank you."

"It was not meant to be a compliment, señorita," the king snapped.

"Perspective." Finn shrugged.

"Please listen!" Alfie said before his father could kick Finn out of the palace. "I'm smiling because we have proof! We have a lead on Los Toros—it's Delegado Culebra."

"What?" his mother asked. "Where is this coming from?"

"We found this teacup—" Finn began before Alfie hurried to explain instead.

He told them how he and Finn had been investigating since the start of the summit. How this was all related to Kol, who had the same Los Toros tattoo. How they'd confirmed that the tattoo was the mark of Los Toros by meeting with the Tattooed King, though Alfie certainly edited that part of the story a bit, and how Finn had learned about Kol's obsession with teacups.

"Here, see for yourselves," Alfie said before tilting the cup so that his parents could see the Los Toros engraving at the bottom. "This was found in Culebra's office at his ráfaga mill. This can't be a coincidence. Culebra has every motive to do this. He was against the summit from the start—and he hates us for being on the throne instead of him and his family. If we get answers from him, we can find out who else is involved and why. We can clear our names in the eyes of the Englassen royals."

His parents looked at one another quickly, and Finn had the feeling that they'd been together long enough to speak without words.

The king's gaze hardened. "And you have reason to believe that this organization was involved in Dezmin's death?"

Finn watched Alfie take in a shaking breath before nodding. "Yes. I know you don't like to hear about what I learned from Sombra's magic, but when I asked to know why Marco Zelas was involved in Dezmin's assassination, it showed me the tattoo."

His mother straightened, her eyes sharp. "If we had no heirs to continue our line, if we were killed, the Culebra cousins would be next in line for the throne."

Finn's eyes went wide. She hadn't put any of these pieces together. She'd thought Culebra was just an angry, power-hungry delegado. She hadn't realized there was so much history between the families.

"If we get him to confess, we can prove to the Englassen royals that we had nothing to do with this, that it was an enemy of ours, not an ally, who did this," Alfie said.

The king thought for a long moment before crossing the room and taking his son by the shoulders. "You have broken a ridiculous number of rules, but I am so proud of you. Come, let's tell Maria to round up the guardsmen and head for Culebra's estate."

Alfie shot Finn a bright look as his father guided him out of the room. "I'll be back!"

And then Finn was left alone with the queen of Castallan.

After a long moment of silence, Finn coughed awkwardly into her fist, wishing she could twirl a dagger between her fingers but stopping herself because maybe it probably wasn't a good idea to whip out a weapon in front of a queen.

"I don't know what to do with you," the queen finally said, her eyes assessing Finn.

"Hopefully nothing," Finn retorted. The queen only tilted her head. Where Alfie looked at Finn with softness, Amada's gaze was sharp. As if she would do whatever was necessary to cleave the secrets out of Finn. Finn fought the urge to step back and raised her chin instead, inviting the scrutiny. As she held her gaze, Finn noticed that the queen had given Alfie his dimples, and his nose too.

"When you left the city," Amada said, "my son was distraught. Except for when his brother passed, I'd never seen him so sorrowful. So lost."

Finn had to look away then, her eyes finding the king's desk instead of the queen's face. "I didn't mean—"

"You never meant for it to happen, but it did." The queen walked to Finn, her eyes still assessing, and Finn didn't know what to do but stand still. "You hurt him then, but every time you're around him he is . . . different. Bolder. Brighter. He trusts himself because he trusts you."

Finn could feel her face warming.

"You bring trouble whenever you're with him, but you bring something great out of him too," Amada said. "I suppose that's a worthy compromise."

Amada made her way to the door and opened it, as the guard who stood beyond it bowed at her presence. "So I hope you'll stay this time, Finn."

"Wait," Finn called. She was going to leave the prince for good. The least she could do was help him with one more thing. The missing cloak was her fault, and when they interrogated Culebra the prince was going to want to ask the man where the cloak was. Finn could do the hard part of telling his parents for him.

The queen turned, her brows raised.

"I need to tell you something. It's about the vanishing cloak."

A CULEBRA IN A CAGE

Long after midnight, Alfie, Finn, and his parents watched Delegado Culebra kick and scream as he was dragged through the palace dungeons.

"Hijo de puta, let me go!" he shouted as he was thrown, silk pajamas and all, into his cell. "What on earth is the meaning of this?!"

Adrenaline burned through Alfie. What if he and Finn were somehow wrong? What if the teacup was just a coincidence? What if they'd jailed an innocent man in the middle of the night for nothing?

Finn squeezed his arm. When he looked at her, he could tell she knew what he was thinking.

"We're right," she said, watching as the man hollered. "He did it."

"How do you know?" Alfie asked, his voice quiet.

"When you've worn a lot of faces, you know how one looks when they just got caught."

"I am an honorable delegado of this great kingdom!" Culebra shouted, indignant. "This is outrageous! Release me at once."

"What is truly outrageous is that we did not suspect you in the first place, Culebra," King Bolivar said, his voice rumbling low like thunder.

"I have no idea what you are talking about," he said, his chin high.

"If you admit to your crimes now," said Alfie's mother, stepping forward to grip the cell bar with her hand, "we will show you mercy."

"You are mistaken, Your Royal Highness," Culebra said, his nostrils flaring angrily. "I am an important man. My allies will not stand to see me imprisoned like some kind of—"

"Criminal?" Alfie said. "That is exactly what you are—we have proof. So stop with the maldito theatrics."

When Culebra only glowered silently in reply, Maria, head of the royal guard, stepped forward with the teacup in her hand. "Do you recognize this cup that was found in the private office in your ráfaga warehouse, Delegado Culebra?"

A flash of shock registered on Culebra's face before he collected himself. "Is drinking tea an illegal offense?"

"No, but being part of a gang and killing delegados is," Finn said.

"I have no idea what you are talking about." Culebra looked her up and down and gave a sniff. "Who the hell are you?"

"The people behind the bars don't get to ask questions. Try again later," Finn sniped.

"If you recognize the teacup, then you must also know of the bull insignia engraved inside. The very same symbol as the gang that has been killing delegados," Alfie said, drawing Culebra's gaze back to him. "Or are you going to keep lying to our faces?"

Maria stepped into the cell and gripped the delegado's arm. The cells were enchanted with written spellwork to block magic as soon as an individual was thrown inside. Alfie knew there must be some sort of spell used to hide the tattoo, but with Culebra's magic blocked, it should be clear as day now. Maria pulled up his silk sleeve and there it was, on his left forearm.

The facade finally dropped then. Culebra's expression changed from the indignant glare of a disrespected noble to a snarl of pure fury.

He turned to Alfie. "You, who dabbled in dark magic that almost destroyed this kingdom. You, a sorry excuse for a future king. *You* dare accuse me of this?"

Alfie nodded, his face hot. "I do."

"Watch your tongue, Culebra," the king said, but the delegado didn't seem to hear him.

"If not for your family's poor leadership Los Toros wouldn't even exist!" Culebra hissed. "People had high hopes for Prince Dezmin until he came up with this ludicrous plan to make peace with Englass. I knew then that there was no hope for your family to do anything but ruin this kingdom."

"Is that why you started Los Toros?" Finn finally said, twirling a dagger in her hand. "Is that it? Can we get to it while we're still young?"

"I had no choice!" Culebra seethed. "You are a shame to this throne, to our legacy. We formed a group to stop you from putting peace with Englass before the well-being of your own people. You brought our enemies to our borders—and for what?"

"To help end the same slavery and abuse our ancestors suffered!"

Alfie found himself shouting back as he stepped closer to the bars. To hear the delegado speaking ill of Dez's dream struck a raw nerve. "To make this world a better place for all who live in it."

Culebra spat at the ground. "Let them stay enslaved and suffer as our people suffered. Let them pay the maldito price."

Alfie shook his head. This man had no empathy, he wasn't worth arguing with, but Alfie still had one more question.

For months he had known that Los Toros had something to do with his brother's death, and now he finally would learn the truth.

"When I was under Sombra's influence and asked why Marco Zelas was a part of Dezmin's assassination, it showed me the bull tattoo," Alfie said, his voice shaking.

Both his parents turned to him. They had disregarded his words before, not wanting to hear anything more about what Alfie had seen or done while he'd had access to Sombra's magic. But now, with Delegado Culebra before them, they couldn't deny that Alfie's claim held weight.

"Why did you kill my brother?" Alfie asked, his voice so low he could hardly hear himself.

Culebra scowled up at Alfie, leaning closer to the bars. "Because your filthy brother didn't deserve the throne. We formed this group as soon as he announced this ridiculous summit to the delegados." His gaze moved to Alfie's parents then. "All of you were supposed to die that night so that a true king could lead," Culebra said, raising his chin. It was him and his family who would be next in line if Alfie's whole family was killed. "Your disgusting allegiance to Englass is why we stole the vanishing cloak and destroyed it rather than let your family keep it."

Alfie's heart pounded. He'd hoped that maybe he could get the cloak back now that Los Toros were caught, but now not only did he know that a wondrous piece of their history had been destroyed, but his parents knew too.

"You had no right!" Amada said, and Alfie stared at her, shocked. She wasn't surprised by Culebra's words. How did she already know about this? But when Finn gripped his arm and looked at him, he knew she had told his mother the truth about the cloak.

"I thought I'd spare you," Finn said, her voice quiet.

"The cloak?" Bolivar said, looking confused before turning to Amada. "You knew the cloak was missing?"

Amada shot him a gaze that promised an explanation later.

"It's better off destroyed than in the hands of this family," Culebra spat. "When he was still alive, I felt sick to my stomach imagining Dezmin wearing it to his coronation."

"You would do well to keep Dezmin's name out of your mouth," a voice sounded from behind Alfie. It was Luka, his face flushed from running down to the dungeon once he'd heard the news. He gripped Alfie by the shoulder, a look of solidarity on his face.

Alfie knew he still had much to apologize for, but Luka shook his head, as if reading his mind. There would be time for that later.

Alfie turned to Culebra, his eyes stinging. It was a strange combination of relief and pain to finally know the truth—though it was a relief he wouldn't wish upon anyone. "Dezmin was twice the man you'll ever be. He would've been the greatest king Castallan has ever seen."

Culebra's violet magic was moving rapidly, and Alfie wondered if he was holding something back. Or maybe his anger, not a lie, made his magic move that way.

"We'll never know, will we?" Culebra mocked, pulling Alfie from his thoughts. "Because your pathetic, Englass-loving brother is dead. Your family may still draw breath now, but someone else will soon finish the job. This I swear—"

"That's it," Finn said, pulling a dagger from her sleeve and stepping forward, pushing Alfie behind her—but the queen beat her to it.

"*Sofocar!*" Amada shouted, her hand thrown forward, tears streaming down her face.

Culebra clutched at his throat as Amada spoke the suffocating spell over and over again.

Alfie stared at her, wide-eyed. "Mother, stop," he said, his voice thick.

"Mi amor, let him go," Bolivar said, the fury in his eyes wavering at the sight of her succumbing to her own anger.

"Let me do right by my child," she seethed, her jaw tight.

Culebra's face was purpled as he choked and gasped.

"Mamí," Alfie begged, taking her face in his hands. "Please."

"He took my baby from me," she shouted, pulling herself free from Alfie's hold. "He deserves to die."

"Dez wouldn't want this," Alfie said gently, wiping his eyes with the back of his hand. "He wouldn't want it."

Amada seemed to finally hear him, and with a gasp, the queen dropped her hand.

Culebra fell forward, his hands on the ground as he took in a choking breath.

Bolivar pulled the queen into his arms. "We are safe from him. It's all right, mi vida."

Alfie wrapped his arms around them both, feeling a painful chapter in their lives finally coming to a close. Luka joined them, folding Alfie into his embrace. They finally knew why Dez was murdered. Alfie had been so afraid of living his whole life without knowing why. Now that he did, he didn't feel better, but he felt more ready to move on.

"Everything I did, I did to protect this great kingdom from the rule of this disgusting family and—"

With a *thwack*, Finn knocked the man out, striking his temple with the butt of her dagger.

"What?" Finn asked when everyone stared at her. "He talks too much."

"I don't know what happened with the cloak, but we will discuss it later," the king said, his narrowed eyes still on Culebra, his arms still wrapped protectively around Amada. "Now that Culebra has confessed, we will soon have his associates and everything we need to prove to the Englassen royals that we had nothing to do with this."

After Culebra was woken up for more interrogation, he admitted to being the head of Los Toros, to orchestrating Dezmin's murder, and to planning the killings of delegados to stop the summit from happening. When that didn't work, he planned Vesper's assassination in order to end any peaceful relations with Englass for good.

He also gave up the names of other members of Los Toros. The guards were sent to apprehend them, and in each home they found yet another teacup with the bull insignia.

They were still interrogating members of Los Toros when the sun rose. Alfie assumed they would be for several days.

In the morning, after Finn had left to fill in Emeraude and gain her freedom from being thief lord, and with more than enough evidence, Alfie's parents called for the Englassen royals to meet them in the throne room for proof of their innocence.

When the Englassens arrived, surrounded by a retinue of guards, they looked bleary-eyed and irritated, especially Marsden. But Alfie had to hope that they would listen.

"We know you have likely already decided whether you will continue this summit or leave," Bolivar said, his voice carrying through the room. "But we ask that you hear us out once more. We have put a stop to the threat against both of our kingdoms—and have the individual responsible for the attack on your daughter in custody."

Vesper turned to Alfie, her eyes filled with surprise and hope.

Amada nodded at the guardsmen stationed at the doors, and Delegado Culebra was brought forward, his chains clanging loudly against the tile floor. He shouted and screamed, but was muffled by a thick gag and rendered harmless by a magic suppressant.

"This man stood to inherit the throne after my family." The king's voice quivered for a moment. "He is responsible for the murder of my son and planned the assassinations of the rest of my family, and also masterminded the anti-Englass killings. He is our common enemy. He wished to sabotage this summit to destroy any chance of our kingdoms making peace."

The Englassen royals stared at Culebra in disgust as he thrashed on the ground, his eyes wide with fury.

Marsden frowned. "And how are we to know that this is not a ruse?"

Alfie closed his eyes before answering. "Remove his gag, let him speak. You will hear the truth in his voice."

After a nod of approval from Amada, the guard uneasily removed the gag.

Culebra drew in a hungry breath and reeled on the Englassens. Without the chains holding him down he would have leaped right at them. "I killed their filthy son and your daughter should've been next, Englassen scum!" he shouted at Alistair, spittle flying from his mouth.

Looking unconvinced, Marsden stepped closer to Culebra. The Englassen prince was uncomfortably calm as the delegado demanded his death over and over. "You should never have been allowed on our land. You shouldn't be allowed to live—"

There was so much hate in his voice that Alfie felt ill.

Marsden nodded at the guard, who forced the gag back into Culebra's mouth.

"He hoped to take the throne for himself and end all talks of peace," Amada said, her eyes cold. "He took our son from us. He is no accomplice of ours."

"I see," King Alistair said, looking disturbed. "We are glad to know that your family is not involved with this."

Vesper stared at the man, clutching her mother's arm in fear. Queen Elinore looked pale, her face drawn tight as Culebra was dragged out of the room by the guards.

The Englassen king and queen leaned close to one another, talking quietly, and Alfie hoped that this summit would, against all odds, end in peace instead of burnt bridges and war.

But when King Alistair stepped forward once more, Alfie knew that peace was still far from their reach.

"We appreciate your efforts to prove that you were not working with these criminals to harm our family, but the risk that you put us through has been far too great. This summit should have never happened with such a threat at large. We will take our leave today."

Vesper looked at him then, her face crumpling.

He was going to have to marry her.

FREEDOM

"Well, muchacha," Emeraude said with a warm smile. "You did everything I asked and more. Not only did you find out what Kol was up to, but you also uncovered the truth behind Prince Dezmin's death, may he rest in peace. You've done well."

This morning Finn had gotten all the information she needed from Culebra and his goons. Kol had been hired by them to help kill Alfie with the promise of a hefty sum and no red-cape interference in la Familia's activities when Culebra became king. Her work was done now, so she was here to collect the vial of blood Emeraude had to track her with. The fact that Kol had been working with delegados to kill a royal was enough to disqualify her line from being thief lords. Finn was free.

She tried to stifle the warm feeling of pride in her stomach. "I thought you weren't a fan of royals."

"I'm not." Emeraude shrugged. "But no one should lose their child like that. He seemed like a nice boy."

Finn rolled her eyes. "You're such an abuela."

Emeraude laughed, pulling Finn into a hug, which Finn stiffly returned. "And your abuela will still be around if you ever want to come visit." She handed Finn the vial of blood. "You are free to go." She looked at Finn and gently cupped her face. "What happened to the boy? The one you were afraid of losing?"

Finn's fingers twitched, wishing for a blade to play with. "It was better to let him go than to lose him. I'll give him a chance at a new destiny."

Emeraude nodded, her gaze softening. "Sometimes it's the best thing you can do for those you love."

Finn didn't move to deny it this time. She only nodded, scrubbing at her eyes with the back of her hand.

"Before I forget," Finn said, her voice thick. "My second-in-command, Anabeltilia, would make a great new thief lord for this quadrant. She would work with you, learn from you. You should pick her. You wouldn't have a puppet, but you'd have a good new leader. Someone who actually knows what they're doing."

"The flaca always following you about?" Emeraude asked.

"Anabeltilia," Finn corrected her with a laugh. "She may be scrawny, but she's smart. I wouldn't have figured any of this out without her."

Emeraude nodded, and Finn felt a plume of pride catch alight in her chest at the thought that her words carried weight with this woman. That she trusted her judgment. "I'll consider her. At the very least she'll have a place in my ranks if she wants it."

"Good," Finn said. Now that that was over with, she was ready to leave San Cristóbal for good.

"Your life is yours now," Emeraude said, squeezing Finn's

shoulder gently. "Go live it."

Finn nodded, her eyes stinging. She took in a deep breath and walked away from Emeraude, refusing to look back.

Her life might finally be hers again, but she didn't even want it anymore.

THE APOLOGY

Alfie paced in his rooms, his stomach in knots.

He didn't have to marry Vesper, he knew that. But if he didn't, he could be inviting war to his shores and death on countless magically enslaved Englassens.

It wasn't fair.

His stomach twisted at the thought of Finn's face when she heard the news that he would still be marrying Vesper. She'd left to tell Emeraude about Kol so that she could finally be free of her duties as thief lord, so he hadn't had the chance to tell her yet.

Her face had been filled with light when they'd finally found proof that the royal family hadn't been involved with Los Toros, and he knew why.

If he and Vesper didn't have to get married, then maybe he and Finn . . .

His face used to grow warm at the thought of Finn, but now he felt cold and lost.

The Englassen royals were leaving soon and he only had so much time to make a choice: to marry Vesper and save her people not only from their enslavement, but also from certain death should the kingdoms go to war, or prepare for war and let them all be slaughtered. Marsden still wanted that needless bloodshed, Alfie could see it in his face. If he couldn't convince his parents to do it, then he would simply wait until it was his time to take the throne.

Alfie couldn't live his life looking over his shoulder, fearing the moment when their enemies would declare war and he would have to order the killing of so many innocents. Not when he could marry Vesper and stop it from happening.

But what about Finn?

His heart ached, but at that moment, he remembered what Culebra had said in their meeting after the first Los Toros murder.

I waste no sympathy on Englassens, thank you very much.

Wouldn't he be just as bad as Culebra if he was willing to sacrifice those Englassens for his own happiness? His shadow wriggled at his feet, looking as uncomfortable as he felt.

He thought of Finn, the way her eyes blazed when they'd finally caught Culebra. Her gaze asking him a question. He knew he'd answered it, but now he felt like he'd told her a lie.

Alfie pulled the parchment out of his desk and stared at their exchanges. What could he write? Gripping his quill tight in his hand, Alfie wrote the only words that felt right.

I'm sorry.

He tucked the parchment back into the drawer, his hand lingering on his desk.

He wished he were a different person. The type of person who would write something else.

I don't want this.

Please don't let me do this.

Run away with me.

But Alfie was not that person. He never had been and never would be. He left the parchment in the drawer and walked out of his room, his shadow slumping behind him.

He trudged down the hall, each step weighing a ton, knowing that he was making the right choice for the world.

But not for him.

Though his mind told him to go to the throne room, his feet carried him elsewhere—to Dezmin's rooms.

He hadn't visited in so long, but he needed to feel his brother's presence. With a shaky breath, Alfie stepped into Dez's rooms and shut the door behind him.

His eyes scanned the rooms, forever looking for the places Dez had lived—sitting at the desk reading, stargazing on his balcony and beckoning Alfie to come see a constellation, kneeling before the glass cupboard where he kept his carved figurines.

In ghost stories, haunted places were always characterized by a spooky presence, unseen by the eye but felt by the soul. A presence that made the hairs stand on the back of your neck and gooseflesh erupt on your skin.

Dez's rooms were clean and untouched, empty. No presence to

be seen or felt. Yet they felt more haunted than any of the tales Alfie had grown up hearing.

Alfie perched on the edge of Dez's bed, cradling his face in his hands.

"I don't want to do this," he said into his palms, hoping that wherever he was Dezmin could hear him. "But I know you would."

Dezmin would make any sacrifice necessary to end Englass's practice of magical enslavement. His happiness would always come second to that. Why was it so hard for Alfie to do it? Why couldn't he be more like Dezmin?

Why couldn't it have been him who had died instead?

Alfie raised his head out of his hands and wiped his stinging eyes. He made to rise from the bed and leave but stopped when he caught sight of Dez's carved figurines.

Something was different.

Alfie opened the glass cabinet and crouched in front of it, certain that his eyes were playing tricks on him. But his eyes weren't deceiving him. The figurines looked . . . wrong somehow.

A playful tiger now seemed frozen mid-snarl, its nostrils flared. Even the once-silly figurine of the puffer pig looked oddly threatening.

At the sound of the clock striking noon, Alfie started and shook his head. He must be misremembering what the figurines looked like. After all, it had been a long while since he'd been in this room. He didn't have time now to examine the figurines and think mournfully of Dez.

If he wanted to make Dezmin proud, he needed to propose to Vesper and end magical enslavement for good.

With one last glance at the now unfamiliar figurines, Alfie rushed out of the room, shutting the door behind him.

When he arrived in the throne room to stand beside his parents, Luka stood on the other side of his parents' thrones. The sweeping room was flanked with red-caped guards waiting for the Englassen royalty to bid their farewell.

From his seat, the king gripped Alfie's arm. "We have done all we could, Mijo."

The queen leaned toward him, her eyes warm. "Your brother would be proud."

Alfie looked away because he knew that there was more he could do—and he would do it today.

As the king and queen talked quietly, Luka made his way to Alfie's side. They stood awkwardly for a long moment. They hadn't spoken about the fight they'd had the night before.

"I shouldn't have left last night," Luka finally said.

"No," Alfie said, stopping him mid-sentence. "I shouldn't have blamed you." The anxiety over proposing to Vesper made his words rush out in an honest jumble. "I was upset and scared, so I placed the blame on you."

Luka shook his head. "I could've behaved better, helped you more. I left you and Finn to handle it all by yourselves."

Alfie remembered Luka's words from the night before.

Maybe you should've let the poison kill me that night.

"No, I should've talked to you after everything that happened with Sombra," Alfie said. "But I was afraid that you hated me for what I did to save you. If you do, I understand. But know that I will never regret saving you. *Never.*"

The two squeezed each other's forearms.

"You're going to do it, aren't you?" Luka said, his eyes searching. "You and Vesper . . ."

Alfie gave a solemn nod.

Luka pulled him into an embrace only to break away when the approach of the Englassen guards echoed through the throne room. The Englassen royals entered behind them, looking as tense as Alfie felt. Vesper's eyes met his, a question brewing in them.

"We have come to bid you farewell," Alistair said.

"Wait," Alfie said, forcing his voice to be calm and measured. "Please give my family one last chance to prove our dedication to this alliance."

King Alistair shot him a long look as Marsden impatiently glanced at the palace doors as if barely stopping himself from just walking out whether his parents stayed to listen or not. "Prince Alfehr, I fear there is nothing left to be said."

"Father," Vesper interrupted, her eyes desperate. "Please listen to him."

Alfie and Vesper met eyes. She nodded at him, ready.

"In order to cement the peace between our two kingdoms, I would like to humbly ask for Princess Vesper's hand in marriage."

A gasp sounded behind him and he knew it had come from his mother, but Alfie didn't pause.

"With our kingdoms bound by blood and love, we will be truly united. The loan would become a gift that Englass would not have to repay." Alfie cleared his throat, wishing he could stop, but the words kept coming out of his mouth like vomit.

"Alfehr—" his father began, but Alfie raised a silencing hand toward his father.

"You have long told me that I am the future of this kingdom," Alfie said, his eyes on his parents. "Please, let me lead." Alfie turned back to the Englassen royals. "The only thing I ask is that the immediate end of your caste system is built into our wedding contract. When Vesper and I marry, our kingdoms will become allies and we will help shoulder the financial burden of ending the caste system and rebuilding your economy."

"What?" Marsden said then, his voice hushed with shock. This would ruin his plans of war and he knew it. "You can't be serious. Vesper would never—"

Vesper shot him a look as she stepped forward to take Alfie's arm. Alfie could tell she had waited her whole life to silence Marsden and make her own decision regardless of what he wanted. "It's what I want, Mother and Father. Please." She looked at Alfie, summoning a small smile. "Let us do this for the future of both our peoples."

King Alistair looked too shocked to speak, until the queen took his arm and they spoke quickly among themselves.

"Very well," Queen Elinore finally said. "Let us discuss this possible engagement."

THE EXPLANATION

"Alfehr, have you lost your mind?" his father shouted in his study.

"No," Alfie said, feigning confidence even as his shadow twisted at his feet.

"How could you make this decision without consulting us first?" Amada said. "The people will riot, and it's a huge financial undertaking to make the loan a gift. But it's also your life, Alfie. You're giving away your life."

"I know," Alfie said to her, his eyes stinging.

Amada watched him for a long moment, seeing through him with ease. "What are you not telling us?"

Bolivar looked between them. "What do you mean?"

"He wouldn't do this if there was something going on that we didn't know, Bolivar," Amada said, her eyes on Alfie. "What is it, Mijo?"

After taking in a shaky breath, Alfie explained everything. How Marsden thirsted for a war with Castallan, a war that they would win at the cost of many lives, especially the magically enslaved. His parents stared at him, shocked into silence.

"If I don't marry Vesper we are inviting a war onto our shores. A war that we will win, but at what cost?"

"S-Still," the king sputtered. "That doesn't mean you should marry her."

"It's too much of a sacrifice, Alfehr," his mother said.

"It isn't too much of a sacrifice," Alfie said, his heart breaking as he spoke. "A whole country will be freed from slavery and a war avoided. I am not too important to make that sacrifice."

"Yes, you are!" his mother argued. "You are the future king of Castallan."

Alfie nodded, his throat burning. "I know. That's exactly why I must do it. I am the future king of Castallan. I am a product of my ancestors' struggles and victories." He took his mother's and father's hands. "I am a product of two great parents who have raised me to know that my role comes with power and privilege and that I must use it for good. I cannot stand by and let Englass hurt others the way they did our people, and I will not let a war take a single Castallano soldier from us. Not if I can stop it. I was born to sacrifice myself for the greater good. I must do this."

Tears streaked his mother's face. Without a word, the queen pulled him into a fierce embrace. When Bolivar joined in, gripping him tight, Alfie knew his fate was sealed.

ONCE OR NEVER

I'm sorry. Those were the two words Finn found written on the parchment as she walked out of Emeraude's headquarters after updating her on what had happened.

Finn didn't need to think twice to know what the words meant.

If I were to get married to Vesper, I would never expect to hear congratulations from you. Instead I would apologize. Because if I married Vesper, I would be giving her something that already belonged to you.

Exposing Los Toros hadn't worked. He was going to have to marry her anyway. Finn knew it in her bones. And she would willingly break every one of those bones to go back to a world where that wasn't true.

What was worse was it shouldn't have even mattered. She wasn't going to stay in San Cristóbal, in his life. What she'd seen in the diviner's parlor had made sure of that. So what did it matter if he married someone else?

The answer was that it didn't. It didn't matter.

"And yet you're so mopey," Ignacio joked at her side. "Haven't you ever read any stories before, Mija? Princes end up with princesses and thieves end up in prison."

After staying up all night with the prince and then heading straight to Emeraude, Finn didn't even have the energy to fight it.

"This is for the best, isn't it? With you long gone, he'll likely live a long life," Ignacio mused.

"Sure," Finn heard herself mutter. "Whatever you say."

Her mood was so lackluster that Ignacio faded on his own with little fanfare. Maybe that was the key to getting rid of him. If she made herself feel hopeless all the time, he hardly needed to show up to do the job.

Maybe this was life now.

Finn walked aimlessly through the Pinch, and when she got tired of that she walked aimlessly through the Bash. Then the Bow. Night dropped like a curtain. Suddenly the moon was overhead and the only proof of how long she walked was the pain in her aching feet.

The palace swelled on the horizon, so tall it looked like a ladder to the stars themselves. Without a thought, Finn started walking toward it.

He was going to marry Tomato Head. Fine. So be it.

But not before she had her say.

She wouldn't tell him everything she'd learned from the diviner, not about the dagger that would slash his middle. That wouldn't be happening anymore anyway now that she was leaving. But she would tell him that her destiny belonged to him and his belonged to her. And that no matter who he married, or even if they never saw each other again, nothing could change that.

* * *

Alfie sat slumped in an armchair in the library.

He had asked all the library attendants and scholars to leave. He needed this space for himself.

It was so quiet it was as if he was underwater, which was an apt description because he felt like he was drowning.

Drowning in grief for his brother, who could finally rest in peace while Alfie himself felt renewed pain after hearing the vitriol coming from Delegado Culebra's mouth. Grief for what the future held for him. Grief for what he'd lost.

Grief for Finn.

She hadn't responded to his message and he wondered if those two words would be the last she ever read from him.

Luka had stayed in the library with Alfie for hours, but eventually Alfie had asked him to leave too. He knew that his cousin wanted to go find James. Luka probably wanted to be the first to tell him that soon he'd be free, and who was Alfie to stop him. He needed quiet anyway.

He'd been afraid that his parents would be disappointed in him for what he'd done. That would have been much easier to accept. But they weren't disappointed—they were sad for him, just as he was sad for himself. Somehow, that was worse.

"I figured you'd be here," a voice called from the far side of the library where the double doors stood.

It was Finn, and she looked as tired as he felt.

"Finn," he said, happy to see her and instantly so sad too. Because if their goodbye had already happened, then, in a way, he'd already moved beyond it. But now she was here and that meant the pain had yet to come.

But still, he rose from his seat and walked toward her.

"I went to your room but you weren't there," she said, giving him a tired smirk as she met him halfway. "And I thought to myself, if I were a bookish prince, where would I be?"

Alfie couldn't bring himself to laugh. "You weren't wrong."

They both came to a stop when they stood before each other, barely a foot apart.

"I have to tell you something," she said.

She looked afraid, and that scared Alfie more than anything. He could count the things Finn was afraid of on one hand.

"What is it?" he finally asked, his eyes searching.

"I bumped into your kooky diviner the other day," she said uneasily.

Alfie blinked at that. The last person he wanted to think about now was Diviner Lucila. He'd been forever angry about her telling him he didn't have a future, but now he was even angrier that she hadn't told him that *this* would be his future—a dead brother he would always miss, an unwanted marriage with an Englassen princess, the loss of a thief who brought nothing but chaos yet always seemed to make him feel whole. Couldn't she have warned him about this? He looked at Finn's face—her true face, unguarded.

Couldn't the diviner have told him about what he was going to lose?

"Did she say something to you?" Alfie said, his throat tight. He knew the pain of hearing of a future he did not want.

"She did," Finn said. Her voice was quiet as her shadow twisted at her feet.

Alfie watched as his own shadow edged closer to hers. "Whatever she said to you, it doesn't define you. Don't let her—"

"She told me something about you," Finn blurted, cutting him off.

Alfie's stomach dropped. What new blow could the diviner deliver now? What had she told Finn that would make her look at him like this, with fear in her eyes?

"She told me that when she tried to divine you, she couldn't see your future because there was a missing piece and without it, she couldn't properly read you."

Alfie nodded, not wanting to hear the story again. "I know," Alfie said, feeling himself deflate at the memory. "It seems I'm incomplete."

"No." Finn shook her head, her eyes darting to her feet. "No, you're not."

Alfie looked at her for a long moment. "What do you mean?"

"She told me that she found the missing piece, the thing so entwined with your destiny that she couldn't read you until she found it."

Alfie's heart pounded in his chest. "What is it?"

She looked at him then, her eyes blazing. "Me."

"You," he breathed. For a long moment his mind went blank, taking in the information and giving nothing back.

"I didn't believe her either," Finn said, throwing her hands up. "It doesn't make any maldito sense. You're a prince and I'm . . ." She shook her head. "Us being entangled like that makes no sense. But she was sure," Finn said. "And now I am too. No matter who you marry, that won't change. You will always be entangled with a thief, you hear me?"

Alfie could barely hear her anymore. He stared at her in shock.

"Well, that's all I wanted to say." When Alfie still didn't respond, she blew a stray curl out of her face in frustration. "Say something!"

That was enough to jar Alfie back to the present. His body moved just as his mind caught up with him. He took her hands in his, turning them over to rub soft circles into her palms. "All my life I thought I was broken. So broken that I didn't deserve a future, but that was wrong." His voice sounded foreign to him, as if it were coming from another body. Everything was foreign to him now. With one word from her, his future had been rewritten, reclaimed. Alfie looked at her surprised face, wanting to remember the details to recall over and over again for the rest of his life. It was so rare that she looked so lost and then, the more he spoke, so found. "It wasn't true at all," he said, a laugh parting his lips, surprising him with the strange joy bubbling inside him. "I wasn't broken; I was just waiting for you." He could do nothing but say it again. "*I was waiting for you.*"

Finn's hands, once soft and pliant in his, moved slowly, lacing their fingers together. She looked at him the same way she had four months ago when he'd told her that she didn't need to help him stop Sombra if she didn't want to, that he would never force her. She was looking at him with that expression of fearful trust. As if in trusting him she was diving off a cliff's edge, but she was strong enough to take that step into oblivion so long as he was meeting her at the bottom.

Before she could say another word, Alfie gripped her hand and pressed it to his chest, just as she had when he'd nearly lost his mind in the Clock Tower. She'd put his hand on her chest so that he could feel her heart beating steadily, to help him calm down. But Alfie didn't want her to think he was calm; he wanted her to know that this was how she made him feel. His heart beat fast under her palm.

Finn's eyes shifted from his face to her hand on his chest. Alfie looked at her, hoping that she understood what he was trying to say. Then her lips curved into her signature smirk and Alfie knew she understood. Her hand shifted up, away from his chest to the back of his neck. She pulled him down into a kiss, and Alfie was lost in the heat of their shared breaths, the soft rustling of their clothes as they moved against each other, the playful press of their noses as they broke apart only to come back for more.

He didn't know what possessed him to engage his *propio*. It was as if it happened by accident.

Or maybe a touch of fate.

But when he looked at her, he didn't see her red magic. He saw something entirely different.

"You're purple," Alfie gasped.

With his *propio* engaged he could see the magic running through her had shifted from her signature myriad of reds to violet. "The color of your magic has changed." He'd never seen anyone's magic change in his entire life. It was enough to make him forget about the kiss.

For a moment.

"Purple is good," she muttered. She didn't seem to be listening. She cornered him against the wall and with one hand tilted his chin up before pressing her lips to his neck. "I like purple," she said between kisses.

Alfie found himself forgetting about this strange magical discovery. For one long, delicious moment his mind went alarmingly quiet before the part of him that lived in the library prodded him. How could someone's magic suddenly change color? The only time he'd seen anything like this was when Sombra had infected the people with his evil, dyeing their magic black. But this was different. Sombra was gone.

"Wait, wait, wait," Alfie said, pushing her back gently by the shoulders.

"Really?" Finn complained.

Alfie forced himself to look at her again, just to make sure he was right. He engaged his *propio* and saw it again. Her magic was purple, but now his hand was on her shoulder, playing with the neckline of her shirt, and Alfie was shocked to see that his hand was purple too.

"Qué?" Alfie said aloud.

"What is it?" Finn demanded. "Is there something on my face?" She swiped under her nose.

"No," Alfie said. "No, there's nothing wrong with your face."

Alfie wasn't sure who moved first, but then they were kissing again.

"Wait," he said again when they broke apart for air.

"Why?" she said, throwing her hands up.

"We're both purple, Finn. The colors of our magics have changed. They match. I've never seen this and I don't—" The realization struck Alfie like a wave, sweeping him under.

Finn was red. He was blue. Together, they made purple.

"It's you and me, together. Blue and red." He looked at her in wonderment. "I've always been able to change my own magic to match someone else's and work within their spellwork, but I didn't know that I could actually change the color of their magic." It was an extension of his *propio* that he hadn't expected.

"You didn't change my magic," she said, resolute. "You stole some of mine and I stole some of yours back."

"Then we're both thieves now," Alfie said.

"An even trade," Finn said, and between her words Alfie could hear what she didn't dare say.

You give me all of you. I give you all of me. A fair trade.

When she tilted her chin up, no doubt with a retort on her lips about how bad a thief he would be, Alfie pressed his lips against hers once more.

Finn pulled back suddenly, and it was as if Alfie had been doused with a bucket of ice-cold water.

"Wait," she said, her eyes wide.

Now it was Alfie's turn to breathlessly ask, "Why?"

Finn tilted her head. "If our magic matches, does that mean we can travel together again. Like before?"

In the heat of the moment he hadn't thought of that. If his magic could mix with hers, making their magic match, then the portals he traveled through should recognize Finn as an extension of himself. He'd only been able to do it before when he'd caught some of Sombra's essence in the dragon figurine. But they probably could do it again now.

Alfie's stomach tightened at the thought of the screams he had heard within the magic.

"Maybe," he said, shrugging uneasily. "I don't know."

"You still hear the screams?"

Alfie nodded. "I heard them on my way back from the Tattooed King."

"Let's try," she said, her eyes searching and finding his hesitance. "I'll be with you the whole time."

Alfie swallowed. Maybe this would be the last time he would have the courage to brave the realm of magic and the sounds within. With Finn at his side he found he could do almost anything.

"Very well," Alfie said, fingering the glass doorknob in his pocket. He still carried it about as a force of habit. "Where do you want to go?"

"Your rooms," Finn said, her chin high.

Alfie's spine straightened. The doorknob fell from his hand and sank into the floor. He pretended he'd dropped it on purpose. He took her hand. How had their kiss changed the colors of their magic? How would he replicate it? He'd felt connected to her, emotionally and also physically.

Alfie closed his eyes and thought of their bond, of how much he would miss her, of how much of himself he'd discovered because of her. And then he could feel himself pouring into her. This time more give than take. He wanted her to match his blue. Blue was the color he'd assigned to transporting to his room; he needed them both to match that.

Sweat beaded at his forehead. When he opened his eyes, Finn was a beacon of blue.

"Purple again?" Finn asked when he stared at her for too long.

"This time we're blue," he said ruefully, remembering that this might be the last time they were anything together.

Alfie turned the doorknob and the floor opened to the tangles of magic he'd once traveled with ease.

"Ready?" Finn asked.

"Not quite," Alfie admitted, but with one look from her he smiled and together they stepped into the magic.

He watched the colors of magic play on Finn's skin, waiting for the wailing to begin, waiting for her to look at him in fear at the sound of magic rejecting him, but it didn't happen. The magic gently deposited them into his rooms without a sound.

He sighed in relief, a great weight on his shoulders turning light as feathers.

"No sound," Finn said breathlessly. "That travel is weird, but somehow I missed it."

Alfie could only nod, watching the exhilaration bloom on her face. There were no screams, and he knew why.

It had to be Finn.

Maybe combining their magic had healed the rift between him and the realm of magic. Maybe the magic saw the love he was sacrificing for the greater good and called it even. Alfie couldn't be sure. All he knew was that only she could've done it. Only she could have freed him from that.

And still, he was going to marry someone else.

"What?" she asked, annoyed. "Why are you looking at me like that?"

"I'm trying to decide which is worse," Alfie admitted, his heart aching in his chest. "Having you for one night or never having you at all."

Finn was silent for a long moment, long enough for Alfie to

know that she wasn't sure of the answer herself. She didn't say a word but, instead, pulled her shirt over her head and wriggled out of her trousers, cursing under her breath when they tangled around her ankles. Then she was standing in nothing but her underthings. Two daggers were secured at her waist and ankles for safekeeping. If his mind had been able to make a joke, he would've laughed and said, *Of course you've got extra daggers.*

"Well," Finn said, stepping out of the puddle of clothes and toward him. She was so close that he could feel the heat radiating from her bare skin. He couldn't help but step forward, like a flower turning toward the sun. "Have you decided?"

Alfie ran his thumb over her jawline, swept it over her full top lip. "Yes."

This small slip of time was theirs to savor, but his mind forever sprinting ahead of him, Alfie was painfully aware of how quickly this time would disappear. Of how he needed to make sure to cherish it. Of how soon it would be over.

Of how soon she would be gone.

"Stop thinking about it," she said, closing the distance between them. "Be here. Stay here."

And then Alfie let the idea of time, of responsibility, of the future, fall to ash.

There were buttons that were annoyingly difficult to undo, eliciting a curse from her and a laugh from him.

"It'd only take a second if you'd just let me use my dagger. . . ."

"No, no," he chuckled, undoing his buttons himself. "I'll do it. Please stay unarmed for once in your life."

There was talk of the night when the two had met, masked and mischievous. After all, when something comes to an end, it's only natural to speak fondly of its beginning.

"You looked like you were going to wet your maldito pants at that cambió game," she laughed while he fingered a frizzy curl on her forehead.

"Perhaps." He shrugged, too content to be bothered. "But if I remember correctly, I was the one who went home with the prize, wasn't I?"

At that Finn huffed, her fingers twitching as if she longed to summon a dagger, but the annoyance fell away just as quickly as it came. In a smooth, liquid motion, she hitched her leg over his waist, silencing him with a kiss as she guided his hands to grip her hips.

There were questions and answers.

"Where will you go?" he asked. He didn't know if he should know the answer to that. If he knew where she went, he might follow her.

But perhaps that wasn't such a bad thing. Or maybe it was the worst thing.

"You asked me that the last time we said goodbye," Finn said, her cheek leaning against the sore spot on his shoulder where she'd bitten him. He wondered how long the mark would last. "I didn't tell you then, and I'm definitely not telling you now."

He looked at her, the question gnawing at him. "You can't make an exception? Just this once?"

Finn tilted her head, and Alfie could tell what she said next would hurt him just as much as it would heal him. Haunt him just as much as it would sustain him for the years ahead—the years without her.

"You are my exception, Prince. I would have never come back here if you weren't."

Alfie pressed his forehead to hers and fell into her embrace, done with questions for the night. The rest of that stolen time could be counted in laughter, in the brushing of their noses, in the swell of their matching breaths and intertwined fingers. But it could never be counted in minutes. Some things simply overwhelmed the cold business of seconds, ticks and tocks. Some things were untouchable. When he held her and moved with her, he could convince himself that he had lived a whole lifetime here in this moment.

But time could not wait forever, and as the sun began to rise they sat on the edge of the bed, their feet dangling over the side, both knowing that once their toes touched the ground it would be over.

When Alfie sat still for too long, Finn made a move to step down, to get it over with.

"Wait," Alfie said, grabbing her hand. "Por favor."

If this was the last thing they were going to do, then at least let it be done together.

Alfie took a breath and squeezed her hand. "Okay," he said. "I'm ready."

Finn smiled ruefully, her eyes shining. "Liar."

Together, the prince and the thief stepped out of their oasis and back into reality.

THE CLOAK

Two days later, the marriage contract had been drawn and Alfie had
successfully guaranteed the freedom of thousands of Englassen people while Marsden sulked on the other side of the table.

Two days after that was his betrothal ceremony.

The morning had been one of anxiety and pampering, an odd
combination that Alfie could not enjoy even if he tried. And he was
not trying.

Alfie was taken to the palace baths, where he was scrubbed with
salts and then slathered with lotions. His hair was massaged with
coconut oil while his nails were filed and shined. Then came the
long process of having his ceremonial armor placed on him—plate
after plate of the gold pieces weighed him down with the pressure
of today. Now would usually be the time when his parents would
present him with the vanishing cloak so that he could take it into
the ceremony and wrap himself and Vesper in it, but there was no
cloak to give.

Culebra had made it clear that the cloak was gone, destroyed.

His parents knew the story of what Alfie had done with the cloak now that Finn had told his mother, but they hadn't spoken about it. There had been the betrothal ceremony to plan, in addition to dealing with the riots that had exploded in the city after the betrothal announcement. There hadn't been much urgency to discuss the cloak when it was already gone for good, but Alfie knew they would want to talk about it today.

Alfie stood stiffly in his rooms, his spine straightening to keep the armor from pulling him toward the floor. He wanted to sit on his bed, but sitting was hardly comfortable in this armor. Then he stared at his bed and couldn't help but think of Finn.

Had she left already?

Did it matter? Whether she was still in the city or not, he would never see her again.

"Breathe, sourpuss," Luka said, pulling Alfie out of his thoughts. "Today is a big day; don't make it worse by staying in your head when I'm right here to offer more scintillating and distracting conversation."

"You know," Alfie said, mustering a small smile. "Telling me to breathe is the same as telling anyone else to hold their breath."

"What can I say?" Luka quipped. "I live to challenge you."

Luka had come to keep Alfie company while he waited for his parents to arrive to ready him for the ceremony, and Alfie was thankful for it. Without him he would do nothing but spiral about the betrothal, the fact that he'd lost the cloak.

The fact that Finn was gone from his life.

A knock sounded at his door.

"Come in," Alfie said, his stomach tight.

His parents strode into his rooms, their faces solemn. This wasn't what he had expected they would look like on the day of his betrothal ceremony, but then, he'd never expected his life to take this path.

"May we have a moment alone with Alfehr?" his mother asked Luka.

"Of course." Luka squeezed Alfie's shoulder. "I'll see you at the ceremony." Alfie's eyes followed Luka as he left. Then it was only him and his parents and all that lay ahead for this day.

"Are you ready?" his father asked as they came to his side.

"Yes," Alfie lied. "Of course."

"This isn't what we imagined for you," his mother said as she fixed the crown on his head.

"I know," Alfie said. "It's not what I imagined for myself either."

"We know why you've chosen this path," Bolivar said. "We're proud of you for putting the enslaved before yourself, but we wish you did not have to."

Amada's eyes grew glassy. "If we'd postponed the summit like you'd suggested, then maybe things wouldn't have gone so wrong. Maybe you wouldn't have to—"

"Mamá," Alfie said, pulling her gently into a hug. He didn't want to dwell on what could have been. This was his reality now. "It's all right."

"So," Amada said. "As you know, Finn told me what happened to the cloak. I've told your father."

"You're upset with me," Alfie said. He would rather have them shout at him than sit in this silence.

"Oh, absolutely," she said. "When I told your father the details we were already planning the tongue lashing you would get. You gave away something that was not yours to give."

Alfie looked down at his feet. He couldn't argue with her. He'd lost something completely irreplaceable. "What stopped you?"

"Our very kind hearts," the king said before looking at his wife. "And fond memories."

Fond memories? Alfie only stared at them.

"You know," Amada said, "your father was supposed to marry someone else."

Alfie blinked. "Qué?" His parents had told him that they were a love match, a couple who chose each other as opposed to being set up, but they'd never said that his father was betrothed to another.

"She's right," the king said, his hand finding Amada's. "I was betrothed to another woman from a more powerful family. Your mother and I met at my engagement party." He kissed her palm. "I was hers by the end of the night."

Alfie stared at them. His parents were not rule breakers. They lived on the idea of decorum. Or so he'd thought. "You were unfaithful to your fiancée . . . with Mamá?"

Bolivar and Amada burst into laughter. "It's as if you think we've never done anything wrong in our lives," Amada said, wiping the tears from her eyes.

Alfie rubbed the back of his neck, suddenly embarrassed by his own shock. "You've never spoken about it. How could I not be surprised?"

"That is more than fair, Mijo. Not even your brother knew." Bolivar straightened Alfie's armor. "It was hardly a traditional meeting, but it is what we wished for you."

Alfie could only nod. It was what he'd wanted too, and if wanting were enough, he would be marrying someone different today.

"That wish won't come true," Alfie said. "But Dezmin's wish will. That's something, isn't it?"

His father squeezed his shoulder. "Yes, that's something."

"But what does that story have to do with me losing the cloak?" Alfie asked.

"Well," Amada said, her tone lighter than Alfie had expected. "Your father gave me his heart that night years ago, even though it wasn't his to give either. It had been promised to someone else, but he gave it to me anyway." She cocked her head at him, her eyes searching. "I have a feeling you gave Finn the cloak for the same reason."

Alfie nodded, his eyes stinging.

Amada's hand found his cheek. "Oh, Mijo." She pulled him into her embrace and Alfie fell into it, tucking his head into the crook of her neck the way he would when she carried him as a child. "Don't get me wrong. We're furious that you lost it."

"Completely livid," his father added.

"But it's not as if Englass has ever had much respect for our customs. We'll have the ceremony without it." She pulled free from the embrace and gave him a hard look. "But you'll have to answer for it later."

Alfie nodded, his heart lightened.

"Now chin up, Mijo," the king said while tapping Alfie's chin. "You're getting betrothed today."

THE PROPIO SEER

The day of Alfie's betrothal ceremony, Finn sat in Kol's office, drinking.

She was waiting to hear back from Emeraude about who would replace her as la Madre. Then she could leave for good.

She was free. Free to live a life searching for those gold eyes, but never finding them.

A knock sounded at her door.

"I said take the day off!" Finn barked.

An elderly man opened the door. "Perdóname, I was told that la Madre wanted to see me?"

Finn squinted at the viejo. "Who are you?"

"I used to work with Kol. She called me the *propio* seer."

Finn stared at the man. "Anabeltilia said you couldn't be found. I even went to your place in the Pinch to check and you were long gone."

The man cocked his head. "I was never contacted by anyone by that name. And I live in the Bash, not the Pinch. I was asked in a letter by someone called Emeraude to come see you to talk about some strange *propios?*"

Finn was surprised that Anabeltilia hadn't found him if he'd just been in the Bash this whole time. The girl had even sent her to his supposed apartment in the Pinch. . . . She must've been mistaken about his address. Well, it hardly mattered now.

The man looked at her then and his eyes lit up with recognition that Finn did not reciprocate. "Ah, you're the girl Kol was talking about."

Finn's skin crawled as his eyes roved over her. He didn't look at her lasciviously, the way some men did. Finn could tell that when he looked at her, he was seeing beyond the physical.

Somehow, that was worse.

"You know me?" Finn said, her fingers twitching for a dagger.

He shook his head. "I don't know you, but I know what you can do." He pointed at the shadow at his feet. It moved slowly with age, just as he did. "You can change your appearance, within limits of course. Kol told me as much. But now that we're face-to-face I see that you can change others' too, almost as easily as you can change your own." He looked at her harder, as if a piece of her were far off in the distance. "And you can—"

Finn raised a silencing hand. "I already know what I can do, viejo," she said, hoping to shut him up. She didn't need anyone else to lecture her on the new part of her *propio.* "I took Kol's place."

"Coño, you're the one who did her in?" The old man looked at her again, a hint of respect in his eyes.

"You can go," Finn said, slurring her words. "The questions I needed to ask you don't matter anymore." Los Toros were caught. She didn't need his help.

"You know," he said, "Kol asked me to look into you too."

Finn froze at that. "What?"

"Yes, just before Equinox, if I'm remembering correctly."

He said it casually, as if the whole world hadn't nearly broken in half at the Equinox Ball.

"She knew you could change your appearance, but she wanted to be sure that she knew every shade of your *propio* so she could properly block it. She asked me to look into you, but I caught the flu and couldn't. She didn't want to wait, so she just went on what she already knew."

Finn stared at him. This man falling sick was the only reason why Kol hadn't known to fully block Finn's *propio*. The only reason why Finn had been able to use her abilities to transform the prince and make their trip to the Clock Tower possible.

"The letter stated that you wanted help on identifying the men with those strange *propios* who killed the delegados, but I've traveled long and far under Kol's service, cataloguing *propios* all the way down to the southern tip of Castallan, where pingüinos waddle about on the ice, and I've never even heard a rumor of such *propios*." He gave a shudder. "I would say the culprits aren't from Castallan."

Even in her drunken haze, Finn sat up. "What?"

"They must be foreign. I would know of men with such *propios* if they lived here. Kol paid me to be thorough."

Finn shook her head. Why was she even talking to this man? She already knew who Los Toros were, didn't she? She was far too drunk for this useless conversation. "You're free to go. I don't need this information anymore."

But when the old man left, she couldn't stop thinking. If Culebra ran Los Toros, then how could the group be from another kingdom?

THE MAP MARKED WITH BLOOD

They must be foreign. I would know of men with such propios *if they lived here.*

As Finn stared at the map that Anabeltilia had left her, the words of the *propio* seer echoed in her mind. Something wasn't sitting right.

Finn chewed her lip as she looked at the red tacks marking the map where corpses had been found, begging her mind to glean something from the map, but finding nothing.

Finn was staring at the X's when the answer flared to life in her head like a flash of lightning.

She grabbed a quill from Kol's desk and began connecting the X's in curving lines. In moments an image began to come through.

Finn gasped—the three murders formed a bruxo's triangle with the palace directly at its center. Los Toros had set up some sort of written spellwork to span the capital. She didn't know if the *propio* seer was right about the threat being international, but right now it didn't matter. All she knew was that there was a threat and it was coming for the prince and his family today. But what were Los Toros using the bruxo's triangle for? Was it like the legend Alfie had spoken of, spellwork that would crack open the ground and let the city fall into the depths of the world? Something that would hurt everyone within its lines?

A sudden realization made Finn's blood run cold. Each of the three points of the bruxo's triangle represented a murder. The point in the middle, where the palace was, must be the same, wouldn't it? The vision of the prince being stabbed in the stomach played in her mind.

"They're going to kill him," Finn said, her heart pounding against her rib cage. They'd thought that Los Toros had been caught, but the gang still had one more trick up their sleeve. "They're going to kill him to complete whatever spell they're doing."

Not if she could help it.

Finn nearly ripped the map off the wall and turned toward the door, but leaning against it lazily was the last person she wanted to see—Ignacio.

"And where exactly are you going?"

Finn squared her shoulders. He wasn't real, she knew that. But he also was—if he followed her everywhere for the rest of her life, how could he not be real? What was more real than the fear she felt at the sound of his voice or the sight of his chilling, knowing smile.

"Get out of my way," she snarled.

With a cluck of his tongue Ignacio shook his head at her. "You were finally choosing the right path, leaving this place. You understood the truth. That little prince's influence made you soft. But you yourself are anything but soft. You have no place here, with him. And now you want to run back into this mess." He gave her a disapproving look. "It's disappointing, Mija."

"You're wrong," she bit out, though doubt was creeping in, staining her like blood seeping in a white shirt. "You don't know anything about me."

In the blink of an eye Ignacio was in front of Finn, suddenly monstrously tall and looming over her. "*I made you!*" he shouted, his eyes turning full black, just as they were when he carried Sombra's magic. "You act like you aren't an extension of me. As if you could be like him," he spat, disgust in his tone. "But you *are* me, Mija. You are my legacy. You have brought me to life beyond death. And what could be greater proof of that than this new shade of your darling little *propio*." He cupped her face with his cold hands, his fingers long, his nails sharp and dirtied.

"That boy can tell you whatever you like, but it doesn't change the truth. You are my daughter. Mine," he seethed, coming so close that his breath puffed on her face. "You are my legacy. You are *me!*"

"No," Finn snapped. She was tired of not knowing who she was. Tired of thinking she needed someone to tell her instead of just knowing it for herself. "I don't need you to tell me I'm bad, and I don't need Alfie to tell me I'm good. I am not you!"

"Oh really," Ignacio said. "You control others whenever you feel like it. No consequences." He grinned wildly. "Just for fun. Who does that sound like to you, hmm?"

His words overwhelmed her like a wave, sweeping her under, but then something sparked in her mind. Something that carried her to the surface and let her gulp fresh air.

"No." She shook her head at Ignacio, finally understanding something. "You're wrong."

"I'm never wrong when it comes to you."

"Yes, you are," Finn said, and she could feel herself smiling. In the face of this horrible ghost, she was smiling.

"Take that look off your face. Don't forget, I can love you and—"

"—and hurt me, yeah, yeah, yeah. I know," she scoffed. She finally understood. She couldn't stop laughing. "I'm not you at all."

Ignacio opened his mouth to speak, but Finn wouldn't let him. "You just told me yourself. For you, controlling others is fun; there was no sacrifice, just fun. You lost nothing while you took everything from them, from me. But that's not the way it is for me. Whenever I control someone else, it costs me my freedom too. I have to move with them," she shouted, her eyes stinging. She couldn't help but think of the man she'd hurt in the tattoo parlor. She'd felt his fear and pain as if it were her own while Ignacio felt nothing but pleasure when he controlled others. "Every time I take over someone else, I feel their fear—I feel it, it hurts me. The same way it hurt me when you forced me to do all the horrible things you commanded. I'm nothing like you. This power may be like yours, but the way it feels for me, is nothing like it did for you. Part of you is in me, I'll admit that," she said, resolute and sure in herself. "Part of you will always be in me. Maybe that's why my *propio* has developed the way it has. But I will never find joy in controlling others the way you did. Never."

Ignacio stared at her, speechless, but Finn didn't have time to think about him; her mind was crackling with energy.

She hadn't returned to Castallan for Alfie to tell her she was a good person. She didn't need the prince for that—part of her had already known it. She'd returned for Alfie. Just Alfie.

And with the prince in danger, she didn't have time for this nonsense anymore.

"So you can just get the hell out of my head, hijo de pu—" But when Finn looked up, Ignacio was already gone, vanished. She knew, deep within, that he would never be returning.

"Yeah, see yourself out," Finn said to the empty room, needing to have the last word even when it came to a ghost.

Finn rushed toward the door before skidding to a stop as Anabeltilia walked in.

"Well, don't you look energized," she said.

"There's no time to explain! Los Toros are planning something for the betrothal ceremony. I talked to the *propio* seer—"

Anabeltilia stared at her. "What are you talking about?"

"I've got to stop it! Get la Familia ready to fight!" Finn dashed down the stairs and through the empty pub and made her way to the door. Anabeltilia followed her halfway down the stairs. "Get to Emeraude and tell her—" Finn felt a sudden prick at her neck. She touched it and pulled out a quilbear quill, just like when the bull-masked thief stole the cloak from her.

"Finn!" Anabeltilia shouted from the stairs as Finn began to fall to the ground. Anabeltilia was no fighter; whoever had knocked her out was going to take her without a problem. As her vision swam, Finn just hoped she would wake up in time to save the prince.

Finn woke to the smell of blood.

She was sitting at Emeraude's table, her hands and legs tied to the chair.

Before her, Rodrigo and Elian sat at the table in their usual seats. At the head of the table sat Emeraude, a wide smile cut into her throat, the dagger still lodged in the side of her neck. Her head sagged over the back of her chair, so far that Finn couldn't see her face, only her chin. The decorative blades jutted out of the wall behind her, glinting in the lamp light.

"Coño," Finn breathed.

"Ah," Rodrigo said. "You're finally awake. Ready for another boring thief lord meeting? Emeraude," Rodrigo called to the corpse. "What's the news of the day?"

"What's going on?" She couldn't look away from Emeraude's throat. When they said nothing, Finn shouted louder. "*Why would you do this?*"

Rodrigo pulled a rolled-up map from under his arm. It was the one from Finn's office. "It seems you already know. We had people watching you at Kol's pub, of course. And once you loudly announced that you were going to stop the betrothal we had them knock you out and deliver you straight to us for safekeeping."

It struck her then, like a pail of ice water dumped over her head. "You knew. You knew Los Toros were up to something big." Her eyes darted between them, her fingers itching for a dagger. "You both knew. You're in on it."

Elian rolled his eyes.

"Yes, muchacha, we're in on it," he said, nodding at Emeraude's still body. "And once the betrothal ceremony had been finalized, we finally got approval to kill her—a reward promised to me by Prince Marsden himself. But we didn't expect you to figure anything out. Well done."

"What?" Finn stared at him. She'd thought the culprits were Los

Toros, not the Englassens. "Prince Marsden?"

The words of the *propio* seer struck her then: the threat was *foreign*. He was right.

All along it had been Englass. Englass and Los Toros were in on this together.

"Ah," Rodrigo said with a grin. "Elian, I think she's finally getting it."

"I don't understand," Finn said, her mind abuzz. "What are Los Toros planning? What are they doing tangled up with the Englassen royal family?" She shifted in her seat, tugging on her restraints. Why hadn't she learned desk magic? She could've untied these ropes with a word.

"Los Toros and Englass are one and the same," Rodrigo said as he leaned back in his chair and threw his leather-booted feet onto Emeraude's table. "Working toward a common goal of performing some clever spellwork today."

"Will they lock us in the capital and kill us?" Finn asked. "Is that what they're doing with the bruxo's triangle?"

"Of course not," Rodrigo said with a bark of laughter. "What profit do they make if everyone's dead?"

"What is the maldito spellwork?" She bared her teeth at them, making the stone floor shake with her anger. She was tired of waiting for answers. "*Tell me!*"

For the first time since she'd met him, Elian spoke. "Spellwork that unwrites the magic inside you."

Finn stared at him. He waited all this time to speak and he chose to speak nonsense. "Stop speaking in maldito riddles!"

"He's telling the truth," Rodrigo said. "Englass will claim

Castallan once more, and written magic is how they'll do it."

"Explain it to me," she growled. When he only smiled at her, Finn shouted and fought with such force that she rocked her chair on its legs. "Tell me!"

"You're quite demanding for someone tied to a chair, but fine. I'll tell you. Back when those Englassen pendejos colonized us, they tried to break our connection to magic the old-fashioned way. They destroyed our books, forbade us from speaking our language, and only allowed us to use elemental magic if it was in service to them."

"I don't need a maldito history lesson," Finn growled.

"Are you sure?" His eyes swept over her, slow and judgmental. "You don't look like you've had much of an education."

Anger flared inside her. Emeraude had been forced under the heel of a man who'd sought to own her and instead of being ground to dust, she'd sent her monstrous husband straight to his grave. All that only to be taken down by these pendejos.

"They've developed written spellwork that will sever Castallan's connection to magic forever. No Castallano alive will be able to remember even a word of their mother language. No connection to language means no magic. The effect is quite stunning. The victims become docile, obedient, amicably soulless. Not an ounce of fight left in them."

Finn's stomach dropped. It was unthinkable.

"And you two?" she said, her voice hushed and strained with anger. "You'll get to remember."

"But of course. We've been marked safe," Rodrigo said, pointing to a chain around his neck, the very same one that Elian wore.

She'd noticed it during her first thief lord meeting, but she'd thought nothing of it. She felt so stupid now.

"A talisman to exempt us from the spellwork," Rodrigo went on. "It's only fair. After all, we helped provide what they needed. You did too, in your own way. The vanishing cloak was key for the spellwork. A great cultural artifact is needed for the spellwork and only the cloak would do. With the mess of high-profile crimes you committed, tracking you down and getting the cloak back was simple. Thank you for your service," he said with faux gratitude. "We got the cloak from you before the summit even started because the Englassens needed it early to prepare it for tonight. Now the betrothal ceremony will get us the final piece."

Finn stared at them. The bull-masked thief had taken the cloak to deliver it to the Englassen royals for a ritual that would rob her whole kingdom of its magic. Everything had become painfully clearer, but still, there were some things she didn't understand.

"Why the betrothal? Why all the murders and the drama if you've had the cloak this whole time? Why make Alfie marry her if they just want to enslave the kingdom?"

"Well, the spilling of Castallano blood needed to happen for the ritual to work, hence the murders, but the final piece is the blood of the royal family, willingly given," Rodrigo said. "Complex magic requires complex ingredients. It's not as if Princess Vesper could bat her eyes and ask Alfie if she could please have his family's blood," Rodrigo laughed. "Lucky for us, part of the Englassen betrothal ceremony is for the families to exchange blood. So to get the final ingredient we needed to create the type of political climate that would convince that bleeding heart Prince Alfie that he needed to marry Vesper. Her near assassination and the guilt at leaving all those poor Englassens enslaved was enough to get him to pop the question." Rodrigo clapped his hands, grinning. "And there you have it."

Finn could only stare at him. Los Toros' murders were done for the spellwork, but also to manipulate Alfie into having to marry Vesper. All the threats to the Englassen royals had been fabricated. They'd made it seem like Alfie's family had endangered them just to guilt Alfie into this marriage, into giving them the final ingredient for their horrifying spellwork.

"The humiliation of it all is quite delicious to Prince Marsden. Thanks to him, soon we'll have a new king to answer to." Rodrigo took a shot of rum. "Long may he reign."

Finn blanched. "You're cowards."

"I think the term you're looking for is geniuses," Rodrigo said.

"Let me go. I can still stop it. There's still time for you to realize what an idiot you are for doing this," Finn said through gritted teeth. "Let me go."

"Absolutely not," Rodrigo said. "We don't want you interrupting your friend's nuptials, do we?"

Elian shook his head, looking bored as usual.

"Plus, we kept you alive because we want to see the transformation happen." Rodrigo leaned forward in his chair. "I want to watch the light fade from your eyes as Prince Marsden completes the ritual. No, you're far too important to release. You're our guest of honor!"

Finn clenched her jaw, looking at the dagger lodged in Emeraude's neck. "You're making a mistake."

Rodrigo smiled. "What makes you so sure?"

Finn looked at him. "This."

She cocked her head sharply to the left, and thanks to her stone carving, the metal dagger flew out of Emeraude's throat and lodged itself in Rodrigo's. He choked and gasped as he bled out.

Before Elian could make a move, Finn rocked backward until her chair hit the ground. On the earth floor Finn twitched her fingers and summoned up shards of stone to slice through her restraints. She shot up from the ground to see Elian watching Rodrigo choke and gasp, but the boy did nothing to help him, only turned to her.

As Elian watched her with his blank eyes, a sour fear curdled in her belly, paralyzing her where she stood. Before she could pull the blades from the wall behind him, he caught her in his *propio* and dredged up a fear inside her that was so intense she couldn't move.

Ragged breaths burst from her lips in labored gasps. She could scarcely breathe. He was trying to do to her what he'd done to the thief lord before him—scare her into a heart attack or to at least make her pass out. Then he'd finish the job while she was unconscious.

But Finn had an idea.

She pushed against the fear and forced herself to move, to change herself into Elian and seek out the connection between them. In the blink of an eye he was under her physical control. If she moved, he would move. But best of all, she no longer felt any fear. In fact, she felt nothing.

She'd been right; the boy could control others' emotions because he had none. When Finn puppeteered people, she felt what they felt, and Elian felt *nothing*. Finn had always wanted to feel nothing, but now she felt lucky for every tear shed, every bout of rage she'd ever experienced. This boy was empty, and she needed to end him before he ended her.

Finn took a step backward and Elian mirrored her, his eyes widening with surprise. She'd never seen him look surprised. Without a word, Finn broke into a backward run.

He realized his fate before it tore through him.

Finn slammed into the wall behind her and so did Elian, but the wall behind him was full of Emeraude's machetes, jutting out blade first. One surged through his left hip, another just below his collarbone.

Finn had expected to feel the pain of the blades, but the boy was numb with shock. He hardly made a sound as the life seeped out of him. Finn released him from her hold then, letting his body twitch and shudder at its sudden wounds. The fear in Finn's chest slowly receded. When Elian finally stopped breathing and fell still, his eyes looked no more lifeless than they always had been.

Gasping, Finn dropped to her knees, clutching at her chest, happy to feel her heart pounding after it had been so calm while she puppeteered Elian. She could feel again.

She staggered to her feet, gripping the table for support as she rose.

Finn looked at Emeraude's corpse, her eyes stinging. "I don't have time to give you the burial you deserve," she said. She longed to hear Emeraude's light laugh along with her insistence that Finn take another slice of flan, but the room was as silent as the corpses within it.

But then again, Finn already knew what Emeraude would say to her.

Muchacha, killing those pendejos is a good enough funeral for me. What are you waiting for? Get going.

Finn gave the corpse a nod. "Goodbye, Abuela." She turned on her heel and ran into the night.

The fate of an entire kingdom weighed on her shoulders, but all she could think of was the prince standing at the altar, danger closing in on him from all angles as he offered his blood in good faith.

Was that when a knife would sink into his belly and steal his life away like she'd seen in the diviner's quarters?

Finn shook her head. If they were going to try to take some royal blood, then it would be hers.

As she ran, Finn put her hands on her face and engaged her *propio*, molding her features into the face of the boy she hoped to save.

THE BETROTHAL CEREMONY

As Alfie entered the great ballroom for the betrothal ceremony, flower petals rained from the ceiling in an endless, gentle cascade.

The falling flowers were red, gold, and blue—a combination of Englass's and Castallan's colors. Alfie wanted to lie down and let the flowers bury him where he stood.

He stood at the start of a great aisle down the ballroom to the altar where Vesper, his parents, and his soon-to-be in-laws awaited. On either side of the aisle stood the finest nobility of both kingdoms, here to witness the promise of their great union, one that would save both Alfie's and Vesper's people from war but leave his heart to die in the process, buried under these maldito flowers.

At the end of the aisle, in Castallano wedding garb, Vesper stood waiting. Alfie made his way to her.

"Today we gather to join two families in blood, pride, and prosperity," the minister said. "Would the mother and father of the groom present their palms."

Alfie's parents stepped forward, their faces stiff. His mother met his eyes, as if asking him if he wanted to call this off, as if telling him that if he ran down the aisle and out the doors, she would be right behind him. But Alfie just gave her a barely perceptible nod.

The king's face was drawn and somber, accepting of what was to come. When the minister sliced his palm, letting the drops fall into a vial, he didn't even flinch. They did the same to his mother, and Alfie had to stop himself from grimacing at the finality of it. The minister would collect the blood of one family in one vial and the other in the second vial. Then he would mix the two together, a symbol of the joining of families and of the children to come from their union.

While Castallano betrothal ceremonies were ones of passion and vows and romance, Englassen ceremonies were logic, practicality, and blood.

After Prince Marsden and his parents offered their blood, the minister turned to Alfie and Vesper. "And now the bride and the groom must present their palms."

Alfie and Vesper faced each other and held out their palms to the minister. Alfie met her eyes, hoping to find calm reassurance there. But comfort was nowhere to be found. Vesper looked stone-faced.

Calculating.

Cold.

Before Alfie could question it, the minister had sliced through his palm, guiding the droplets into the vial to join the blood of his parents.

As soon as the minister released Alfie's hand, Vesper looked away, and Alfie wondered if she was regretting this as much as he was. But before the minister could speak again, a great rumbling shook the floor of the palace.

In an explosion of rock and debris, countless members of Los Toros in horned masks sprang up from the ground, like thorny flowers bursting through the grass. Their stone carvers must have tunneled beneath the palace, waiting for the betrothal to begin before they struck. Alfie was so shocked he could hardly move. He could feel his heart beating fearfully in his chest. He'd thought this was over, that they were safe, but he'd been wrong.

The banquet hall exploded with screams as the masked killers drew their blades and twisted the elements at their command.

Guardsmen tried to protect both royal families, but Los Toros fought them off, conjuring walls of rock and twisting flames to push them back.

Before Alfie could move to strike, a masked man held the Englassen king with a knife to his throat. The entire Englassen royal family were held at knifepoint.

"We asked you to take care of this kingdom, to keep Englass out, but you did not perform your duty; you did not protect your people."

"Stop this!" Alfie shouted. "Please, we can come to a peace. There is no need for bloodshed. *Please*," he begged.

"We promised you that we would stop Englass from becoming part of this kingdom," the masked man said. "And now we will make good on that promise."

The masked man pressed the blade flush against the Englassen king's quivering neck and Alfie's mind fell blank at the prospect that he was about to watch a king murdered before his eyes. But it wasn't the Englassen king who fell.

The masked man pulled the dagger away from the Englassen king's throat and threw it with precision. The blade sailed forward and sank into King Bolivar's chest.

Alfie's father gave a gasp—a hollow sound that Alfie knew came only from the dying. He slumped sideways against Alfie's shoulder, dead.

With her face and body molded to match Alfie's as best as she could, Finn dashed up the palace stairs. The doors were flanked with both Castallano and Englassen guards. Changing into the prince was the best plan she could come up with to get into the palace and stop the wedding.

"Open the gates!" Finn said, grasping for the deepest abilities of her *propio* that let her mimic voices.

"P-Prince Alfehr?" a guardswoman sputtered, her eyes wide. "How are you— What—"

Finn paused. The Englassen guards stilled, looking at her. If she shouted that this betrothal ceremony was an Englassen coup, the guards would attack. She needed to find a way to get Alfie out of there safely. Even if it meant she would be in danger.

"The prince at the wedding is an imposter! This is all a plot to assassinate Princess Vesper—"

But Finn never finished the sentence. A bull-masked figure leaped from behind the Englassen guards and, too late, Finn recognized this moment as one she'd seen before in her vision.

She hadn't seen Alfie get stabbed; she'd seen herself get stabbed while disguised as him.

The blade arced and sank into Finn's lower stomach. Finn had done her fair share of stabbing, but she'd always been quick enough, clever enough to avoid a knifing like this. The bite of it was so intense that she couldn't scream. She could only curl forward, feeling her body shudder around it. Waves of pain rippled away from the bleeding wound, as if it were the epicenter of an earthquake destroying her body from the inside out. She could feel her *propio* melting away, her body returning to its natural state in order to save energy to heal.

The Castallano guards began to rush forward, but without a moment's hesitation, the Englassen guards began to cut them down, one by one, with practiced swings of their sabers.

Finn stumbled onto her knees, her hands pressed tight against the weeping wound as the woman removed her mask. Beneath it was a face Finn knew.

"If Emeraude hadn't called on the *propio* seer herself, you wouldn't even have made it this far. Soon you'll join that useless vieja," Anabeltilia said.

"You don't get to call her that," Finn bit out, her body still curling with the pain of the wound. "Why? Why did you do this?" She'd even vouched for the girl to Emeraude. She'd thought that she and Anabeltilia were alike. They'd been through the same struggle that left scars on their bodies and their hearts. She'd thought she could trust her. But Finn had been wrong.

"I was supposed to be next," she said. "Now I will be. It was exhausting pretending to be in awe of Emeraude and helping you with all your clueless plans. But you're too late anyway, Face Thief. The ceremony has begun and the blood has been given, but I'm happy to let you go witness the rest."

Finn pressed a bloody hand to the ground and forced herself onto her feet. She let the scream of pain building inside her fuel an angry, feral growl. She wanted to run Anabeltilia through for betraying her, for acting like a begrudging friend and lulling Finn into a false sense of trust. But she had no time. Not now.

"Get out of my way."

Anabeltilia only smirked and stepped aside. "By all means."

When the Englassen guardsmen tried to stop her, Anabeltilia waved a hand. "Let her go. There's nothing she can do now but watch."

So Finn limped as fast as she could through the palace doors and down the halls. The halls were littered with dead Castallano guards. She was too late, this she knew. But if the prince was going to die today, he wasn't going to die alone.

Finn ran, leaving a trail of blood behind her as she chased an uncertain future.

Alfie could hardly breathe.

He was lost, swept away by the sight of his father's corpse. So lost that when the double doors to the ballroom flew open and Finn barreled through, shouting something, Alfie couldn't hear it. A curtain of silence seemed to descend all around him.

He could not hear his mother screaming as the guards wrenched her away with rough hands. He couldn't hear it, but he knew it was happening. Finn was dashing down the aisle to get to him, knocking out guard after guard with her stone carving only to be tackled to the ground by three of them.

He didn't remember moving, but he was on his knees clutching his father's limp hand.

"Papá," he gasped, staring into his father's unseeing eyes. "Papá, please."

Alfie didn't want to engage his *propio*, didn't want to confirm what his heart already knew to be true, but he did. His father's green magic was gone; all that was left was a shell. Alfie wanted to surrender to the grief, to go numb under the weight of it, but he couldn't because he was too confused.

Why would Los Toros do this if they were targeting Englass? What purpose did killing his father serve?

"Well done," Prince Marsden crowed, clapping his hands in delight as the masked man who had held him captive let him go. Los Toros released the Englassen royal family and instead moved to stand in front of them. To protect them.

Alfie looked at Vesper. Her gaze was indifferent, distant.

"Why?" Alfie said, his voice hoarse and broken. "*Why?*"

"I must protect my country and its values, Prince Alfehr," she said. Her previous shyness was gone and Alfie knew it had to have been an act. "You ought to understand that."

"And thanks to you we have what we need," Prince Marsden said, snatching the vial of blood away from the minister. "Royal Castallano blood, willingly given." He turned the vial this way and that, his eyes tracking the movements of the blood.

"What?" Alfie said, still breathless, still so lost that he could barely speak.

"This kingdom's true owner is Englass," Marsden said, raising his chin. "And it will be so again now that we have your blood."

"We will never bow to you," Queen Amada shouted, fighting against the guards that restrained her.

Without a word, Marsden strode to her and struck her across the face. The queen's head swiveled painfully to the left from the force.

Anger welled inside Alfie, driving him to his feet, but the Englassen guardsmen grabbed him, holding him fast. He could see a group of men holding Luka back as well. They seemed prepared to handle his strength. This was all planned. Everything had been a lie.

"Keep your hands off my mamá!" he shouted.

Queen Amada didn't even flinch. She turned back to the Englassen prince and spat in his face.

Marsden gave a disgusted sigh. "Castallano savagery," he said before snapping his fingers. A servant handed him a handkerchief and he wiped his face. "How predictable."

"What would our blood do for you that would make this worth it?" Alfie roared, fighting against the guards who held him. "Why?"

"They're going to use your blood in some spell to take our magic away," Finn croaked from where the guards held her against the ground. "All Castallanos' magic. Make us mindless slaves."

Alfie's eyes went wide. "What?"

"That's right," Marsden said, his tone gleeful. "Bravo to you, bleeding stranger. We needed your blood, Prince Alfehr, to complete the spellwork that will make you ours again. Your fall will be my greatest legacy."

"You must understand," Vesper said, stepping ahead of her brother. "My country wouldn't have survived a war, and your people are better off under our rule anyway. No one else will have to die. It's the best option—"

"No!" Alfie cried, his jaw clenched tight. "Don't speak to me about what's best. Don't you *ever* speak to me. I should have known the night you proposed, you never saw us as people. You only saw us as possessions, things to own! You disgust me."

Finn had been right all along.

When people own you once, it's hard for them to look at you as anything else. Trust me. I would know.

Vesper's mouth closed, a flash of hurt in her eyes before her gaze became stony once more. Alfie couldn't believe he'd ever thought they could be friends.

"I must say, it was far too easy to get you to trust her," Marsden said. "I needed to act bullishly cruel so that she would seem the perfect angel in comparison. You fell for it so easily. I couldn't believe she convinced you to take us out to the Pinch to witness that murder."

Alfie's head spun with the new information. Of course. Going to the Pinch had been their plan all along. Having Vesper witness one of the anti-Englassen murders would make things all the more difficult for Alfie, and her promising to never tell her parents made him trust her more. It had all been a ruse.

"With the help of Delegado Culebra and his allies, we created the illusion of Los Toros in your kingdom. Culebra recruited Castallano members with the promise of power and riches, and we sacrificed them as we saw fit."

Alfie thought of the bull-masked people who had spoken the self-killing magic at the final cultural exhibition. They'd all just been Marsden's lambs to slaughter.

"He put on quite the show when you interrogated him," Marsden said with a smirk. "Soon he'll be running this kingdom in my name. We tasked them with killing delegados in the name of an anti-Englassen movement to seed some much-needed discord. We needed some pressure to get you to agree to marry Vesper, and making it seem as if you'd put my whole family in danger did the trick. It wasn't difficult. All the while, you agreed to have our guardsmen stationed throughout the city, so they were able to move freely and draw the intricate written spellwork around the city."

Alfie stared at Marsden, the information falling into place in his mind.

"And the best part is your role in it," Marsden said. "We needed a relic of great power and cultural weight to perform this spell. We were trying to figure out how to break into the royal vault to find something when we learned that you had already given your precious vanishing cloak away to some thief! All we had to do was locate her and take it back. She wasn't hard to find with the string of high-profile crimes she left in her wake." A servant stepped forward and handed the cloak to Marsden. "We even made sure to tell the thief girl that the cloak would be given to a true Castallano king who would never make peace with Englass, just to be sure you'd be thrown off our scent."

Fury roared inside him. He could hardly breathe. "There is no magic that could take our magic away from us. It doesn't exist."

"It didn't exist," Marsden corrected him. "Until we developed it."

"And now with the blood of the entire royal family, given in good faith, the cloak, and the spellwork that our guardsmen wrote around your despicable capital when you agreed to let us station them throughout the city, we need only speak the words and you will forget your native tongue. The murders were strategically placed as sacrifices for the spellwork. Your father is the last one. And with the sacrifice of the current king, this spell done over your capital will amplify to your entire kingdom. You all will lose your connection to spoken magic. And this kingdom will be ours again."

"You monster!" Alfie shouted.

"Ah, it wasn't just me, Alfie. I've got to give credit where credit is due. James, come forward and take a bow."

Alfie gasped as James stepped forward, his head hanging with shame.

Marsden clapped. "After James broke Englassen law, we saw him as the perfect candidate to test some experimental magic that pulls *propios* from one body to another. We hear that was something you were once interested in, Prince Alfehr. James now has multiple *propios*, which made killing your delegados easy and gruesome— traveling through matter, manipulating bones, speed, and even an illusionary *propio* so that he always looked Castallano when the murders were done."

Alfie understood now. James's magic had always looked like a strange dark color. Not a color at all, but a dark mixture of multiple shades, as if a child had dumped all his paints together. It was because he carried multiple colors. This must've been why James always looked so ill. The human body wasn't meant to hold so much magic. But if James was the murderer, why had James's magic been blue when he and Alfie fought in the Pinch? If Alfie had to guess, he'd say that James's magic probably turned one color based on which *propio* he was using. When Alfie had fought him in the Pinch, his magic had been blue to match the *propio* of becoming transparent. So when Alfie looked at James's magic in the palace, when James wasn't using any of his *propios*, his magic was a dark, murky mix of colors as opposed to the blue he'd seen in the Pinch.

"You're lying," Alfie said. He had once wanted to take Xiomara's *propio* as his own to free Dez, even though he knew the risks of having two *propios* in one body were unthinkable, but he had been willing to try it for Dez. The idea of even more *propios* was absurd. The body just wouldn't support it.

"How astute of you," Marsden said. "You're quite right. My healing magicians are certain that poor James here only has a short time left to live. His body can't handle the strain of so much magic." He looked at James, disgust in his eyes. "Which is why he's looked so pitiful and sickly as of late. But he still got the job done, didn't you, James?"

"How could you?" Luka shouted from where he was held by the guards.

James looked at him with anguish. "I'm sorry. I didn't want—"

"Come now, don't be too angry with him," Marsden interrupted. "I threatened to kill him and his whole family if he told you a word about what he was made to do, and bless his heart, he still wanted to help you. Such a sweet boy." Marsden gripped him by the neck and James cried out. "At the last cultural exhibition James was supposed to keep Master Luka distracted so he wouldn't jump into the fray when Los Toros tried to assassinate Vesper. We knew his strength would be an issue if we didn't have a plan to keep him away. But James couldn't say no to Luka and interrupted the whole plan, jeopardizing everything."

James looked away from Marsden, fear in his eyes.

"I punished him, of course, and confined him to our quarters for the last few days," Marsden said. "You know, I'd promised him that if he did as I asked, his family would be returned to him, safe and sound."

James looked at Marsden, a fragile hope in his eyes.

"And I kept my promise," Marsden said. "Your family is safe."

Relief flooded James's features.

"After all," Marsden went on. "They were the first test subjects for this culture-severing spellwork. Since the spellwork was a success three weeks ago, we've kept them safe to monitor the effects of what happens after the spellwork is complete." He patted James's shoulder. "So they're in very good health, I assure you."

"What?" James gasped, his face going pale. "You promised. *You promised!*"

Marsden snapped his fingers and Englassen guards grabbed James and pulled him away. Marsden didn't even seem to hear James. His eyes were on Alfie and Alfie alone. "Now your family are blank, soulless bodies. Obedient, pliable. Exactly how all Castallanos will be in a matter of minutes."

Alfie was so terrified that he couldn't hear James's screams of grief anymore. He could only hear his heart racing. That was what happened when someone wiped away your connection to your culture, your ancestry. You became nothing, no one. And if Marsden had successfully performed the spellwork on others, he was no doubt capable of performing it on Castallanos too.

This was what would happen to his people and he could do

nothing about it. Finn groaned where she was held down by the guards, bleeding onto the tiled floor. Luka fought but the guards pricked him with quilbear quills, making him fall slack. Queen Amada looked as if she'd already died.

After everything, this was how his kingdom would end. Soulless, lost, enslaved.

"Now, let's get on with it, shall we?" Marsden placed the vanishing cloak on the ground. He took the mixture of blood and poured it about the cloak. Then he dipped his fingers in the blood and began writing in Englassen. The bloody script on the ground glowed, and in a panic, Alfie tried to cling to his memories, his knowledge of his heritage, to think of the words he'd grown up hearing, the lovely lilt of Castallano that curved his tongue when he spoke. He tried to hold on to the culture that rang in his bones as clear as a bell.

As the blood writing faded, Marsden looked around triumphantly. But Alfie felt no different. He waited, waited to feel his culture being wrenched away from him, but . . .

. . . nothing happened.

Alfie looked around the room in confusion. Everyone seemed unaffected. The Englassens had been so confident, but something had gone wrong. Thankfully, something had saved them from that terrible, magicless fate. Hope swelled in Alfie's chest. He was alert, alive with magic. He could feel it inside him.

Finn glared at Marsden and spoke, shattering the silence. "Come mierda, hijo de puta."

"In case you didn't know," Alfie said in perfect Englassen. "She just told you to eat shit *in Castallano.* We still have our language. Your spell didn't work."

Marsden's pale face reddened. "What do you mean it didn't work? We have everything, we did everything—" Marsden gestured wildly at James. "We tested it on his family. It worked!"

Alfie didn't know what mistake they'd made in the casting, but something had happened. He should've felt lucky, but Alfie almost wished that it had worked; then perhaps he wouldn't hurt as much as he did in this moment. He would be blissfully ignorant of his life falling apart around him.

"You failed," Alfie said with a broken laugh. "*You failed.* And you killed my father for *nothing!*" he shouted, his voice cracking. "Nothing at all but a failed experiment."

He wanted to be happy, to be glad that his culture hadn't been wrenched away from his people. But his father's dead body lay at his feet, and he could feel nothing but pain. Castallan had been robbed of yet another king, his mother robbed of her husband, and Alfie robbed of his papá. He'd lost the man who had hoisted a young Alfie up onto his shoulders so that Alfie could know what it was like to feel tall. A man who had sometimes looked at Alfie fondly before saying, "You have your mother's dimples, you know? The same face. That was the first thing I noticed about your mamá. She smiled and I was done for." And Alfie would listen, pretending his father hadn't said that to him many times before.

King Bolivar was gone.

Tears streaked his face and the world grew blurry around him. At first he thought it was his tears and the grief that had turned everything gray, but by the way everyone looked around, confused, he knew he was not the only one who'd seen it. The world seemed to be cast in shadow, the sun a dull orb and its rays lacking glow. They'd been plunged into an endless twilight. A chill moved through the air, washing over Alfie like long-nailed fingers through tangled hair. Something had changed.

Something was wrong. Was Englass's spellwork starting to work? Had it just been delayed for some reason?

In the space just before the altar, at the head of the aisle that Alfie had walked up, a black crease blossomed in the air. Alfie hadn't seen anything like this since Xiomara had opened the void to rid this world of Sombra's evil magic. A chilling fear trickled down his spine, making his throat go painfully dry.

Two hands reached through the crevice, pushing space open as if it were mere curtains, and out stepped a familiar figure. Alfie could only stare, panic racing through him.

There, standing before Alfie, as if not a moment had passed, was his brother, his eyes black as night.

His father was dead and Dez was alive. Nothing made sense anymore.

It struck him suddenly that this was probably why the spellwork hadn't worked. This was why Englass hadn't robbed Castallan of its magic.

They had needed the blood of every living member of the royal family to complete the spell.

Since Dez had been alive in the void, they didn't have his blood to perform the spell. Dezmin's arrival had nothing to do with Marsden's failed magic at the betrothal ceremony. That much was clear from Marsden's shocked face. This had not been part of his plan. This was something else. Something worse.

Dezmin scanned the room, delight in his black eyes. "It seems I'm interrupting an important event. My apologies." He turned to Alfie then, his smile widening. "Didn't you hear your brother calling for you?" Dezmin asked, and beneath his voice was the echo of something sinister, something that was not Dez at all. "I couldn't get his annoying screams to quiet until the transformation was finally complete. I was certain you'd make the connection."

Alfie's heart pounded in his chest. The sounds he'd heard while traveling through the magic hadn't been the realm of magic rejecting him—it had been Dezmin crying out in pain, being overtaken by something dark. He'd thought that combining his magic with Finn's had somehow ended the screams, but in reality the screams had gone quiet because his brother had been snuffed out by whatever this evil creature was.

"Then he even managed to change the adorable little figurines in his bedroom," he went on. "And still you didn't put it together. But don't fret; I'm happy to oblige."

"Who are you?" Alfie asked. "What have you done to Dezmin?"

"Believe it or not," the being said with Dezmin's voice, "I'm happy to see you again. It's been far too long."

The truth struck Alfie like a physical blow, like a shock of lightning. He gasped, his shadow wilting at his feet.

Sombra twisted Dezmin's face into a cruel smile. "Hello, Alfie."

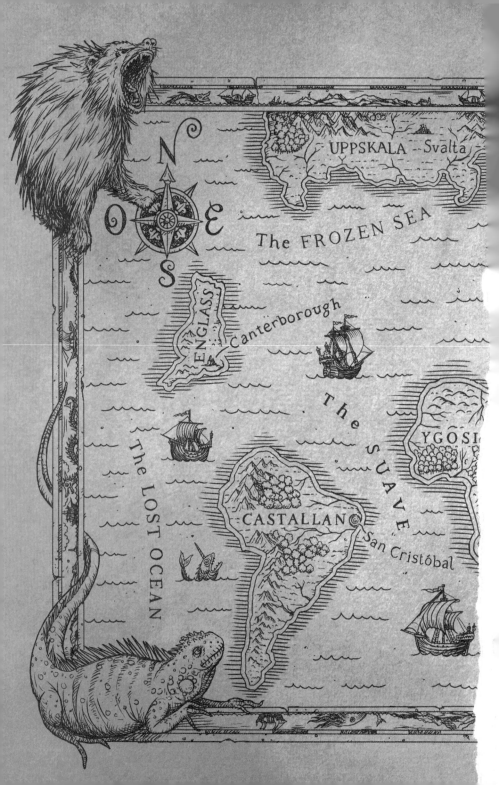